LITTLE GIRL LOST

Katie Flynn has lived for many years in the Northwest. A compulsive writer, she started with short stories and articles and many of her early stories were broadcast on Radio Mersey. She decided to write her Liverpool series after hearing the reminiscences of family members about life in the city in the early years of the twentieth century. She also writes as Judith Saxton. For the past few years, she has had to cope with ME but has continued to write.

Praise for Katie Flynn

'Arrow's best and biggest saga author. She's good.'
Bookseller

'If you pick up a Katie Flynn book it's going to be a wrench to put it down again'
Holyhead & Anglesey Mail

'A heartwarming story of love and loss'
Woman's Weekly

'One of the best Liverpool writers'
Liverpool Echo

'[Katie Flynn] has the gift that Catherine Cookson had of bringing the period and the characters to life'
Caernarfon & Denbigh Herald

KATIE FLYNN

LITTLE GIRL LOST

arrow books

Published by Arrow Books in 2006

2 4 6 8 10 9 7 5 3 1

Copyright © Katie Flynn, 2006

First published in Great Britain in 2006 by
William Heinemann

Arrow Books
The Random House Group Limited, 20 Vauxhall Bridge Road,
London SW1V 2SA

www.randomhouse.co.uk

Addresses for companies within The Random House Group Limited
can be found at: www.randomhouse.co.uk

The Random House Group Limited Reg. No. 954009

A CIP catalogue record for this book
is available from the British Library

ISBN 9780099486992 (from Jan 2007)
ISBN 0 09 948699 7

The Random House Group Limited makes every effort to ensure that the
papers used in its books are made from trees that have been legally sourced
from well-managed and credibly certified forests. Our paper procurement
policy can be found at: www.randomhouse.co.uk/paper.htm

Typeset in Palatino by Palimpsest Book Production Limited,
Grangemouth, Stirlingshire
Printed and bound in the United Kingdom by
Bookmarque Ltd, Croydon, Surrey

Chapter One

December 1910

As Sylvie turned to walk along beside the river it was raining; soft fine rain which blew gently with the breeze, scarcely visible but nevertheless a force to be reckoned with. It blew against Sylvie's cold cheeks, gave the surface of the river the aspect of frosted glass, and added a satiny gleam to the paving stones beneath her feet.

Sylvie turned up the collar of her dark coat and shivered a little; what the devil was she going to do? She had spent the evening with her sister, Annie, who lived not far from where she was now standing, and of course she had told her everything. Annie was older than she by a full dozen years, and ever since her awful problem had become clear Sylvie had been certain, in the back of her mind, that Annie would have the answer to her predicament, as she had solved so many of Sylvie's problems in the past.

But this problem, it appeared, was one which even Annie could not solve. 'Wharrever made you *do* it, queen?' she had kept repeating with increasing querulousness. 'You know your Len's temper, none better, and Robbie's years older'n

1

you! What's more, if he were anyone's pal, he were our Bertie's. So why did you do it?'

After four or five repetitions of this question, Sylvie could have screamed aloud. Surely it was obvious? She had been tremendously flattered when Robbie, her big brother's pal, had come home on leave from his ship and had taken notice of the little girl who had suddenly become a woman. He had been sweet to her, bought her presents, taken her to the picture house, even let her ramble on about her marriage to Len, because with Len in prison she had needed someone to talk to, someone who would not simply moralise and remind her that Len had already served over half his sentence and would soon be free once more. Robbie had even been good with little Becky, buying her sweets and chocolate bars, a pencil box, a colouring book. Then, on his last evening at home, he had taken Sylvie to see a pal . . . only the pal had been out, and the house had been empty. Robbie had pretended to be surprised, had apologised humbly for putting her in a difficult position, and had begun kissing and cuddling her . . . and then the kissing and the cuddling had turned into something else, something a deal more dangerous, and before she knew it . . .

I was a wicked girl, Sylvie told herself miserably now, wiping the misty rain from her face. I married Len because I was expecting his child, but at least he wanted to marry me and was pleased as punch when Becky was born, even though he had hoped for a boy.

Of course she had not actually wanted to marry Len, or anyone else for that matter. But her mother had insisted that Sylvie let Len make an honest woman of her. 'You'll have to marry him, queen,' she had said lugubriously. 'Them Dugdales is a big fambly, and they've a deal o' money and influence round here. Times ain't easy, and if I were to say you was goin' to keep the baby but you wouldn't marry their Len . . . well, I'd lose me job for a start, and so would your brother, and the chances are the Dugdales would go to Father O'Reilly and he'd say we had no choice – you had to marry the kid's father or be excommunicated or wharrever. And you'll be well looked after by that Len. He's a good worker, never short of a bob or two, and he's crazy about you, no kiddin'. Then there's the child. Mrs Dugdale's for ever on about havin' a grandchild . . . oh aye, they'd make a great fuss of a baby, believe me. You'd both be in clover for the rest of your lives.'

But it wasn't fair, Sylvie told herself now, walking drearily through the rain and looking down at the murky waters of the Mersey as she passed. They talked me into marrying Len when I knew very well it were a mistake – I were only sixteen – and once the knot were tied I realised he were jealous of every feller who looked at me twice and wouldn't listen to reason . . . and he sulked whenever something went wrong and expected me to live in the pub with his parents and scarce poke me nose outside it except when he or his ma and pa were with me . . .

And then he went too far when he was breaking up a fight in the pub and a feller ended up in hospital badly injured. Len didn't know his victim were sufferin' from a weak chest and the scuffers came runnin' and Len ended up in Walton Gaol, and has been there for the last two and a half years, and I'm stuck with Ma and Pa Dugdale and I've been a fool and oh, oh, how I wish Len was in the nick for good, because when he finds out . . .

Her mind somersaulted at the thought of what would happen if – or rather when – Len discovered her secret. He hadn't been due out of stir for another six months and she had trusted to luck – and her sister Annie – to think of a solution before then. Only his awkward old grandfather had been and gone and died, and the authorities had agreed to let Len out of the nick for the funeral, and Sylvie was sure that the moment he set eyes on her . . . oh, God, no one else bar Annie knows, but Len will know, and he'll bleedin' kill me and chuck me body in the bleedin' river, sure as my name's Sylvie Dugdale, and it'll serve me right.

The rain was beginning to fall faster and in her despair Sylvie had been keeping her eyes on the ground, so she did not see the man approaching until he was almost upon her. For one awful moment she thought it was Len, and even when she realised her mistake she jumped sideways

4

clumsily, anxious that they should not collide. Unfortunately, she did not see one of the bollards which lined the bank at this point until she had bumped into it. She stumbled, tried to right herself, and the next thing she knew she was struggling in the ice-cold water of the Mersey. Terrified, hampered by her winter clothing and unable to swim, she opened her mouth to scream and felt the water rush down her throat, the currents drag her down.

Why does it always perishin' well rain when I'm comin' off duty? Brendan O'Hara asked himself as he strode along the embankment, gazing morosely ahead and screwing up his eyes against the drops blowing into his face. His helmet gave him some protection, but he knew that when he got back to his lodgings he would have to wring as much water as he could out of his heavy cape before he hung it on the back of his bedroom door. There was one good thing about being on a late shift, though: Mrs Taggart, his landlady, would be in bed, and with a bit of luck the kitchen would still be warmed by the fire in the big old-fashioned stove. That meant he would be able to make himself a cup of tea and maybe even fill a hot-water bottle to take to bed with him. If neither of Mrs Taggart's other lodgers had got soaked, he would let down the drying rack from its position up against the ceiling and hang his cape over that. Cheered by this thought, Brendan rubbed his cold hands together and increased his pace; the sooner he got home – except that he still found it difficult to call No. 48 Hunter Street home – the sooner he could be curled up in bed.

Despite the fact that he had now lived in the city for almost two years, Brendan still missed the leprechaun-haunted bogs of Connemara, where he had been born and bred. His father had scraped a living on a tiny farm, breeding sheep, growing potatoes and cutting turfs of peat to sell to town dwellers. It had been a hard life but the O'Haras had been luckier than most and had managed to feed themselves and have enough money over to educate their two sons at a local school. But the sad truth was that the farm could not support both boys; it was a matter of necessity that Brendan, the younger by five years, should get employment away from the farm, and if possible send back money to help towards his parents' keep as they grew older.

When Declan, the elder brother, suggested that Brendan might apply for a banking post with a friend of his in Galway, Brendan had been horrified; he had always worked out of doors and had no desire whatsoever to take on an office job. Instead, he had joined the Merchant Navy and managed to get work aboard a cargo vessel plying between Liverpool and South America. At first he had been content with the life, but by the time he was twenty he had had enough of the sea and decided to take work ashore – if he could get it, that was, for there was a good deal of unemployment, not only in Ireland, but in England as well.

He had thought about the Army, for several of his relatives were military men, but then his favourite uncle, his father's youngest brother, Sean, invited his nephew to stay for a weekend. Sean was a police constable in a small village not far from Ormskirk. He was married to a plump and comfortable local woman, and they had two nicely behaved little boys, and as far as Sean was concerned no life could be pleasanter than his. 'The Lancashire Constabulary clothes me, pays me a decent wage, provides me with a grand house and then lets me get on with the job,' he had told Brendan contentedly. 'I'm a countryman and this is a country patch. I get on well with everyone, even when I catch 'em scrumpin' apples from a neighbour's orchard, or poachin' on the estate, and when Sergeant Cobbold retires in two years' time, then mebbe I'll get his job, move into his house, and enjoy a better salary, though of course I shall cover more ground than I do now.' He had looked quizzically at his nephew. 'Ever considered joining the force, lad?'

The truth was of course that Brendan had never given it a thought, but he began to look into it, and had liked what he saw. In due course he had applied to join the Liverpool Constabulary, and since he was over six feet tall and had always taken a pride in keeping fit he had passed the medical without trouble and had actually enjoyed the initial training. He had hoped to be posted to one of the outlying districts of Liverpool, but instead had gone to Hatton Garden, where he knew he was gaining much-needed experience. At first he had lived in police barracks and it was only recently that he had been permitted to go into digs. He was given a lodging allowance, of course, and had moved in with two other constables of a similar age.

Brendan was an easy-going sort of fellow and got on well with constables Collins and Simpson, and the three of them, though they often grumbled over her strictures, liked Mrs Taggart well enough and knew themselves to be a good deal more comfortable than they had been in the barracks.

Just now, however, Brendan was more concerned with getting out of the rain than anything else so he quickened his pace. He saw the slight figure ahead of him, and automatically found himself wondering what a woman was doing out on such a night. Almost certainly she was up to no good, because even as Brendan looked, he saw her turn up her coat collar and shrug her head as far down as she could. No doubt she had been trying to filch something, though what it could be Brendan had no idea. The shipping was all in the docks, apart from such craft as the Mersey ferries and one or two small fishing boats, and there would be little enough to steal from any of them.

Brendan saw the woman jerk up her head and guessed that his helmet had warned her that a policeman was approaching, for she swerved, and then, to Brendan's complete astonishment, appeared to dive into the river.

There was a tremendous splash, closely followed by a sort of gurgling gasp, and Brendan, breaking into a run and casting aside his cape and helmet, suddenly realised why she had been walking along the embankment so late and on such a night. Suicide! He knew it happened, but this was the first time he'd seen despair in action and it galvanised him, so that he ripped off his tunic and shed his boots without a second thought. He would have to go in after the young fool, but oh, Gawd, what a horrible prospect! He jumped into the water feet first, and gasped as the icy cold crushed the breath out of him. He could see the woman's dark coat ahead, for the garment had trapped air and floated to the surface. Teeth juddering, Brendan reached the coat in a couple of strokes and thanked God when his hands grasped the body still within it. Halfway to the nearest set of steps, swimming strongly on his back, he realised that this would-be suicide was not a mature woman but a young girl, and a beautiful one at that.

As he hauled her up the slippery concrete steps and laid her on the flagstones, the uncaring street lamps shone down on a mass of wet, ash-blonde hair and a small white face, whose huge dark eyes were fixed imploringly on Brendan's own.

Brendan grinned at her but his teeth were chattering so much that he had to wait a moment before actually speaking. 'You're all right,' he said huskily, at last. 'You aren't going to drown, but if I don't get you under a roof pretty quickly we'll probably both die of exposure.'

As he spoke, Brendan stood up and heaved the girl to her feet. Her knees began to buckle but Brendan looped an arm round her waist so that she did not fall, then glanced despairingly at the clothing he had cast off. Putting it on again would be madness but he dared not leave his uniform, let alone his grand boots, here, where anyone might pick them up.

Looking wildly about him, he saw a pile of timber alongside one of the nearby buildings and carried the girl across to it, sitting her down and bidding her, rather brusquely, to stay just where she was. Then he ran back to his clothing, crammed his wet feet into his boots, picked up the rest, and returned to the girl. She was sitting where he had placed her, water running off her to mingle with the puddles on the flagstones, and shivering so uncontrollably that Brendan began to wonder how on earth he was to get her into some form of shelter before she simply died of cold. But there was his tunic. He wrapped it round her and buttoned it up, then plonked the helmet on his own head. Then he hauled her to her feet. 'You've got to keep moving or you'll freeze where you stand,' he said. 'Movement helps; can you put your arm round my waist?'

The girl nodded and Brendan slung his cape round the pair of them and urged her into motion. Even in his cold and sodden state, he could not help grinning inwardly at the sight they must make, like some peculiar two-headed turtle, or a couple of drunks indulging in a three-legged race. Fortunately, however, his digs in Hunter Street were not too far distant. They paused for breath under the Dockers' Umbrella and Brendan looked searchingly into his companion's face. She was breathing quickly and still shivering, but he thought she looked marginally better. Starting off again, they threaded their way along Water Street and Dale Street, and by the time they turned left into Byrom he could see that there was faint colour in her cheeks; she looked a good deal better and the shivering had stopped. Swift movement, Brendan told himself with satisfaction, was clearly beneficial both to someone just fished out of an icy-cold river and to the fisher-out.

It was probably no more than twenty minutes since he had rescued her, though it felt more like an hour, that the pair of them stumbled round to the back door of No. 48. Even in his present predicament, Brendan quailed at the thought of going in by the front door and trekking Mersey mud all over his landlady's new linoleum, to say nothing of the strip of drugget which ran from the front door along the length of the hall. However, he knew the hiding place of the back-door key and reached up to the lintel. He opened the door and pushed his companion into the kitchen, which felt gloriously warm even though Mrs Taggart had banked down the fire for the night. Brendan thrust the girl into one of the old easy chairs, stoked up the fire and then, with a curt reminder to her to stay where she was, went across the kitchen and up the stairs to his own room. He grabbed a couple of blankets off the bed, then stole downstairs again and let himself into the kitchen as quietly as possible. Draping the blankets over the chair nearest the fire, he smiled reassuringly at the girl. 'I'm going up to my room to change,' he whispered. 'You get your wet things off and wrap yourself in these blankets. I shan't be gone more than a couple of minutes, and when I come back I'll wring your clothes out over the sink, stir up the fire again, and hang them over the clothes horse.' He looked enquiringly across at his companion. 'Understand? And don't you move out of this kitchen, right?'

The girl nodded. 'Right,' she agreed weakly. 'And – and I haven't thanked you for saving my life. I can't swim, you see. I'd have been dead in two minutes flat if you'd not grabbed me.'

Brendan bit back the words *Then why did you jump in if you didn't want to drown?* saying instead: 'Never mind that. We've got to get your stuff dry because none of my clothes will fit you and you'll be wanting to get home.' He picked up the kettle, went over to the sink and filled it, then carried it back to the fire and stood it over the flame. 'I'll be back before this boils and I'll make us both a cup of tea.'

He left the room and was halfway up the stairs before it occurred to him that the presence in the kitchen of a soaking-wet girl, naked but for a couple of blankets, might well raise a few eyebrows. On the other hand, one look at her clothing would convince the most hardened sceptic that this was not an orgy of seduction but merely a rescue, which, after all, was part of his job.

He was downstairs again, as he had promised, just before the kettle boiled. The girl had dried her hair on the kitchen roller towel and was looking a good deal more cheerful, though she eyed him rather apprehensively as he handed her a cup of tea. She had spread her clothes out on an old clothes horse which she had pulled around the fire and Brendan, blushing, hastily looked away from the steaming garments. He said, approvingly: 'That's right, alanna. We'll have you respectable again in no time, which will be just as well because I don't fancy having to explain what's just happened to my landlady, or to the other fellows who lodge here for that matter. Suicide's a crime, you know, though how you can punish someone who's already dead I've not worked out.'

He settled back in his chair as the girl's large eyes – he saw now that they were an unusually brilliant blue – rounded in astonishment. 'Suicide?' she squeaked, forgetting to keep her voice low. 'Suicide? Wharrever do you mean? I were walking along the embankment, mindin' me own business . . .'

'Keep your voice down,' Brendan said, his tone anguished. Indignation was all very well but he had no desire to find himself explaining a situation he did not yet fully understand to either Mrs Taggart or Simpson and Collins. 'All I can say is, miss, that I saw you dive into the water, and naturally I thought that . . .'

'Well, you want to think before you think,' the girl said rather confusedly, but this time she kept her voice low. 'I were walkin' along, havin' a bit of a weep, to tell you the truth, and all of a sudden you loomed up out of the rain and mist, lookin' twice the size of any mortal man. You scared me so much that I jumped to one side, hit the bleedin' bollard and went head first into the river. It were an accident, and I'll swear to it on the Bible if you like.'

Brendan felt a wave of relief at her words. Now he came to think of it, he remembered the cry that she had given when she hit the water, and also her eagerness to be rescued, for she had not struggled in his grasp as he began to tow her towards the steps. Besides, what reason could such a beautiful girl have to kill herself? For he could see now that she was indeed beautiful, with a fragile loveliness which had become clearer now that she was warm and dry. But she had said she was crying, so she could not have been exactly happy as she

14

walked along by the river. Come to that, what had she been doing in such a spot, all alone, and so very late?

He put the question to her and saw the faint pink colour rush into her cheeks. Clearly wanting to gain time, she raised the cup of tea to her lips, staring at him over the rim as she sipped. Then she seemed to come to a decision and put the cup down. 'I'll tell you, but remember, I'm tellin' *you*, not a policeman,' she said. 'If you went and split on me and if – if it got around, I could be in real trouble . . . well, I could be dead, to tell you the truth. You saved my life tonight and it would be a wicked old waste if you lost it for me tomorrow. Can you understand?'

Brendan smiled at her. 'I'll do my best,' he assured her. 'And I certainly won't split on you, I can promise you that; I wasn't on duty anyway, even though I was wearing my uniform. So go ahead. By the way, I'm Brendan O'Hara; I saw the ring on your finger so I guess you're married, though you scarcely look old enough, but I can't call you missus!'

The girl held out a hand, smiling trustfully up at him. 'How do you do, Mr O'Hara? Or should that be Constable O'Hara?' she said as they shook hands. 'I'm Sylvie Dugdale – and I'm married to a feller called Len. You may know his parents; they keep the public house down on the Dock Road. It's called the Ferryman. It's a big pub and Len's an only child, so after we were married we moved in with his parents, and I live there still.'

'I know it – it's on my beat,' Brendan said.

'Well, Len's in gaol; he were sent down for assault two and a half years ago,' Sylvie said. 'You might be thinkin' I was cryin' 'cos I want my husband out of gaol, but you'd be wrong. Len is horribly jealous and – and if I hadn't been in the family way, I never would have married him. Oh, I expect you think I'm dreadfully weak, but I was only sixteen and my mam works for the Dugdales and so does my brother Bert. If my father had been alive it might have been different, but Mam – and Father O'Reilly – told me, that the baby was as much Len's as mine, and that it would be wicked to make the child a bastard because of a mere scruple.' She laughed bitterly. 'A scruple! The truth is, Len wanted me, and his parents have always spoiled him rotten, so he begged and pleaded . . . and then he got violent. He broke three of me ribs . . . I tell you, I were downright perishin' delighted when he landed in Walton Gaol.'

'I see,' Brendan said inadequately. His own happy childhood had not prepared him for the unhappiness and marital misery which was so often brought to the attention of the Liverpool police. But this girl, with her frail and tender beauty, should surely have been spared that. The very thought of any man raising his hand – or worse, his belt – to this slender, defenceless creature was sickening. Yet it had not broken her spirit; there was resolution in the tilt of her chin and strength of character in her large eyes. 'So why were you crying?' Brendan enquired, adding apologetically: 'Of course, if I'd known you had a child, I'd never have thought you were trying to commit suicide.'

At the mention of her daughter, Sylvie's face softened. 'Yes, you're right. Becky makes everything worthwhile. Despite her father, she's the most beautiful little thing, and I have to say his parents adore her, and they're kind enough to me in their way.'

There was a short silence whilst Brendan mulled over her words. At length he said, tentatively, 'That's no reason for you to be crying, in such a place, and at such a time, too.'

Sylvie sighed. 'It's rather a long story,' she said. 'Are you sure you want to hear it?'

Brendan nodded emphatically, and as Sylvie began to speak he realised that this was a much-needed release, and that simply sharing her story would help her more than any sympathetic words of his could do.

'Before I was married me name was Sylvie Davies, and we lived next door to a family called Wentworth. Sally Wentworth and I were bezzies, even though she were two full years older'n me. We went everywhere together, to and from school, on our mams' messages . . . we even shared treats when one of us had something nice. It were grand having a bezzy like Sally. She had an older brother called Rob who was ever so good to us. We thought he was wonderful; he was always slippin' us pennies for the picture show. I suppose I had a bit of a crush on him when we were kids.'

Brendan waited patiently whilst Sylvie gazed into the fire and, he presumed, thought lovingly of her childhood. However, when the silence stretched, he prompted her, as gently as he could. 'And . . . ?'

'Then Robbie went away to sea and when he did come home, which wasn't often, he didn't take much notice of Sally and me,' Sylvie said. 'Well . . . I was a married woman with a kid and Sally was working at the jam factory. About four months ago, he came home on a long leave and found Len in prison and myself at a loose end. He said he felt sorry for me and took me around a bit. I was flattered and didn't realise where his kindness was leading until . . . until . . .'

Brendan gazed at her. He could guess what must be coming next but felt he had to hear the full story from her own lips. 'If you mean he persuaded you to – to go to bed with him, then I understand why you were crying,' he said slowly. 'But you'd better tell me, in case I've got it wrong.'

Sylvie sighed and bent her head, pleating a piece of blanket, then smoothing it out again. Brendan reflected that it must be taking a deal of courage to relate her story to a stranger and was tempted to spare her the pain of more revelations, but suddenly she raised her eyes and looked at him squarely. 'Yes, I'm pregnant,' she said baldly. 'I'm almost four months gone and Len's coming out of gaol tomorrow to attend his grandfather's funeral. He'll take one look at me and he'll guess because I shan't be able to look him in the eye – oh, I'm so ashamed – and then he'll kill me because Len's jealous as a cat an' strong as an ox. Oh, he may not do it tomorrow, but he'll do it just as soon as he gets out of jug, I'm sure of that. I went to my sister Annie tonight because I thought she'd tell me what to do, but the only idea she had was – was doing something awful, wi' hot baths and drinkin' a bottle o' gin . . . other than that, she didn't seem to have any ideas at all.'

Brendan looked doubtfully across at her. He could well understand why she had been crying and thought that, had he not already decided she was a decent kid, he might have suspected that her dive into the river had been deliberate after all; she had reason enough for a desperate act, God knows. However, he could not help disapproving strongly of what she had done. He knew Len Dugdale might be a violent man but this did not excuse her behaviour. She had broken one of the Ten Commandments by committing adultery, an act so dreadful that Brendan thought she would never be able to forgive herself, let alone expect forgiveness from others. However, it would scarcely help to say so. Instead, he smiled at her, saying bracingly: 'Well, alanna, I won't deny you've done a terrible bad t'ing because you must know it yourself, but—'

'It wasn't just me what did a terrible thing! Why, the terrible thing was being tricked into an empty house by Robbie so he could have his way with me,' Sylvie said wildly. 'So far as Robbie was concerned it was just a bit of fun. I wrote and told him what had happened as soon as I knew but he hasn't replied. Why should he? It isn't fellers what pays for a bit of fun – it's us women. I did think about gin an' that and those old women in the courts what'll do away wi' a baby before it's born, only girls die, don't they, and it's a mortal sin as well . . .'

'Life is unfair,' Brendan agreed, thinking that this Robbie had probably got a girl in every port. If I ever get to meet him, my fist and his nose will have something to say to one another, he thought vindictively.

'And I know Len will kill me when he gets out of Walton,' Sylvie continued.

'No he won't. I realise you'll have to go to the funeral tomorrow, but Len won't attend the wake afterwards, if that's what's worrying you, and he'll have a couple of warders with him from start to finish. You must put a brave face on it and simply steer clear of him, apart from saying hello and so on. Remember, even though he's been slammed up for a couple of years he must have seen you at visiting times, so he's very unlikely to notice any change in your shape. Why, I fished you out of the river with every garment clinging to you and I couldn't tell.'

This seemed to cheer Sylvie, for she gave him a tremulous smile. 'But as soon as I do begin to show, his horrible old mam will write to him, or visit him in prison,' she pointed out. 'And if it ain't Ma or Pa Dugdale, it'll be someone else; you know how folk love to pass on gossip. Come to that, I'm not too sure what Pa Dugdale might do if he found out. They'll know the baby isn't Len's, of course, so they might light into me straight away and not wait for Len.' An enormous shudder shook her small frame and made her thick, silver-blonde hair shiver. 'I try not to be a coward but it's hard when you can still remember the pain; I did tell you Len broke three of my ribs once, didn't I? And he tramped on me toes until me feet were black and blue.'

Brendan stared at her. He knew adultery was terribly wrong but it was nothing compared with what Len Dugdale had done to her, and if this Robbie Wentworth had had a morsel of sense he would never have dreamed of seducing a married girl, exposing her to such grave danger. Brendan leaned forward in his chair, gazing earnestly into her small pale face. 'You're right; you can't stay at the Ferryman until the baby is born,' he said gruffly, for he did not want her to see how her predicament had touched him. 'I don't mean to save your life one minute and let some bug— I mean some brute half kill you the next. I don't know when Dugdale's due for release but that isn't important, not really.' Sylvie was gazing at him with wide-eyed admiration, so once again he spoke rather to reassure than to inform. 'I'll attend this funeral tomorrow – where's it to be, by the way? – just to keep an eye on you. But as soon as it's over and Dugdale's safely back in gaol, I'll put my mind to solving your predicament. I'm sure there's a way out – there has to be.' He rose to his feet and began to gather up Sylvie's clothing, now nicely dried out, though very crumpled. 'The pub will have shut some time ago but I dare say you can get into the Ferryman without being noticed. Anyway, I'll walk you home, so if you need a boost in through a window . . .'

Clutching the blankets to her and holding out one hand for the clothes, Sylvie rose to her feet. 'You are good,' she said fervently. 'I never thought I'd be glad to fall in the perishin' Mersey, but I reckon it were the best thing that could have happened to me. To tell you the truth, when I hit the water I thought of the only advice Annie had give me – you know, hot baths and a big glass of gin – and I wondered if a cold one wouldn't do just as well.' She smoothed a hand gently over her still flat stomach, smiling with a tenderness that caused Brendan to swallow convulsively. 'But as I said, girls die when they try tricks like that.'

'Right, and now tell me when and where old Dugdale's funeral is to take place,' Brendan said quickly, not wanting to go into any moral issues now.

'Oh, the funeral! It's at eleven o'clock tomorrow

morning, at St Anthony's, on the Scottie, and then at Anfield Cemetery. Can – can you really come? Only you've been so good, constable, that I wouldn't want you to get into trouble on my account.'

'I'm off duty tomorrow morning, having been on nights for a whole week, and you'd better start calling me Brendan because I'm going to call you Sylvie,' Brendan said briefly. 'And of course I'll come to the funeral, though I'll come in civvies, not in uniform. I won't speak to you but I'll hang back as we come out of church and you can tip me the wink, somehow or other, if there's trouble brewing. And now I'll pop upstairs and get my old coat and cap whilst you dress yourself.' He smiled at her. 'See you in ten minutes, if that's long enough?'

'That'll be fine,' Sylvie said. 'See you presently, then.'

Chapter Two

By the time Brendan and Sylvie had dressed themselves as warmly as they could, and Brendan had
borrowed a large black umbrella from the coat
stand in the hall, the rain had almost stopped.
Brendan tried to slow his long stride to match
Sylvie's, but she tucked a small hand into the crook
of his elbow and kept pace with him, chattering
almost gaily, though in a quiet and subdued voice,
as they traversed the dark and windy streets.

Brendan knew the Ferryman well; it was a
seamen's pub, of course, but every such place had
its regulars. Men – and occasionally women – who
lived in the neighbourhood preferred to drink at
a place not far from home; a place furthermore
where they were known and could sometimes
drink on tick if the landlord was aware of their
circumstances and knew he would get his money
on pay day. The Ferryman was a very large
building: an elaborate Victorian mansion, with
four short fat towers capped by curly slate-roofed
turrets. The place attracted a crowd of hangers-on,
of course, lads either too young or too penniless
to buy a drink at the bar, so Brendan always kept
a wary eye on it whilst on his beat. Mr Dugdale

and his wife had two barmen and it occurred to Brendan to ask his companion which of these burly gentlemen was her brother. She shot him an amused look.

'Neither of 'em,' she assured him. 'My brother Bertie's the cellar man. He's short with reddish hair and limps because he were a seaman once and got knifed in a brawl. That's why he came ashore, because the knife had cut a tendon or something behind his knee and he couldn't keep upright on the deck no more. But he's really strong – you have to be to do his job. He's older than me. He's thirty.'

'I've got a brother . . .' Brendan began, but his companion was talking again.

'My sisters are older than me as well – Annie, Ellen and Reet. None of 'em are married yet, though Ellen and Reet are both engaged to seamen and hope to get wed next summer. Annie is me favourite sister 'cos she brought me up, more or less. She's different. She's got a real good job as housekeeper at the big hotel on Church Street, opposite St Peter's Cathedral. She says she won't ever marry 'cos all men are brutes; she'll have a career instead. She still comes home when she's off duty, though she lives in the hotel most of the time. She's got a dear little room where we can talk without the family overhearing; in fact, that's where I went this evening. But she's moving to a London hotel soon, so we shan't see so much of her,' Sylvie finished.

Brendan blinked, taken aback by the volume of information, but he realised that she was simply chattering to ease the strangeness of walking the dark streets with someone she scarcely knew. Also, he guessed it was a brave attempt to take his mind off what she had already told him, so he answered her in kind. 'You're lucky to have a big family near enough to visit and your sister Annie sounds grand,' he told her. 'I've only got one brother and no sisters at all, and since, as you've probably guessed, I'm from Ireland, I can't see any of 'em except on my annual holiday. But I've an uncle living in Lancashire; he's a village bobby, a grand feller, so when I get the chance – when I'm off duty, that is – I visit him and his family for a bit of a change from city life.'

He had hoped to make her feel more at ease and this seemed to do the trick, so he beguiled the rest of their walk with a description of the little farm in Connemara where he had been born and where his parents still lived. She exclaimed over the fact that his mother and father were both nearing seventy – her mother was only fifty – and this led to Brendan's explaining that, as a general rule, the Irish married much later than their English counterparts. 'For 'tis economical sense to save up for a home of your own before marrying,' he told her. He did not add that both priests and parents encouraged late marriages because if a woman was forty before she wed she was unlikely to have a large family.

'I wish it were like that here,' Sylvie said, rather dolefully. 'I were only seventeen when I had Becky and Len's a lot older than me, o' course.'

By this time they were approaching the Ferryman and Brendan drew her to a halt where there was a dark patch between two hissing gas lamps. 'Look, alanna, how long do you reckon it'll be before your ma-in-law – or someone else – realises you're in the family way? Only it's pretty clear to me that you'll be in danger if you stay in Liverpool once the Dugdales know there's a child on the way. Is there anywhere that you and Becky can go, where the Dugdales won't find you?'

'I don't know of anywhere,' Sylvie said miserably. 'I've tried to think of a good reason for goin' away, only even if I did, neither Becky nor meself can live on air. At present, of course, the Dugdales pay for just about everything.' She smiled brightly up at him, though there was trouble in her large eyes. 'What do you think I should do?'

Brendan sighed, but not aloud. She was so young, so trusting, and so very pretty. As they walked, he had been thinking hard, and now he came up with an idea, if not a solution. 'I t'ink what you'll have to do is to leave Becky behind, because you know they love the child and would never abandon her,' he said slowly. 'Then you could tell them you've been offered a live-in job with a rich family. You could say they have come over from America to visit their relations in Ireland, so will only want someone for six months and are prepared to pay well. You'd have to beg them, very prettily, to take great care of Becky because your new employers would not consider taking on anyone with a child of their own. And then you could go to my cousin in Dublin, have the baby, get it adopted, and return to Liverpool. You can give them my cousin's address so they can write, and you can write back. Only . . . only will they believe it, do you think, or will they smell a rat?'

'Oh yes, they'll believe it. They know I'm desperate for a home of my own, and of course Len hasn't been earning while he's been clapped up,' Sylvie said. 'And even Len was getting sick and tired of living under his parents' roof. The only thing is, it would be dreadfully hard to leave Becky – though I suppose it wouldn't be for very long, really. But won't your cousin mind, Brendan?'

Brendan patted her shoulder reassuringly. 'She's a grand girl is Caitlin O'Keefe, and I'm sure she'll be happy to get you out of trouble once I've explained everything to her. And if you can't get a job over there, then I'll send you enough money to keep you going until the baby's born,' he said. 'Caitlin's married to a feller called Pat. They've a grosh of kids and live in a couple of rooms off Francis Street, in a place called Handkerchief Alley, but Caitlin's got a heart as big as a bus and we've always been good friends. I'll write and ask her if she'll take you in and I'm sure she'll do her best to help you, particularly if in return you give a hand wit' the kids and the cleanin' an' such.'

Sylvie clasped her hands round his arm and then, to his great astonishment, stood on tiptoe and kissed his cheek. 'I don't know what I've done to deserve all the help you're givin' me,' she said humbly. 'But I thank you from the bottom of my heart.' She glanced down at herself. 'How long will it be before Caitlin's reply to your letter arrives, do you think?'

'Well, I'll do me best,' Brendan said. 'But if all goes according to plan, I'd hope to get you off to Ireland in two or three weeks.' He took her arm and began to lead her towards the Ferryman. 'If someone happens to have seen us together, just tell 'em the scuffer were a bit doubtful as to why you were on the streets so late at night and insisted on accompanying you home.'

'But you aren't in your uniform,' Sylvie objected. 'Anyway, nobody will be awake, not at this hour. Ma- and Pa-in-law sleep in the big double bedroom overlookin' the main road, but Bertie will have put the back-door key on the nail above the lintel when he left. He keeps the lock oiled so I can get in without a sound and be in my bed five minutes after that. Becky won't wake; she sleeps like a log, the little darling. She shares my room, of course, but she hardly ever wakes me. Ma-in-law will have put her to bed at around seven o'clock; I work evenings, cleaning in Lewis's on Ranelagh Street when the store closes, and I often go on to Annie's after that, so they won't have wondered where I am.'

'Oh, I didn't realise you worked away from home. That'll make things a good deal easier,' Brendan said. 'What time do you finish your cleaning job? I could meet you at the back entrance of Lewis's if I were off duty.'

Sylvie tilted her head in thought. 'I'm usually done between nine and ten,' she said. 'It would be grand if you could meet me out of work; why, you could walk me home and we could talk – then it would be you that Len tore limb from limb!' She gave his hand a quick squeeze to show that she was joking. 'It's ever so good of you, Brendan. I do Monday to Friday at the store.'

Brendan took her elbow and steered her round to the back of the pub, lowering his voice to a confidential murmur. 'Is that the back gate? Yes, I reckon it must be; don't they lock it at night?'

'No, because the dustmen come early, sometimes before anyone's up,' Sylvie said, raising the latch and slipping into the cobbled court-yard beyond. She dropped her voice to a murmur so low that Brendan had difficulty in catching her words. 'There's no need to come any further and you've a fair walk home. See you tomorrow!'

Brendan, however, accompanied her to the door and reached up to the lintel to hand her the key from where it hung on its nail. 'I don't know how you would have fetched it down if I hadn't been here,' he remonstrated. 'You're not tall enough to reach the lintel, let alone the key.'

In the tricky moonlight, he saw her lips curve into a mischievous smile. 'See that bucket?' she whispered. 'Bertie always leaves it there, upside down, so all I have to do is step on to it real carefully and fetch the key down in a trice. Now you know all my secrets . . . and there's no one I'd rather trust than yourself.'

Brendan was about to bashfully disclaim when she took the key from him and turned it in the lock. Then she stood on tiptoe and kissed his cheek before opening the door and slipping inside, closing it softly behind her.

For a moment, Brendan just stood there as the key clicked in the lock, listening to the soft patter of her receding footsteps. Then he walked slowly and cautiously across the back yard, let himself out of the gate, and stood in the jigger leaning his broad shoulders against the tall brick wall. After a moment, his hand stole up and touched his cheek. He had been kissed by other girls, but he had never before felt the giddying, wonderful feeling that had swept over him as Sylvie's mouth had gently touched his skin for the second time. Am I in love, he asked himself, with a girl I scarcely know who's married to a feller with a deal more money than I'm ever likely to have? Yet I've been brought up to believe that marriage is for better for worse, for richer for poorer, and that divorce is a real sin. I'd never be able to call Sylvie mine.

It was not a bright or hopeful picture that Brendan painted as he strode through the dark streets towards his lodgings, so it was strange that he smiled blissfully as he walked, and was still smiling when he climbed into his bed at last.

In her own bed, Sylvie smiled, too. She liked that young constable, really liked him. He was good-looking, of course, and very tall, with the typical Irish dark blue eyes and black hair, curly as a lamb's fleece. But she told herself that this was not why she liked him. He was reliable, sensible and very much on her side. She loved Annie dearly but it had not been her sister who had been able to suggest a solution to her problem, but the young constable. He was going to try to arrange a temporary home for her, with his cousin in Dublin, until the child within her was born.

He had saved her life, of course, and she was grateful on that count, but she reminded herself that had he not loomed so suddenly out of the driving rain she would never have tripped over the bollard and landed in the water. Not that it was his fault; she had been too full of her own troubles to watch where she was going.

He was so sympathetic, too. She could still remember the way his eyes softened when she told him of her troubles; remembered, too, how those same eyes had hardened when she spoke of her broken ribs, her crushed and blackened toes.

Snuggling down beneath her blankets, Sylvie

thought, rather guiltily, that she had not been strictly truthful about those broken ribs. The blow which had done the damage had been aimed at a young man who had had one drink too many; he had seen Sylvie coming into the bar one night to collect empty glasses and had grabbed for her, making a very rude remark as he did so. He had not known she was Len's wife, of course, but unfortunately he had turned away at the crucial moment, making an even ruder remark, and Len's heavy fist had already been travelling far too fast to stop. She had dropped like a stone, gasping for breath, crying out to Len that he had killed her, which at least had saved the customer from the well-deserved battering he might otherwise have received. It had been her first intimation that Len could be violent, however, and she had been frightened by the murderous look on his face as he had crossed the bar. But Len had assured her that he was truly sorry for hurting her, had taken her to the nearest hospital explaining, more or less truthfully, that she had accidentally intervened in a 'bit of bother', and had been hurt by sheer bad luck. A doctor had strapped up her ribs and Len had treated her like a princess for weeks.

However, she had told him that he should never hit a man foolish with drink and endeavoured to make him promise to think before flying into a rage again. He had said, humbly, that he would try to do so, but even then she had doubted his ability to control his temper and had been anxious that his anger should never be directed at her.

'I know it were an accident, but next time it might be me chin, or me eyes,' she had said aggrievedly as they lay in bed that night, for the strapping tugged at her injured ribs and even breathing was a painful business. 'You'll have to watch that temper of yours, Len Dugdale, or you'll find yourself in real trouble.'

'But I can't bear to see another feller reachin' for you,' Len had mumbled. 'You're so pretty that every man who looks at you must want you like I do. I know you'd never have married me if it weren't for Becky comin' so of course I'm scared all the time that you might meet someone you liked better'n me.'

Sylvie had sighed. 'I shan't, because I've got you, and Becky, and a nice home,' she said diplomatically. 'Besides, I married you, didn't I? So I'm not likely to look at another feller in – in that sort of way. Why, whatever would Father O'Reilly say?'

Len had given a relieved sigh and laid a heavy arm across her shoulders. 'I'll try to remember that, 'cos I know you're a good girl, and won't play me false,' he had said. 'I know I ain't handsome, nor I ain't clever, but I'm crazy about you, little Sylvie.'

Sylvie, with her ribs still tweaking whenever she moved, had decided that in future she would stay behind the counter and let someone else collect the dirty glasses from the bar, and tried to dismiss the incident from her mind. It was not as though she had ever given him any cause for jealousy; she supposed that some men were jealous by nature and the women who married them had to be aware of the fact.

The affair of the crushed toes was a case in point. Len had been painting the window frames on the outside of the pub one Saturday afternoon and she had been holding the ladder when a passing workman had wolf-whistled, following it up with a shout of: 'Wish you would hold my ladder, queen.'

Sylvie had turned her head, the way one does when one is addressed, and had heard from above her a growl of rage which many a tiger would have envied. Len had leapt down from the ladder intent, she realised, on mayhem, and his heavy boots had landed crushingly on Sylvie's sandalled feet and knocked her flying. Sylvie had shrieked – two of her toes had later proved to be broken – and the ladder, relieved so suddenly of Len's weight, had also descended on her. The workman, though hampered by two heavy buckets full of whitewash, had made off down the road with amazing speed, the whitewash sloshing out of the buckets as he went and making curious patterns all along the flagway. Len would undoubtedly have followed him and wreaked revenge, but he could scarcely do so with his wife lying moaning on the pavement, a ladder on top of her and green paint everywhere. Instead, he had dragged her clear of the ladder and apologised anxiously, adding bracingly: 'But you ain't much hurt, I can tell; you've a good healthy colour. C'mon, let me help you indoors an' make you a nice cup o' tea.'

Sylvie had been absolutely furious. Her head ached from the blow the ladder had given it, her crushed toes were sheer agony and here was her great oafish husband telling her that there was nothing wrong with her. And when she had tried to stand, she was unable to do so. 'My . . . my feet . . . you landed on my feet,' she had gasped. 'Sometimes I really hate you, Len Dugdale.'

He had been sorry then, had picked her up in his arms, and carried her tenderly into his mother's kitchen. But on this occasion he had refused to take her to the hospital. 'I dursn't show me face there again, not after last time,' he had mumbled, looking appealingly at his mother. 'Send Bertie to Dr Hislop. He'll come round if you give Bertie half a crown so he's got the money in advance.'

The doctor had arrived, examined the bump on her head and the state of her toes, and accepted without so much as a blink the explanation that the ladder had slipped and both Len and ladder had descended on poor Mrs Dugdale. Indeed, why should he not? The pavement outside was covered in green paint, the walls were splashed with it, and both Sylvie and Len bore traces on their skin, hair and clothes of their recent encounter with green hard gloss. It had taken several hours of careful work with turpentine before the two of them were clean once more, and all Sylvie's clothing had been ruined and had to be thrown in the dustbin.

The doctor had said he thought two of Sylvie's toes were broken, but because they were so badly mangled he could do little about it. He had bandaged her feet lightly and had told the Dugdales, rather grimly, that young Mrs Dugdale must not attempt to walk for at least four weeks, and possibly six. Then he had promised to come in again next day and had left, advising Len to get to work on the pavement before folk walked through and spread the paint even further.

Now, smiling at the recollection, Sylvie told herself that she had not really deceived the young constable. Both accidents had been occasioned by Len's jealousy, and there had been other incidents, less dramatic, but just as painful for her. Once, at a family party, a cousin of Len's had given Sylvie a peck on the cheek during a game of Forfeits. Because he was a cousin, and there were a great many people present, Len had said nothing. She had forgotten all about it until they were in their own room that night, when he had suddenly seized her by both shoulders and shaken her till her teeth rattled. 'Don't you ever let a feller kiss you again,' he had said menacingly. 'Because next time it won't be just a shaking you'll get, it'll be a black eye. Then see if the fellers want to touch you!'

She had flared up, of course she had, pointing out that it was scarcely her fault that his wretched cousin had seen fit to kiss her cheek – if you could call it a kiss, that was. 'And if you start hitting me, Len Dugdale, you'll wake up one morning and find me an' Becky gone,' she had said. 'How would you like that, eh?'

He had mumbled what she now realised was his usual defence when attacked. 'It weren't my fault; I only gave you a shake because I love you. I told you before I wouldn't have other fellers payin' attention to my wife. Ma and Pa always said you was flighty, but I didn't believe 'em – still don't, only it's in me mind that they could be right . . .'

Sylvie had told him crossly that this was no excuse for his behaviour and had listened to his promises of future saintliness with considerable disbelief. Len wasn't a bad-looking bloke. He had thick, dark brown hair, very dark eyes and a strong, cleft chin, but he reminded Sylvie of a prize bull she had once seen being led through the streets on the way to a show. The bull had had a big, bland, handsome face, but there was a look in his eye which said, plainer than words, that he had a mean streak as wide as the Mersey, and if you overstepped the mark he'd see you regretted it.

Then, of course, there had been the incident with Ronnie Evans, and Len had been sentenced to three years in Walton Gaol. Sylvie had always known that it had not really been Len's fault. Had the man been normal and healthy as Len had believed him to be, then he would simply have muttered off home with a few bruises, or perhaps a black eye. But he had recently been diagnosed as having tuberculosis. Resentful, frightened and feeling ill, he had come into the Ferryman to drown his sorrows and had become belligerent, for he was not used to strong drink. He had been with two or three friends who had watched his descent into drunkenness with some amusement, but of course when Mr Dugdale had called upon Len to evict Ronnie his pals had rushed to his aid, and what should have been a simple ejection rapidly became a scrum in which half the customers had eagerly joined.

Len had landed the troublemaker a punch in the solar plexus and the man had gone down. Len, Sylvie knew, would never have put the boot in on purpose, but he had surged forward to grab another troublemaker, and had kicked and trodden upon Ronnie without realising it. The young man was probably unaware of it, being then in a drunken stupor and incapable of so much as a groan of protest, but when the fracas began to clear Ronnie's pals discovered him and carted him off to hospital, muttering dark threats about how Len would be made to pay for nigh on killing a sick man.

Ronnie had been in hospital for weeks; at one time the medical staff had feared for his life, but he had pulled round. A good many customers had wanted to speak up for Len in court, and of course the Dugdales had done so, but the fact that Ronnie had tuberculosis and would not, in any event, have much of a life before him had caused Len to be found guilty of inflicting grievous bodily harm and sentenced to three years in prison.

Sylvie was sure that Len's stay in Walton Gaol would have taught him a lesson, and knew that, had it not been for her present condition, she would have been looking forward to his release. Becky could not even remember her father, and Sylvie herself would not be sorry to give up the job at Lewis's, which she had taken on to make up for the sudden loss of income when Len was sent to gaol. Still, with Constable Brendan O'Hara on her side, things seemed a good deal brighter now than they had looked only a few hours previously. Sylvie yawned. She had no need to worry. Brendan would look after her; he had promised to do so. It would be a wrench to leave Becky, but it would not be for ever, and far better for the child in the long run if her mother could avoid discovery, and the inevitable rupture from the Dugdales that would follow.

Beyond her window, she heard the clock strike three. Gracious, this would never do. She had to be up in four hours' time to help Ma Dugdale clean out the big room where the wake would be held and to make mounds of sandwiches, sausage rolls and little cakes. Sylvie had had many sleepless nights since confirming her condition, but now she closed her eyes resolutely, and was soon deeply asleep.

'Mammy! Mammy, *will* you wake up? Grandma Dugdale called you ages ago and Granny Davies is helping with the breakfast, 'cos you ain't around. Have you forgot it's the fune-er-al of Great-grandpa today?'

The shrill, insistent voice brought Sylvie slowly up from fathoms deep. She opened her eyes with some difficulty, for the lids felt as though they were weighted down with lead, and saw the blue gaze of her daughter fixed anxiously on her face. Sylvie moaned and discovered, as she moved, that her whole body was one enormous ache and her head was thumping like a trip hammer. She sat up on one elbow and tried to smile at Becky. 'Be a little angel, queen, and ask Granny Davies if she could bring me up a cup of tea,' she urged. 'I – I had an accident last night and didn't gerrin till terrible late and I don't feel so good this morning. Tell 'em I'll gerrup as soon as I've drunk me tea.'

Becky's small, rosy face lit up. 'I'll tell 'em,' she said, importantly, pounding out of the room. 'I'd bring it up meself only I's too little.'

This made Sylvie chuckle and somehow chuckling made her feel less dreadful, even as the events of the previous night came back to her mind. Someone was actually on her side – she was not going to have to struggle on alone. She would see

Brendan O'Hara today at the funeral and they would probably manage to exchange a few words.

Reluctantly, Sylvie swung her legs out of bed and stood up rather shakily, then sat down abruptly, hearing footsteps on the stairs. She would have to tell her mother some tale because of her muddy and crumpled clothing, but she did not think that the truth would be too well received. After all, though she often visited Annie after work, she had never before left her sister's neat little room and gone wandering off beside the Mersey. Explaining how she came to fall in the river would have been straightforward enough, but explaining what she was doing walking alone in the heaviest rain they'd had for weeks would be nigh on impossible. But the footsteps were getting closer; hurriedly, Sylvie rehearsed her story.

'Morning, chuck,' her mother said breezily, pushing the door open and stumping, flat-footed, across the room. The tea in the large earthenware mug slopped on to the linoleum as she approached but this did not appear to worry her, and she gave her daughter a wide and gummy grin as she handed over the mug. Mrs Davies was a large, fat woman with untidy grey hair which she pinned into a bun on top of her head each morning, but which had usually descended to hang in witch locks around her face by the time she reached her place of work. She was easy-going, placid and hard-working, and Sylvie was carelessly fond of her, though she had grown used to the astonishment with which people greeted the announcement of their relationship, for no two people could have looked less alike than Sylvie and her mother. Mrs Davies's small blue eyes squinted towards her large and bulbous nose, and her skin was red and roughened, whilst she had lost all her teeth long before Sylvie was born. She had acquired a set of false ones from the dentist on Brougham Terrace but seldom bothered to wear them, though Sylvie knew she would do so for the funeral as a mark of respect. Her mother had liked old Mr Dugdale, who had lived in the front turret room, and never complained when she had to climb three flights of stairs carrying his breakfast or his shaving water. In fact, she never complained about anything her employers asked her to do provided she was given time off to attend morning and evening service on a Sunday, and an hour off each day to clean the church and give what she described as 'a brush and a whitening' to the front steps of the priest's house.

Sylvie's eyes ran over her mother's large and untidy figure, currently clad in a drooping brown dress and an enormous calico overall. Her thick woollen stockings were concertinaed round her legs and she wore ancient gym shoes on her feet. There were large holes in both toes through which one could see bare skin, for her stockings were always tattered and worn. Sylvie sighed. 'Morning, Mam,' she said. 'You aren't thinking of

43

going to the funeral in that dress, are you? Only it'll be a big do, 'cos the old feller were well liked.'

Mrs Davies bridled. 'Course I ain't. I'm stayin' at the Ferryman to look after Becky and see to the grub. Wharrabout you, young lady?' She tutted and one of her eyes swung sharply up to stare at the ceiling for a moment, as it always did when she was uneasy. 'Young Becky said as you'd had an accident last night, which from the state of your clothes I don't doubt. What did you do – fall in the Mersey?'

Sylvie jumped, then turned it into a shrug. 'It were rainin' cats an' dogs so I nipped in to see our Annie, hopin' the rain would stop. I stayed wi' her for ages but it was still pourin' down when I come out. I'd missed the last tram so I were hurryin' along the street and I slipped.' She wrinkled her nose disgustedly. 'I went down in a puddle of mud and muck; someone had emptied a load of rubbish out on the flagway, I reckon. I were real shaky an' this mornin' I ache all over. A feller come along and give me his arm back to the pub. That's why I didn't wake this morning when Ma Dugdale shouted me.'

Her mother nodded, as though satisfied, but Sylvie was dismayed to see a knowing look cross the older woman's face. 'This young feller what helped you home,' she said, picking up the big tin jug and pouring water into the round china bowl which stood on the washstand. 'Handsome, were he? Anyone I know?'

44

Sylvie went over to the washstand and dabbled her fingers in the water. In normal circumstances, she would have pulled her nightgown over her head and had a nice strip-down wash, but she felt it would be unwise in her present condition. Speaking casually, she said: 'It were a scuffer actually, though he weren't in uniform. He were ever so nice, real fatherly. He wanted to knock the Dugdales up so's they could make sure I hadn't broken nothing, but I wasn't having that. So he just said I should call a doctor if I felt poorly later, and went off home.'

Her mother nodded. 'Aye, that sounds reasonable,' she said, and Sylvie realised, with a stab of dismay, that her mother did not believe her story but would go along with it. And it isn't so far from the truth, Sylvie thought resentfully, soaping her old flannel and beginning to wash her neck and face vigorously. I wonder why she doesn't believe me, though? I'm sure I sounded as convincing as anything.

Her face was covered with suds and she was in no position to say much when her mother suddenly spoke. 'You and Annie, you ain't a bit alike to look at; Annie being brown-haired and brown-eyed, and pretty tall and hefty, like meself. But one thing you do have in common: when you're tellin' your old mam a story – a lie, that is – a special sort of tone comes into your voice. Oh aye, I always know when you or our Annie is letting her imagination run away wi' her.' She clucked impatiently. 'Tek off that bleedin' nightie and have a good strip-down wash, 'cos you're streaked with mud, you know, and it won't do for the old lady to start asking questions.' Her mother always referred to Mrs Dugdale – though not in her hearing – as the old lady, despite the fact that they were almost of an age.

Sylvie rinsed the soap off her face and neck, then turned to glare at her mother, now seated comfortably on the bed and staring at her with a very odd sort of look. 'Haven't you got any work to do, Mam?' she said, trying to sound friendly but hearing the querulousness creep into her voice without much surprise. Aggravating old devil! Why on earth was she hanging around up here when she doubtless had a thousand tasks awaiting her attention downstairs?

'Oh aye, but I can spare you five minutes,' her mother said. 'Unless you don't want to take off your nightgown in front of your old mother? If so, of course, I'd best be off.'

Sylvie felt the heat creep up her neck and invade her face, and guessed she was as scarlet as a beetroot. She was beginning to say, frostily, that it was all the same to her if her mother had time to spare but that on such a busy day, with the funeral in a few hours, she would have thought . . . when she was rudely interrupted.

'No need to get naggy at your old mother just because you're in the family way,' Mrs Davies said. 'An' no need to tell me it ain't Len's 'cos though

46

I'm no professor I can still put two 'n' two together 'n' make four. You'd best get round to Mrs Grundy what lives in Nightingale Court; she helps young gels in trouble, or so I've heard.'

Sylvie stared, round-eyed, at this astonishing parent of hers, then pulled herself together. 'I don't know what you mean,' she said briskly. 'Besides, old Ma Grundy kills people, or so the talk in the bar goes.'

'Len'll kill you when he gets out of jug if he finds you've been carryin' on wi' that Robbie Wentworth,' her mother pointed out. 'I blame meself, though I'm sure I done me best to bring you up decent, but it's a bit late to start layin' blame. First it were Len takin' you down the jigger so's there weren't no choice but for you to marry him, and now it's young Wentworth. Told 'im yet?'

Sylvie was about to reply when she heard a faint hail from below. Hastily, she tore off her night-gown and began to soap off the mud from last night's adventure. 'I've not seen Robbie for ages, but you're right, of course, I am in a spot of trouble,' she said. 'There is a way out, though, and now I come to think of it you could help me ever so much, if you would. But I can't explain now, it's too complicated. We'll talk after the funeral.'

Brendan attended the funeral as he had promised, scarcely recognising Sylvie at first, with her bright hair covered in a black felt hat and her small figure also shrouded in black. Len, however, was easy to pick out. He was in the front pew with a warder on either side of him, and though the warders were burly Len Dugdale dwarfed them. Brendan had known he must be a big man but thought that inactivity and prison food had probably increased the other's weight by several stone. Sylvie, in the pew behind, was tiny in comparison with her hulking great husband.

The church was packed and there were several policemen present, including a sergeant who had once, he told Brendan, walked Brendan's own beat. 'The old feller was a very different kettle of fish from the Dugdale that's in charge now,' he said nostalgically. 'If you went to the back door in them days you'd get a mug of porter if the bar was open, or a big cup of tea and a lovely buttered scone if it weren't. He'd ask you in to sit by the fire for five minutes so's he could tell you any gossip which might be useful, and you'd go on your way feelin' that a policeman's lot weren't so bad after all.'

Brendan had listened wistfully. The present landlord of the Ferryman did not encourage police visits, though he was always polite. But at this point in the sergeant's reminiscences the notes of the organ rang out, and the service began. When it was over, the priest announced that they should vacate the pews one at a time, starting at the front, and Brendan got a really good look at Len Dugdale as he, the two warders and a couple of policemen processed solemnly down the aisle and out into the morning freshness.

The entire congregation left the church in an orderly manner and followed the six black horses, with their nodding plumes, across the city to Anfield Cemetery. Brendan was devoutly thankful that the heavy rain of the previous night had given way to a clear blue sky, though the wind was brisk, making him glad to turn up his coat collar.

The grave was already dug and Brendan joined the others as the priest began to intone the words of committal. He was standing directly opposite Len, and as Mr Dugdale moved forward and threw a handful of earth on to the coffin Brendan was astonished to see large tears begin to run down Len's podgy cheeks. When his father turned to him, however, he knuckled his eyes briskly, then bent to pick up some earth and lobbed it gently down on to the coffin. After that, most of those present followed suit, including Sylvie, and when she stepped forward Len gave a strangled sob and tried to join her. The warders were having none of it. They had stood unobtrusively enough beside him, but when he turned towards his wife both men snatched simultaneously at his wrists and the policeman behind him clapped a hand on his shoulder and leaned forward to mutter something into his ear. It seemed to bring Len to a conscious-ness of his surroundings for he sighed gustily and bent his head, and presently the gravedigger seized his spade and began to shovel the earth briskly back into place. This was the signal for the landlord of the Ferryman to invite the assembled company back to the pub where refreshments awaited them.

Immediately people looked more cheerful, and the procession leaving the churchyard strode out briskly, eager to be back within doors out of the knifing wind.

Brendan saw Sylvie, who had been surrounded by her family, drop behind them for a moment as the crowd manoeuvred its way out of the cemetery, and seized the opportunity to have a quick word. He reached her side and bent his head, keeping his voice down and not so much as glancing at his companion. 'You all right? I called in to have a look at the rota in the nick on my way here and it looks like my next day off will be in three days' time. I've written to Caitlin asking her to reply as soon as possible.'

Sylvie had glanced up at him as they drew level but she was quick-witted enough now to follow his lead and look straight ahead. 'Things have changed,' she said softly. 'My mam knows and I'm hoping she'll help us. So mebbe it'll be easier to gerraway. We'd best talk, though . . . you're free on Friday? I'll be doin' Ma-in-law's messages and that'll include visitin' Charlotte Street for fish. I reckon I'll be there about ten in the morning; how would that be?'

Brendan hesitated. The market was a pretty public spot, especially on a Friday, but then sometimes it was easier to be missed amongst a crowd. And if either of them saw someone they knew whilst they were together, they could simply move apart. After all, the pub in which she lived was on his beat; it would be natural for them to exchange a few words. He said as much and Sylvie gave a quick little nod. 'Right, and if something happens, and I can't get to the market, then we'd best meet outside Lewis's after work,' she said.

Brendan was about to reply when they reached the gates and he saw that the Dugdales were waiting for their daughter-in-law. Hastily, he dropped back again, walking so slowly that he was soon overtaken by the last of the mourners. He saw Len and the warders approach the family group. Len spoke, his father answered, and the big woman he knew to be Mrs Dugdale surged forward as though she were about to embrace her son, but her husband grabbed her arm, restraining her, and the warders began to lead Len towards a cab which was standing by the kerb. They bundled him into it, and as Brendan emerged from the cemetery Len leaned out of the window. 'Not long now, queen,' he shouted, clearly addressing his wife who stood, hands clasped, gazing towards him. 'Only another five months an' I'll be home. Oh, Gawd, I can't wait!'

He might have said something else but was jerked back into the cab. The driver whipped up his horses and the last Brendan saw of Len Dugdale was one beefy hand, raised in farewell, as the cab disappeared.

*

Sylvie abandoned her parents-in-law as soon as she could. Fortunately, they were deep in conversation with relatives, some of whom had come a considerable distance to attend the funeral. Folk had been genuinely fond of the old man, but he had been ninety-two and had been bedridden for the past three years. Now that the serious business of burying him was over they could talk and even laugh once more, so it was an easy matter for Sylvie to jerk at Ma Dugdale's sleeve and tell her that she intended to hurry ahead. 'I know Mam will be setting out the food and brewing tea,' she hissed into her mother-in-law's ear, 'but there's even more people comin' back than we expected, so I reckon we'll need at least another couple of loaves of sandwiches, an' mebbe a few more cakes and scones. I can pick them up from Sample's if I hurry, and still be back in time to give a hand before most folk arrive.'

'You do that. You ain't a bad girl, even though you scarce said a word to our Len,' Mrs Dugdale said grudgingly. 'Poor lad, he were longing to hear your voice, but you didn't go near nor by.'

'Nor did you; we were told not to try to approach him,' Sylvie said smartly, stung by the injustice of the remark. 'I'll be off then. There's Becky, too. She'll be under Mam's feet I don't doubt, though she'll be doin' her best to help.' This time she did not give her mother-in-law a chance to reply but turned and began to wriggle through the crowd. She was lucky enough to see a tram going in the right direction and jumped aboard, alighting straight outside the bakery she had intended to visit, so that she was back at the Ferryman and slicing bread well before the funeral party arrived.

Becky was delighted to see her and was full of her own helpfulness, though she plucked, disgustedly, at her droopy black dress. 'Grandma Dugdale said it were made for Cousin Bertha when she were my age and she were taller and fatter than me, an' I want to change now,' she said as soon as she saw her mother. 'Great-grandpa called me his pretty little rose when I wore me pink cotton; he wouldn't want me lookin' plain an' ugly in this nasty dress.'

'Black shows you're sad because Great-grandpa isn't here any more,' Sylvie said, slicing bread like a machine.

'I can be just as sad in pink,' Becky said obstinately. 'I can be sadder, 'cos I'll be thinkin' about Great-grandpa an' missin' him instead of thinkin' about me dress. How can I be a little ray of sunshine in this horrible old thing? Oh, did you see me daddy, Mammy? Did he give you a present for me? Is he comin' back to the house? Grandma Dugdale said as how he were bound to bring me a present now he's workin' away, though she thought he would be too busy to come back to the Ferryman. I hope he brings me a leprechaun, 'cos he's in Ireland, ain't he? An' I'd like a little green feller of me own.'

Sylvie laughed and rumpled her daughter's flaxen hair. She and Mrs Dugdale had bought a tiny doll which they meant to present to Becky as a gift from her father. 'Yes, I did see Daddy and he sent you a big kiss and – and a little parcel, which he gave to Grandma Dugdale. Now be a good girl and don't ask Grandma to give it to you until all the guests have gone, because it's bad manners.'

Becky began to ask why it was bad manners, but at that point the door flew open and Mr and Mrs Dugdale, closely followed by their guests, began to stream into the big room behind the bar. Mrs Davies, flushed and beaming, grabbed the kettle off the stove and began to pour hot water into the urn which stood ready, and very soon they were all too busy to answer questions.

It was past four o'clock in the afternoon before the last guests departed, and Sylvie carried Becky, clutching her father's present, up to their room to change her out of the dreadful black dress and pop her into her cot for a much-needed snooze. It had all gone off rather well, Sylvie told herself, slipping out of her own dress and lying down on her bed. She would snatch a couple of hours' sleep herself before going off to work. For a little while she lay there looking forward to her meeting with Constable O'Hara, but soon weariness overcame her and she fell asleep.

Chapter Three

'Mr O'Hara! You told me last night to wake you at seven, so I'm doing it even though, so far as I can recall, this is your day off – or have they changed it again?' The voice echoing hollowly through the door was his landlady's and Brendan rolled over and groaned before shouting a stentorian reply.

'Thanks, Mrs Taggart. You've a wonderful memory, so you have, for 'tis still my day off, though almost every shift I've worked lately has been messed about. But I'm going out today to see my uncle so I need to be up and about early.'

'If you're respectable, there's a cup o' tea in me hand which I'll bring in so's you can drink it afore coming down to breakfast,' Mrs Taggart said.

Brendan assured her that he was extremely respectable and she came into the room, a small neat woman, her grey hair braided into a long plait and wound like a crown on top of her head. Brendan, accepting the tea with many thanks, thought how lucky he was to have found such a comfortable billet. Policemen had to be careful when they chose lodgings, or they might find themselves living in what amounted to a den of thieves, might even find themselves prosecuting the person in whose house they lodged. That was why the authorities always vetted one's digs before allowing one to move in, though this had not been necessary in Mrs Taggart's case. She was the widow of a police sergeant and had been letting her rooms to policemen ever since her husband's death, ten years earlier.

Because of her knowledge of the force, she was understanding of the lives her lodgers led, knowing very well that they were not at fault when they did not come in for meals, worked double shifts, or were simply forced to go on duty instead of taking the only day off they had been allocated, perhaps for as long as three weeks.

However, there had been no mention of his working today when he had signed off from his night shift, so Brendan was determined to get out of the house and stay out; if the force was unable to contact him he might actually get his day off for once.

By half-past eight he was making his way towards the market. He knew Sylvie could not possibly arrive at such an early hour, but he still felt he would be safer away from the house. He was wearing civvies, of course, and not the ones which the police force recommended either. They told the men that their off-duty wear should be blue suits and bowler hats, but Brendan knew there was no actual rule which insisted on this, so today he was clad in a navy blue seaman's jersey, and a pair of heavy-duty denim trousers, tucked into short rubber boots. On his head he wore a woollen hat, for the December day was cold, and despite his height and the way he carried himself he was sure that he did not look like a policeman. He realised how right he was when Sylvie failed to recognise him, though she had known he would not be in uniform. Her incurious eyes looked him over without recognition and it was not until he hissed her name that she looked again, and her slow, enchanting smile broke out.

'Brendan!' she said joyfully. 'Oh, I was beginning to wonder whether you'd forgotten we were meeting here. I've bought my fish and the rest of my messages. Do you know Dorothy's Dining Rooms? They deal mostly with market traders so I think we could pop in there and have a quiet talk over a cup of tea.'

'Yes, I know it. I've been in there once or twice; they do a good special for ninepence.'

Presently, they found themselves a quiet corner table and ordered tea from an elderly waitress, who looked as though her feet were killing her. Sylvie was wearing the long black coat, black stockings and black boots in which Brendan had first seen her, but she had added a black head square which she wore pulled forward so that it half hid the upper part of her face, as well as completely covering her hair. Brendan thought it extremely unlikely that anyone would recognise either of them; folk looked at policemen's uniforms rather than their faces and, for economic reasons, nine out of ten married women in the city habitually wore black.

The tea arrived, and as soon as the waitress had departed Sylvie began to speak. 'My mam knows I'm expecting a baby. It wasn't so much my shape as – as because she guessed. She watched me wash the morning after I'd fallen in the Mersey and instead of pulling my nightdress off and getting on with it I – I sort of dabbled around. Then she asked me outright. I tried lying but me heart wasn't in it, and anyway it's a good job she does know, because she'll help me, though only on certain conditions.'

'What conditions?' Brendan asked suspiciously. He wondered whether the old lady might imagine Sylvie's lover to be a rich man who could hand over money in exchange for her silence, but Sylvie soon disabused him on that score.

'She agrees that I must leave Becky behind, though I still hate the thought of doing that. But she says it wouldn't be right to involve the child in deceit, and besides you couldn't expect her not to mention that she had a baby brother or sister when we came back to Liverpool, which would put the fat in the fire and no mistake.'

Brendan laughed. 'You're right there,' he agreed. 'Any more conditions? From what you've told me, your mother is a sensible woman with her head screwed on the right way, and it's grand that she means to help us. Fire ahead, then.'

'She says I must promise her faithfully that I'll get the baby adopted and come back to Liverpool just as soon as I can. She says if I went off and never came back it would put her and Bertie in a horrible position. But there's no fear of that – they know I'd never desert Becky.'

'Fair enough. What reason are you going to give for leaving the Ferryman?' Brendan asked. 'Did your mam help with that, too?'

'Oh yes, that's the best of all,' Sylvie said, dimpling at him. 'I would never have thought of it, but she says we must say that some relatives of ours who went to America years and years ago have come to England to meet various members of our family. She means to pretend to entertain them, and to discover that they need someone to look after their small child when they go over to Ireland to visit the rest of the family. Mam's pa, my grandfather, came from Donegal, you know. She'll say they're rich and will pay well, and Len's ma and pa will agree to my going because I'll be earning money so's Len an' me can have our own place when he comes out of clink. Me mam's worked for Mrs Dugdale for years and years, and though the old girl might not believe me, she trusts my mam. We won't tell Bertie, or anyone else, that there are really no American relatives and I do think it's a brilliant idea, don't you? And of course we'll say that the Americans won't employ someone with a kid of their own, because they want me to concentrate on their little one and not worry about mine.'

'Right,' Brendan said, digesting this. Like Mrs Davies, he could see no alternative to Sylvie's leaving Becky behind, especially since she had made it plain that her in-laws would accept the loss of herself for six months or so with equanimity, but would never consent to losing their grand-daughter for so much as six days, let alone longer. So now he smiled encouragingly into the small face opposite his own. ''Tis hard on you to be without your little girl for so long, but 'tis for the best, I'm sure of it,' he said consolingly. 'Besides, you'll have Caitlin's kids, and the new baby, until you can find a grand new home for it. Then you can come back to Liverpool wit'out a stain on your character. Why, once Len is away from his parents' place, he may become easier to live with; it does happen, I'm told.'

'I don't know about that,' Sylvie said doubtfully. 'But Brendan, I probably won't be earning a good wage, unless your cousin can find me a job.'

Brendan did not tell her that he intended to send Caitlin money each month, but he had already told his cousin that he would do so. Instead he said that when Sylvie got back to Liverpool she should pretend that she had been robbed, though he personally was sure that she would get work in Dublin.

'An' me cousin won't be after you for money 'cos she and Pat are pretty comfortable,' he said, feeling the heat rise to his cheeks. He had told Caitlin that the money was to be a secret between them. 'An' now, alanna, I think you must write to Robbie again, explain the situation and say you'll be in desperate need of money for the next six months. Once he knows there's to be no scandal, I'm sure he'll help. After all, it is in his interest to do so.'

'Yes, that's true,' Sylvie said thoughtfully. 'The Wentworths live next door to me mam and if it were common knowledge what Robbie had done he'd be afraid to show his face at home, and I don't think he'd like to be thought badly of. What's more, he an' Len were thick as thieves – good pals, I mean – when they were in school, before Robbie went to sea and Len married me, and I guess Robbie wouldn't want his old pal to know how he had behaved.' She turned glowing eyes to Brendan. 'I'm sure he will help,' she said breathlessly. 'And I think you're the cleverest man, as well as the kindest, that I've ever met. I'll write to Robbie as soon as I get home. Ma-in-law will think I'm doing Christmas cards.'

'It's great your mam's going to help you. We seem to have sorted out most of your problems,' Brendan said comfortably, and stood up. 'You must write to your mam often while you are away, and I'd be glad of a line now and then.'

Sylvie rose to her feet as he spoke and picked up her marketing bags whilst he went over to the desk and paid the bill. When he returned he gave her a reassuring smile. 'I'm sure Wentworth will be in touch before Christmas,' he said, taking the heavier of the marketing bags from her. 'I imagine that you will tell him to write to your mam's address. Don't forget, I lodge at 48 Hunter Street, but I'd rather you didn't call there unless you're in desperate need. And as soon as I hear from Caitlin, I'll come down to Lewis's; you're usually free about nine in the evening, aren't you?'

Almost a month later, Sylvie boarded the Dublin packet, in a snowstorm, bound for Caitlin's home. She had the address in her bulging portmanteau and her heart was high, for she had escaped without anyone discovering her secret. She was beginning to notice a thickening of her waist, which terrified her, and was grateful that very soon now she would be with folk who knew of her condition and understood her plight.

Soon after Christmas, Mrs Davies had asked for a couple of hours off so that she might meet the SS *Arabic*. 'Do you remember me Auntie Effie and her husband, Tom, what went to the States, oh, a good twenty years back?' she had asked her employer. 'Well, me aunt died last year but she were very keen for her daughter to come back to England and meet some of her relatives. The daughter's a married woman now with a little boy of two and a new baby. They won't be in Liverpool long because, as you know, my family hail from Donegal, but I've promised to get them into a decent hotel – they're well off, it seems; quite rich in fact – so I think I ought to meet their ship.'

Mr and Mrs Dugdale had accepted this without question. It was by no means unusual for relatives to want to visit 'the old country', and when this happened the family still in England, and Ireland, were eager to show friendship towards these strangers who had once been close. So Mrs Davies had gone off on her invented errand and when she had mentioned casually, after a couple of days, that the O'Keefes were looking for a nanny before they went to Ireland, someone reliable who would look after their youngsters whilst they were travelling around, Mrs Dugdale had actually suggested that Sylvie should apply for the job. 'And I could look after Becky,' she had said eagerly. 'You say they're payin' well 'n' all found. Our Sylvie could save a lot an' it 'ud be wonderful for Len to come out o' clink an' find a nice little sum waitin' for him. I ain't sayin' I approve of them movin' out because it's right handy havin' the pair of 'em on the spot, but me and Mr Dugdale would be willin' to turn the attic floor into a self-contained flat – that means with its own kitchen an' bathroom – if we could use Sylvie's earnings to mek the changes.'

Naturally, Mrs Davies had agreed enthusiastically, and that evening she had collared Sylvie in order to tell her what had transpired. 'But I never knew the old saying were so true before – you know the one: *Oh what a tangled web we weave when first we practise to deceive,*' she had moaned. 'Where we are to lay our hands on a large sum of money by the time you get back, God only knows!'

Sylvie, however, had brushed this aside.

'Brendan says I may be able to work, so with luck I'll have some money,' she had pointed out. 'As for the rest, I shall say I were robbed.'

So the whole charade had been played out to its obvious conclusion: Sylvie had applied for the fictitious job and been appointed, and had given in her notice at Lewis's. Brendan had booked her passage aboard the packet, waving aside her half-hearted offer of payment. Inevitably, there were times, as Sylvie thought about leaving the Ferryman and journeying to Ireland, when her heart sank into her boots and she truly thought she could never do it. Leaving my beloved Becky will break my heart, she told herself. But common sense reminded her of what she stood to lose should she remain in Liverpool. The Dugdales would turn her out, probably make sure that she never saw Becky again, and that would be far, far worse than an absence of a mere six months. So she squared her shoulders and continued with the scheme.

Mrs Dugdale had professed herself eager to meet the O'Keefes, but Sylvie had vetoed her mother-in-law's suggestion that she should bring Becky to the Pier Head to see her off.

'I've not actually told the O'Keefes that Becky's only three, because I don't want them to think me a heartless mother,' she had explained, with her most guileless look. 'But you come, Ma; it'll be nice to see a familiar face as the ship leaves the shore.'

Mrs Dudgale had actually given Sylvie a kiss as they had said their farewells in the Ferryman's kitchen. 'You're a good gel to want to make a bit of money for our poor lad,' she had said warmly. 'And you don't have to tell me how much you'll miss Becky, because you've always been a grand little mother to her.' She had hesitated, then added: 'And I won't deny you've been grand to Mr Dugdale an' meself; a real help, norrabit reproachful over havin' to work behind the bar when you ain't at Lewis's.'

Sylvie was thinking of this praise as she boarded the ferry. It would make it easier to return to Liverpool, once the baby was born, knowing that Mrs Dugdale would welcome her gladly and not resent her reappearance. Her mother had advised her to pick out a nice family party as soon as she was aboard and attach herself to them, and though this seemed a trifle unnecessary Sylvie did as she was bid. She was presently very glad she had, for as the gangway was removed, and the ship's siren sounded, she saw her father-in-law on the quay-side. He was waving a large red and white checked handkerchief and Sylvie bent down and picked up the child of the young couple to whom she had been talking. 'Wave to my dear old dad, little 'un,' she commanded. 'See him down there? He's the feller with the red and white hanky.'

'I see him,' the little imp exclaimed, putting a plump arm round Sylvie's neck. 'He's gorra big red nose, hasn't he?'

'That's because he's the landlord of a pub, and bends his elbow too much and gets squiffy,' Sylvie said untruthfully, and regretted it as the child announced, in ringing tones: 'Squiffy? Does I get squiffy? Does my daddy get squiffy?'

Sylvie glanced apprehensively at the child's parents, but they were both laughing. 'No, Daddy doesn't know the meaning of the word,' the young mother said, smiling at Sylvie. 'And now let's go below and have a nice cup of tea before we meet the waves of the Irish Sea, because once we get out there I'm sure drinking tea will be the last thing on our minds.'

Brendan was unable to see Sylvie off on the ferry, because at the very moment the ship sailed he had been on parade at the Rose Hill police station. The constables were standing to attention whilst the sergeant marched up and down the line, demanding to see each man's accoutrements, which meant that one produced one's truncheon, handcuffs, whistle, and occurrence book and pencil. When the sergeant had closely examined all these objects, he went up and down the line again, impatiently tweaking at tunics and criticising the shine on the large heavy-issue boots which every man had to buy from his own wages. By the time he released them to go to their beats, Brendan thought morosely that the Irish ferry would be clear of the estuary and her bows would be butting at the grey waters of the Irish Sea. Not that it was anyone's fault, exactly; the sergeant was quite a decent bloke but Brendan remembered the old adage *Never explain, never complain*, which he knew to be all too true, so had said nothing about his wish to wave the Irish ferry off.

Still, he comforted himself now by recalling that they had said their goodbyes the previous evening. They had met briefly, outside Lewis's, both of them sheltering under Sylvie's umbrella since, as on their first meeting, the rain, mixed this time with hail, had been driving almost horizontally. He had checked that she had Caitlin's address right and had given her a packet of envelopes and a pad of notepaper as a parting gift. 'So mind you write to me to let me know all's well,' he had said gruffly. 'I doubt I'll be able to see you off tomorrow, but I'll be thinking of you.' He had patted her shoulder. 'Take care of yourself.'

For answer, she had cast the umbrella aside, thrown her arms round his neck and kissed him on the side of his mouth. 'You are the best and kindest man in the whole world,' she had said sweetly. 'One of these days you'll meet a really nice girl who is free to love you the way you deserve and I envy her.'

He had picked up her umbrella and handed it back to her, saying ruefully: 'I hope you're right, but being a policeman's wife isn't much fun, you know. And now you'd best run off, or I'll miss my quarter and be in deep trouble.'

He had watched her go and then had had to hurry through the driving rain to arrive on time at the point on his beat that he was supposed to have reached. He had had little fear that the sergeant would check on such a wild night but one could never be sure. So far, his record sheet was clean, and he meant to keep it that way.

With an effort, he dragged his mind back to the present. The sergeant had given each man his beat, and the constables were enjoying a few moments of conversation before they went their separate ways. Constable Flanagan, who had been in the police force for almost ten years and had recently got engaged to a girl in County Down, was holding forth. 'I'm goin' to give in me notice at the end of the month,' he announced. 'The sarge told me last week that I can't get wed until we've been engaged for four years and mebbe not then either, if she ain't suitable. I'm sick of bein' treated like a perishin' kid and I'm sick of bad digs and cold food and cold feet. I thought life in Ireland was hard, and so it is, but I've saved a fair bit, enough to buy a bit of extra land so's me dad's place can support me and the wife. Oh aye, I'll be gone by March.'

All the men stared at him admiringly and Brendan opened his mouth to offer his congratulations just as the sergeant bawled from behind him: 'Move on!' and grinning, they scattered. As he walked, Brendan considered what the older man had said. It was true, the police force did not treat its members well, but he took home a regular wage, a much higher one than he could have earned in most other employments, and because one got so little time off saving money was easy. Indeed, he had amassed a considerable amount in his two years on the force, and thought that, if he could stick it for another two or three years, he would be able to buy a small property of his own. Then, because he was not afraid of hard work, he would speedily begin to prosper. The money he would send to Caitlin would not make much difference, particularly as, to his considerable relief, Wentworth had answered Sylvie's desperate plea pretty promptly and had promised fifteen shillings a week for the next few months.

As Brendan began to plod towards his beat, he thought again of Sylvie's fragile beauty and wondered what she was doing right now. He glanced up at the clock above the chemist's shop and calculated that she would not be in Dublin until his shift was half over. Not that it mattered; he could not possibly get news of her for at least a week. Ahead of him, a row seemed to have broken out between two shopkeepers and half a dozen angry customers. Brendan made his way towards them, walking with the deliberate stride which seemed slow, but carried a policeman towards trouble at a surprising rate. 'Hello-ello-ello, what's goin' on here, then?' he enquired jovially. 'Lost a pound and found a penny, ladies?'

Several voices answered him simultaneously. It

seemed one customer, a tall angular woman in the regulation black, with sandy hair pulled tightly back from her narrow face, had accused Mr Binns, who owned the nearby hardware store, of selling her a cracked chamber pot. Mr Binns had said that she must have knocked it 'cos it were sound as a bell when he put it in the paper bag. It then transpired that the sandy-haired woman was the wife of another shopkeeper, who had emerged from his premises and was both backing her up and probably slandering his neighbour, whilst the other women, delighted, milled around, first taking one side, then the other.

Brendan took a deep breath. 'I think everyone, barring the injured parties, should move on,' he said. 'And the rest of us will take a look at the article in question . . .'

It might not have been easy to find one narrow street amongst so many in the Liberties, but Sylvie's fragile prettiness stood her in good stead. She put her bag down for a moment, and as she did so a warm Irish voice addressed her. Turning, she saw a little old man smiling at her. He was dressed in ragged clothes and carried a pile of newspapers under one arm. 'Sure and you look like you could do wit' some help, and amn't I the feller to give you a hand?' he said, pushing his greasy cap to the back of his domed and balding head, and grabbing for her bag. 'Where's you bound?' He looked her shrewdly up and down.

'A pretty critter like you will be headin' for some-where real smart, I guess. Would it be Sackville Street where the big stores are, or Merrion Square, where the smart folk live? If so, you'll be wanting to cross the Liffey; there's a bridge nearby—'

But here Sylvie broke in. 'No indeed; I'm looking for Handkerchief Alley. I believe it's in the Liberties. Do you happen to know it?'

'To be sure, I know it well. It's off Francis Street, so it is, and we'll still have to cross the river,' the old man said. Rather to Sylvie's surprise, he seemed disappointed, but he heaved her bag on to his shoulder and set off, advising her to follow him. Sylvie did so, looking curiously about her as they passed along the busy streets. There were plenty of shops but it occurred to her that the city of Dublin was like a small town, lacking the enor-mous buildings so common in the city of Liverpool. Here, few buildings were more than two storeys high, and despite the fact that it was an icy-cold day the countless children running and playing in the streets were clad in the skimpiest of rags; this was clearly a very poor part of the city, however, and Sylvie decided to defer her judgement until she'd had a chance to look round.

Presently, they crossed the river by what the little man informed her was called the Metal Bridge. It spanned the Liffey in a glorious arc, and halfway across Sylvie paused for a moment to look down into the swirling waters, for the Liffey was clearly a tidal river, as was the Mersey, and it gave her a comfortable feeling of familiarity, for she had begun to feel very much a stranger amongst the jostling crowds. Once on the further bank, she tried to take her portmanteau from her new friend, because he was so very old and did not look particularly strong, but he waved her away, saying gruffly that he'd carried many a heavier burden. If he had been younger and fitter, Sylvie might have been afraid he would bolt with all her possessions, but judging from the way he was wheezing he stood little chance of escaping from her even if he decided to do so. Accordingly, Sylvie merely kept close to him, which she would have had to do in any case, for now the streets were even more crowded than they had been on the other side of the river.

They had walked some way when her companion turned into a street lined with shops and market stalls. 'This here's Francis Street,' he informed her. 'It's a grand street, so it is; you can buy anything you're likely to want here. But we're nearly there.' And to be sure, two minutes later, he turned into an alley lined with tall tenement blocks on either side. He came to a breathless halt, wheezing painfully, and standing her portmanteau down upon the filthy cobbles. 'What's your friend's name, alanna? Which floor's she on?'

Sylvie looked around her. She had been brought up in a Liverpool court and she knew such places were considered slums, but this was a good deal worse than anything she had seen in her city. The tenement buildings looked as though they might collapse at any moment; windows were cracked and broken, with glass missing, the brickwork was crazed with huge crevices, and the smell which lingered most unpleasantly in the chilly air convinced Sylvie that there was little, if any, sanitation. She opened her mouth to comment, to ask if this was really Handkerchief Alley, for she remembered Brendan saying that his cousin and her family lived in comfortable circumstances, but before she could speak there was a great clattering of footsteps from the nearest building, and a woman came out and flung both arms round Sylvie.

'You'll be Sylvie Dugdale, what's coming to stay with us for a while,' she said exuberantly. 'And you're welcome as the flowers in May, so you are. You'll have guessed that I'm Caitlin O'Keefe . . . but who's your friend?' She glanced enquiringly at the odd little man, then beamed. 'Well, if it ain't Sammy, what sells the *Herald* down on the quays,' she announced. 'Everyone knows Sammy. But how come you two have met up?'

'The gentleman carried my bag for me, and the truth is I were glad of it, 'cos it's a deal heavier than I thought,' Sylvie admitted. She fished a threepenny bit out of her purse and handed it to the old man. 'Thank you very much indeed,' she said formally.

Sammy snatched the money eagerly and grinned, revealing a mouthful of broken, blackened teeth, then disappeared with a mumbled word of thanks. Caitlin shook her head sadly at her guest. 'A penny would have done . . . or a ha'penny, come to that,' she said. 'But come up and meet the family. We've got the whole of the top floor; we get it cheap 'cos the roof leaks.' She led the way into a small hall and then began to climb the stairs, which were rickety in the extreme, with holes at intervals. Sylvie realised that her hostess, whilst chattering gaily, was placing her feet only on the soundest of the steps and hastily followed suit; she had no desire to plunge down one of the holes and break a leg before she had even reached the O'Keefes' dwelling.

On the second landing, Caitlin paused for breath and took the portmanteau firmly out of her visitor's grasp. 'I'll carry it now, seein' as you're in the family way,' she said. 'Did Brendan tell you – oh, but I was forgettin', he couldn't tell you anything about this place because he's never seen it – that there's thirty-six stairs up to the top landing, and that's quite a climb when you ain't used to it.'

'I expect I'll soon grow accustomed,' Sylvie said, rather breathlessly. 'Besides, there are a great many steps up to our room in the Ferryman, so I am quite used to climbing stairs. I expect you get wonderful views over the city, don't you?'

They had reached another landing and Caitlin snorted. 'Views?' she said scornfully. 'Not unless

74

you count rooftops and other tenements, to say nothing of washing lines.' She grinned at Sylvie and Sylvie had a good look at her. Caitlin had soft, dark curls and big, dark eyes set in a small face. She was very pretty, though her clothing did nothing to enhance her slender figure, but of course she would scarcely be wearing her best things when doing her housework and minding her children. She was clad in a long dark blue skirt, a blouse which might once have been white but was now a dirty grey, a very long and loopy black cardigan with half the buttons missing, and a tattered black shawl. The clothing all seemed a good deal too big for her. Sylvie, in the new coat, navy serge skirt and leg o' mutton blouse, with its high neck and frilled collar, which Mrs Dugdale had insisted she buy for her 'interview', felt horribly overdressed, for she saw Caitlin's eyes examining her even as she examined the other girl. 'Sorry about me clothes,' Caitlin said, as Sylvie opened her mouth to explain why she herself was so smartly dressed. 'They were my mammy's; she died last year an' left me everything, which weren't much, but the clothes come in useful.' She dimpled at her new friend. 'I'm no hand wit' a needle else I could've altered 'em to fit me better.' She looked, admiringly, at her guest. 'Ain't you just the prettiest t'ing, though? I'd love to be fair, so I would, but we's all dark, from Pat an' meself to our youngest, Colm, who's four.' She heaved the bag up into her arms once more even as Sylvie assured her, truthfully, that she herself was no prettier than Caitlin.

'Brendan never told me a thing about you, except that you had several children,' she admitted as they began to toil upwards again. 'That's typical of a feller, though – they don't waste words on describing someone you're going to meet anyway. Gosh, aren't these stairs steep?'

'Aye, they are that, so they are,' Caitlin agreed, just as they arrived at the very top landing. She pushed open a heavy door to her right, explaining as she did so that the doors on the left led to the children's bedrooms, and the doors on the right to her own bedroom and the kitchen. As she spoke, they had entered the latter, which, to Sylvie's bemused eyes, seemed to contain about twenty people. However, it was a pleasant room, with a bright fire burning in the grate, linoleum upon the floor, scattered with bright rag rugs, and a number of wooden chairs grouped round a large central table. The walls were whitewashed and the pots and pans on the shelves gleamed with cleanliness, whilst the large dresser against one wall displayed a quantity of crockery. Everything was beautifully clean and there was a pleasant smell of food cooking, whilst the open doors of a large cupboard revealed strings of onions, a big bag of potatoes and another of carrots, and a number of shelves crowded with smaller bags, bottles and jars, clearly containing foodstuffs. Caitlin turned towards her, once more dumping Sylvie's bag on the ground.

'Sit you down, my dear,' she said hospitably, then turned to the children. 'Close the doors of the press, won't you? It makes the room look so untidy.' A child obediently trotted across to the cupboard, closed the doors carefully, then returned to stand before her mother.

Caitlin smiled her approval. 'Now come and meet Sylvie, who's going to live with us for a while,' she commanded.

The children rushed forward and then, to Sylvie's amusement, shuffled themselves into size order. They were raggedly dressed, the boys with roughly cut hair and scabbed knees, the girls on the whole tidier and certainly a good deal cleaner. Despite Sylvie's initial conviction that there were at least twenty children in the room, it turned out that there were only eight, three of whom were not O'Keefes.

But Caitlin was introducing everyone. 'Maeve's me childminder and a grand help she is, too. She lives with us, takes care of the kids when I'm at work, gets me messages, washes, irons . . . oh, I don't know what I'd do wit'out her, an' that's gospel truth. Say hello to Sylvie, Maeve; she's goin' to be livin' with us for a while.'

The child, Maeve, smiled shyly at Sylvie. She was a poor, plain little thing and Sylvie had already noticed that she dragged one foot as she walked and held one shoulder higher than the other. She had limp dark hair and a small and skinny body, but Caitlin assured her visitor that Maeve was

77

nearly twelve and a very capable young person. 'And this is Clodagh, me eldest,' Caitlin continued. 'She's eight. Then come the twins, Fergal and Seamus – they're six – and then Grainne – she's five – and me youngest, Colm – he's four.' She smiled brightly at Sylvie and pointed to the last two children in the line. 'Maeve looks after these for their mam while she's out at work. I expect Brendan told you that I've got a job in Switzers, which is a big store on Grafton Street. I'm in the ladies' gowns department and sometimes I model the clothes and walk up and down so's the real ladies can see what a ball gown or a smart suit looks like wit' someone inside it. The money's a great help even though Pat has a job in a bank on Sackville Street. He's real clever, is Pat. He were always top of the class when he were in school, so one day he'll probably be a bank manager.' She dimpled at Sylvie once more. 'Same as I'll be head sales lady in Gowns.'

'Brendan didn't mention it,' Sylvie admitted apologetically. 'You see, we were only able to meet secretly because the Dugdales kept an eye on me for their son, Len.' She looked speculatively at Caitlin. Just how much did Caitlin know? If it was as little as she, Sylvie, had been told about the O'Keefes, then she had better grit her teeth and start explaining at once. 'Look, I think you and I will have to have a quiet talk. I feel really bad that you might think I've come to you under false pretences, and—'

'We'll take your t'ings along to your room and

start unpacking; Maeve will keep the kids occupied until dinnertime,' Caitlin said briskly, picking up Sylvie's bag once more and ushering her out through the kitchen door. 'I'm afraid you can't have a room all to yourself – you'll be sharing with Clodagh, Grainne and Maeve – but you've a bed to yourself.' She flung open a door as she spoke and ushered Sylvie into a rather small room with low attic windows and a wooden floor whose planks rose and fell like waves on a stormy sea. There were two galvanised buckets strategically placed beneath the stained ceiling in horrid anticipation of the next downpour, for when Sylvie looked up she could actually see sky through one of the wide cracks which ran across the plaster. In addition to the buckets, there was a big brass bedstead upon which rested a feather mattress, and beside it, crammed between the window and a tea chest which clearly did duty as a dressing table, was a narrow pallet.

'That's yours,' Caitlin said proudly, pointing to the pallet. 'It used to be Maeve's but she's going to head 'n' tail it wit' the two girls. I know the pallet's kind of narrow,' she added apologetically, when Sylvie did not speak, 'but when you get a job you can buy yourself something a bit more comfortable. We've a grosh of markets in Dublin where everything you can think of can be bought second-hand.'

'Sorry, I was thinking of something else,' Sylvie said. 'And that bed will be fine until I start to get bigger, of course. But – but you said I might gerra job. Who on earth will employ me when I start to show?'

'They'll employ you first because of that hair and then because you don't talk wit' a brogue so broad that the smart ladies can't understand you,' Caitlin said wisely. 'I have to calm me tongue down in Switzers, I can tell you. I reckon you'll get a good two or three months' work behind you before they start to get suspicious, and then there's other jobs where they don't care what you look like so long as you sell the goods, or clean the premises, or iron the linen. But come on, alanna, you were wantin' a quiet talk and now's the best chance we'll get, so fire away.'

For a moment, Sylvie wondered whether she should trim her story a little, make it more accept-able, but then decided that this would be silly as well as unfair. So she took a deep breath and began. 'Well, it all started when me husband, Len, was sent to prison . . .'

By the end of February, Sylvie was beginning to grow accustomed to her new life, though she missed Becky almost unbearably. She even missed the Ferryman, and of course often longed for her mother's sturdy common sense to comfort her when she was worried. The truth was that despite Brendan's reassuring words, the O'Keefes were pitifully poor by Sylvie's standards. Wages were dreadfully low and rents higher than they should have been, and Sylvie felt obliged to give Caitlin as much of Robbie's money as she could afford, though Caitlin said repeatedly that it was not necessary; they had got along without it before and God knew Sylvie didn't eat all that much.

But however difficult the circumstances, Sylvie could not but love the O'Keefes. They were a wonderfully warm and friendly family, and when she had been in the city a few days Caitlin had taken her along to Switzers. She had heard that there was a vacancy on the Gloves and Haberdashery counter, and the staff member who had interviewed Sylvie had given her the job at once, though she had had to accept what had seemed a pitiful wage. 'But if you give satisfaction, your money will go up after your month's trial,' the woman had explained and Sylvie, wearing her tightest corset, had thought, hopefully, that she might earn for another month or two before her condition became obvious.

But that had been some weeks ago and now, as Sylvie slid behind the Gloves and Haberdashery counter in Switzers, she reflected that her happiest hours in Dublin were spent here, where the smell was not of poverty but of beautiful leather and suede, floor polish, and the perfumes used by all their lady customers. Through the window opposite she could see large flakes of snow descending from a grey sky. They were coming down very slowly and gracefully, but Sylvie thought of the overcrowded little bedroom in Handkerchief

Alley, the ice on top of the water jug, and the snow which would melt and come trickling through the ceiling, and shivered. To be sure the O'Keefes were better off than most, and her own contribution must help, but the hole in the ceiling remained and when she had asked Pat, rather pettishly, why he did not go up and make the tiles good, he had reminded her first that it was winter, and next that the tiles were extremely slippery.

'I've no desire to find meself shooting down towards the alley and ending up a mangled heap on the cobbles,' he had told her. 'The landlord won't raise a finger and we do get the place cheap. When spring comes, I'll mebbe get to work wit' canvas and tar, but until then, the buckets don't do a bad job.'

Sylvie knew she should not grumble, that the O'Keefes were treating her with great generosity, but she still felt somewhat aggrieved. Pat had patched the ceiling in the boys' room so that it scarcely leaked at all, and she did so hate lying in her bed at night and listening to the tinkle of water running into the buckets, knowing that she must get up and empty them out of the window – praying to God there was no one below as she did so – then carefully replace them in their strategic spots. Having performed this task, she would climb back into bed and be kept awake for what felt like hours, because water falling into an empty galvanised bucket is even noisier than water falling into a full one. Of course, she could always rouse Maeve, inform her that the bucket was full and ask her to empty it, and this she had done on several occasions. But once, when Maeve had been truly exhausted and very deeply asleep, Sylvie had been unable to rouse her. Consequently, she had had great difficulty heaving the overflowing buckets up to the window, which meant that a good deal of water had leapt from bucket to floor where, of course, it had run down between the floorboards and ended up falling on to the sleeping heads of Mr and Mrs Cavanagh in the flat below.

Sylvie had not been unduly worried because she had not known in which room the old couple slept, until Mr Cavanagh had come storming up the stairs at two in the morning, vowing vengeance on whoever had 'peed on the bloody floor and near on washed me and the wife out of our bed'. He had thundered on the wrong door to begin with and Sylvie, guessing what had happened, had heaved the blankets over her head and feigned sleep. Had he knocked first on Caitlin's door, she and Pat would no doubt have explained and apologised, but unfortunately he had chosen the boys' room. Shock-headed Seamus had come to the door and seen an opportunity to get the girls into trouble, or so Sylvie had thought to herself, for the twins were a couple of devils. He had pushed past Mr Cavanagh and thrown open the girls' door, and in the light of the tall candle which Mr Cavanagh held had pointed out the buckets and the telltale wet patch even now spreading further across the floor. Maeve had sat up immediately. 'It's dat sorry I am, Mr Cavanagh,' she had said in her small, high voice. ''Tis all my fault, for I didn't hear the bucket was almost full till it was so heavy I couldn't move it wit'out help. I did me best but I'm afraid I spilt some before I got it to the window.'

Mr Cavanagh had been beginning to say, grudgingly, that he supposed it were really the landlord's fault when Grainne and Clodagh, too, had sat up. 'You said it were pee, Mr Cavanagh, and it weren't nothing of the sort,' Grainne had said in an injured voice. 'Our mam gives us two big jerries what we keep under the bed; we pees in dem, not on der floor.'

Mr Cavanagh had grunted and then chuckled, and this had emboldened Sylvie, in her turn, to sit upright and say, in a bemused voice: 'Whatever's happening? Where am I?'

Nobody had deigned to enlighten her, however. Grainne, Clodagh and Maeve had already snuggled down and Seamus had been ushering old Mr Cavanagh out of the room, but the boy had given Sylvie a contemptuous glance just before he closed the door and Sylvie had felt, uneasily, that he knew very well who had spilt the water and thought her a coward to let the blame fall on Maeve.

Next morning she had tried to apologise to Maeve for not confessing that it had been she who had been responsible for the Cavanaghs' dousing. But Maeve had ducked her head and mumbled:

'Sure and it might have been me, and anyway, amn't I supposed to wake up before the buckets are filled, so's I can empty them wit'out any spillages? The t'ing is, I should've emptied 'em before I got into bed – that's what I'm meant to do – but I was so tired I forgot. Dem twins had me playin' hide 'n' seek round half Dublin afore they let me catch 'em.'

Sylvie had promised to remind Maeve, in future, to empty the buckets before she slept, or to do so herself before she climbed into her own bed. It seemed to rain twice as often in Dublin as it had done in Liverpool, and doubtless would snow twice as often, too, or was that simply the impression given by an unsound roof rather than a sound one?

'Miss Dugdale! I've told you before that no good sales lady ever stands behind the counter wit' her mouth wide open, gazing into space. Even before the customers start coming in, you should be checking the goods, cleaning down the measuring rule, winding up the ribbons, putting the gloves in size order . . . ah, here comes Mr Leggatt. Look lively, girl!'

Sylvie shot a malevolent look at the speaker whilst beginning to open drawers to check the goods therein. Miss O'Leary was head sales lady on Gloves and Haberdashery and had appeared to take against Sylvie from her very first day at the store. The fact that Sylvie was married, though she was always referred to as Miss Dugdale at work, seemed to exacerbate her resentment, but Miss Spencer, who also worked on Gloves and Haberdashery, had assured Sylvie that the head sales lady disliked all her employees. 'We're young and she's old, we're pretty and she's plain, we had a decent schooling else Switzers wouldn't have took us on, and she's thick as pease porridge,' she had said cheerfully. 'What's more, the customers like us so our sales figures are better than hers. Still an' all, she's not as bad as some. Mr McDonald, in Gents' Tailoring, says that his head of sales takes all the credit when one of them sells a deal of stuff to a customer. He'll come swanning up and have a few words with the customer, perhaps he'll fold a shirt or pretend to check the price of a pair of socks, and then he'll put his initials on the bill and swear to heaven that it were his sale.'

Sylvie had stared round-eyed at her companion. The two girls had been walking back to the Liberties along Great George's Street and Sylvie had let her pent-up breath go in a whistle of astonishment. 'Well, I'll never grumble about old O'Leary again, and I'll thank God fasting that I'm not in Gents' Tailoring,' she had said devoutly. 'In fact, Switzers is a nice place to work. At home, in Liverpool, I worked in a big store as well, but I were just a cleaner, going in when the shop was closed. This is much nicer.'

'I reckon it pays better, too,' Miss Spencer had said. Although she had lived in Dublin all her life, she had managed to shed most of her brogue and could, when necessary, speak with only the lightest of Irish accents. Her home in the Liberties was not far from Handkerchief Alley, but right from the start she had warned Sylvie not to mention her home address if she could possibly help it. 'There's as bad slums round the back of O'Connell Street,' she had informed her new friend. 'Why, I've a cousin living on Henry Street in what were once a great mansion. There's eleven of them livin' in two rooms. But it's a good address, see?' Sylvie had not seen, not really, but she soon realised that people like Miss O'Leary despised folk who lived in the Liberties, so she kept her address to herself as far as she could and thanked God that the words Handkerchief Alley held no menace for the Dugdales. Since Sylvie was living there with the rich O'Keefes from America, they assumed without question that it was a nice area.

Now, Sylvie finished tidying the first glove drawer, which was perfectly tidy anyway, and glanced across at Miss Spencer, who was industriously rolling lace round a white card. Sylvie sidled nearer the other girl, intending to ask her where they should take their sandwiches, for it was no day for wandering the streets, but at that moment a customer approached the counter. She was tall, slim and elegant, wearing a powder-blue costume under a rich fur cape, but the gloves she held in one hand were grey and Sylvie's budding sartorial instinct told her that they should have been blue. Anticipating this, she drew out the third drawer down – gloves, blue to purple, all sizes – and began to lay out the contents upon the long wooden counter. The woman's elegant brows rose. 'You're very quick,' she observed, in a low, rather pleasant voice. 'I was about to ask you to show me some blue gloves but I see you realised what I must be wanting.' She examined the items Sylvie had already laid out on the counter. 'Yes, those match my suit exactly, though they are rather thin. However, my chauffeur is only just outside the door, for there's little traffic about today, so I shan't be out in the cold for long. Have you a size five and a half?'

Thanking her stars that she had sorted the gloves, Sylvie produced the desired size and flicked the price ticket over so that the customer did not have to ask how much the gloves would cost. The woman smiled and nodded, then asked to see a warm scarf in a similar shade. When that had been produced and approved, she suggested that Sylvie should show her a length of French lace with which to trim a ball gown she was having made.

Bringing out a variety of lace and spreading it tenderly along the counter, Sylvie thought that the day had begun well, despite the snow. She hoped it would go on even better because it was so nice to have pleasant things to write home about.

She wrote every night, trying to space the letters evenly so that one went to her mother, one to the

Dugdales, one to the wretched Len in prison and one to Annie. Occasionally, she wrote to Brendan, and these, in fact, were the only letters in which she could be completely frank, knowing not only that he would never give her away, but that he had no opportunity to do so, since he knew neither the Dugdales nor the Davieses and had, in any case, been temporarily seconded to the Rose Hill district, so that now he did not even have to pass the pub or the court in which her family lived whilst on his beat.

She received news of Becky every time her mother or Mrs Dugdale wrote and she found a certain consolation in making a great fuss of Grainne. Despite the fact that Grainne was almost two years older than Becky, they were rather similar, for Becky was big for her age and very bright, whereas Grainne was tiny and a little slow.

As soon as she had arrived in Dublin, Sylvie had decided that all her letters home, even the ones to Annie and her mother, must carefully give the impression that Handkerchief Alley was in a smart area of Dublin, that she lived in a grand house and that her only employment was that of nursemaid to the O'Keefe children; not of course to the children of Caitlin and Pat, but to those imaginary American cousins. They had never told Annie that the story had been a fabrication, so it was only her mother who knew the truth, but after the most fleeting consideration Sylvie had decided it was far too dangerous to confide in her mother in writing. Mrs Davies was so scatterbrained that she might easily leave her letters lying around where anyone could read them, or simply hand them to Mrs Dugdale, if that lady should happen to ask whether she'd received news of Sylvie lately.

The morning wore on. By lunchtime the stream of early customers had subsided to a trickle, for the snow was whirling down with increasing force and when Sylvie peeped out through the windows she saw a white world, only the roadway being kept more or less clear by the constantly passing traffic.

''Tis a good t'ing we can eat our dinners in the staff room,' Miss Spencer said as Miss O'Leary dismissed them, with an admonition to hurry back early, should the weather improve. The two girls often took their sandwiches down by the quays so that they could watch the shipping coming and going along the Liffey, but there was no chance of that today. Instead, they hurried to the staff room and began to eat.

When they had finished, they went to the ladies' cloakroom, and Sylvie took the opportunity to have a quick peep at herself in the full-length mirror. She thought apprehensively that her waist was definitely thickening now. The baby had started moving recently and Caitlin had accompanied Sylvie to the Daisy Market, where they had bought a skirt with an elasticated waistband, and a large and comfortable smock, though naturally she could not wear either garment at work. The sales girls were expected to turn up in black skirts and white blouses and now, looking at her profile in the mirror, Sylvie realised that it would not be long before someone beside herself noticed her expanding figure. She had hoped that Miss O'Leary might allow her to continue to work whilst her condition was not obvious to customers, for her sales record was excellent and the counter high, but now she realised that this was most unlikely. With the weather worsening, Gloves and Haberdashery could well manage without her, but she was still determined to do her very best to please Miss O'Leary in every way possible.

Returning to Handkerchief Alley that night, fighting her way through what amounted to a blizzard, she wondered, not for the first time, how her small daughter was taking her absence. She had asked both her mother and her mother-in-law this question and had not received very satisfactory answers. Mrs Dugdale had replied, rather smugly, that she had no need to worry her head on Becky's account. The child adored her grandparents and seemed not to miss Sylvie at all. She and Mr Dugdale had moved Becky's cot into their room when they discovered that she did not like sleeping alone and now she seldom mentioned her mother, save to ask whether Sylvie would bring her a doll's pram when she got back. *If you'll send me the money I'll buy a doll's pram for you and you can give it to her when you come home*, Mrs Dugdale had written. *There's a nice one, second-hand o' course, in Paddy's Market for half a crown. I'll put it in the cellar until you gets back, so's she won't see it ahead of time, or you can pay me back later if you'd rather.*

Mrs Davies's letter on the same subject had seemed rather more cagey. Like her employer, she had said that Becky was perfectly happy and did not seem to miss her mother too much, though doubtless she would greet her return with joy. *But I'll be glad when youse back,* her mother had written laboriously. *Becky's getting pert and saucy; I can't give her a smack, but you could. It's hard on her, though. She don't remember her da and she's beginnin' to forget you. We'll all be a deal better when youse home.*

By the time Sylvie reached Handkerchief Alley she must, she thought, look like a snowman. She was extremely cold; her fingers and toes were completely numb and as she shook the snow off herself and began to climb the rickety stairs she thought how nice it would be to sit down in front of the fire and be fussed over by Maeve. Caitlin was working late, otherwise the two girls would have walked home together. Maeve, however, was a good little soul and would probably already have the kettle on and a slice of bread impaled on a stick, so that Sylvie could enjoy tea and toast as well as the warmth of the fire.

As she entered the kitchen and began to struggle out of her wet coat, the baby kicked sharply, and despite herself Sylvie felt almost affectionate towards it. This was a rare emotion since the baby had been nothing but trouble and though she was grateful for the money Robbie sent, she resented her need of it. He had seduced her, and then simply walked out of her life leaving her with all the responsibility for the child they had made together. But when she felt the little chap kick out like that – she was sure it would be a boy from its vigorous movements – she could not help remembering how Len had wanted a son. Oh, he adored Becky, thought the sun shone out of her, but he had made it pretty plain that when they had another child he hoped it would be a boy. Well, this one was certainly a little feller, Sylvie told herself, but Len would have no claim on it, would never so much as see it.

'Sit down, sit down, and get yourself as near the fire as you can without scorchin',' Maeve was saying as she took Sylvie's soaking coat and hung it across the clothes horse. She clasped Sylvie's hand in her own small paw and tutted. 'You're cold as death so you are! But as soon as the tea's brewed you shall have a cup and a nice piece of toast wit' butter on.' She turned to Clodagh, sitting cross-legged on the hearthrug. 'Clodagh, darlin' child, will you toast a slice for poor Sylvie when you've done your own? She's frozen cold and I dare say famished as well.'

Clodagh said placidly that Sylvie could have the piece now almost ready for spreading and Sylvie watched contentedly as Maeve limped round the room, pouring milk into a mug and adding tea from the big brown pot. She was beginning to warm up, and started to tell Maeve that Caitlin had popped into her department just before closing time to ask her to let them know at home that she would be late. ''Tis stocktaking,' she said. 'We had a grand month in Switzers. We nearly sold out of some lines so they want to re-order, but before they can do so they have to stocktake.' Sylvie was just thinking how nice it was to feel warm when her chilblains decided to take a hand. As they thawed out the pain was dreadful, and Sylvie moaned.

'What's happenin'?' Maeve asked, hurrying to her side. 'Is you hurt, Sylvie?'

'It's me bleedin' chilblains,' Sylvie said, groaning. 'Oh, why didn't I remember how they hurt when they get warm? I shouldn't have got so near the fire.'

'You can't stay cold all your life just to prevent your chilblains from hurtin' you,' Fergal said piously. 'You should have sat at the back of the room until you thawed out.' He was the easier of the twins to deal with, but now Sylvie glared at him.

'Thank you so much, Mr Clever,' she said, her tone heavy with sarcasm. 'And wasn't that the advice I was handin' to meself, without any help from you? Besides, it's too late. Oh, I'll have to scratch, and scratchin' makes chilblains much worse, everyone knows that.'

'Hold my hand, Sylvie, then you won't be able to scratch,' little Grainne said at once, while

Clodagh gave it as her opinion that no one could stop chilblains hurting, whether you scratched 'em or not. 'Mammy says to dip your hands into the water bucket so's they thaw out gradual.'

'Into a jerry full of pee, you mean,' Seamus said coarsely, though Sylvie knew that it was a cure much valued in the area. He leaned across and took the pointed stick from his sister. 'Can I have the next slice of toast, Maeve me darlin'?'

By the time March came in and the market women were selling little bunches of snowdrops, Sylvie's secret was out, at least as far as the O'Keefe children were concerned. On her way to get the messages with Maeve, with all the children accompanying them, Sylvie had slipped on a wet step and fallen. It had not been a bad fall and she was scrambling to her feet when Maeve, rushing to help her up, had said anxiously: 'Are you hurt, alanna? Is the baby all right?'

'What baby?' Clodagh had said suspiciously, and of course Sylvie had had to come clean, though she had not told anyone that the baby was not Len's. The children appeared to accept the fact that Sylvie had come to stay with them so that she might be looked after while her husband was in prison.

Shortly after this, Miss O'Leary had suddenly noticed that her newest employee was in the family way. She had been in the staff room, finishing off her lunch with an apple, when the head sales lady had asked her to pass her down a register of employees kept on a high shelf. Sylvie had reached up . . . and Miss O'Leary had suddenly given a sort of strangled gasp.

'Miss Dugdale, I believe you have something to tell me,' she had said, in her most icy and repressive accents, and Sylvie had known that the game was up.

'Yes, Miss O'Leary, I'm expecting a child,' she had admitted, trying not to sound ashamed, for although she was known as Miss Dugdale in the store everyone knew that she was married, and there was nothing disgraceful in a married woman's giving birth to a child, she told herself defiantly. Miss O'Leary was a silly old maid, but surely even she could not pretend to be shocked over such a natural occurrence?

Miss O'Leary, however, had thought otherwise. 'You must have known that you were in the family way when you took the job,' she had said crossly, when she ordered Sylvie to accompany her to the office and was sorting out her cards. 'I've wasted valuable time and effort on training you to be a useful member of the department, and this is how you repay me! Well, I don't imagine you will expect a reference, not after the way you've behaved.'

'But Miss O'Leary, I simply have to work,' Sylvie had said pleadingly. 'If you won't give me a reference and I can't get a job, how can I manage?'

'That's not my problem, Miss Dugdale,' Miss

O'Leary had said primly. 'And now I begin to wonder whether you really are married, or whether you came to Ireland when you found you were in a – a difficult situation. Because of the shame, you know.'

Sylvie had sighed and shrugged, letting her shoulders droop. 'I can show you my marriage lines, Miss O'Leary,' she had said quietly. 'But if you are determined not to give me a reference, then there's no point.'

Miss O'Leary, looking a trifle harassed, had handed Sylvie her cards. 'You'll have to collect your money at the end of the week, and to tell you the truth, Miss Dugdale, the only places who will employ a woman in your condition won't be looking for references,' she had said, and her voice had been a good deal kinder. 'I know it's hard, but after the baby's born – I take it the cousin with whom you are living will give an eye to it? – then you can come back to me again. If I've not managed to find someone suitable – and I might not, because the next couple of months are by no means our busiest, and I shan't be in a hurry to take someone on – then I might consider taking you back.'

Sylvie had thanked her humbly, if a trifle guiltily, left by the end of the week, and found work in a large laundry on Marrowbone Lane. She came home after her first day completely exhausted, hardly knowing how to drag herself up the three creaking flights of stairs. Reaching the kitchen, where Caitlin was bustling about laying the table and putting the finishing touches to the meal they would presently eat, she flopped into a chair and gave an enormous heartfelt groan. Caitlin looked round and then, without comment, poured Sylvie a large mug of tea. 'You poor little t'ing,' she said kindly. 'I worked in that laundry when I were carryin' Clodagh and I swore I'd never do it again. But I reckon after a few days you'll get into the swing of things. I did, at any rate.'

Poor Sylvie gazed at her friend with lacklustre eyes. 'The weight of wet sheets when you're carting them from the rinsing water to the mangle,' she said hollowly. 'And then hanging them out on the lines and heaving the prop across. And there's water everywhere, and steam pourin' out of the coppers so's every inch of skin is all slippery. I were wringin' wet in ten minutes and I stayed wet all day. Oh, Caitlin, if only Miss O'Leary had took me on as a cleaner!'

'Yes, but they've always got folk eager to take a cleaner's place, and so far as I know there's no vacancies in that line,' Caitlin assured her. 'You could look for cleanin' work in a private house, but the money's just terrible and at least the laundry pay's fair, so you'd best stick to it, alanna.' She smiled encouragingly at the other girl. 'Tell you what, you'll be a good deal keener to go back to Liverpool when you're leaving the laundry than you would have been over leaving Switzers.'

Sylvie had never told Caitlin how she missed Liverpool and her old home and comfortable life, because it would have been both rude and ungrateful, but she felt a real pang of longing for a whole roof over her head and a hot meal on the table which she had not helped to prepare. However, she could scarcely say so. Instead, she laughed and said that no doubt Caitlin was right. Laundry work must become easier as one grew accustomed, and anyway, once the baby was born, she would be returning to Liverpool and would, no doubt, get her old job at Lewis's back. 'And now that I've got experience as a sales lady I can apply for a better job when I get home,' she added. 'I'm grateful to Miss O'Leary for that, at least.'

Caitlin agreed that this was true and presently Pat came breezing in and they assembled round the table to begin the meal. Rather to Sylvie's surprise, her aches and pains grew less as she moved round the room after supper, clearing the table and washing the crocks. In bed that night, however, her mind returned to the problem of what she should do after the baby was born. She had told her in-laws that the job in Ireland would last about six months, so the baby should be a few weeks old before she crossed the sea once more. She meant to wean the child before she left, then to offer it for adoption, but Caitlin had once said, with surprising firmness, that she should wait at least six weeks after the birth before returning home.

'They won't take a baby away from its

mammy until it's six weeks old, I've heard, so you may have to stay a wee while longer, alanna.'

So now Sylvie helped to lay the table for next morning's breakfast, played a guessing game with the children and told Grainne and Colm a story, then made her way to bed. Snuggling down beneath her thin blankets and thanking her stars that it was not raining, she decided that there was no point in worrying over the hard work in the laundry or, for that matter, her return home after the baby's birth. She had never been a worrier, had inherited her mother's calm and placid temperament, and, telling herself that fretting would only make matters worse, she settled down to sleep. So far something, or someone, had always turned up in the nick of time to solve her problems for her. Think of how providentially Brendan had come into her life! And then the job at Switzers, which had been so perfect for her, had come vacant within two days of her arriving at Handkerchief Alley. She could think of a dozen occasions upon which she had been rescued from some scrape or other by the intervention of fate, and it would happen again.

Satisfied that she had no need to be anxious, Sylvie slept.

Chapter Four

'Ah, you're back. Nothing happened yet?' Caitlin said. 'I wonder should we have a word with the nurse.'

Maeve looked up and smiled as Sylvie entered the room. The little maid of all work was wielding the heavy iron on her mistress's best white blouse and now she held it suspended for a moment. She noticed how pale and tired Sylvie looked after a day in the laundry and admired the other girl's courage in continuing the work when her baby was due any day.

Sylvie sighed and shook her head at Caitlin's suggestion. 'No, I don't need to see the nurse. I've always been vague about dates. I were late with Becky, so this one will probably be the same. And don't they say boys are always later than girls? But oh, I'm fed up with looking like an elephant, and feeling like one, too.'

Caitlin laughed. 'You are pretty large,' she acknowledged, 'but you don't look a bit like an elephant; you're far too pretty.' She turned to Maeve. 'Make us all a cup of tea, there's a good girl.'

Maeve stood the iron down in the grate and

limped over to the teapot. She was distressed by Sylvie's obvious exhaustion and had been wondering how she could help. Surely there must be something she could do? And now, suddenly, she knew what it was. She carried the brimming cup over to Sylvie, who took it eagerly, curling both hands round the mug. The month was May and the trees in Phoenix Park were in full leaf, but a chilly wind had begun to blow as evening drew on. Maeve turned to Caitlin. 'I've been thinking,' she said slowly. 'That there laundry's turble hard work, I've heared you say so a dozen times. I know I's only twelve, but I reckon if I were to go round Marrowbone Lane and tell 'em Sylvie were near her time, they'd be quite happy to let me take her place. I'd make 'em pay me the same as what they pays Sylvie and hand the money over at the end of each week,' she finished.

She looked from one face to the other as she spoke and was secretly rather upset when Sylvie snorted. 'You? Why, you'd never manage the weight of the wet sheets, you're so little and thin. And then there's your lame leg . . . no, they'd never take you on.'

Caitlin was kinder. 'You're a dear little soul, Maeve, but the work really is very heavy and I don't believe they employ any youngsters,' she said. 'Besides, who'd help around the house, give an eye to the kids, do me messages and so on, while I'm at work? I really couldn't spare you, alanna.'

Maeve flushed with pleasure, feeling the heat rush to her cheeks. Caitlin was so kind and good. Maeve had always known how lucky she was to have got the job with the O'Keefe family. Her mother, a widow with ten children, had been absolutely delighted when Caitlin had called on her, offering to give one of her girls bed and board in return for looking after her five children, keeping the house decent and doing all the little jobs which Caitlin herself, earning good money at Switzers, could no longer cope with. Caitlin had looked at the three eldest Connolly girls, tall Bridget, pretty Eileen, and Maeve, with her lame foot, limp hair and plain little face. She had smiled at them all but her dark eyes had lingered longest on Maeve, and must have read the desperate appeal in her face, for it had been to Maeve she had addressed herself. 'D'you like children, alanna? Are you good wit' the little ones?' she had asked. 'Your sisters is grand girls but they'll be wantin' proper jobs in a year or two and I want someone who'll be happy to look after the O'Keefes for years and years!'

'I love children, so I do, and they love me,' Maeve had said eagerly, for once not feeling shy because this lovely lady looked so kindly upon her. 'I's only nine, so I won't be after leaving you for ages – if you take me on, that is.'

'Right. Then if you're agreeable, Mrs Connolly, Maeve can come back with me now and meet the family. Then she can come home and pack her things, and return to Handkerchief Alley tomorrow morning, if that suits,' Caitlin had said.

Mother and daughter had exchanged a quick glance. Despite her youth, Maeve had been too wise to say she only had the clothes she stood up in – that she owned nothing which was worth packing and taking with her – but Mrs Connolly got round the problem. 'I'll send one of the girls up wit' a few t'ings, so she can start right away,' she had said. 'Eh, but I'll miss our Maeve, always so willin' to give a hand . . . you've got yourself a bargain, so you have, Mrs O'Keefe.'

'And I'll pay you sixpence a week, seein' as you'll have to get someone else to help with your chores,' Caitlin had said tactfully. 'Come to think, no need for her to bring clothes; I've a cousin living two streets away what works for a family in St Stephen's Green; they're for ever givin' her skirts which she passes on to me 'cos she's only got sons. Most of the stuff is too big for my Clodagh yet, but they'll fit young Maeve a treat.'

Naturally, Maeve had felt a little tearful because she was leaving the home she knew and going to strangers, yet by the time they reached Handkerchief Alley she knew she was doing the right thing. Mrs O'Keefe had told her to call herself Caitlin and her husband Pat, and had talked soothingly of the life that Maeve was to lead. She had even apologised for the three flights of stairs but had said, with a chuckle, that at least once you were in the flat it was all on one floor.

She had taken Maeve round the flat and Maeve had been delighted and astonished when she was told she would have her own little bed. She had not even complained when Caitlin had filled a large tin bath with hot water, added some sort of strong disinfectant, and scrubbed every inch of Maeve's skinny little body. Even her hair had been scrubbed, then cut short and combed with a steel comb because Caitlin had told her, kindly, that there were tiny insects called nits in her hair, which she could pass on to the other children if they were not ruthlessly eradicated.

Then – wonder of wonders – she had dried Maeve on a rough towel and given her beautiful clothes to wear: a clean navy blouse with no buttons missing, a grey skirt and some grey woollen stockings, and some knickers, as well as a pair of plimsolls with only a tiny hole in the toe of each. Maeve had never owned a pair of shoes in her life and had always gone barefoot, so the plimsolls were precious indeed. She had longed to go home and show off to her sisters, but that would not have been fair on the O'Keefes. Instead, she had settled down to work as hard as a human being can. She did the messages, pushing the two youngest children and purchases round the streets of Dublin in an old wooden box on wheels. She cleaned the house, kept the children amused whilst their mother was at work, peeled mounds of spuds, gutted fish, skinned rabbits, and did it all cheerfully because she loved the O'Keefes and wished, desperately, to prove that Caitlin had done the right thing in choosing her rather than her older, and better-looking, sisters.

She had now been with the family for three years and thoroughly enjoyed her life, so it had been no small sacrifice to offer to do the job in the laundry in Sylvie's place. But Caitlin had asked her a question and she must answer it, though it went against the grain to do so. 'Who'll help in the house, look after the kids and run your messages? Why, Sylvie, of course,' she said at once. 'Sure and wouldn't we just change places, like the princess and the pauper in the storybooks? And you wouldn't be losing me, Caitlin, 'cos I'd be back here as soon as me work finished every day, so if there was something Sylvie couldn't manage, then I'd see to it as soon as I got home.'

Caitlin had been sitting in one of the shabby old fireside chairs, keeping an eye on the heavy black pot suspended over the fire. But now she jumped to her feet and gave Maeve a big hug. 'You're the kindest little creature I ever did know. And I believe you could do it, as well. The women in the laundry is awful kind – they'd teach you the easiest way of doing things, same as they did wi' Sylvie. Besides, if it were too much . . .' She turned to Sylvie. 'Well, what d'you think? You wouldn't lose by it.'

Maeve turned, rather anxiously, to Sylvie, and found the other girl heaving herself out of her chair. 'Oh, Maeve, if you truly think you could cope, I'd be that grateful, even if you only did it for a couple of days. You could say that I'm sick and you're standing in for me,' she said, and Maeve was astonished to see tears in the girl's big blue eyes. 'The weight I'm carrying around means I start off tired. It would be wonderful to do ordinary things and of course I'd take great care of the children, I promise you I would.'

Maeve beamed at her. She still thought Caitlin was the prettiest person in the whole of Dublin, but now she acknowledged that Sylvie ran her a close second. Also, the English girl's combination of silver-fair hair, blue eyes and rose-petal complexion was something rarely seen in Ireland. Since her arrival, Sylvie had not taken a great deal of notice of Maeve, though when she wanted the younger girl to do something for her she always asked very prettily. But now she is smiling at me, Maeve thought, delighted to have won the older girl's thanks. She's really very nice and I'll do my best to satisfy the folk at the laundry so that poor, pretty Sylvie can have an easier life.

Maeve was as good as her word and must, Sylvie thought, have worked really well, since at the end of a week she brought home the same money that Sylvie had been earning, and handed it over without a word of complaint. The youngster admitted the work was hard but she enjoyed the companionship of the older women, and because she was always eager to give anyone a hand she was popular too.

Sylvie, for her part, quite liked everything to do with her new domestic duties save for looking after the twins. Seamus and Fergal were fiends incarnate, accompanying her when she went to the shops after school and then running off before they could be asked to help fetch or carry. They were supposed to chop kindling for the fire and to cart coal and water, tasks to which they had taken without much enthusiasm under Maeve's gentle rule, but which they saw no reason to perform for Sylvie. Lugging coals and hot water up three flights of stairs was no joke in her condition, but Sylvie knew better than to complain to Caitlin of her sons' behaviour. Should she do anything so unwise, the twins would wreak immediate revenge: a dead mouse in her bed, her blanket damped with – she hoped – water, or a rotten old potato pushed into the toe of her boot so that she discovered it the next time she put it on. And the twins would look her straight in the eye and deny that her complaint had anything to do with them.

Still, a bit of aggravation from the twins was nothing compared to the dreadful slog at the laundry, and for the first time Sylvie began to appreciate Maeve. She looked so skinny and frail, she dragged her left foot, which turned inwards at an odd angle, she held one shoulder higher than the other, her skin was sallow and her hair stringy, and she was plain as a boot. But she had courage and determination and had made it clear that she thought Sylvie deserved the help she was giving her. Sylvie began to show respect, even affection, for the crippled child, and was delighted when it seemed to make the O'Keefe children like her more. Clodagh had always been polite, but now she became friendly, talking eagerly about the birth of the little baby whose advent Sylvie awaited, and promising to help to look after the little one, to take it for outings and to give it its bath.

Relieved of the cruelly hard work at the laundry, Sylvie went to bed early, got up late, and told Caitlin most of her hopes and most of her secrets, too. She told her friend about the dreadful Robbie, about how Brendan had helped her with no thought of any sort of reward, and even about Len and the Dugdales.

'I reckon you're lookin' forward to goin' home, once the babby's born,' Pat said one evening, ignoring a sharp warning glance from his wife. Sylvie was uneasily conscious every now and then that Pat thought his wife and Maeve spoiled their guest, but she smiled very prettily at him and said that, yes, she would be glad to go home in many ways, though she would miss the O'Keefes horribly.

'Oh aye?' Pat gave her a shrewd glance, letting his eyes travel from the top of her head to her slippered feet. 'Well, it won't be long now before the babby's born, be the looks of ye.'

'It can't come too soon for me,' Sylvie said

fervently, for the sheer size and weight of her was exhausting, even without the laundry work. She went to bed that night actually hoping that the birth would indeed be soon, yet when she awoke in the small hours with a nagging pain in her back she suddenly realised that she was not so sure; she had forgotten the pain which had accompanied Becky's arrival into the world, but here it was again, at first just a nagging discomfort but very soon as sharp as if someone was endeavouring to pull her insides out.

She told herself to be brave and sensible; no point in shouting out before the pains were coming every five or six minutes. But soon she forgot her own good intentions and began to groan, to moan, and quite quickly to give breathy little shrieks the moment the contractions started.

It woke the children, of course. Maeve slipped out of bed and ran through to Caitlin, who returned with a shawl wrapped round her night-gowned shoulders. 'Get the girls up and put 'em in the kitchen, on the sofa; they can spend the rest of the night there,' she told Maeve. 'Oh, and boil the big kettle and fetch me through the ragbag. Then wake Seamus and Fergal and tell 'em to get old Nanny Clarke from Meath Street.'

Nanny Clarke was one of the nine-day nurses much prized by Dublin women. She would take complete control of the birth, tending the mother during her labour and only sending for a doctor if something went wrong. After the child was born, she would truly come into her own, ensuring that the mother remained in bed whilst she did all the washing, cleaning and even cooking which the new mother would otherwise have had to do. Naturally, she was well paid for this service, but Sylvie had been glad to employ her, knowing that she could not expect Caitlin to take on such extra work, and that Nanny Clarke deserved every penny.

Caitlin waited until Maeve had left the room, and then turned to Sylvie. 'By the sounds you're makin' it shouldn't be long now, especially as it's a second baby; it's usually only the first what comes slow and difficult,' she said reassuringly. 'I durst not give you a drink, not until Nanny Clarke says it's all right to do so, but I'll heave you up in the bed so when you start to push you'll have more leverage, and I'll sponge your face. I found that a great help, so I did, when I were birthin' me own babies.'

Sylvie moaned, but thanked Caitlin in a cracked whisper when the rag was used to wipe the sweat from her brow, and when Nanny Clarke approved a cup of tea she drank it thirstily – and vomited it up only seconds later. She heard the two women conferring, then Nanny turned Maeve out of the room, examined her patient, and said, after poking and prodding for what felt like hours, that this looked like bein' some time.

'But it's her second child; I thought second children always came easier,' Caitlin said.

'Usually, but not always, alanna.' The old woman settled herself on the truckle bed, for Caitlin had insisted that Sylvie should transfer to the larger and more comfortable bed for the birth, and said philosophically, 'I'll have a cup o' tea, wit' somethin' warmin' in it, so's me strength keeps up, since I don't reckon we'll see the child afore mornin'. She turned to Sylvie. 'I'm tellin' you, it'll be a whiles yet afore you sees this babe, so you'd best try to get some sleep.'

Oh, very amusing, Sylvie told herself sarcastically, as another pain arrowed through her back and reappeared like a red-hot iron in her stomach; fat chance I've got of sleeping with all this going on. Doesn't the woman know I'm in agony? But she did not say it aloud. This was clearly going to be a very different birth from that of her darling Becky and she was going to need all the help she could get. It would not do to antagonise anyone, particularly not Nanny Clarke who was, according to Caitlin, the best midwife in all the Liberties.

Nanny Clarke had been right. It was not until the second day after Sylvie's labour had started that the child was finally born and, as it happened, Nanny Clarke and Maeve were the only people present at the time. Caitlin was in the kitchen, preparing a meal, and had just sent Maeve in to enquire whether Nanny Clarke needed anything, when the girl found herself grabbed and told that she must provide something for Sylvie to pull against. Maeve had held out both hands to the frightened girl on the bed and Sylvie had seized them in a grip so hard that afterwards Maeve found she was bruised black and blue. 'Pull, pull, and then I can bear down,' Sylvie said, and Maeve obeyed.

This was not, by any means, the first confinement she had attended but she thought that it was the strangest. Twice during her labour, Sylvie's pains had ceased completely and Maeve knew that the midwife had been as mystified as any of them. But now it seemed that things were really going right, and indeed this stage of her labour proved to be of short duration, for Maeve had barely been in the room ten minutes before Nanny Clarke gave a grunt of satisfaction. 'Sure an' haven't you got a lovely little girl?' she said. Maeve stared as the old woman hung the baby upside down and slapped its tiny buttocks so that it would draw in a breath for its first cry.

She glanced at Sylvie, at the white sweat-streaked face, the damp silver-blonde hair, and then Sylvie's eyes flew open. 'A *girl*?' she said incredulously. 'But – but I were sure it were a boy.'

Nanny Clarke grinned. 'Well, I aren't one to be making a mistake, alanna, and this 'un's a girl, you tek my word for it,' she assured the young mother. 'Never mind, eh? The next 'un will be a boy, sure as I'm standin' here.'

As she spoke she had been wrapping the baby in a clean piece of sheeting, and now she handed the child to its mother, smiling as she did so, then turning away to fill a basin with warm water, commenting that she would give the child a good wash when Sylvie felt she could part with the little 'un for a moment. Maeve could not help noticing that Sylvie took the child without a great deal of enthusiasm, saying pettishly as she did so: 'Well, I'm sure I'm glad it's arrived at last, but . . . oh, my God!'

She was staring at the baby with a look of horror on her face and Maeve moved nearer, taking a good look at the child for the first time. To her, it looked like all newborns, with a small, reddish, wrinkled face, tightly closed puffy eyelids and a rosebud mouth, which even as she watched began to make sucking motions. 'I think she's very pretty,' she murmured. 'What'll you call her, Sylvie? And – and why are you staring at her like that?'

'Because she's a girl and I expected a boy,' Sylvie answered feebly. 'I'm sure she's very pretty but . . . but she's got ginger hair! Oh, poor little thing, ginger hair's ever so unlucky; in the old days they said all red-haired women were witches!'

Before Maeve could answer, Nanny Clarke waddled across the room and took the baby. 'Many a babe's born bald, or wit' a crop of hair black as soot, but they rubs most of it off an' then their real hair comes,' she said reprovingly. 'This ginger fluff will just go. You want to thank your stars, young woman, that she's whole and healthy, and the pair of you is still alive.'

Sylvie lay back on her pillow and smiled at Maeve. 'You know I can't keep her,' she whispered, 'so I dursn't let myself grow fond of her. I shall rely on you, Maeve, to take good care of her. You do understand, don't you?'

'I'll do my best,' Maeve whispered, 'and it won't be hard, 'cos I do love little babies, so I do.' She thought the baby's ginger hair was rather appealing and had not really understood what Sylvie had meant. She glanced at her, smiling shyly. 'Would you be after fancyin' a cup o' tea now, Sylvie? And mebbe a bite of bread and jam? If so, I'll nip across to the kitchen and fetch it in no time. You'll feel better wit' some grub inside you.'

Sylvie had been lying with her head turned away and her eyes closed, but at Maeve's words she opened them, looked round and gave the younger girl a rather wobbly smile. 'Oh, Maeve, you're ever such a good kid, and I'm sorry for what I said about ginger hair. It's all nonsense, of course,' she said, in a thread of a voice. 'As for tea and a jam butty, I'd love it. And you might tell Caitlin the baby's come and it's a girl.'

When Maeve had gone to fetch the tea, Mrs Clarke picked up the baby and followed the younger girl across the room but paused in the doorway to address her patient. 'You've had a hard time of it, m'dear; best try to snatch some sleep while the tea brews,' she said. 'Mrs O'Keefe and the children will be wantin' to have a hold of the little 'un. Best I take the babby to them rather than have them crowdin' in on you when you're weary from the long labour.'

Sylvie murmured her thanks as the door closed behind the old woman, then began to consider her reaction to her first sight of her newborn daughter. Had she given herself away? She had been horrified when she had looked into the small crumpled face, for the baby was the spitting image of Robbie Wentworth! In the back of her mind there had been half-formed, nebulous plans to introduce the child to the Dugdales, when she was older, as a long lost relative of the O'Keefes, or even the child of a friend, but one glance at the baby's face made her realise that this would not be possible. Everyone would see the likeness, which would undoubtedly grow stronger as time passed. She had declared that the baby had ginger hair, but in fact it was more sandy, just like Robbie's, and worst of all was the mole, shaped like a tiny apple, on the child's right cheek. Robbie's sister Sally, and Robbie himself, had just such a mole, and in the very same position. Should the child ever turn up in Liverpool, no one could doubt who had fathered her!

However, she had known, really, that taking the child back to England was not going to be possible.

She had told Brendan she meant to have the child adopted and that was exactly what she must do. Girls, she believed, were easier to place than boys, so perhaps it was as well that the child was a girl, yet somehow she knew she would have parted with a boy more easily. Boys were tougher, more independent; she hated the thought of her little girl going to a home where she might not get the love every child deserves.

Sylvie's eyes filled with tears but then she remembered what Maeve had said and scolded herself for her foolishness. Maeve was a kind little soul; she and Caitlin, between them, would make sure that the baby went to someone who would truly love her. Satisfied, Sylvie turned her face into the pillow and was soon asleep.

Brendan awoke to find the June sunshine streaming in through his bedroom window and falling across his face. He groaned and rolled over, desperate to get back to sleep, but the truth was he had worked so many double shifts and snatched so little rest between that sleep eluded him most of the time. However, he had been granted two whole days off since it must have been obvious, even to his superiors in the police force, not renowned for their concern for the well-being of their men, that he would not be much use to anyone when asleep on his feet.

The trouble was, superintendents and above did not know, or at best had forgotten, how to walk a beat themselves, let alone work double or treble shifts, and so did not realise that men in the last stages of exhaustion were often too tense to sleep, and kept waking up, convinced that their alarm clocks had gone off, or that they were due in at the station.

However, Brendan had come off duty at six o'clock the previous evening and had slept deeply until this moment, which could not be bad. He glanced at his watch on the bedside table and saw that it was fifteen minutes short of eight o'clock. If he got up now, Mrs Taggart would undoubtedly make him a breakfast, and he knew it would be a good one because he had missed so many meals over the past couple of weeks. On the other hand – Brendan stretched luxuriously, feeling warm and comfortable, and not terribly inclined to move – there was the possibility that he might fall asleep again and it would be good to catch up on lost slumber. He grinned to himself. What a pleasant dilemma! He could choose between sinking back into sleep, relaxing in his comfortable bed, with the golden sunshine falling like a blessing upon him, or he could get dressed and go downstairs to enjoy bacon, fried bread, a couple of fried eggs and possibly some kidneys, as well as plenty of crisp brown toast, butter, and Mrs Taggart's own orange marmalade. He sat up in bed. Once he had thought about Mrs Taggart's breakfasts, his rumbling stomach informed him that it did not mean to let him sleep whilst it was so empty. So, yawning hugely, he stuck his feet out of bed and padded over to the washstand. Cold water in winter made washing a misery, but now it was pleasant to lather his face, neck and torso with lovely cool water and plenty of Pears soap, and then to dry himself on the brown and white striped towel which Mrs Taggart had provided.

As he washed and dressed, Brendan considered the events of the last few weeks. Civil unrest had been growing for some time, inflamed by the poverty of the city and the fact that the rich seemed to feel it their duty to oppress the poor whenever the opportunity occurred. Prices rose all the time, yet wages remained obstinately at subsistence level. Women wanted the vote, which seemed a natural enough wish to Brendan, but it was being vigorously denied them, both by the government of the day and those on the Opposition benches. Yet changes were going on all the time. A fellow called Henry Melly broke records when he flew an aeroplane round the city and across the Mersey in only forty-one minutes, and a new laboratory for the treatment of diseases had just been opened at the Mill Road Infirmary. These were momentous happenings, yet Brendan had read somewhere that Liverpool workers were amongst the worst paid in the country.

Sighing, he pulled on his boots and stood up. He was just a humble scuffer, with no need to understand anything but his orders, yet he could not help wondering at the orders he was given.

The seamen for instance, who had been the first to go on strike, had only wanted a rise in wages of ten shillings a month, which was not much to ask considering how prices had risen. Brendan had always been a great reader and though his work now limited the amount of time he could give to his hobby, he still read the newspapers avidly and caught up on current affairs by visiting the library on William Brown Street whenever he had the opportunity. Thus, he had realised some time ago that trade was booming, which meant in its turn that workers worked harder, for employers wanted to line their pockets yet more richly, but had no desire either to employ more men or to pay them more money. Even now, with the dockers and transport workers taking part in the strike – and joining their unions in ever-increasing numbers – the employers preferred bully-boy tactics to a calm discussion which might lead to the end of the strikes.

Poor old King George, Brendan thought. He had succeeded to the throne barely a year before and it looked as though his was going to be a troubled reign. Not that kings had to do double shifts, lucky beggars! Neither did they have to face angry crowds armed only with their truncheons, whilst the crowd could be carrying broken bottles, cricket bats and other unusual, but effective, weapons of war. It was protecting the blackleg workers in an effort to break the strike which had kept him out of his bed for three nights running. And of course, there had been constant confrontations with the strikers. Brendan, beginning to descend the stairs, put a cautious hand up to the side of his face where the lump caused by a docker's hook was just beginning to go down. Still, the strikers always seemed to come off worse, for most of them had almost no money and large families to feed. They were desperate all right, but the police force did not employ weaklings and it was impossible not to fight back, particularly when there were hundreds of strikers all wanting to score a hit on any scuffer who represented the authorities who were denying them the right to a half-decent wage. Nevertheless, Brendan felt bad about it, and knew that many of his fellow policemen felt the same. But orders were orders, and order was order. They had to obey the one and keep the other and that was all there was to it.

'Mornin', Mr O'Hara,' Mrs Taggart said, as he entered the kitchen. 'I never thought to see you so early, not after the way you've been workin' lately. You poor fellers must be cursin' these perishin' strikes as much as the rest of us, I don't doubt. They say food will run short if the dockers refuse to unload the ships, but I've managed to get a nice piece of bacon, and there's eggs and a loaf . . . I'll try to see to it that me lodgers don't starve.'

'I slept a good twelve hours and I reckon that's enough,' Brendan said, sitting down at his usual place. 'Then I thought it were about breakfast time, and that was enough for me stomach to decide to go on strike an' all . . . "No more sleep for you, me laddo," me stomach said, "not until I'm fed an' watered."'

Mrs Taggart laughed. 'I'll heat the pan,' she said, then walked across to the dresser and picked up an envelope. 'Letter for you; Irish stamp, so it'll be from home,' she informed him. 'You're in luck, though I've not heard anyone say that the postal service is part of these here strikes . . . not yet, at any rate.'

She handed the letter over and Brendan saw at once that it was from Sylvie. He opened it with his heart in his mouth, for she had seemed very down in her last letter; the baby had been overdue, the heat was killing her, and she was no longer working at the laundry but was beginning to miss the companionship of the other laundry workers and had actually been considering returning to work, hard though it was.

So he opened this letter with some trepidation, then smiled with relief. The baby had arrived; not the expected boy, but a girl. She had not yet named the child. Did he know the exact date when Len would be coming out of prison? She had had a bad time birthing the baby, and Caitlin thought she should stay in Dublin until the baby was six weeks old. She did not ask about Becky, for her mother and mother-in-law both kept her posted, but sometimes, she told Brendan, she felt her little daughter would scarcely remember her when she did return.

The letter, which was short, ended with the usual sentence. *Well, I must close now and write to the family*, she said. *Many thanks for all your help, Brendan, and for your last nice letter. See you soon. Yours faithfully, Sylvie.*

'Everything all right at home?' Mrs Taggart enquired. She put down in front of him a plate bearing, in addition to bacon, eggs and fried bread, a pile of new potatoes, cut into discs and fried in the bacon fat. 'Get outside of that little lot,' she commanded comfortably. 'Then there's toast and butter, and some of my marmalade, and a nice big mug o' tea. What'll you be doing for the rest o' the day? If I were you, I'd tek a walk to settle the food down like, and then I'd get back to bed, catch up on me beauty sleep.'

Brendan thought this a good idea and said so, trying to eat slowly so that he would not be plagued with indigestion, something which most beat coppers had to contend with due to missing so many meals and then bolting the ones they did manage to get in order to return to their duty. However, his breakfast finished, he realised he was far too wide awake to return to bed, and, seeing what a fine day it was, he decided to go out for a stroll. He owed his parents a letter and could write that – and one to Sylvie – when he returned. He had been meaning for ages to find out exactly when Len would be coming out of prison, hoping that Sylvie would be able to come back before that date, but now it sounded as though she was unlikely to do so. He knew she had been dreadfully homesick, particularly at first, missing Becky, her family and her friends, and he guessed too that she hated the filth and poverty of Handkerchief Alley. However, as time went on, her friendship with Caitlin had compensated for the temporary loss of her Liverpool connections and she had loved the job in Switzers, though she had been sad when the firm had dismissed her, as her condition grew more obvious.

Brendan had never visited Handkerchief Alley but he had spent some time in Dublin and knew the slums to be a great deal worse than those in Liverpool. Sylvie had assured him however that Caitlin's home was a little palace compared with those of her neighbours and this had relieved his mind. It would have been too bad had he found he had sent Sylvie to a dreadful, disgusting place instead of to the refuge he had promised her.

It was a warm day, so Brendan slung his jacket across one shoulder and sallied forth into the sunshine. He had been heading for the Free Library on William Brown Street and was still thinking about Sylvie and her troubles when he saw that the entire area ahead of him was thronging with people. He groaned inwardly; it looked as though he had walked right into the beginning of another riot, and on his first day off for ages, too. He was thankful that he was not in uniform and would have turned round and found an alternative route but for the press of the crowd;

they were all going in one direction and he was being carried along with them. Strong though he was, he found it impossible to retrace his steps.

The people surged into the huge space of St George's Plateau and Brendan saw that a speaker, perched high on the steps, was already addressing the crowd. Squinting over the heads of those in front of him Brendan recognised Tom Mann, the socialist and labour leader. He admired Mr Mann but sensed that there would be trouble when he saw a large body of police beginning to shove their way through the crowd, shouting at the men before them to disperse or they would regret it. But the crowd did not intend to disperse; they had come to hear Tom Mann speak and did not mean to let themselves be sent home like naughty schoolboys, so the warnings were ignored, though shouts were exchanged. If the police had behaved less violently, Brendan thought afterwards, the trouble would not have escalated the way it did, but very soon truncheons were being flourished – and used – and people were beginning to run. Horrified, Brendan saw men fall, saw those who came behind surge over them. But he was power-less to interfere, for now he was being carried away from the plateau and back in the direction of his lodgings. All around him he saw the white and frightened faces of men who had only wanted to listen to Tom Mann and had ended up bruised and battered. Many were blood-streaked, some nursing arms which might later prove to be broken; others limped on crushed and painful feet. Glancing back, Brendan saw members of the police force, many of whom he knew, with the light of battle in their eyes hitting out mercilessly at men who had no weapons to defend themselves with. It was the first time he had been at a riot – if you could call it that – without the protection of his uniform and his fellow officers. And he realised the terror that the force inspired in ordinary people. For a start, most of the police were taller and better fed than the men they were harassing, and they knew how to wield their truncheons for the most punishing effect. When you took into account the fact that all the men in the crowd were out of work and had already come perilously close to starvation, it was no wonder that they fled, only anxious to get home where they might nurse their hurts.

Brendan turned away, sickened by what he had seen. A man near him was weeping as he cradled crushed and bleeding fingers; another was swearing a steady stream of profanity as he hitched his filthy jacket up over a shoulder which he carried with great care. We treat them worse than animals, Brendan thought disgustedly. And there was no need for it, no need at all. They weren't rioting, poor devils, they were simply trying to listen to a man they admired, a man who might one day be able to help them improve their lot in life.

He made his way back to his lodgings in a

thoughtful mood. He had joined in police charges without ever really seeing how wrong such actions could be because he had been with his fellow policemen, defending them as they were defending him. Now, however, he was seeing such behaviour through the eyes of the oppressed, recognising the needless brutality, the pleasure in violence which he had read in more than one constable's face.

He arrived back at his lodgings and was greeted with mild surprise by Mrs Taggart, who looked him up and down before remarking that he had better clean himself up a bit. 'There's soup and sandwiches in half an hour and by the look of you you'll have worked up quite an appetite by then, despite your big breakfast,' she said.

Brendan looked down at himself and was surprised to see that there were smears of dirt on his jacket and blood on his shirt. He knew he had not been hurt at all but guessed that, in the press of the crowd, blood and dirt had got transferred from the wounded to everyone within reach. 'Okay, I'll have a good wash. And you're right, Mrs Taggart, I have worked up an appetite. I got caught up in a meeting on St George's Plateau and there was a bit of a scuffle. Not being in uniform I wasn't involved, but I reckon I must have brushed up against fellers who bore the brunt of the police dispersal.'

'Very likely,' Mrs Taggart said, then heaved a sigh. 'It's a tough life, bein' a copper,' she observed.

'Especially when you're lined up against your own kind, so to speak. My Albert found it hard, but it's what they pay you for, he used to say. Just you remember that, and it won't seem so bad.'

Brendan looked at his landlady with considerable respect, for she had clearly read his feelings on the matter. 'I will,' he promised. 'Thanks, Mrs T. And now I'll go to my room and make myself respectable.'

Brendan managed to get his two days off, but as soon as he put his head round the station door at the end of that time he was told to report to Rose Hill police station, where an extra man was needed, and from then on he almost forgot what it was like to have a proper sleep in his own bed. The seamen refused to let the dockers unload their cargoes and the dockers themselves refused to work. Then the transport workers refused to move supplies which had been unloaded by blacklegs from the quayside. The army were called in, and in the heat of the riots Brendan almost forgot about Sylvie, and was honestly surprised to discover, from someone who had been drinking at the Ferryman, that Len Dugdale was out of prison and would very shortly be looking for work.

'He was a docker before he were sent to gaol, but there's nothing doing down the docks right now, unless you're prepared to outface the pickets,' Brendan's informant said. 'Of course he can help out in the pub, but if the ale runs out there won't be much call for him there either.' He chuckled. 'I dunno if he can drive a tram, but I doubt it. I reckon he'll be wishin' hisself back in jug before he's much older.'

'He ought to join the force; we aren't allowed to go on strike,' Brendan said wearily. He had been set to guard a warehouse full of grain, but it had been fired by insurgents, so he and his fellow policemen had spent an exhausting night fighting the blaze. 'Anyhow, the bosses have got to listen to reason sooner or later; let's hope it's sooner, because I'm fairly worn out.'

But the bosses did not listen, or not immediately at any rate, and Brendan continued to work all the hours God sent and to drop into his bed, when at last he got time off, almost too weary to sleep.

Then, when he had been promised a forty-eight-hour break and had fallen asleep at last, he was roused by Mrs Taggart, her grey hair in curl papers, a shawl clutched round her nightgowned form and a drooping candle in one hand. 'They've sent a young feller round to rouse you out,' she told him, yawning. 'There's been trouble down at the docks and they need every man they can get; will you go?'

'I suppose so,' Brendan said wearily, putting his feet out of bed. 'I suppose they want me to report to Rose Hill?'

'No, Hatton Garden. I'll get you a nice cup of tea whiles you dress,' Mrs Taggart said. 'I know it must feel like the middle of the night, but it's only ten o'clock so if things go well you could yet get yourself a proper night's sleep. I still had my lamp lit, otherwise the lad could have knocked until kingdom come and I'd just have pretended to be asleep.'

Brendan grinned at her. 'Thanks for that,' he said, reaching for his uniform trousers, for he had gone to bed in his underwear, too exhausted to undress. 'And I'd be grateful for the tea, so I would. I wonder what's up? But I dare say I'll know soon enough.'

He did. Rioters had tried to break into a warehouse alongside the Goree Piazza; the army had been sent in, and the police were wanted to contain what had begun to look like a very ugly situation. To his relief, Brendan found that the night air, despite being very warm and almost muggy, woke him up properly, and he was able to be a real help to his fellows when it came to defending the warehouse. And, as always, the sight of the army with fixed bayonets was enough to scatter the crowd, so that after no more than an hour Brendan was able to return to the Hatton Garden nick and receive his orders to stand down.

'Go back to bed, lad,' his sergeant said. The poor feller looks as tired as I feel, Brendan thought, and was glad to obey the command, though as he made his way through the dark streets he felt inclined to lean against a wall and just nod off while he had the chance. However, he knew this would never do, and kept doggedly on, forcing himself to walk as though on his beat.

He might have continued thus, more asleep than awake, had he not happened to glance sideways as he passed the mouth of a jigger and see, between the sagging brick walls, a man – no, two men . . . three – coming towards him. Had the men continued to advance, Brendan would have thought little of it, but they hesitated, clearly seeing his uniform in the dim light of the gas lamp overhead, and then one of them muttered a word of command and all three charged passed him, almost knocking him over. He grabbed at them, caught the edge of a shirt which came apart in his hand, kicked out, felt his boot connect with a shin and shouted . . . then one of the men turned and pushed Brendan violently in the back. Unprepared, Brendan went down like a ninepin and by the time he had recovered his wits and scrambled to his feet, the men had disappeared and he was alone in the mouth of the jigger.

Or not alone. The men had been up to some mischief and now that the sound of their boots had receded he could hear something else, another sound, and one he did not like: a moaning, like the sort of noise a cat makes when injured.

Bristling with indignation, Brendan marched into the narrow passageway, expecting to find an animal in a bad way . . . and found what he at first thought to be a pile of clothes hard up against a dilapidated wooden door. He bent over the pile but could see very little. Then he remembered he had a box of matches in his pocket and lit one, bent once more . . . and swore beneath his breath. Breathing stertorously, blood-dappled, the elder of the two looking as though his head had been caved in by a vicious blow, were Len Dugdale and his father.

There had been no hope of an early night after that. He had summoned assistance, seen the two men safely delivered to the nearest hospital, and returned to the station. He had had to write out a long report and then his sergeant had announced that he was leaping to conclusions when he had written that he thought the Dugdales had been deliberately targeted. 'They was decently dressed and known to most villains on our patch,' the sergeant had said portentously. 'I reckon it this way, meself. They might have got mixed up in that riot, been seen by the fellers, noted as bein' men o' property, so to speak, and follered. Then the rioters beat 'em up and robbed 'em. How does that sound?'

Brendan was doubtful. He had barely been able to see the features of any of the men as they rushed at him out of the darkness, but he had a strong feeling that they were probably connected in some way to the young man Len had been sent to prison for injuring. He knew, as did everyone else, that the poor fellow had died only a couple of months before, knew, too, that it had been tuberculosis that had killed him and not the fracas with Len; but you try telling that to the chap's relatives, he thought grimly. Oh yes, if he had to make a guess, it would be that the attack had been motivated by revenge and not the urge to rob, though both men's pockets had been empty when they were admitted to hospital.

He thought the sergeant might think differently when, a week later, the hospital reported that Mr Dugdale senior had died in the night, but he was wrong. The sergeant merely said that they would 'prosecute immediate enquiries' and let it be known that the two men had been attacked for gain, almost certainly by some of the men who, earlier in the evening, had attacked the warehouses in the Goree Piazza.

Others had been too busy over the strikes to take much interest in the affair, though when Brendan voiced his doubts to his landlady, she commented at once that in her view it was almost certainly a revenge attack.

'Whenever there's trouble, like them riots, someone uses it to their own advantage,' she said darkly. 'I remember when Mr Taggart were put into hospital; they tried to tell me it were "someone in the crowd", that the blow weren't meant for anyone in pertickler, but when he were safely home again, Mr Taggart told me it were a feller whose son he'd banged up for . . . oh, well, for something he'd done wrong. Revenge, see? It's easy, in a crowd, to get yourself a big cudgel and hit someone what you think has done you wrong and, by and large, you get away with it.'

'Aye, you're right there,' Brendan said. 'But they were robbed, Mrs Taggart, and I'm pretty sure the attackers were all strangers to me. Even if I did know 'em, I didn't recognise them 'cos it were pitch dark, and besides, they knocked me down; by the time I got to me feet they were long gone. Still, you never know, something may turn up.' But he spoke without much optimism for the city was still seething with unrest and how could anyone pick out three men from amongst the crowd of rioters, many of whom had been armed, desperate men who might well take to robbery with violence if the opportunity occurred?

'Morning, Caitlin. Sorry I'm so late but I've been awake half the night with the baby whining and grizzling. I fell asleep around five, I s'pose. Maeve woke me when she took the baby, but somehow or other I just drifted back to sleep again. Any porridge left?'

Caitlin looked up. She had been scrubbing out the big, blackened porridge pot but had saved a bowlful for her guest; she indicated it with a jerk of her head, then said a trifle reproachfully: 'Yes, there's yours. You know, you do rather put on Maeve, alanna. It isn't her job to get your baby fed; it's you who should be taking her round to Mrs O'Mara.'

Mrs O'Mara had lost her own baby shortly after

134

Sylvie's child had been born, and when Sylvie's milk had dried up after a couple of days Mrs O'Mara had been glad to earn some money by feeding Sylvie's little one.

'I do take her round sometimes,' Sylvie said. 'But Maeve likes doing it, you know she does, Cait. And I'm quite willing to get her messages for her . . . only aren't you going to the shops yourself today? I heard you telling Clodagh last evening that she needed new boots and I thought . . .'

'Oh aye, we're going shopping at the markets,' Caitlin owned. 'So there's no need for you to put yourself out. Besides, it's Maeve's day to visit her own mam and the family, so likely she'll take the baby with her.' She looked speculatively at the younger woman. 'You've not been round there, have you? I reckon you should visit them and see how Maeve lived before we took her on.'

'Well, all right, I'll pop round there later,' Sylvie said. She looked surprised. But not half as surprised as she'll look when she sees how Maeve's family live, Caitlin thought with an inward smile. She liked Sylvie, of course she did, but she thought her very selfish, using her undoubted beauty to get what she wanted and rarely considering anyone but herself. Perhaps when she had visited the Connolly family she might appreciate Maeve rather more. Pat had said several times that their guest did not know how lucky she was, for the O'Keefes had a much better lifestyle than most of their neighbours.

But now Sylvie was sitting at the table eating porridge, and since the children had long since disappeared Caitlin decided that it was high time she had another go at the younger woman. 'Sylvie!' she said. 'That child of yours will be two weeks old in a couple of days and still no name to her. It's shameful, so it is. Why can't you just pick a saint's name – Mary, Bridget, something like that – and have her christened, decent like? If something were to happen – which the good God forbid – and her wit'out a name, how would you feel? She's your own dear little girl when all's said and done. I know you had a bad time birthin' her, but even so . . .'

'I'll think of a nice name soon,' Sylvie said, looking hunted. 'Or . . . I wonder if Maeve would like to have the naming of the baby? She's that fond of her . . . and she looks after her so well, and . . . remember, Caitlin, I mustn't let myself love her or take too much of an interest in her 'cos when I go back to Liverpool I've got to forget all about her. Please try to understand.'

Caitlin sighed. She did understand what Sylvie meant but someone had to name the baby. Never in all me born days, she found herself thinking, did I meet a woman who puts things off the way Sylvie Dugdale does! True, the baby would have to be left behind, but that was no reason for not giving her a name.

'Mam, there's post for Sylvie!' Clodagh entered the kitchen on the words, holding out two envelopes, which Sylvie took with a word of thanks. She glanced at the writing, then at mother and daughter, both looking enquiringly at her, and smiled her pretty smile.

'One from me mother-in-law and one from me mam,' she said. 'I do hope Becky's all right.'

She ripped open the first envelope, then gasped and handed the single sheet with its short scrawled message to Caitlin. Caitlin read it aloud. 'Come back, Sylvie, we're in bad trouble. Mr Dugdale's sick unto death; they say at the hospital he may not last the night, and Len's pretty bad. It were a riot . . . he got bashed on the head . . . you must come home. Becky needs you. We all need you.'

Sylvie had ripped open the second envelope, saying as she did so: 'This one's from me mam.' She began to read aloud, as Caitlin had done. 'Dear Sylvie, Len come out of prison a couple of days gone. He and his da went down to the docks to see if Len could get work there. They was gone a long time and then a scuffer come to the door and told Mrs Dugdale her men had been injured in one of these here riots. They're mortal bad. Sylvie gal, you must come back. Please come at once.'

'What'll you do, Sylvie?' Caitlin said after a long pause. 'I know you'll have to go back, but . . .'

'I'll leave as soon as I'm able,' Sylvie said at once. 'I can't stay here, not with everyone at home in such trouble.' She turned imploring eyes on Caitlin. 'You know I can't take the baby with me but I'll leave money with you so you can pay Mrs

O'Mara and – and buy anything the kid needs. I'll get in touch just as soon as I've sorted things out.'

'I'm awful sorry about your da-in-law and Len, and we knew you'd be leavin' once we'd found someone suitable to take the baby . . .' Caitlin began, then saw Sylvie was already at the door. 'Hold on a moment . . .'

'Can't wait,' Sylvie called over her shoulder as she headed for the stairs. 'I have to fetch Maeve back, because I must talk to her about taking care of the baby.'

'Yes, I dare say, but . . .'

'It's no use, Mam,' Clodagh said prosaically, going over to the sink and beginning to wash up the crocks. 'She'll be back in a moment; it ain't far to Maeve's mam's place. And when she does come back, you tell her she'll have to name the baby afore she goes and pay Maeve extra whilst she's away. It's only fair . . . you said yourself the Dugdales were well off.'

'That wasn't me, that was your da,' Caitlin said. 'Not but what I agree – they've got a big pub so they have, down by the docks, and it's always busy; Sylvie's told me so many a time.' She got to her feet and began to dry the delft as Clodagh put it on to the draining board. 'I suppose Sylvie must go back but it *is* her baby, not ours, so it puts us in a difficult position.'

'I don't see that,' Clodagh said as she turned away from the sink. She dried her hands on the roller towel behind the door, and began to stack the dishes and spoons as her mother dried them. 'Sure an' didn't she say she'd have the little one adopted?' she said, putting the clean dishes back on the dresser. 'You know she can't take her home, Mammy.'

'Yes, I know, but to tell the truth, Clodagh me love, she's not a pretty baby and you know how folk in these parts dislike ginger hair. There's kids by the score wantin' good homes who would be picked before Sylvie's little 'un, so I think that's a horse which won't run.'

Clodagh, a practical child, sniffed. 'Well, babies don't eat much, anyway, and if that feller of hers dies she'll be able to take the kid back to Liverpool,' she remarked. She grinned at her mother. 'Though everyone'll know he couldn't possibly be the father, since he were in prison.'

Caitlin blinked. The things children picked up from casual conversations! She frowned at Clodagh. 'Nonsense! I dare say Len has broken a bone or two, but that'll be the worst he'll have suffered and he isn't likely to die from a broken arm. Now go and get your jacket . . . unless you don't want to come with me to the Daisy Market?'

As she had hoped it would, the thought of the new boots which were to be bought put every-thing else out of Clodagh's head. She gave a squeak of joy and scooped up her mother's big marketing bag. 'I'm ready,' she said. 'Oh, I do love buyin' new boots, so I do.'

Chapter Five

A week after the letters had arrived, Sylvie found herself aboard the ferry heading for Liverpool. Leaning against the ship's rail, she contemplated the last week, which had been exceedingly hectic. She had gone round to the Connolly place and had been appalled by the building, which was a crumbling three-storey tenement, with gaping holes in the wooden stairs, no glass in the windows and precious few tiles on the roof, to judge by the rich growth of mould which seemed to cover all the walls. The Connollys all shared one miserable damp room. Most of the children appeared to sleep in the pile of rags close up against a leaky window frame, while their mother shared a straw pallet bed with her two youngest sons, and the room had been criss-crossed with lengths of clothes line since it appeared that Mrs Connolly took in washing, though how she ever managed to get it dry was a mystery to Sylvie. The room had been fiercely clean, though the furniture, if you could call it that, was mainly tea chests and half-barrels which stood against the wall so that, when seated, one could lean back on something. Sylvie had never seen so pitifully poor a place, yet from the moment Mrs

Connolly had greeted her warmly and ushered her inside, she had realised that despite the poverty and lack of material goods the Connollys were a very happy family. The room might have been small, but Mrs Connolly had assured her guest that this was an advantage, so it was, since it was easier to keep warm when you were all cuddled together. 'Two of me boys sell newspapers, though 'tis only Thomais who's licensed; Paddy has to scarper when the polis come round. Still an' all, 'tis a great help so it is, to have a few extra pennies comin' in.' She had beamed at Sylvie. 'I dare say Maeve's telled you that me eldest, Bridget, has a live-in job. She's kitchen maid at a big house on the outskirts of the city, but she's a good gal an' comes home for her day off, and always brings bits 'n' pieces for us. The cook sometimes gives her a grand fresh-baked loaf and a bag of apples, or the remains of a pie. Now and again it's a dress, or some trowsis what may fit one o' the boys. An' she hands over as much as she can afford from her wages, sometimes as much as half a crown.'

'Well, isn't that lovely?' Sylvie had said rather feebly as her hostess had paused expectantly. 'And what about your second daughter . . . is she still at home?'

'Oh aye, she helps by sellin' oranges for one o' the market women, but there ain't much money in it,' Mrs Connolly had said, rather sadly. Then she had brightened. 'But our Maeve's a grand help, so she is. Whenever she comes home, she scrubs the stairs, does me messages, carts me laundry . . . she even irons a great pile of sheets which is the job I hate the most 'cos of the rheumatics acrost me shoulders. Oh aye, she's a good little girl is our Maeve.'

All this while, Maeve had been making and pouring three cups of very weak tea, with the baby slung across her shoulder and apparently fast asleep. She had handed Sylvie a chipped and handleless cup, full of straw-coloured liquid, saying with a shy smile: 'It ain't as good as you'd get with the O'Keefes, but tea's a turble price, so it is.' She had glanced enquiringly up at Sylvie. 'There's bread and a smear o' jam but I'll doubt you'll be hungry yet.'

'No, I'm not hungry,' Sylvie had assured her, 'but I've come round, Maeve, because something bad has happened back in Liverpool, which means I must go home straight away. As you know, I can't take the baby, but Caitlin has agreed to keep her for the time being. Only – only I'm afraid it will be you who has the real responsibility, so I need you to say you'll look after her before I can make any plans. I'll pay you every week,' she had finished hastily, though she could tell from Maeve's beaming smile that the girl had no intention of refusing the favour.

After that, it had been easy. She had explained about the letters, telling Maeve that both her father-in-law and her husband were in hospital and that she must return to Liverpool at once. Back at the O'Keefes', she had told Caitlin that Maeve had agreed to look after the baby and that she meant to leave two whole pounds with Caitlin, though she also intended to give Maeve five bob to cover more immediate expenses. She had smiled winningly at Caitlin as she spoke and had thanked her profusely for agreeing to keep the little one. She had then told her friend that she meant to go along and explain matters to Mrs O'Mara, but even as she walked quickly across the kitchen Caitlin had grabbed her arm and swung her round, shaking Sylvie's shoulders quite hard as she did so. 'You'll do no such t'ing until I've had *my* say,' Caitlin had said, and Sylvie had noticed, with a stab of surprise, that the other girl's cheeks were pink with annoyance. 'You'll not land me and my man wit' a nameless, godless child! You either have her christened or you take her to Liverpool wit' you. Choose!'

If it had not been for that remark, Sylvie thought now, feeling the freshening breeze on her face as the ferry left the shelter of the estuary and moved out into the open sea, she would have left at once, but she had stayed to see the baby christened Catherine Mary, as Catherine was the anglicised form of Caitlin's own name. 'But you can call her Mary, so's there's no confusion,' she had said kindly. Only then had she been free to depart and she had wasted no time. She had packed all her belongings in her big suitcase and there had been emotional farewells, of course, for she was very fond of Caitlin and liked Pat well enough, though she suspected her liking was not reciprocated. If I had had more time, she told herself now, gazing rather bleakly back across the choppy waves to where the small, grey town of Dun Laoghaire nestled against its green hills, then I could have made him like me, made him see that I'm a good person, that having a baby who's not your husband's doesn't make you all bad; but she had not had time.

Maeve had wept a little and thrust Catherine Mary into her arms for a last cuddle before the boat sailed. Sylvie had accepted the child, but after the briefest of moments had handed her back to Maeve. 'It's no use, Maeve; she's already more your child than mine and that's how it has to be. I hope to God someone real lovely adopts her but I know you'll not let her go to anyone bad.' Then she had kissed Clodagh, and Grainne, and had tried to kiss the twins and Colm, only the twins had given raucous shouts and broken away from the family group on the quay, and though Colm had not managed to escape she had seen him rub her kiss off his cheek as soon as he thought himself unobserved. She had smiled wryly to herself, reflecting that boys were very different from girls, and had then climbed up the gangway to find herself a seat whence she could wave her good-byes in more comfort.

But now Ireland was little more than a blue-grey hump, in the distance and the dancing green sea and white-tipped waves were all about them, and with some astonishment Sylvie realised that she felt free and young again, as young as she had been before she had married Len Dugdale. She guessed that this was because on the ferry, she was between two lives; she had left behind in Ireland the little daughter whom she dared not love, and was not yet enveloped in the trials and tribulations of the Dugdale family. In Ireland, the O'Keefes – and presumably the Connollys – had known she had been a bad girl. They had never held it against her, had treated her with great kindness and generosity, but she realised now that this had cast a shadow over her life with them. They would look after the baby until she was old enough to be adopted and would see she went to a good family; but now Sylvie herself must concentrate on the troubles which lay ahead, and they were different troubles, not directly the result of her behaviour.

Smiling, Sylvie got to her feet and decided to walk round the deck. It was better than just sitting and waiting, particularly as the choppy sea was beginning to have its effect on those passengers with weak stomachs. Only a few feet from her, several women and a couple of men were leaning over the rail and . . . Sylvie hastily withdrew her gaze from their heaving shoulders and started to walk along the smooth decking.

Sylvie had not known precisely what to expect when she reached the Ferryman, but as soon as she got within sight of the pub she realised that something truly bad had happened. The blinds were drawn and the pub was closed, although it should have been open, and when she let herself into the cool dark bar and put her suitcase down to ease the ache in her arm, her mother-in-law came rushing across the sawdust-covered floor to give Sylvie a hard hug and to press her tear-wet face against her daughter-in-law's smooth cheek. 'Oh, Sylvie, I'm that glad you've come home, though your mam told me you would,' she said brokenly. 'Mr Dugdale passed away yesterday afternoon . . . the funeral's arranged for Thursday because we weren't sure when you'd be back. We've had the scuffers in and out ever since it happened. There's been no peace for anyone, but now you're back things will be easier, I'm sure.'

Sylvie had returned the hug rather shyly. 'Oh, Ma, I'm most dreadfully sorry that Pa's died,' she said sincerely. 'But how is Len? You said he was pretty bad . . .'

'Len took a deal of punishment, but the surgeon who's sewed him up an' set his bones an' that hopes he'll pull through,' Mrs Dugdale said. She picked up the suitcase and set off for the back regions of the pub, gesturing for Sylvie to follow her. 'We can visit him this evening, both of us. They won't let children in, you know, but if we go while your mam's here – your mam's been wonderful, Sylvie, a tower of strength – then she'll give an eye to Becky.'

Sylvie looked round the kitchen. 'Where is she? Oh, in kindergarten, I suppose.'

Mrs Dugdale shook her head. 'She's been that upset over her grandpa – and her daddy, of course – that I've not sent her today,' she said. She bustled over to the stove and lit the gas under the big, blackened kettle. 'I've no doubt you could do with a cup of tea, you poor dear, so I'll just make one and then we'll call your mam down to share it with us. She and Becky are making the beds together.'

Sylvie smiled. 'I can't imagine Becky making beds . . .' she was beginning when the kitchen door flew open and her mother surged into the room, closely followed by Becky. Sylvie gave a little gasp. Becky's beautiful hair was confined in two short, fat yellow plaits, and her small figure was swathed in an enormous apron. In the six months since Sylvie had seen her last, she had changed a great deal. It seemed to her mother that her round, childish face had been replaced by a much more serious one, and the baby chubbiness which Sylvie had loved had quite gone. This little girl was thinner and a good deal taller, and to Sylvie's dismay, when the child's eyes met her own they were hard and cold, with no vestige of the excitement over a returning mother that Sylvie had expected to see. However, Sylvie ran across the kitchen, holding out her arms. 'Oh, queen, I've missed you so dreadfully,' she said. 'Have you missed me? I didn't have time to buy you a nice present before I left Ireland but we'll go out tomorrow . . .' The words died in her throat. Becky had cringed away from her and her expression was so antagonistic that Sylvie's arms dropped to her sides and she simply stared at the small, flinty face. 'Becky?' she said uncertainly. 'Becky, don't you know me? It's your mammy, back from Ireland.'

The child walked round the table and tugged at Mrs Dugdale's skirt. 'Grandma, is it teatime? Can I have a piece of shortbread as well as a cup of milk, 'cos I'm real hungry?'

Mrs Dugdale looked uneasily at the child. 'Wharrever is the matter, chuck?' she asked. 'You've not said hello to your mammy, nor given her a hug. Don't you pretend you've forgot her!'

'Why not? She forgot me,' Becky said resentfully. 'Can I have a piece of shortbread, Gran?'

Her grandmother began to remonstrate once more but Sylvie interrupted her. 'It doesn't matter, Ma. Becky an' me will have to get to know one another again,' she said, with forced cheerfulness. She crossed the room and gave her mother a warm hug and a kiss on the cheek. 'Oh, Mam, it's wonderful to be back and I truly have missed you.'

The funeral was well attended for the Ferryman was a popular pub and Mr Dugdale had made many friends. Becky, though she had been shy and awkward with her mother at first, had been reconciled when Sylvie took her to Lewis's to buy her a black crêpe dress, and had also purchased at the same time a beautiful straw hat with poppies round the crown and long scarlet ribbons which tied into a big bow at the back. 'You won't be able to wear it until the funeral's over,' Sylvie had told her small daughter, 'but then a crêpe armband will be quite sufficient and you can put away the black dress.'

'Why can't I wear my lovely new hat to the funeral?' Becky had asked plaintively. 'It's the prettiest hat I've ever seen, but what's the good of it if I can't wear it? I want all me pals to see it while it's still new, an' everyone's comin' to the funeral.'

Sylvie had laughed. Young though she was, Becky was already deeply conscious of her appearance, just as Sylvie had been, and indeed still was. 'Well, at least you won't have to go on wearing black for months and months like members of the royal family did after King Edward's death last year. In fact, they only came out of mourning in time for the coronation last month.'

Grandma Davies had trimmed the plain black straw bonnet, which Becky was to wear at the funeral, with a small bunch of artificial violets. 'Purple's allowable,' she had said, smiling at her granddaughter. 'Now no more grumblin', because you loved your Grandpa Dugdale, didn't you? And wearin' black shows you're sad he's gone, see?'

Becky had appeared to understand and now she stood beside her mother whilst the coffin was lowered into the grave. It was a brilliantly fine day, but as the first handful of earth rattled against the coffin Sylvie remembered that other funeral and how she had caught Brendan's eye, and how they had left Anfield Cemetery after a hurried conversation. She wondered if he was here today, but the crowd was so dense that it was next to impossible to pick out one man.

She was still searching hopefully, however, when the service finished and the crowd began to make its way back to the road. Someone fell into step with Sylvie; she glanced sideways and saw it was Mrs Barratt, a neighbour of her mother's. She opened her mouth to thank the woman for coming but Mrs Barratt was ahead of her. 'How's your Len?' she asked, with beady curiosity. 'I seen him almost a week ago when I were visitin' me Uncle Fred.' She clicked her tongue. 'Eh, he looked mortal bad. More stitches and plaster than anything else if you ask me.'

'He's still very poorly,' Sylvie said cautiously; she was shocked anew, every time she visited Len, by the state of him. But they had been trying to keep their worries from Becky, who was not allowed in the ward and so had no idea how ill her father was. 'I'm afraid he won't be home for a few weeks yet. The sister told me they'd not let him come home until he's – he's more himself.'

'If you ask me, the only way he'll come out of

there will be in a box,' Mrs Barratt said bluntly. 'Mind, they say surgeons can perform miracles these days,' she added hastily, clearly reading the shock and disgust in Sylvie's eyes.

Beside them Becky tilted her head up, looking from one face to the other. 'Why should he come home in a box?' she asked curiously. 'Mammy says he'll come home in a hansom cab.'

'So he will, love,' Sylvie said. She had meant to issue an invitation to Mrs Barratt but the woman's crudely expressed opinion had changed her mind. 'Come along, Grandma is waiting for us in the nice carriage that brought us here.' She turned to the older woman. 'It may interest you to know that my husband is thought by the doctors to be on the road to recovery,' she said coldly. 'Thank you for your interest.'

She turned away decisively, ignoring Mrs Barratt's muttered, 'I were always one to speak me mind,' and lifted Becky into the waiting carriage with a real sense of relief. Until this moment, she had not realised how much of her antagonism against Len had disappeared since visiting him in hospital. He was so different now! Because he had been unconscious for so long, she supposed, he had grown thin and pale, and though the stitches which had criss-crossed his face had been removed they had left livid scars. The doctor had assured her that the marks would fade, and she in her turn had assured him that they were unimportant. What mattered was that Len should come to himself once more and begin to lead a normal life, for his mother was finding it difficult to run the pub with no man to help her. Bertie did his best, as did the two barmen, but Sylvie knew that it was not enough. Mrs Dugdale yearned for her son's help and was growing increasingly anxious over the state of him, and Sylvie, doing the books and the ordering, cooking meals and generally helping out, realised that at least she was no longer worrying about her own problems. Ireland, the O'Keefes, and the baby, no longer seemed important. Her life for the moment was here. As she had promised, she would send money to Dublin every week until the child was adopted, but what a blessing that Caitlin and Maeve, between them, would take care of the child until then . . . though Sylvie sometimes found herself wondering whether any adoption would in fact be arranged, for Catherine Mary, with her gingery hair and fretful wailing, was not a fetching child as Becky had been.

They arrived back at the Ferryman and hurried into the large room where the funeral tea was to be held. Mrs Davies greeted them with relief and very soon Sylvie was so busy pouring ale and porter, making big pots of tea and handing round sandwiches that she had no time to think about Len or to worry over what would happen if Mrs Barratt were right, if he did emerge from hospital only to join his father and grandfather in Anfield Cemetery.

When the wake was over, the food and drink all gone, and Becky in bed, Sylvie made her way to the hospital. Len was in a large ward, but on this particular evening the curtains round his bed were drawn, and when she slipped into the little cubicle these formed it was to find Brendan sitting beside the bed apparently talking to the unconscious Len. Sylvie stopped short, too surprised to speak, but Brendan got to his feet and took both her hands, squeezing them warningly. 'Evenin'. You must be young Mrs Dugdale,' he said cheerfully. 'I don't suppose you know, but I'm the feller who found your husband and your father-in-law in that alley at the back o' the docks. I'm a policeman and the Ferryman's on my beat, so I've been popping in just to check all's well. And I've been visiting Mr Dugdale here because the ward sister said the more visitors he got – visitors who talk to him, I mean – the sooner he'd come round. But now you're here . . .'

'Thank you so much, constable,' Sylvie said politely. Her voice was cool but her face, she knew, was flushed and her eyes bright. Without stopping to think why he had addressed her as a stranger, she began to say that she had meant to call round in Hunter Street, but she found her voice abruptly cut off by one of Brendan's large hands which came up to cover her mouth. 'I'll just say me farewells to your husband, Mrs Dugdale,' he said. 'Because I've come to believe he hears every word I say, though he can't speak for himself, not yet.'

He had removed his hand from her mouth as he spoke, realising that Sylvie had got the message: it was neither safe nor kind to talk in front of Len as though he could neither hear nor make sense of what was said. Now he turned to the bed. 'Evenin', Mr Dugdale. I'm on duty for the next six days but I dare say I'll find a moment to pop round and have a word. You see, I'm still not too sure how you come to be dumped in that alley, because when a feller's hurt in a riot folk mostly leave him lie where he fell, and I'd like to know a bit more detail when you're able to tell me.' With that, he leaned over the bed, picked up Len's large, unnaturally clean hand, and shook it slightly. Then he gave Sylvie a quick smile and made his way out through the curtains and back down the ward.

Sylvie stayed with Len for about twenty minutes. For once, she was at a loss as to what she should tell him. She knew her mother-in-law had decreed that Len should be told nothing worrying and had not spoken of his father's death in front of him, though she, personally, did not believe that he could hear a word she said. The doctor in charge of Len's case, however, thought otherwise, so Mrs Dugdale had chatted about customers, the doings of the staff, and Becky's funny little ways. So far, Sylvie had really not been able to talk to him with any ease; the dark secret which had taken her to Dublin hung over her like a pall, and she was afraid she might let something slip which would give her away. Having seen Brendan, of course, she guessed that he would hang about outside so that they might talk, for so sudden had been her departure from Dublin that she had had no opportunity to tell him that she was returning. However, there was the shopping expedition with Becky to mention, and the fact that she had bought the child a beautiful straw hat, trimmed with poppies. She also talked a little about how kind her mother's American cousins had been to her, understanding that she needed to save her money and never pressing her to spend it. 'Because I know you are as keen as I am myself to have a home of our own one day,' she said now. She took hold of his large hand and squeezed it and felt a thrill of excitement course through her when he returned, very slightly, the pressure of her fingers. 'Len? Oh, Len, I'm almost sure you squeezed my hand! Can you squeeze it again, chuck? Oh, do try!'

But the hand within her own remained motionless and Sylvie concluded that she had either imagined the movement or that it had merely been a twitching of the long unused muscles. Besides, she told herself as she said her farewells and kissed his unresponsive cheek, what difference would it make if he did regain consciousness? From what the medical team had told her, it would be months, rather than weeks, before he could work again.

She left the hospital building and saw Brendan waiting for her. She joined him and he walked beside her as she made her way back towards the pub. He glanced at her, his eyes smiling. 'I was at

155

the funeral but I didn't come back to the Ferryman,' he said quietly. 'I guessed you'd returned to Liverpool as soon as you heard what had happened, and I knew you'd visit Len, but I didn't try to contact you in case it started folk talking; better that we meet naturally, like now.' His glance ranged appreciatively over her. 'You're looking very well, alanna. It seems Dublin air suited you. Now, how is the baby?'

'Oh, Catherine Mary, you mean?' Sylvie said airily.

'Catherine Mary? Sure and isn't that a pretty name? What about her surname, though? Will she be known as Catherine Mary Dugdale, or Catherine Mary Davies?'

'I called her O'Keefe; I hope you don't mind,' Sylvie said rather guiltily. 'Caitlin thought it were best, seein' as how she'd passed me off as her cousin. I don't know how Pat felt – he's the O'Keefe after all – but he never objected, not to me at any rate.' She looked rather anxiously up at her companion. 'Caitlin is the kindest person in the world, but – but I don't think Patrick liked me very much. I did my best, helping in the house, looking after the kids, buying treats for everyone on me pay day, but I always had the feeling he resented me.'

Brendan nodded thoughtfully. 'That's understandable in a way,' he said. 'I dare say he felt you were a responsibility, but I hope he were never unkind. I never knew him well, not like I knew

Caitlin, but he seemed a pleasant sort of feller.'

'He is a nice feller and I shouldn't have criticised him,' Sylvie said remorsefully. 'I dare say he disapproved of my having the baby by Robbie when I were married to Len.'

Brendan gave her another appraising look, followed by a grin. 'You don't say?' he said, and there was a definite laugh in his voice. 'Now tell me about Catherine Mary; what does she look like? Does she take after you, or Robbie?' His face softened, the quizzical look being replaced by one of great sympathy. 'I'm a feller so it's difficult for me to understand how a mother feels, but it must have been like tearing your heart out to leave the little 'un behind.' He stopped walking abruptly. 'Who's feeding her? Catherine Mary, I mean. She needs her mother's milk, doesn't she?'

'I found a wet nurse livin' nearby; my milk dried up before the baby was more than a couple of days old,' Sylvie said, rather awkwardly. She felt that this was not a subject she should be discussing with a young man. 'As for who she resembles, it's Robbie. She – she's got ginger hair, like his, and I dare say some people would think her as plain as a boot, but she's too young yet to know what she'll look like in a year or two!' Brendan started walking again and Sylvie trotted along beside him. 'Are you going to continue visiting Len? Because if so, maybe we could meet outside the hospital and exchange news,' she suggested rather breathlessly, for Brendan's natural stride was a good deal longer than hers. 'I've agreed to pay a – a young woman to look after the baby until she's old enough to be adopted.'

'It's for the best that she should be adopted and go to someone who could care for her,' Brendan said earnestly. 'Your mother-in-law really needs you, Sylvie, to help her run the pub and to look after Becky, and if you want my opinion, I think you'll find Len's experience will have changed him. So for the moment, you've simply got to play a waiting game. Just remember you're not alone, the way you were in Ireland. You've got your mam, your family, even your mother-in-law; and there's meself of course, anxious to do anything I can to help you.'

By now they were approaching the Ferryman and Sylvie took his hand for a moment, giving it a brief squeeze. 'Oh, Brendan, you are good. You've already helped me out of the most dreadful trouble, but everything's such a mess,' she said miserably. 'Becky can't forgive me for leaving her. Oh, I've been silly and selfish, I know that. All the bad things I've done have been because I married someone when I was too young to know what I was taking on. Only one good thing has come out of all this and that's your friendship. Thank you, thank you.'

Brendan grinned at her. 'You aren't the first person to get into a muddle because she jumped into marriage and then found she'd made a mistake, and Becky will come round once she knows you're not going to leave her again,' he assured her. 'Chin up! You're here where you belong, with Becky and the rest of your family, and Caitlin will make sure that Catherine Mary goes to a good home.'

Sylvie smiled gratefully at him. She really did like Brendan and told herself that he would make some woman a fine husband one day. Unfortunately, however, it could not be herself, not whilst Len lived.

Brendan had stopped outside the Ferryman and was gesturing for her to go inside. 'All this civil unrest – the riots and that, and the strikes – mean I'm never sure when I'll be on duty,' he told her. 'I can't say when I'll get to the hospital again, but I've been visiting the Ferryman on a regular basis, doing my best to see there's no trouble here since the tragedy, so no doubt we'll see each other from time to time.'

Sylvie stood for a moment with her hand on the door, watching Brendan making his way along the crowded pavement, then went slowly into the house. Sighing, she crossed the empty bar and headed for the kitchen; there was work to be done and she'd best get on with it, for tomorrow they would be open for business once more.

Chapter Six

It was a cold day. Sylvie was washing up the breakfast dishes. Len had come out of hospital some
weeks before Christmas, mainly because the
medical staff felt they could do nothing more for
him. He had recovered consciousness all right, but
he couldn't talk, and he could neither walk nor
get up from the bed they had made for him in the
room behind the bar; in fact, he was not the Len
that Sylvie had known. If he knew who she was,
he gave no sign of it, nodding his thanks when
she took him a meal, and smiling a slow, rather
stupid smile when she asked him a question, or
reminded him gently that Mrs Dugdale was his
mam, Becky his little daughter and she herself his
wife.

Mrs Dugdale had told him, with tears, that his
father was dead, but Sylvie was sure he had not
taken it in, nor did he respond in any way when
friends came calling, or customers shouted a
greeting across the bar. Right now, however, Becky
was sitting on her father's bed, chattering away
about the events in her life whilst waiting for her
grandmother to take her shopping. Sylvie listened,
smiling to herself, but then turned from the sink,

remarking as she did so that since Len was nearly asleep, Becky might as well begin to get ready to go out. Becky, who could sometimes be difficult, stared at Sylvie for an unnerving moment and then remarked: 'He likes to hear me talk; Grandma Dugdale says he does, so what do you know?'

'I know you're a rude little girl,' Sylvie replied sharply, stung by her daughter's words. 'And Grandma Davies is about to go down to the market for some messages. If you want to go with her, you'd best behave yourself.'

'I *am* going with her,' Becky said loftily. 'You can't bleeding well stop me.'

Sylvie opened her mouth to say that indeed she could just as Mrs Davies entered the room. 'Come along, Becky. I've got so many messages that I need your strong little arms to help me carry them home.'

Becky shot a triumphant look at her mother. 'Told you so,' she said impudently, rushing across the room and snatching her coat off the peg on the back of the door. 'If there's so much shopping, Grandma Davies, why don't we have us dinners at the Dining Rooms by Paddy's Market? I do love to have me dinner out.' She turned to her father. 'Is there anything you want, Da? Would you like a few sweeties?'

Len made no reply and Becky ran over to the bed and gave his hand a pat. 'I'll get you some sweeties anyway,' she promised. 'Ta-ra Daddy.'

She went to pass Sylvie but her mother grabbed

her by the shoulder, stopping her in her tracks. Sylvie knew that Becky's pertness was not entirely the child's fault; between Grandma Dugdale, Grandma Davies and herself, Becky was over-indulged to say the least, but Sylvie had decided that this behaviour must be nipped in the bud before it became a habit. Accordingly, she pulled Becky round until the child was facing her, and then said quietly: 'You will go nowhere, Becky, until you have said you are sorry for speaking to me so rudely. And you certainly shan't have your dinner out, for rude children get punishments, not treats.'

For a moment, Becky stared at her mother defi-antly, then she flung both arms round Sylvie's neck. 'I'm sorry I were rude, Mummy,' she muttered. 'But it's what Cousin Alfie said to his mammy when she telled him to fetch a sack o' spuds from the greengrocer on Heyworth Street.'

'Alfie's a rude, naughty boy,' Sylvie said, repres-sively. 'Don't copy him again. Now off with you, queen, or you won't be home in time for your dinner.'

Sylvie waited until Becky and her mother had disappeared, then donned coat and hat and let herself out of the pub. She shoved her gloved hands into the pocket of her winter coat and decided that if she got the job she was about to apply for, she would buy new gloves and a smart hat with her very first wages. She had been unable to get work outside the pub since returning from

Ireland, but a week previously there had been an advertisement in the *Echo* for a sales assistant in Lewis's Hat and Glove department. Sylvie remembered how happy she had been when she had worked in Switzer's and had told her mother-in-law, with an edge of defiance in her voice, that she meant to apply for the position. Mrs Dugdale was a good deal easier to deal with than she had been, but she had looked doubtfully at Sylvie. 'But you work at the pub in the evenings, and you find that hard enough,' she had pointed out reasonably. 'And you work pretty hard during the day as well; we all do. I don't deny it would be nice for you to get out of the old Ferryman now and again, but this 'un's a full-time job . . .' she had tapped the newspaper as she spoke, 'which means eight till six, longer some nights.' Her face had softened. 'Why, you'd see almost nothing of Becky, and I know how you value your time with her, the little darling.'

'I think perhaps I've been trying too hard with Becky,' Sylvie had said slowly. 'I'm beginning to believe that she'd appreciate me more if she didn't see so much of me. She knows how desperately I need her love, especially since poor Len isn't able to – to love anyone right now. So if I take a job away from the pub, I'll just make sure I spend an hour with Becky before bed each evening. And you must admit, Ma Dugdale, that the money would come in useful.'

Mrs Dugdale had agreed, rather doubtfully, that

this was so and Sylvie had answered the advertisement and been granted an interview this very morning. She knew she was looking her best. Her flaxen hair had been plaited and then coiled into a large bun, whilst the dark hat perched upon the top of her head was enlivened by a big chiffon scarf of palest blue wound around its crown. Her navy blue skirt and jacket had been brushed and pressed, and her dark winter coat, which matched her hat, looked smart enough to impress most people. All in all, Sylvie thought, if appearance and experience were all that were required, she really should get the job.

As she made her way towards Ranelagh Street she thought about the money she sent every month to Caitlin for Catherine Mary. She had been paying for the child out of her savings but these were running low; another good reason for getting a job.

Turning into the imposing entrance of the big store, Sylvie congratulated herself on the fact that it was not raining, for to arrive soaked to the skin would not be a good start and she had not thought to bring an umbrella. A commissionaire in a smart uniform was standing just inside the door. As she approached him, he sprang to attention, smiling down at her. 'Good morning, madam. Can I help you?'

Sylvie gave him her warmest smile. 'I've come for a job interview with a Miss Snape. Could you direct me to her office, please?' she said. 'I'm a little early, but . . .'

'I'll take you as far as the lift meself,' the commissionaire said grandly. He led her across the store, which was half empty at this early hour, called the lift for her, and told the bellboy who worked the machinery that the lady wanted the top floor. Then he stepped back and saluted, wishing her good luck.

Two hours later, Sylvie emerged from Miss Snape's office. She had got the job and was to start the following Monday. Wages, terms and conditions had been explained to her and she had been given a tour of the store and been introduced to various members of staff including, naturally, Miss Beamish, who ran the Hat and Glove department, and her two assistants.

Sylvie had been delighted with everything. It would be wonderful to work here, away from the smell of stale beer and cigarette smoke, and from the odour of ill health that hung around Len no matter how hard she and her mother-in-law tried to dispel it. And it would be lovely to receive a proper wage, for though Mrs Dugdale paid all the normal household expenses she rarely handed over any actual money.

She headed for the outer doors of the store with a light heart, feeling she had won back her independence. If she wanted to buy Becky a present, she would be able to do so, and she would send Caitlin a little extra, so that the almost forgotten baby in Dublin would also benefit from her change in circumstances.

'Congratulations, miss.' Sylvie looked round sharply and saw the commissionaire beaming at her. 'You've gorrit, haven't you? I saw Miss Snape giving you the royal tour a while ago and she never does that if a gal hasn't made the grade.' He leaned closer, lowering his voice. 'You'll be happy here, miss, we're a decent bunch and we stick together. Why, when I was . . .' He stopped short; the floor-walker, a tall elegant man with slicked-back grey hair and a tiny toothbrush moustache, was approaching. The commissionaire snapped to attention. 'Good day, miss,' he said, turning away.

'Oh . . . good day,' Sylvie said, and shot through the swing doors and on to the pavement. The sky was grey but the rain still held off and she felt disinclined to go straight back to the pub where her mother-in-law would immediately find her a dozen jobs to do. For a moment, she stood uncertainly on the pavement, then decided she would go round to Hunter Street; if Brendan was off duty she could tell him her news and she knew he would be satisfyingly pleased, because he was still very much her friend and would rejoice with her over her good fortune. He still visited Len, sitting on a chair by the bedside and talking quietly to the other man, but he made no effort to get Sylvie to himself and she thought, rather sadly, that the admiration which had kindled his eyes when they had first met seemed to have cooled.

As luck would have it, she saw Brendan ahead of her when she approached the next side street.

He was in uniform and Sylvie recognised the man to whom he was talking as his sergeant. So this would be one of the 'quarters' which Brendan so often referred to. Sylvie now knew that this meant he had to be at certain spots at regular intervals so that he could be checked by the sergeant on his beat, though this did not always happen by any means. However, it would not do to interrupt them, so she waited until the sergeant walked ponderously away. Then she fell into step with Brendan, smiling up at him.

Brendan looked down at her, his slow smile beginning. 'You look very smart,' he said. 'Where have you been?'

'I was coming round to Hunter Street, hoping you'd be off duty, and I know you won't want to hang about seeing as you're walking your beat, but I simply had to tell you my good news. I got the job; that's why I'm all dressed up.'

Brendan stared at her. 'What job?' he asked incredulously. 'Surely you work at the Ferryman? I don't think Mrs D. could manage without you.'

'Oh, I think I must be going mad. I quite forgot I hadn't seen you for a couple of weeks so you wouldn't know I was being interviewed at Lewis's today. I'm a sales assistant on Hats and Gloves, with a real salary. Oh, Brendan, I couldn't be more thrilled.'

'That sounds very nice,' Brendan said slowly. 'But how will you manage, Sylvie? I don't think Lewis's employ part-time staff and I know Len makes a good deal of work ... and there's Becky ...'

'Mother-in-law will simply have to employ someone else during the day, but I'll be there evenings,' Sylvie explained, rather impatiently. She was disappointed in Brendan's reaction, for he did not seem to share her delight. 'Don't you realise, Brendan, that I'm little better than a servant at the Ferryman? I don't get paid, you know, but Ma-in-law takes it for granted that I'll work from seven in the morning till midnight, six days a week, and hardly ever have so much as half an hour to myself.'

'Oh, I didn't realise,' Brendan said, rather blankly. 'But surely taking on a full-time job will mean you have even less time to yourself? I mean, you can't call working behind a counter exactly relaxing, can you?'

'It'll be wonderful after working in the Ferryman. And I shall have a bit more money to send to Caitlin – for the baby you know,' Sylvie said quickly. 'I've been sending half a crown most months from the money I saved up while I was in Ireland, but it's beginning to run out and I can't ask Mrs Dugdale to hand over cash.'

Brendan grinned and gave her hand a discreet squeeze. 'Sorry. I hadn't realised what a difficult position you're in,' he said, with obvious sincerity. 'Many congratulations; you've done well to get a job with so much unemployment around. Tell you what ... wait on, when do you start?'

'Next Monday,' Sylvie said at once, delighted that her friend was on her side after all. 'I've got to buy clothes for work, but they pay me back after six months if I've proved I'm capable of doing well. So I've got the rest of the week to prepare myself for my new life.'

'Right. And my next day off is Thursday. What a pity it's winter, but even so, we might have a day out to celebrate. Ever been to Southport? We could catch separate trains, if it would make you feel more comfortable, and explore the town, have a meal in a restaurant, and do a bit of shopping. I can't suggest taking Becky because she'd talk about it to your mother-in-law and it wouldn't do; you do understand, don't you?'

'Yes, of course I understand, and I'd love a day out in Southport,' Sylvie said, beaming up at him. 'Oh, Brendan, I can't wait till Thursday!'

Brendan watched Sylvie out of sight. He was excited at the thought of a day out with her, though he told himself that this was simply because he enjoyed her company. He also told himself that he had once had a crush on her, but now he was more sensible and simply regarded her as a friend. He admired the way she helped to look after her sick husband, as well as assisting her mother-in-law in the running of the pub. He also thought she was bringing up Becky beautifully, despite the occasional interference from two doting grandmothers.

A passer-by greeted him cheerfully, making

some comment about the weather, and he touched his helmet and murmured a reply. The woman had a plump baby on her hip and Brendan smiled at it, reflecting that Catherine Mary would be about the same age as this one. He knew very little about the baby, save that she had ginger hair. He remembered Sylvie saying that the child was plain, but when he had mentioned it to his Uncle Sean's wife she had told him, rather scornfully, that all small babies looked alike. 'Young mams is all the same; they worries about the oddest things,' she had assured him. 'You tell your young friend that probably by now the baby's hair will have darkened, or lightened; changed, anyway.'

But Brendan had felt it was better not to say anything, for Sylvie had given the baby up and that was the end of the matter.

Another woman came towards him with a crowd of small children at her skirts, and they smiled a greeting; Mrs Mabel had no children of her own but looked after other people's and was popular with the mothers as well as their offspring. The youngest child was redheaded and beamed up at Brendan, showing tiny pearly teeth and a dimple in one cheek. Brendan found himself wishing that he could nip over to Dublin one fine day and take a look at young Catherine Mary. It would not do to admit to Sylvie that he was curious about the baby she had been forced to abandon to Caitlin's care, but perhaps one day he really would drop in on his cousin when he was heading for home leave and see how the child was getting on.

Brendan continued on his way, deciding he would write to Caitlin when he got home and see how things stood. If she needed money, he could always spare a bob or two . . .

Maeve was in the kitchen finishing the clearing away of the breakfast things. She had taken the children to school earlier, for though Clodagh, Grainne and Colm could be relied upon to go into their classes and remain there all day, the twins were another matter. They hated school and had to be handed over to their teacher, who was then responsible for them until school ended in the afternoon.

In fact, apart from Maeve herself, the only other person in the kitchen was Catherine Mary. The child sat on the hearthrug, playing contentedly with a large wooden spoon with which she was banging an empty cocoa tin, producing a pleasing amount of noise, though she added to it every few minutes with triumphant shouts.

Maeve looked down on the curly head, which had darkened to a pleasing shade of chestnut, with most tender affection. She adored Catherine Mary, thought her the cleverest and most beautiful child in the whole of Dublin, and had been delighted when the little girl had started to say 'mum-um-m' when Maeve picked her out of her bed in the mornings.

The bed was just a cardboard box and it was growing too small for her, so Maeve meant to go round to the market stalls in Francis Street to see if she could beg an orange box – a large one – from one of the stallholders. The market women were generous people, understanding the difficulties of rearing large families with wages so low, and Maeve had little doubt that she would get her orange box.

The baby on the floor began to gabble and Maeve looked round quickly, then picked up the nearest object, which happened to be a heavy iron ladle, and hurled it across the room at the large rat which had emerged from a hole in the skirting board. The rat paused for a moment – the ladle had missed it by at least three feet – then turned round and scuttled for the kitchen door, which stood open. Maeve shuddered. She hated rats and Handkerchief Alley was having a plague of them at present. Pat did his best, blocking holes and insisting that food should be kept in tins, but even so, rats were likely to appear when one was off one's guard, and at night, as she lay on her little straw pallet, Maeve could hear them pattering around in their constant search for food.

Sighing, she went and picked up the ladle, giving the child's curls a reassuring pat. If only my aim were better, she thought, but perhaps it was as well that she had not hit the creature. The thought of a wounded rat, perhaps turning on the baby, or at the very least having to be despatched

172

by herself, was a horrible one. There were traps, of course, but the rats had grown knowing and were seldom caught by such means. Fergal and Seamus had managed to account for several of the creatures, for they were good shots with a boot or a brick, but by and large the rats were winning. Every day, Maeve imagined, mother rats were giving birth to little pink babies which in due course would become a menace to the dwellers in Handkerchief Alley, spreading disease, defiling food and making the mouse population which had dwelt there before them seem positively benign in retrospect.

On the homemade rag rug, Catherine Mary attacked her cocoa tin once more, and Maeve picked up the coal scuttle and put more fuel on the fire, then went to the dresser and got the housekeeping purse out of the top drawer. She had a list of messages and wondered whether she should ask again at Mr Farrington's chemist shop just off Francis Street whether he had a rat poison which would not harm small children. Such a thing had not been available the last time she had asked, and with the alley positively swarming with small children it would be extremely dangerous to use anything that they might find and put in their mouths.

'Wish we had a terrier,' Seamus had said wistfully, only the previous day, when he and Fergal had returned from a trip into the country, both bearing large swedes beneath their coats. 'When we were robbin' the farmer of these here turnips, or whatever they are, one of the fellers told us to come up to the barn and see some sport. They'd got four terriers, grand little chaps wit' white bodies and brown ears, and they set 'em to clear out the rats what had been eating the farmer's grain. The feller give us big sticks and said to hit any rat what tried to get away and to mind out we didn't hit the dogs by mistake. There must ha' been a hundred rats in there but the terriers were quick as a flash, honest to God they was, Maeve. It were grab, crunch, toss, and another rat had bit the dust. By the end of a couple of hours, I'm tellin' you, there weren't a rat alive on that whole farm. Eh, I wish we could have a borrow of a terrier; that'd soon sort out the buggers in Handkerchief Alley.'

Maeve had agreed, wistfully, that it would be just grand to hire the services of such a dog, but she knew it was impossible. No farmer in his senses would agree to let someone from the Liberties march off with his terrier, suspecting, probably rightly, that he would never see it again. Clodagh had once said, tearfully, after a trip into the countryside to gather berries, that she believed rich farmers thought folk in the Liberties would scrunch up post and wire fencing for their dinners, so violently had they reacted to the presence of her and her little sister making their way along a leafy lane and picking blackberries as they went.

Maeve had laughed at the time but she did

understand what Clodagh had meant. The only thing the farmer owned nearby was the post and wire fencing which surrounded his field, so his violent shouts that 'them thievin' little buggers' should get off his land had seemed somewhat unnecessary. After all, what use would two little girls have for post and wire fencing unless, of course, they really could take it home and gobble it up.

Chuckling to herself at the recollection, though she supposed there was nothing really to laugh about, Maeve dressed the baby in the warm coat – rather too large for her – which she had bought from a stallholder in the Iveagh Market last time Sylvie's money had arrived. She did not have to glance through the window to know that it was cold outside, for despite the fire, which was always kept burning in the kitchen, icy draughts came through the ancient cracked wood of the window surrounds, and fairly whistled up the stairs. Maeve unhooked her own coat from the back of the door, slipped it on, and buttoned it up. It had once belonged to Caitlin and it was growing threadbare now, so Maeve added a large shawl before picking up the baby and settling her on one hip. She then muffled both of them in the voluminous folds, and set off down the treacherous creaking stairs. Recently, Pat had cut her a little crutch from a trimmed tree branch, which was very useful, but when she had the baby in her arms it was more of a hindrance than a help.

She reached the inner hall and shivered. It had obviously snowed in the night and the wind had blown a small drift in through the sagging front door to pile up against the opposite wall. Horrible, horrible winter, she thought, taking the twins' homemade handcart down from where it stood against the wall and plonking the baby in it before letting herself out into the street. If she had not had so many messages, she could have kept the baby on her hip, but she would need the hand-cart, for she had a deal of marketing to do, besides hoping to acquire an orange box. Quickly, she took off the shawl and wrapped it round the baby, shivering as the cold struck her anew. Catherine Mary was like a little hot water bottle held against her hip, but it was more important to keep the baby cosy than to warm herself. How I wish spring would arrive early for once, she thought as she pushed the handcart out on to the cobbles. When the weather grew milder, there would be clumps of snowdrops under the trees in Phoenix Park, and crocuses would poke blue, purple and gold noses up through the leaf mould, but while it was so bitterly cold spring seemed far off indeed.

'The top o' the day to you, Maeve me little love!' Mr and Mrs Cavanagh were returning home after a shopping expedition, and Maeve felt a stab of guilt. When the weather was foul, she usually popped into the Cavanaghs' after taking the children to school to ask if they had any messages, but this morning she had completely forgotten, so the old couple had had to brave the cold, and the snow, to buy their own small requirements. 'Oh, Mr Cavanagh, Mrs Cavanagh, I'm so sorry,' she said repentantly. 'The truth is it was snowing when I got back to the alley and I was so anxious to get meself and the babe back into the warm that I clean forgot to call on you. And today's Friday an' all.'

Friday was fish day and Maeve knew that the Cavanaghs, who liked a piece of fresh cod, would have had difficulty in obtaining it, for the boats in Dun Laoghaire would not go out in severe weather. The Cavanaghs, however, were smiling cheerfully at her. 'Sure and aren't you a good little soul?' Mr Cavanagh said genially. 'But we had to go out ourselves this mornin'. The lady what used to employ Mrs Cavanagh to mend sheets and such said she'd some white work which needed doing. There were a rent in a fine lace tablecloth which she wanted mending and she planned to lace-edge half a dozen plain napkins to match it. She'll pay well for the work and she agreed Mrs Cavanagh could do it in her own home provided she could finish it by Sunday morning. So we had to go and fetch it.' He flourished a large oilskin shopping bag. 'It's in here, and if it's finished in time we'll be two bob the richer!'

'That's grand, so it is,' Maeve said sincerely, beginning to move away. She did not suggest that she might have collected the tablecloth and napkins from Mrs Cavanagh's old employer because she knew that no lady would hand over a beautiful lace tablecloth and six snowy napkins to a little ragamuffin from Handkerchief Alley. Still, it did mean it had not been her fault that the Cavanaghs had had to leave their home and face the snowy conditions outside.

Maeve began to hurry, thinking to herself how grand it was to have boots on her feet. When she had lived at home, bare feet were taken for granted, even in weather such as this, but Caitlin sent her children to Our Lady's school on Baggot Street where every single child wore not only boots, but also a smart uniform. Caitlin had sighed over the expense but she and Pat thought education tremendously important, so every morning the children were dressed in neat blue jerseys, with pinafores for the girls and dark jackets for the boys, and boots of course, always well polished. As soon as they returned from school, clothes and boots were snatched off them and stowed away in the press, ready for next day. And of course, such precious clothing would be handed down to younger brothers and sisters when it no longer fitted the child for whom it had been bought.

Maeve, of course, had never attended Our Lady's; in fact, she had rarely attended school at all, though Caitlin had taught her to read and write, and doing the messages had speedily helped her to understand the value of money and to be able to add up in her head quicker than most people could do it with pencil and paper. Sometimes she dreamed of being able to send

Catherine Mary to Our Lady's and she tried to save up her pennies so that she might buy a uniform jersey, though she doubted that she could ever run to boots. But this was daydreaming, and she knew it. She would never be able to afford the fees which were charged at Our Lady's; even the penny a day asked at St Joseph's had been too much for her poor mother, though the Vincent St Paul's Society had paid for the schooling of both her older sisters, which just went to prove how poverty-stricken poor widow Connolly was, because everyone knew that the Vincent St Paul's Society would make you sell every little thing you possessed before they would stump up so much as a penny piece. Caitlin had once told her that the Society's money could only be handed over after something called means testing, which meant that the Society's representative came into your home and made sure that you had nothing before they handed out help.

By now, Maeve had reached Mr Farrington's chemist shop and she popped in to enquire about rat poison, only to be told once again that there was nothing less dangerous available. Then she continued to hurry along Francis Street, nipping into the butcher's shop for scrag end of mutton to make a stew, and into the grocer's for tea, sugar and rice. Her last but one call was at Cullen's dairy, where she bought a couple of pints of milk before turning back towards home, because she intended to make a rice pudding for the evening meal. She had left the greengrocer until last, because she meant to wheedle an orange box from him and that, and the potatoes and stewing vegetables she would buy, were the heaviest items on her list.

She was turning into Handkerchief Alley when she saw two large boys, looking rather furtive, emerging on to the main street. One was carrying something, swinging it casually yet seeming to try, at the same time, to keep it out of sight. Maeve stared, then limped across the space which separated them, her face beginning to flush as hot blood rose to her cheeks. The boy was carrying a cat, swinging it by one leg, and Maeve could see that the creature was not dead for it was trying feebly to free itself from the boy's grip.

'Put that cat down!' Maeve shouted, skidding to a halt in front of the boys.

The lad holding the cat tried to put the creature behind his back. 'It ain't nobody else's cat, it's just a rotten old stray what steals scraps out of the dustbins and chases the pigeons,' he said defensively. 'We're goin' to chuck it in the Liffey where it'll drown, an' a good thing, too.'

'You'll do no such thing!' Maeve said, not mincing words. She was a good deal smaller than both boys but her indignation at such cruelty overrode any fear she might have felt and besides, right was on her side. When she guessed, from the way the boys' glances slid past her, that they meant to make a break for it, were actually looking forward to seeing the cat's dying agony as it sank below the waters of Anna Liffey, indignation gave her strength. She lunged forward, punching the cat holder so hard that she knocked all the wind out of him. He bent forward, coughing and wheezing, and even as his grip loosened Maeve caught the cat round its body and swung it into her own arms. It was pathetically thin, more skin and bone than anything else, and trembling violently, but to her astonishment and pleasure, even as she tucked it in the crook of one arm, it actually began to purr.

'Good puss, good little cat then,' Maeve said. She gave the boys one last glare, then returned to the handcart. Catherine Mary was asleep, unaware of the drama which had just been played out before her, so Maeve seized the handle and began to walk along the alley just as the snow began to fall once more, the big soft flakes landing indiscriminately upon cart, baby and Maeve herself.

In the hallway, with the outer door pushed shut, Maeve had time to examine her new acquisition. It was quite the filthiest cat she had ever seen, so dirty that she could not even guess at the colour of its coat, but it had huge golden eyes, enormous pink-lined ears, and a tiny pink nose which it had somehow managed to keep clean. Maeve smiled down at it. 'If I let you go them bleedin' boys will come back for you sure as my name's Maeve Connolly,' she told it. 'They live in the end house on Lamb Alley, so they won't have far to walk. What's more, you're too little an' weak to fight your own battles yet awhile, so I think you'd best come home wit' me. Caitlin's ever so kind, so I'm sure she won't turn you away, an' when you're a big chap you'll be a rare help in keepin' rats an' mice down. Besides, you won't be no charge on her because I'll pay for your food until you're big enough to hunt for yourself. Now, I'll take you and baby up to the flat and come back for me messages, because heaven knows how I'd get up the stairs carryin' everythin' else as well as the pair of you.'

Presently, with baby, cat and shopping safely stowed in the kitchen and Catherine Mary still slumbering peacefully, though now in the new orange box instead of the old cardboard one, Maeve was able to turn her attention to the cat. She soon discovered that it was crawling with fleas, but that was no surprise. Life in Handkerchief Alley was a constant battle against bed bugs, lice, fleas and other pests, and this was something she could deal with. She filled a basin with warm water and dumped the cat in it. It surfaced, blinking its big golden eyes and mewing pitifully, but it made no attempt to scratch. Maeve was able to lather it thoroughly with carbolic soap and saw, with satisfaction, the fleas floating off. She knew that, though the horrid little creatures were immune to most things, they could not live for more than a few seconds in water, and this was an easy method of getting rid of the pests.

She rinsed the little cat's fur and as she dried it she saw with pleasure that it was a dark, smoky grey, with four white paws and a white chest. She thought it would grow into a handsome cat. I'll give it as much food as I can possibly afford, and if I go down by the quays when the fishing boats are coming in I'm sure there'll be all sorts of scraps – fish heads and that – which other folk won't want, she planned busily. Emerging from the towel, the cat began to purr again, and Maeve hurried across the kitchen and took a saucer down from the dresser. She poured a little of the milk she had just bought into it, then went to the food cupboard, putting a hand out towards the bread crock. As she moved the lid, something else moved and she saw a medium-sized rat coming towards her. Maeve gave a shriek, she couldn't help it, and stepped hastily back, allowing the rat to dodge past her and make for the hole she had already noticed in the skirting board. There was a noise from behind her, as menacing as a snake's hiss, and when she turned round Maeve saw the cat leap from its perch on the kitchen table straight on to the floor. The rat gave a startled squeak and redoubled its speed, but the cat almost caught it, though how such a small creature would have tackled a rat Maeve had no idea. The cat sat down by the hole, then tested its depth with a sensitive paw. Maeve hastily picked it up; she had no desire to lose her new friend, for the rat she had seen earlier that day had been as big as the cat, if not bigger. She carried it over to the table but did not leave it there since it had turned in her hold so that its big golden eyes might remain fixed on the hole into which its enemy had disappeared. Still with it clamped beneath her arm, Maeve got a piece of bread from the crock and crumbled some of it into the milk. Then she stood the cat down by the saucer. 'Get that lot inside you, little feller,' she advised. 'For whatever you may think, you've a good deal of growin' to do before you can come off best against a rat.'

She had half expected to have to fight to keep the cat, but when Caitlin returned from work that evening and found her family gathered round the small grey creature she was delighted, and welcomed it warmly. 'Sure and just the fact that a cat lives here will put off many a rat from climbin' the stairs,' she said. 'When it's bigger they know it'll kill 'em so that makes 'em wary of even the smell of a cat. I wonder why I didn't t'ink of gettin' a cat before, for the good Lord knows they're ten a penny in the Liberties.'

'You're a lovely pussy, so you are,' Grainne crooned, stroking the grey plush of the cat's back. 'You're big enough to catch a nice mousey for your dinner an' I doesn't like mouses when they comes on to me piller, though rats is worse, of course.' She turned to Maeve. 'What'll you call him – is he a feller or a girl?'

'He's a feller; a little tomcat,' Maeve said, with confidence. She had taken the cat down to the Cavanaghs to enquire as to its sex, and had been assured by the old man that it was a tomcat. 'I thought I'd call it Tiddles, unless you've got a better idea.'

'I don't like Tiddles. Let's call him Tommy, 'cos he's a tomcat,' Grainne said. And though several other names were bandied about, it was finally decided that Tommy it should be, and when Pat came home he agreed that the cat would be a grand addition to the household.

'But you'll have to keep him in the flat for a few days to be sure he knows he lives here, for cats is independent; he'll likely want his freedom, particularly since he's a tom,' he said.

Caitlin laughed. 'Fellers is all the same,' she remarked. 'They all want their freedom, so long as it's give 'em wit' two good meals a day and a warm bed o' nights.'

The baby was sitting with the other children and now she reached out small hands towards the cat. Caitlin gave a squeak of dismay and jumped forward, but Maeve, seeing her anxiety, waved her back. 'It's all right, Cait,' she said reassuringly. 'Catherine Mary's been playin' with Tommy all afternoon, and they're fine together.

Pat turned away from the group on the hearthrug towards where his wife was prodding a fork into a large pan of potatoes. 'Where's me dinner, woman?' he demanded. 'You said yourself us fellers want two meals a day as well as our freedom, so the sooner it's on the table, the quicker the man of the house will be satisfied.'

Chapter Seven

July 1914

'Mum! Sorry I's late for me dinner but I met up wi' Wilf, so we played wi' his pals – relievio. It were grand!'

It was a warm summer day and Sylvie was making vegetable soup for Len, patiently pushing an assortment of vegetables through a hair-sieve. She turned a hot face towards her daughter. 'Oh, Becky love, I'm glad you're home! And I do hope it really was relievio you were playing, and not skipping leckies. It's not that I don't like Wilf, but he's been brought up to do all sorts – he thieves fruit and coal, never pays a penny to ride a tram when he can steal a lift . . .'

'He doesn't have any pennies,' Becky said placidly, helping herself to one of the biscuits cooling on a wire tray beneath the open window. 'Is Dad's soup ready, Mam? If so, I'll take it through to him. And we weren't skipping leckies, honest to God.'

'I'm glad to hear it, because it's dangerous. I had a friend once who ended up . . . lame, because she . . .'

She stopped short, uneasily aware that she had been about to cite Maeve's experience as a lesson to Becky, who knew nothing of her Irish life. Becky, however, was concentrating on the biscuit whilst peering at the vegetables her mother was preparing with such care.

'Dad used to skip leckies when he were a kid,' she said suddenly. 'He doesn't think it's dangerous – he telled me so.'

Sylvie turned and stared at her daughter. 'Told you so? Darling, he can't talk! Or do you mean Granny Dugdale told you?'

Her daughter stared at her. 'Course not. I *said*, Dad told me.'

'But he . . .'

'Oh, talking!' Becky said contemptuously. 'You can tell folk things without *words*, Mam! I said I'd been skipping leckies wi' Wilf, and Dad nodded, touched his chest and grinned. If that wasn't saying he'd skipped leckies and thought it were fun . . . well I *know* that was what he were saying!'

'Yes, I do see . . . and you're right, because I guess all boys skip leckies, partly for devilment and partly to get a free ride.' She tipped the thick puréed vegetables into a pan and put it over the flame, then turned curiously to her daughter. 'Do you and Dad often talk like that? He's never tried that with me.'

'I expect you're too busy to take the time, 'cos it does take a while 'til you get used to it,' Becky said wisely, after some thought. 'But you ought to try, Mam. Dad does love to talk about the past. Him and me chats away of an evening, about what

I've done, and what he did when he were a boy.'

Feeling remarkably small, Sylvie agreed that, in future, she would try to follow her daughter's example. She did so the following evening and soon realised what a difference it made to Len's whole attitude. She told her mother, who nodded approvingly. 'Out of the mouths of babes and sucklings,' she said. 'Just fancy, Len's been making hisself understood to our Becky for ages and we never knew! Ah well, I reckon things will begin to look up from now on. He'll be talkin' proper before you know it.'

It was not quite as dramatic as that, but Sylvie, watching more closely now, saw that Len really was beginning to improve, and knew they had Becky to thank, though they all took the hint and talked to Len, encouraging him to mime replies or to nod or shake his head according to how he felt.

'You'll soon be back behind the bar, calling "Time, gentlemen, please", Sylvie said one day, but though he smiled and made a thumbs-up sign, she saw the sad look in his eyes and knew her husband did not believe he would ever fully recover. But he might be wrong; the doctor was growing optimistic as Len became able to answer simple questions with a nod, a shake of the head, or even a shrug of the shoulders.

'Miracles do happen,' Dr Hislop assured the Dugdales. 'Keep trying, and you never know – he may surprise us all yet.'

*

Brendan came off duty actually longing for a cold bath, because August bank holiday always meant extra work for the force and today had been no exception. Everyone had been in a holiday mood, surging to and from the ferries which would take them across the Mersey to New Brighton, where they might enjoy the funfair, or disport themselves on the long golden beach.

Brendan let himself into the house and went straight upstairs. When Constable Collins had left, Mrs Taggart she had decided not to replace him but to turn his room into a proper bathroom.

Brendan undressed, filled the tub with cold water and stepped into it, the breath hissing between his teeth as hot flesh and cold water met. He sat very still for a moment, then relaxed and slid below the water until only his head was clear of it, and very soon it was enjoyable and he could reach for the soap and begin washing. At this point, his mind turned to the Dugdales and Sylvie, since he intended to visit the Ferryman later. The last time he went, Sylvie had said that she thought Len enjoyed his company. Becky had become a useful member of the household, helping to entertain her father, doing a great many jobs about the house and accompanying her mother when she went to get the messages. She was doing well in school and frequently read the *Echo* to Len when the women of the house were too busy to do so, for the pub was flourishing and Sylvie's job kept her busy during the daytime.

Brendan soaked his face, neck and hair and ducked right under the water to rinse himself off for one delicious, cooling moment.

Climbing out of the tub, he patted himself dry and began to dress. Every year, he returned to Ireland for his holiday, and sometimes, as his savings grew, he looked into buying a farm or smallholding of his own. He knew he was a country-man at heart, thought he could succeed on the land, yet could not bring himself to seriously consider moving so far away from Sylvie. A married woman, she was clearly beyond his reach, yet the love which had been born the night he rescued her from drowning simply refused to die. Steadfastly, that love had grown until he admitted, though only to himself, that he was unlikely to look at another woman. He had never let her see how he felt, never tried to invent excuses to be alone with her – quite the opposite in fact. Long ago, he had taken her to Southport to celebrate her getting a job in Lewis's, and as they walked along Lord Street he had put his arm round her and, when she turned to him, had felt such a stab of desire that he had been shocked. He had known then that such proximity was dangerous and must never occur again. He knew it was hard on her to be tied to a man who could not be a proper husband to her, but she never complained. Once or twice, he had been tempted to tell her how fond he was of her, but he always stifled the impulse. It could do no good, could even do real harm, for whilst Sylvie considered him merely as a friend they could meet without embarrassment or awkwardness. If she saw love in his eyes when they met her own it would complicate both their lives, and he had no wish to do that.

He finished dressing, tidied round the bathroom, and headed for the stairs. Brendan sometimes acknowledged to himself that if Len should die, his feelings for Sylvie would surface with a vengeance, all the stronger for having been so long suppressed. The doctor, who called regularly to see Len, had once told Brendan that the man was unlikely to have a long life, for though the wounds one could see had healed, no one knew what was going on inside Len's damaged head.

Brendan reached the head of the stairs and clattered down them. He would have his evening meal and then stroll round to the Ferryman. It was generally frowned upon for members of the constabulary to become regulars in any of the pubs on their beat, but because he visited a sick man his presence in the Ferryman was not held against him. He would go into the public bar, buy a Guinness, and then sit quietly in the corner, sipping it and yarning to the regular customers, and all the while he would be casting quick little glances at Sylvie's delicate golden beauty. Just seeing her partially satisfied his hunger for her. After that, he would make his way into the room behind the bar, where he would sit with Len for half an hour, chatting, reading from the newspaper, and occasionally breaking off to hold a glass to Len's lips.

Brendan descended the stairs and opened the kitchen door, thinking that his evening was all planned, and got a rude shock. Ferdy Simpson turned at the sound of the opening door. He was grinning, waving a newspaper. 'Looks like we're going to war wi' Germany, old feller!' he shouted exuberantly. 'Well, you won't catch me holdin' back, 'cos this is one reason for leaving the chief constable can't deny. A feller's got to fight for king an' country, an' as far as I can see, life in the army can't be no worse than life in the police force. Besides, they reckon it'll all be over by Christmas, so the sooner we get to the recruitin' office, the better off we'll be.' He laid the newspaper he was holding out on the table, and began jabbing a finger at the headlines. 'Asquith won't let the Kaiser gerraway with marchin' into Belgium an' threatenin' the French. What'll it be for you then? Army or Navy?'

'Dunno; I'll have to think about it,' Brendan said guardedly, but already excitement was beginning to course through his veins. A way out, and with honour! He realised now that he had held back from leaving the force because he felt he would be letting Sylvie and the Dugdales down. But to go to war, to defend king and country, was a very different matter from simply leaving the area for more congenial work. Yes, he could join the army, which he guessed was not unlike the police force, whereas the Navy, he was sure, would be very different. He said as much and Constable Simpson clapped him on the shoulder and grinned even more widely than before.

'That's grand, old feller,' he said. 'We'll sign on together . . . can't do it today, of course, but we'll do it first thing tomorrer. Eh, I can't wait to see the sergeant's face when he realises we're off the hook. And it ain't only us; there's a dozen or more I know what'll grab the chance of gettin' out. As for the perishin' Huns, they'll soon cave in when they see we mean business.'

Mrs Taggart, dishing up what smelt like a beautiful mutton stew, sniffed loudly. 'War isn't a game, you know, young gentlemen,' she said reprovingly. 'Folk get killed in wars. Why, my brother Eddie was killed in the Boer War and them Boers weren't nothing like as well armed and well trained as the Kaiser's lot. Why don't you wait a while, see what happens? If it's really over by Christmas . . .'

'If it's going to be over by Christmas, then the sooner we join up the sooner we'll be heroes what helped to defeat the Hun,' Ferdy assured her. 'Why, with our police experience behind us, Brendan an' meself will be officers before we've finished our basic training. I can't wait, meself.'

Mrs Taggart began to dish up the stew and both young men took their seats at the table. 'Wherever we're sent and whatever we do, I don't reckon the grub we'll be given will be up to your standard, Mrs Taggart,' Brendan said as he finished the last

193

delicious mouthful of meat and vegetables. He took a slice of his landlady's homemade bread and wiped it round his plate to clear up the rest of the gravy. 'Do you mind if I slope off now? I reckon I'd best go round to the Dugdales', tell them they won't be seein' me for a while.'

'There's plum pie and custard for afters,' Mrs Taggart said reproachfully. 'Surely you aren't going to miss that? After all, how long will it take to eat it if I dish up at once?'

She did not wait for him to reply but whipped the pie out of the oven and set it on the table, then reached for the jug of custard. Brendan, who had risen to his feet, sat down again and pulled the plate towards him. He grinned up at his landlady. 'Thanks, Mrs Taggart. It looks lovely,' he said. 'And you're right, I'll get outside of this little lot in five minutes and feel better for it.'

Christmas came and went, and the country had accepted the grim reality that war, far from being over, was here to stay. Sylvie and her mother-in-law had joined a sewing guild, making warm clothing for the troops, and Mrs Davies, never a keen needlewoman, did her bit by knitting furiously. Scarves, mittens and gloves, thick socks and woollen caps followed each other from her needles in quick succession, and Sylvie grew used to the sight of her mother serving in the bar with her knitting tucked under one arm, for every young man worth his salt, and that included both the

Ferryman's barmen, had by this time joined one of the armed forces. Bertie, morose and self-conscious, had to stay behind, of course, but he resented his lameness and constantly complained that he could have been as good as any other man had he been allowed to join up. As the news from Europe worsened, Sylvie guessed that he must have been secretly relieved, for the casualty lists lengthened daily, and men sent home from the Front made no secret of the fact that the war was terrible, and that they longed to be out of it.

Right now, Sylvie was returning from a late shift at the munitions factory and was very glad of the thick scarf, mittens and socks which her mother had knitted for her, because the snow lay thick, even on the pavement, and everyone realised that it was going to be a struggle to get through January, for already there were shortages in the shops. It was dark too, and the gas lamps guttered fitfully in the strong wind. She shivered and thought longingly of the tram crammed with her fellow workers. Normally, at the end of her shift, she would have caught that tram, which would have taken her most of the way home, but she had forgotten to pick up her purse when she had left the Ferryman that morning. Pride had prevented her from admitting her stupidity in front of the whole queue and, telling herself that the walk would do her good, she had set off to return to the Ferryman on foot.

She had left her comfortable job in Lewis's very

soon after Brendan had joined up, because workers were needed in the munitions factory. The work was hard, but she and her fellows did their best to enliven the drudgery by singing popular songs and chatting amongst themselves.

Brendan wrote regularly and clearly attempted to keep his letters both cheerful and optimistic, but Sylvie speedily realised that he was trying to spare her as much as possible from the full horrors of the war being waged across the Channel. She read the letters to Len and wrote back whenever she could, though she had very little time. And one good thing had already come out of the war: Len was beginning to respond a little more. He thanked her when she performed some small task for him and he could string short sentences together to make himself understood. To be sure, he was still partially paralysed, but he could now hold a cup to his own lips, though spillages occurred with such frequency that either Mrs Dugdale or Sylvie herself always draped him in a large towel before giving him a drink.

Becky helped with the war effort too, as far as she was able. She knitted scarves, though Sylvie knew that Mrs Davies often unpicked them at night after Becky had gone to bed and knitted them up again before the next day, only without dropping any stitches, something to which Becky was very prone. The child also undertook a good few of the messages on her own, for Mrs Dugdale had acquired an elderly perambulator and Becky enjoyed pushing this round the town and loading it up with potatoes, cabbages and any other food-stuffs on her grandmother's list.

Sylvie still corresponded with Caitlin. The letters from Ireland were innocent enough, since Caitlin rarely referred to Catherine Mary, and when she did so one could have been forgiven for supposing that the child was Maeve's and nothing to do with anyone else. Sylvie still sent a half-crown to Dublin every month, but Caitlin never alluded to it, and Sylvie guessed, with real gratitude, that should she find it impossible to send the money Caitlin would never reproach her. Maeve worked hard in order that Caitlin might keep her job and Sylvie guessed that the girl did just about every-thing for the baby because Caitlin had said, several times, how dear Catherine Mary – now known as Kitty – was to little Maeve Connolly. Sometimes, it did occur to Sylvie that Kitty was no longer a baby, but somehow this seemed so unreal that she never allowed herself to pursue the thought. She was sure she would never see the child again and, for obvious reasons, could remember her only as she had last seen her. Maeve occasionally added an ill-written note to Caitlin's letters, telling Sylvie that Kitty was teething, crawling, walking or talking, but the information meant little to Sylvie. If Caitlin had done as Sylvie had hoped – as indeed she had asked her to do – Kitty would have been adopted by now and there would have been no news to pass on. Sylvie knew it was selfish to wish that this had happened, but she could not help thinking, wistfully, that it would probably have been the best thing; Caitlin was very good but her family was large and her income restricted. Had Kitty been adopted by a well-to-do family she would have had advantages such as those Becky enjoyed, which were now denied her.

She tried to wrench her thoughts away from Ireland and Kitty; the child was no longer any concern of hers, as Caitlin herself had made clear. The half-crown a month was conscience money but she could well afford it; indeed, as the child grew, she supposed she really ought to increase the amount. Then she chided herself. If the child became a burden – a financial burden, that was – then either Caitlin or Maeve must surely write to her. After all, she supposed that, ultimately, Kitty really was her responsibility; she could not expect either Caitlin or Maeve to give the child more than they were giving already. Which was love, a little voice in her head remarked.

Now, as she turned a corner into the next street, Sylvie missed the edge of the pavement and skidded into the gutter, landing painfully on both knees. Hastily, she scrambled to her feet; the street was deserted, so at least no one else had seen her fall. She was just congratulating herself on the fact and taking off her mud-coated mittens to examine the palms of her hands, which were smarting most uncomfortably, when a voice spoke almost in her ear. 'Up a dandy, me darlin'!

Me an' my mate 'ere was lookin' for a fallen woman, an' it seems like we struck lucky at last. Where's you headin'?'

Sylvie was so startled that she nearly screamed, but she managed to bite it back and looked into the face of the man who had accosted her. He was tall and broad, with a red, piggy face, and he was dressed in the peaked cap and British warm of a soldier. Sylvie, who had begun to feel apprehensive, relaxed a little. Brendan was a soldier, and so were many of her friends. These men would not wish her harm.

'Cat got your tongue, missy?' That was the second man, also a soldier, but this one had a thin ferrety face and mean eyes, which seemed to be crowding too close to his long pointed nose. Sylvie did not like the look of him at all, but it would not do to show her feelings. 'Where's you goin'?'

'I'm going to the Ferryman; I live there,' Sylvie said quickly. 'Let me pass, please; I'm already late and my husband will be worried.'

She tried to push past them but the men closed in on either side of her, each one taking an arm. 'You doesn't want to go hurryin' off, missy,' the piggy one said reprovingly. 'You've already had one nasty fall; you doesn't want to have another, do you? We'll give you a hand, make sure you get home safe, like.'

'I don't need a hand from anyone, thank you,' Sylvie said icily. She tried to shake herself free but this merely made both men tighten their grip. 'If

199

you don't let go of me at once I shall be forced to scream, and then you'll be in real trouble.'

The piggy man sniggered. 'Who's to hear you, me love?' he asked derisively, and Sylvie realised, with a stab of sick horror, that the narrow road upon which they stood wound its way between warehouses, of course unmanned at this time of night. No help from that quarter, then. She gave another angry jerk and looked down at the men's feet. She was wearing stout boots, but theirs looked even stouter. Perhaps kicking would not be a good idea. However, she felt instinctively that she must make a move soon, or something really bad might happen.

The men began to drag her along and it was difficult to resist for her feet slid on the snow-covered pavement, and suddenly it began to snow again, small vicious flakes blown almost horizontal by the strong wind. Ferret face began to pull her into the shelter of a narrow jigger which led down between two warehouses, shouting as he did so: 'No need to struggle, you silly bitch; we'll pay you fair an' square if you tell us what your charge is. Then we'll walk you back to the Ferryman, nice as you please; we might even buy you a drink.'

'Let – me – go!' Sylvie shouted. 'Wait till I tell my husband how you've behaved and I can assure you you'll be blacklisted by every pub in Liverpool.'

Both men laughed and Sylvie decided that she

might as well kick as not, since things were clearly desperate. These were not two decent British soldiers; they were a couple of low animals, incapable of listening to reason, anxious only to satisfy their lust. She kicked out viciously, then drew in a long breath and screamed at the top of her lungs.

Even as the awful sound left her mouth, Sylvie reflected, with satisfaction, that a ship's siren could not have done better. The scream definitely startled the men and before they had recovered from their surprise she had begun vigorously to kick, first at a pair of stout legs, then at the skinny ones. The piggy man let go of her arm, but she saw his fist travelling towards her face and ducked just in time, then began to shriek again, whilst scratching, punching and biting every bit of them which came within range. The men tried to subdue her and were beginning to succeed when she heard running footsteps. It was dark in the jigger but she saw the pale glimmer of both men's faces as they turned towards the sound, and in a moment they released her; in fact they released her so suddenly that she fell to the ground, banging her head painfully on the warehouse wall, so that for a moment her senses swam and darkness threatened to descend. However, she had scrambled up on all fours and was kneeling, trying to gain strength to rise to her feet, when hands caught her under the arms and a warm voice, with a country accent, spoke. 'What's been a-going on here, eh? You poor little gal; did them brutes run off with your handbag? I'm sorry I didn't stop them, but I heard your shrieks and thought it was more important to frighten them off than to try to catch them.' An arm encircled her waist and it was the most comforting arm in the world just at that moment because Sylvie felt, instinctively, that this was a good man, as good as the other two had been bad.

'Thank you, oh, thank you,' she gasped. She was shaking all over and her voice came out small and thin. 'If you hadn't come along . . . oh, dear God, I'm so grateful that you heard me screaming.'

'That's all right. I'm happy to have driven them off,' the man said. 'Can you walk, me love, or shall I carry you? I can see you're only a slip of a thing.'

'I can walk, only it will have to be very slowly,' Sylvie said shakily. 'They didn't take my handbag because I wasn't carrying one. I – I think they got the wrong idea about me because I'm out alone and so late, but I'm sure I never . . .' She was interrupted by her own sobs, but her rescuer seemed to understand what she had been trying to say.

'It's all right, m' dear; no need to explain, nobbut it's a bad time of night to be out alone, and a bad place to choose for an evening walk. I don't know whether you lost your way in the snow, but you're awful near the docks, and women who walk by the docks at night . . . well, I dare say you know what I mean.'

Sylvie looked up at her rescuer but could see very little in the flickering gas light, for by now they had left the jigger behind and were on the flagway once more. The snow was still whirling past; tiny, tenacious flakes which clung to every surface upon which they landed, a category which included both Sylvie and her rescuer. The snow made it even more difficult to make out the man's features but she thought he had a broad, tanned face, a countryman's face, and she realised that he reminded her of Brendan. He had the same air of casual confidence, the same warmth, and though he was a total stranger she trusted him implicitly.

'Where do you live, m'dear?' he asked as they paused on the pavement. 'I'll see you safe home, for 'tis no night to be out by yourself. Is it far?'

'No, it's not far,' Sylvie said. Her voice sounded very tiny against the howl of the wind and she had to keep her chin tucked into her coat collar, out of the worst of the weather. 'I live at the Ferryman. It's a public house down on the Dock Road. Do you know it?'

The man chuckled. 'Do I not? I'm a seaman aboard the SS *Mercuria*; Southampton's her home port, but lately we've been transferred to doing the Atlantic run, so I'm in Liverpool every few weeks and naturally enough me and my mates go to the nearest pub, which is, often as not, the Ferryman. I'm not much of a drinking man, mind – home-brewed cider is my favourite tipple – but I enjoy the company and it's a deal better than spending me whole life aboard ship.' He glanced down at her curiously. 'There's a couple of young ladies servin' in the bar . . . would you be one of them?'

'Yes, I do work in the bar sometimes,' Sylvie acknowledged. 'But I work in a munitions factory; it used to be the big fruit and veg market down on Cazneau Street and we do shifts, so I'm not often in the bar these days. My mother-in-law is the landlady, though, so if I'm not actually serving customers, or working at the factory, then I'm probably washing up glasses in the kitchen, or giving an eye to my husband. He's been very ill and needs a great deal of care.'

'Aye, someone told me there were a sick feller in the room behind the bar,' the man agreed. 'But we'd best introduce ourselves. I'm Sam Trescoe, and I come from Plymouth.'

'I'm Sylvie Dugdale, Mr Trescoe,' Sylvie said, then repeated what she had said in a louder tone, since the raging blizzard had seemed to snatch the words from her mouth before they could possibly have reached her companion's ears. She was feeling very much better and realised that, though she was shaken and bruised, she was little the worse for her adventure. As she spoke, they reached the front door of the pub and she pulled Mr Trescoe to a halt. In the glow of light from the bar she saw that he was caked in snow, and guessed that she must be the same. 'We'd best get rid of the snow or we'll trek it into the bar,' she said, and began stamping and banging vigorously until she was pretty well clear of the stuff.

Sam Trescoe did the same, then pushed open the pub door and ushered her into the warmth and brightness of the bar. 'There you are, Mrs Dugdale, safe home at last,' he said, and she saw his eyes widen as she unwound the scarf from round her head and shook out her silvery curls. She thought for a moment that he was dismayed by her dishevelled appearance, but a second glance recognised the admiration in his eyes. She dimpled off at him and, seeing him properly for the first time, realised that he was a very handsome man. He had thickly curling light brown hair and the bluest eyes she thought she had ever seen. For a moment, the two simply stared at one another, then Sylvie remembered where she was and chided herself for such stupid behaviour. She glanced about her but the bar was crowded, and no one seemed to have noticed her entrance.

Beside her, Sam Trescoe stirred uneasily. 'You'd best get into the back and make yourself a cup of strong, sweet tea,' he advised. 'Then you should take a hot bath and get yourself to bed, for I'll be bound you're bruised all over. And I'd best be off back to the Sailors' Home before they let some other feller take my bed.'

He turned as if to go, but Sylvie caught at his sleeve. 'No you don't,' she said firmly. 'You saved me from those fellers, Sam Trescoe, and I've scarcely begun to thank you. Besides, I'm in a bit of a state, aren't I? I'd rather you were with me when I explain what happened to my mother-in-law . . .

that is, if you don't mind sharing that cup of tea with me?'

Sam smiled down at her, his blue eyes dancing. 'I could do with a cuppa,' he admitted. 'And would this be Mrs Dugdale senior?'

Sylvie looked round and saw her mother-in-law bearing down upon them, an anxious frown upon her face. 'Sylvie, me love, me an' your mam have been that worried . . .' she began, then gasped, a hand flying to her mouth as she took in Sylvie's muddy and disordered appearance. 'Wharrever's happened? You look as though someone's fished you out of the Mersey!'

Sylvie's laugh was a trifle forced, for the remark took her back to that other rescue, which had been, in fact, even more dramatic than the recent one. But it had not been safe to tell a soul about Brendan's selfless act, whereas it was perfectly all right to tell both her mother-in-law and her mother, who had just come panting up, what had happened in that ugly little jigger. She would have started her explanation at once, but Sam shook his head at her, then took her arm and guided her behind the bar and through into the back room, whilst her mother and mother-in-law followed, clucking anxiously. Once there, Sam glanced quickly at Len, who seemed to be asleep, then turned to the two older women.

'Mrs Dugdale has had a nasty experience,' he said quietly. 'She's still rather shocked and I think a cup of hot sweet tea would help. If one of you ladies would be so good as to make the tea, the other can get her out of her wet things.'

Sylvie was quite amused to see how both women leapt to obey these gentle commands, her mother-in-law pulling the kettle across the flame and getting the tea caddy off the mantel, whilst Mrs Davies pulled off Sylvie's wet and muddy coat, sat her daughter down in a fireside chair, and began to unlace her boots. Still kneeling at her daughter's feet, she turned to look up at their visitor. 'Thank you for lookin' after my girl, for I'm very sure that's what you did,' she said gruffly. 'As soon as I saw her purse lyin' on the dresser this mornin' I began to worry meself, but then I remembered all her good friends at the factory, and I thought she'd be safe enough to borry some cash off one of them.' She turned back to Sylvie. 'But I guess you forgot you'd no money until you was aboard the tram – something like that, anyway – so you ended up walking. I can see you fell over, but . . .'

At this point, Mrs Dugdale delivered a large mug of strong, sweet tea to each of them and Sam, after a glance at Sylvie, told his side of the story. 'I'd just come ashore and was headin' towards the nearest pub when I heard someone screaming; dear Lord, it was a scream and a half! Enough to frighten most people, which I think it did. It came from a little passageway between two big warehouses, so I thought I'd best investigate, especially when two fellers dashed past me, one o' them shoulder-charging me so that I nearly ended up in the gutter myself. I thought the fellers were up to no good, so I went a bit of the way down the passage. The young lady had been knocked down so I give her a hand to get on to her pins and brought her out. Then I walked her home and here we are,' he finished.

Immediately, two pairs of round, astonished eyes swung towards Sylvie. 'I – I think the men were soldiers . . . well, I know they were,' she faltered. 'It's a wild night and there was no one about so I suppose they thought – they thought . . .'

'Aye, they'd think the worst, 'cos any gal walkin' out in this weather . . .' Mrs Davies began, then stopped speaking as tears filled Sylvie's eyes and began to trickle down her cheeks. At once, Mrs Davies was all concern. She surged out of her chair and put her arms round her daughter's shoulders, giving her an affectionate hug. 'Don't you worry, chuck, we all know you're a good girl. But what a blessing this young gentleman came along before any real harm were done.'

Sylvie pulled a handkerchief from her skirt pocket, dabbed at her eyes, then blew her nose resoundingly. 'Yes, it were a blessing,' she agreed fervently. 'Because I started to fight as soon as – as – I realised what they wanted, and they got really angry. I kicked their shins and punched the fat one on the nose, and scratched and bit, but it would have gone hard for me if Mr Trescoe hadn't chased them off.' She turned to her rescuer. 'Mr

Trescoe, this is my mother, Mrs Davies, and the other lady is my mother-in-law. Oh, and the man in the bed is my husband, Len. I see he's woken up; I'll introduce you, but I expect Len won't understand too well what's been going on. He'll be half asleep still, I dare say. And he's very shy with strangers,' she added.

Sylvie led Sam over to the bedside, explaining to Len that this man had rescued her from a difficult situation, and Len smiled and shook Sam's hand, then indicated that he, too, would like a cup of tea. Sylvie went over to the pot and poured him one, then carried it over to the bed. He could not sit up unaided, but when her mother and mother-in-law would have come over to help him into an upright position Sam waved them back. He went to the other side of the bed, put a strong arm round Len's shoulders, and heaved, telling Sylvie to rearrange his pillows. Then he went back to his place by the fire, whilst Sylvie held the brimming mug to her husband's lips. Slowly, fumblingly, Len put both hands up and grasped the mug himself whilst Sylvie smiled encouragement and reached for the towel to envelop him in case of spillages. Usually Len submitted, but on this occasion he shook his head violently, so violently that the tea slurped out of the mug and dappled both his pyjama jacket and the top sheet. 'No, no, no,' Len mumbled. 'I – I – I do it.'

'Yes, of course, chuck,' Sylvie said soothingly, knowing that she must not interfere again. Len's grip on the mug might be uncertain, but he was still a good deal stronger than she, and a wrestling match over a cup of tea would be sheer foolishness. So she let him hold it to his lips and sank down on the chair so that she might take it from him when he had had as much as he wanted. He turned to her, giving a secret little smile of satisfaction, and then began to sip his tea rather noisily, but with enjoyment. Sylvie relaxed. It was clear that Len did not wish to seem dependent in front of a stranger. She listened to the talk round the fire, and decided she would ask Sam if he would like to visit her husband from time to time. After all, Len had enjoyed Brendan's company, and now, with so many of his old friends fighting in France, or aboard warships, he would surely be glad to see a new face now and then. Sylvie would not admit, even to herself, that she would be reluctant to lose touch with this friendly and delightful young man. But when he insisted upon leaving, it was not Sylvie who begged him to come again, but Mrs Dugdale herself.

'You've been real good to me daughter-in-law, and the way you lifted our Len up higher in his bed was kind 'n' all. It's clear he likes you,' she said. 'You're a long way from home, for you said you came from Devonshire, so whenever you're in the port o' Liverpool you must pop into the old Ferryman. You can share our meal, have a yarn wi' Len about how the war's goin' an' meet our Becky. She's me granddaughter an' bright as a button. Now just you promise me that you'll come again.'

'Well, if you're sure, I'd be real grateful for some home comforts, 'cos the Sailors' Home ain't exactly ideal,' Sam agreed. 'And you must call me Sam, 'cos Mr Trescoe's a rare mouthful.' He turned, smiling, to Sylvie. 'And I shall call you Sylvie 'cos of there being two Mrs Dugdales, both pretty young things, so we want no confusion.'

Sylvie was amused to see her mother-in-law blush girlishly and thought that Sam Trescoe must have spent some time in Ireland since he seemed to have kissed the Blarney stone so effectively. And there was poor Brendan, Irish to the marrow of his bones, but totally lacking in the sort of easy inter-course which seemed to come naturally to Sam. She went to the door to see him off, and noticed that the blizzard had calmed, though there were still small flakes of snow falling from the dark sky above. She thought the trams would still be running and advised Sam to go to the nearest stop and catch one, since it was a fair distance to the Sailors' Home on Canning Place and the snow was deep enough to make walking difficult. Sam laughed and shook his head. 'City snow's nothing compared with the snow on Dartymoor,' he said, deliberately exag-gerating his soft west-country accent. 'Why, in winter, the snow on the moor can bury a whole house an' you can walk by an' look down at your feet, and see a chimney pot. Oh aye, we have real snow on Dartmoor, not this flimsy stuff!'

Sylvie smiled at him. 'And if I believe that, you think I'll believe anything,' she said teasingly. 'But of course this is a seaport and they say the salt in the air stops the snow from laying. Good night, Sam, and don't forget your promise; next time you're in port, you'll come straight round to the Ferryman. Agreed?'

'Agreed. Good night, Sylvie,' Sam called softly. Sylvie watched him until he was out of sight, then turned back into the pub once more, realising that she was positively longing to plunge her aching limbs into the hot bath that Sam himself had suggested earlier.

Chapter Eight

September 1916

'Kitty? Are you ready, alanna? We don't want to be late 'cos you'll be in Sister Enda's class and she's a real tartar, so she is.'

Grainne's head popped round the kitchen door as she spoke and Kitty, sitting at the kitchen table in a ferment of excitement, jumped off her chair and ran across the room to fetch her coat from its peg. Today was to be her first day at school and she was looking forward to it so much! Maeve had told her over and over how important it was that she should learn to read, write and do sums, so that when she was a really big girl, a grown-up in fact, she could get a good job and earn money for treats such as a trip to the cinema, or to Booterstown to play on the sand.

Maeve, who had also been sitting at the kitchen table, got up. Kitty knew she would have liked to accompany her on this important day, but could not possibly do so since she had half a dozen children who had to be picked up from their homes and looked after whilst their mothers worked. She had asked Grainne to take care of Kitty, and Kitty had been delighted since she admired the older girl very much.

Now, Kitty scrambled into her coat and Maeve buttoned her up, then kissed her three times, once on the forehead and once on each cheek, before gently propelling her towards the door. 'I wish I could take you to school, me darlin',' she said. 'But you know it's impossible.'

'It's all right, Maeve, you don't have to worry,' Grainne said soothingly. She held out a hand to the younger girl. 'Come along, alanna. If we get to Baggot Street early enough, I'll play you a game of piggy beds on the pavement.'

'I'm ready,' Kitty squeaked, making for the stairs. She skimmed down them with Grainne close on her heels, and emerged into a pleasant sunny morning, though there was a nip in the air as though the weather wanted everyone to be aware that, with the return to school, summer was over and autumn around the corner.

Despite the earliness of the hour, the streets were already crowded. Kitty fingered the end of one of her short fat plaits, checking that it was still held in place by the green ribbon bow which Maeve had tied earlier. Maeve had been determined that Kitty should look her best for her first day at school, but when they reached St Joseph's and saw the motley crew assembled on the pavement, Kitty felt doubtful as to the wisdom of Maeve's actions. None of the other children assembled wore crisp white blouses, neat grey skirts and black plimsolls without so much as a hole in either toe. Oh, there were smartly dressed children all right, but they were in the bright jumpers and skirts which were the uniform of Our Lady's school, situated on the upper floor of the building. The charges for Our Lady's were high, so Kitty had not been able to follow Grainne and Clodagh there, much though Maeve regretted it.

'Ah, one of the sisters is beckoning you in,' Grainne said in Kitty's ear. 'Bye-bye. You follow the rest.' She gave Kitty a little shove. 'You're the sharpest knife in the drawer, our Maeve says, so I dare say you and Sister Enda will get on a treat.' Most of these remarks went over Kitty's head, for whilst Grainne was speaking the children were cramming into the building and being ushered into rooms on either side of the corridor. 'Go in and sit down. Don't say anything until she asks you your name and then speak up good and clear; she don't like mumblers. Got your sandwich?'

'Yes, and Maeve said to give me teacher a ha'penny and she'd give me a drink of milk,' Kitty said, rather breathlessly. The sight of all the children, none of whom was known to her, was a bit daunting and the teacher, standing behind her desk, more daunting still. To Kitty's eyes, she was a mountain of a woman, even taller than Mr Cavanagh, and somehow even huger because she was dressed entirely in black save for the white cloth which framed her face. She took no notice as Kitty sank into one of the small chairs, but it was obvious that she was counting. Kitty heard her murmuring 'thirty-four, thirty-five, thirty-six', and then she strode over to the door and slammed it shut. Kitty turned to her neighbour, a tiny girl with straggly brown hair and enormous, greenish eyes. 'Me sister brought me here this morning and she said . . .' she began in a whisper, but got no further.

'Silence,' bawled Sister Enda, if this was indeed Sister Enda, for she had not introduced herself. 'Sit still and speak when you're spoken to and not before.' She looked at a group of small girls who stood before her simply because there were not enough chairs to go round. 'Sit down, I said. Are you all deaf?'

The little girls collapsed on to the floor as though someone had pulled a string, animating them all simultaneously, and at least three of them burst into tears. Kitty was sitting quite near them and, embarrassed by their predicament, looked down at her feet, but even as she looked she realised that a large puddle had already reached her toes. Quickly, she picked up her feet; one of the small girls was so frightened that she had wet her knickers and Kitty wanted to keep her plimsolls out of danger.

'You! I said to sit still, and that means not to wriggle or scuffle. Yes, it's you I'm talking to, the one with the plaits. What's your name? Sit up straight and answer properly!'

Kitty stared at the teacher, indignation making her cheeks grow hot. Did the nun think she ought to sit there with her feet in a puddle? And anyway, it was very rude to make personal remarks; Maeve had often told her so. She could have said the girl with the clean white blouse, because no one else was wearing any sort of blouse, let alone a clean white one. But the teacher was staring at her, the small eyes in the round, white currant bun of a face glittering malevolently. Kitty remembered what Grainne had said – something about speaking loudly and clearly – so she sat up straighter in her small chair and did both. 'Please, sister, there's a puddle of pee on the floor and me shoes is new; Maeve said not to get 'em mucky and getting 'em covered in pee would be . . .'

She was still speaking when the teacher surged out from behind her desk, crossed the floor in a couple of enormous strides and lifted Kitty bodily out of her chair. 'How dare you use a word like that in my classroom?' she hissed. 'You will remain standing until I tell you that you may sit. What's your name? I need to . . . oh, oh, oh!'

Kitty followed the teacher's eyes and saw, with real pleasure, that Sister Enda's long black skirt had soaked up a good deal of . . . whatever it was on the floor. Maeve called it pee, and so did Caitlin, so it could not have been that word to which the nun had objected, but for the life of her Kitty could not think of another word which could have been considered rude. She began to ask, rather more timidly, what word she had used to annoy the sister, but she was roughly shoved aside and the small girl from whom the enormous puddle had escaped was seized in her stead.

'You are a disgusting little toad,' the nun said, shaking her wet and weeping victim. 'You can't stay in my classroom in that state; one of you – the one with the plaits – must take you along to Miss Brogan's office. She's the school secretary and keeps a supply of knickers and skirts which she will lend you to wear for the rest of the day. But you must bring them back tomorrow, do you understand?'

Shaken by huge sobs, the small girl nodded and was told, brusquely, that she should say 'Yes, sister', when addressing her teacher. 'And another . . .' Sister Enda looked round wildly. 'Ah, I was forgetting. You're mostly new.' Her eyes raked the room, then settled upon the waiflike child with big green eyes sitting next to Kitty. 'This is your second year, Bridget, so you'll know where the broom cupboard is. Fetch a mop and bucket, and be quick about it.'

Then the three children were ushered out of the door, Kitty wondering how on earth she was to find Miss Brogan's office without calling down more trouble upon her defenceless head. But in fact this proved to be the least of her worries, since Bridget pointed to a door at the end of the corridor as soon as the classroom was behind them. 'That's the room you want,' she said bluntly. 'The broom cupboard is on the first landing.'

She disappeared upstairs, leaving the two small girls to make their way to Miss Brogan's office. However, they had scarcely gone a couple of yards along the corridor when the small girl pulled Kitty to a halt. 'My sister Fanny is one of the big girls in the top class and I'll tell her what you done, and she'll get you,' she said. ''Cos youse is a nasty, horrible tale clat, you, with your plaits and your bleedin' new shoes.'

To say that was Kitty was taken aback would be putting it mildly. The other child was so small and weak, in appearance at any rate, but she had turned on Kitty with the speed and venom of a striking snake. Kitty scowled down at her. She was tempted to give her a good shake but realised that this would only make her little companion crosser. Instead, she spoke as reasonably as she could. 'I didn't tell anyone anything,' she pointed out. 'All I did was move me perishin' feet because of the puddle you'd made. And I never said you'd made it, either – well, how could I? I didn't know who the devil you were; still don't, for that matter. And as for your big sister Fanny, I've got two big sisters, Clodagh and Grainne, so anyone what starts anything wi' me will have them to fight an' all.'

Brave words, particularly as she had no idea whether, in fact, Clodagh and Grainne would wade in if they saw the girl they had always treated as a little sister being bullied. And of course they were not at St Joseph's either. However, she did not need to tell her tiny antagonist that.

The girl stared at her defiantly for a moment, then her gaze dropped to the floor and Kitty realised that the wet knickers had left a trail all along the corridor. Better get the kid to Miss Brogan as fast as she could; they could continue their quarrel once the other girl was clad in dry underwear once more. She tugged at the child's arm but was resisted. 'Cor, will you look at that,' the small girl whispered, indicating the wet linoleum. 'Me mam 'ud crucify me if she knew I'd piddled on the floor.' To Kitty's horror, she turned round and began to trot briskly up the corridor. 'I'm goin' home,' she said over her shoulder. 'I'd rather be crucified by me mam than by that wicked old nun.'

Kitty promptly followed her, grabbed her skinny arm and began to tow her back towards Miss Brogan's office. 'You can't just leave school when you want to,' she said severely. 'I dare say you might get away with not coming back tomorrow – I'll never come into this place again – but you can't leave in the middle of the day with wet knickers, that I do know. I 'spect Bridget will mop the corridor, or mebbe it'll dry out, but it ain't your fault, nor mine neither. We're only little. Now come along to this Miss Brogan, young what's-yer-name.'

'I'm no younger'n you, an' me name's Jane,' the child informed her. 'I's sorry I called you a tale clat 'cos you weren't, but I were that frightened I had to blame someone. As for me sister Fanny, she's likelier to give me a slap than you.' She eyed Kitty curiously. 'What are you called?'

'I'm Catherine Mary O'Keefe, but me pals call me Kitty,' Kitty said, then halted and tapped timidly on the door ahead of them. When no one spoke from behind it, she knocked louder, then walked in boldly, telling herself that she was on an errand for the teacher and no one should reprimand her for doing as she was told. The room was dwarfed by an enormous desk, but it was rather a cosy room. There was a floral rug on the floor, and pretty flower-patterned curtains hung at the window. The huge desk was covered with books and papers, and one wall of the room was shelved with books from floor to ceiling. Kitty gazed at them, enchanted. Maeve read her stories at bedtime every night and Kitty had long ago decided that when she was able to read she would go to the Free Library and borrow a new book every week until she had read every volume available. Now, she wondered whether these books might be lent one day, and glanced at the figure behind the desk. The woman was very small and very thin. She had rather dull, brown hair which frizzed in a curly fringe across her forehead; the rest of it was pulled back into a bun on the nape of her neck. She had a narrow little face, very bright brown eyes behind steel-rimmed spectacles, and paper-white skin. She also had deep lines running from her nose to the corners of her mouth, which gave her a severe look, but Kitty saw that these were caused by smiling, for when Miss Brogan looked up and saw the two children standing before her, she smiled, and the lines deepened.

'Yes, dear? What can I do for you?'

'Please, miss, Jane here has had a bit of an accident so Sister Enda sent us for dry knickers,' Kitty said bluntly, when her small companion did not speak. And then she saw the reason for Jane's silence. Beside Miss Brogan's desk, curled up in a wicker basket, was what looked like a beautiful white lamb, and even as Kitty gasped with delight the lamb raised its head, opened dark and liquid eyes, and yawned, revealing neat little white teeth and a great deal of pink and curling tongue. Kitty loved all animals and would have given a great deal to possess a dog of her own, but neither Caitlin nor Maeve would countenance such a thing. Tommy, the cat, supremo of all rat and mice catchers, was the only animal allowed because he earned his keep and he and Kitty adored one another. But perhaps, if she suggested a lamb . . . she could sell the wool, though during a hard winter such a pet might be regarded as dish of the day by some of the poorer families in Handkerchief Alley.

But Miss Brogan had followed Kitty's gaze and got to her feet. 'Fluffy is very gentle; you can stroke him if you like,' Miss Brogan said. She produced a large box full of assorted garments, chose a pair of knickers and, after a glance at Jane, a faded blue skirt, and laid them on the side of the desk nearest to her visitors. 'These little accidents do happen, especially when you're away from home for the first time,' she said comfortably. 'Pop these on, Jane. I'll put your wet things into a strong paper bag and you can come collect them when school's over for the day. Tell your mammy to rinse them through and dry them out so you can come to school tomorrow in your own clothes. Don't forget to bring back the clothes I've lent you, will you?'

Jane assured her that she would not forget, then took off her wet clothes and scrambled into the dry ones. Then she and Kitty knelt before the basket and adored the fluffy white lamb within.

'Only he isn't really a lamb, he is a Bedlington terrier and the best companion a person could wish for,' Miss Brogan told them. 'You seem two sensible little girls; how would you like to take Fluffy for a little walk during your luncheon break sometimes? Normally, you're not allowed out of school but have to content yourselves with the playroom in wet weather and the yard in dry. But children who exercise Fluffy for me are allowed to walk up and down the street for ten minutes or so.'

Kitty and Jane exchanged gleeful looks. What a piece of luck that they had been sent to Miss Brogan and had shown an immediate interest in her delightful pet. Why, if they were to be allowed to take the little dog for a walk, they might even meet up with friends who were not in school. It was too far to go all the way home, but it was still a sort of freedom, and one probably not granted to many pupils of St Joseph's school. So it was with some eagerness that the children agreed to take great care of Fluffy and suggested that they might take him for his first walk that very day. The weather was warm and sunny, and even a ten-minute escape from the horrors of Sister Enda's classroom would be bliss indeed.

Miss Brogan agreed that they should come for Fluffy as soon as they had eaten their carry-out – she called it their packed luncheon – and then Kitty and Jane retraced their steps, noting with satis-faction that Bridget must have spotted the trail of drops, since there were now vigorous mop marks on the linoleum. They entered the classroom to find Sister Enda still taking names and allocating places. It appeared she had found some more chairs from somewhere, since everyone now had a seat, and the children were grouped, ten at a time, round a number of low tables. Sister Enda was handing round slates and a girl, with her hair dragged back from her face and tied with a piece of string, was handing out slate pencils. Sister Enda glanced at them as they came back into the room, then said briskly: 'Name?'

'Kitty O'Keefe,' 'Jane Maloney,' the girls said in chorus, and Kitty stifled a giggle when the teacher stared at them for a moment before saying briskly: 'Jane, you sit there. Kitty, sit beside her.'

As soon as they were seated, the nun commented that they had been gone an extra-ordinarily long time. Kitty, emboldened by the pleasant visit to Miss Brogan, said firmly: 'Miss Brogan wanted to talk to us. It would have been rude to walk away whilst she was speaking.'

'It's rude to answer me back,' Sister Enda said smartly. 'Speak when you're spoken to, and use my title.'

'I didn't know you had a title,' Kitty said and was once more astonished and outraged when the nun leaned across the table and hit her sharply across the knuckles with a ruler.

'Don't answer back. I've already got you down as a troublemaker, young lady,' she said. Having glared at Kitty for a full minute, she turned away and went across to the blackboard. 'Now that all the wanderers have returned, we shall start work by beginning to learn our letters,' she said. 'This is an "a", this a "b", this a "c".' She had been facing the blackboard, but suddenly she swung round, pointing an accusing finger at Kitty. 'You spoke! After all I've said to you already, you actually dared to speak, when I had neither addressed you nor given you permission to do any such thing. If it weren't the first day you would receive three strokes of the cane, but as it is, I'm warning you. One more word out of place . . .'

'But miss . . . sister, I mean . . .' Kitty said desperately, 'I weren't really speaking, I were just saying that Maeve learned me me letters weeks ago. And I can make words, little ones, and read 'em too. Maeve said to tell me teacher . . .'

But this, it seemed, was too much for Sister Enda. She crossed the room at incredible speed for so large a woman, jerked Kitty out of her chair, snatched her hand and flattened it out, holding it by the fingertips, and brought the ruler down sharply on the palm. It hurt, really badly. Kitty tried to wrench her hand away but the nun had too firm a grip on her fingers, and the ruler descended three more times, hurting abominably, before Sister Enda released her. Kitty knew her eyes were full of tears of pain and rage, but when she looked up into the nun's face she saw that her pain was Sister Enda's pleasure, and refused to let the drops fall. Instead, she sat down hard on the little chair and gazed stolidly ahead of her, until the sister turned back to the blackboard to continue her lesson. Only then did she flick the tears away with a forefinger, determining as she did so that she would never, never return to St Joseph's. Maeve could teach her to read, or Clodagh, but she saw no reason to let herself be beaten by a vicious old woman who just happened to be her teacher.

For the rest of the morning, Kitty sat in her seat with her lips folded in a tight line. She had been hit on her left hand and, since she was left-handed, this made writing almost impossible, or would have done had writing been required. Since all they were expected to do, as yet, was to trace the shape of the first six letters of the alphabet on to their slates, she managed this as efficiently as the other children. Indeed, looking about her surreptitiously whenever the nun turned away, she thought her letters were probably the best she could see, despite her injured hand.

For injured it certainly was. The ruler had raised red welts across her small palm and in one area, where the blows had fallen on almost the same stretch of skin, there was a smear of blood. This actually gave Kitty considerable satisfaction. Maeve won't let me come back here when I show her my hand, Kitty thought triumphantly. Sure and Enda, the witch, has gone too far this time. I dare say Maeve will come round here tomorrow morning and tell the head teacher that there's a wicked woman on her staff. I hope she does. I hope old Enda the witch gets chucked out of the school for ever and ever, 'cos she made a good little girl's hand bleed. I am a good little girl, Maeve and Caitlin often say so; it's that witch Enda who's wicked.

However, there were compensations, playtime for a start. The children at Our Lady's had the run of a reasonably sized garden but St Joseph's children had the yard, which was already marked out with various games. Some of the children had brought lengths of rope with them and Kitty watched, wistfully, as two of the bigger girls swung the rope and others jumped in and out, shouting the well-remembered phrases, rhymes and catches which children have shouted since time immemorial. After watching for a bit, Kitty saw that anyone could play provided they did not spoil the enjoyment of others by getting tangled up in the rope. She said as much to Jane and Bridget – the three of them had kept together –

and Bridget agreed that anyone could play. Presently the three of them jumped in, and managed a good twenty jumps before the rope began to turn too fast for them and they jumped out, pink-cheeked and breathless, and were actually congratulated by one of the big girls on their nimbleness.

Playtime over, the children returned to their classrooms, Kitty, Jane and Bridget glowing from the exercise and feeling very much more cheerful. Bridget, being a second-year pupil, had been able to give them quite a lot of useful advice, including a warning that Sister Enda hated dull children, though she also hated bright ones. 'It sounds as if she hates all children,' Kitty observed, as they formed into a ragged line to file back into the building with the rest of their class. 'And how can she find out whether you're bright or dull if you're never allowed to speak?'

Bridget laughed. 'She'll let you answer when she asks you a question,' she explained. 'Only you've got to answer the way she likes. It's best to say "Please sister" before anything else you say. And if she tells you to sit down when you've finished answering, you're supposed to say "Thank you, sister". Oh, and I forgot to say you have to stand up as soon as she points to you or shouts your name.'

'Why?' Kitty asked baldly. 'Why can't we answer sitting down?'

Bridget shrugged. 'How should I know? It's one of their rules, and if you don't do it they get mad.'

'Then why don't they tell us their rules?' Kitty said plaintively, as the queue began to shuffle forward. 'They haven't told us any rules yet.'

'No, because they like punishing us and if we knew what the rules were, we wouldn't break 'em,' Bridget said. 'Sister Enda loves nothin' more than seein' a new kid crying. Why, look at your hand; it'll be black and blue by morning, I don't doubt.'

'Well, *she* won't know if it is,' Kitty said defiantly, as they squeezed into the building once more. 'Because I'm not coming back, not me. Maeve won't let me, not when she sees me hand.'

Bridget gave a hollow laugh. 'We all says that,' she observed. 'But I reckon you'll be here tomorrow, just like the rest of us. It's strange, because the nuns and the brothers laid into our mams and dads when they were little. I know they did because I heard my daddy tellin' my brother Billy that he weren't whopped half as hard by his teacher as our daddy had been by Brother Claudius.'

Kitty would have liked to say she was different, that Maeve, not being as old as most mothers, would understand, but she held her tongue. Maeve envied her the chance of the proper schooling which she, herself, had largely missed out on. The Connollys had been terribly poor – still were – and Mrs Connolly had needed all her children to work just as soon as they could. Maeve had been taught to read, once she arrived at the O'Keefes', by Caitlin, and had been pathetically grateful, Kitty knew that. Maeve often spoke of sitting beside Caitlin at the big kitchen table, learning first her letters and then how to string them together into words, and words into sentences. Both Maeve and Caitlin had often been so tired that they had fallen asleep over their books and Pat, returning after his own long day, would laugh to find the two of them with their heads on the table, sometimes gently snoring.

Thinking of that, as she re-entered the classroom, Kitty felt a horrid coldness slither down her back. How could she go home when school was over and tell Maeve that she did not mean to go back again? It would break her heart, for she had such high hopes! She had told Kitty over and over that reading, writing and arithmetic were like keys to a big door, behind which lurked wonderful things, things called opportunities. Kitty did not know precisely what an opportunity was, save that it was wonderful. She imagined it must mean nice food to eat, lots of books to read, plenty of turfs for your fire, and trips to the Saturday Rush at the local cinema.

Yet there was something even more precious behind that door, something which Maeve thought she could never have for herself but wanted for Kitty. 'I've got a lame foot and an ugly face, as well as a miserable, scraggy little body,' she had said to Kitty once. 'But you are straight and strong and beautiful. Darling Kitty, you should have everything. But it's really important to get an education.'

Naturally, Kitty had protested that Maeve was not ugly, and that her body was not scraggy, but Maeve had just laughed. 'Never mind that,' she had said. 'I know what I know. Now run along wit' you, I've got work to do.'

By the time she sat down, however, Kitty found she was far more cheerful. She had two friends, and the possibility of more, and she was determined to win the teacher's approval, much though she hated her. For the rest of the morning she did her best to do as Sister Enda said, but she noticed that the woman's eyes were always upon her and knew, with a little shiver of dread, that her teacher was actually hoping that she would overstep the mark in some undefined way. 'You're too perishin' clean, so you are,' Bridget informed her, when they were eating their carry-out. 'You don't blend in wit' the other kids, you stand out. Partly it's your plaits and partly it's that clean white blouse. If I were you, I'd come a bit more raggedy like tomorrer. And now let's go and get Fluffy.' She giggled. 'If Sister Enda knew Miss Brogan was lettin' us walk her dog, she'd be that furious she'd probably make up half a dozen new rules so's we could break 'em an' she could belt us.'

The three small girls were allowed back into the school – it was a fine day, so they had eaten their carry-out in the yard – by the door monitor when they explained that they had been asked to walk Miss Brogan's terrier. The monitor was a large girl of ten or eleven, with thick fair hair and a round, rosy-cheeked face. 'Right, you can go in, all three of you, lucky little beggars,' she said when they had explained. 'Miss Brogan's ever so nice, ever so kind as well, and Fluffy's a good little feller.'

Kitty had been a little doubtful as to the wisdom of all three of them going along to the school secretary's office, since Miss Brogan would only be expecting herself and Jane, but in the event her fears were unfounded. 'Ah, Bridget, I see you've taken our two little new girls under your wing,' Miss Brogan said, smiling down at them. 'Now don't forget, take Fluffy as far as the Liffey – you know the way, don't you, Bridget? – and then come straight back. It should take you ten or fifteen minutes.' As she spoke, she was fastening a red leather collar round Fluffy's neck and attaching to the collar a red leather lead which she handed to Kitty. 'There you are! You'll find he's very good and doesn't try to tug, but you must never let him off the lead because he doesn't understand about traffic and might run under a horse's hooves. He'll want to pause to go to the bathroom when you pass lamp posts, so you must let him do that, and I think you should take turns holding the lead. Slip the loop over your wrist and then hold the strap so he can't escape even if you were to drop the strap for a moment. I'll show you.' She did so, then stepped back, smiling at them. 'Now don't forget, no further than the river. It wouldn't do if you were late for Sister Enda's afternoon class.'

The three children set off in the highest of spirits,

with Fluffy frisking ahead of them. Every now and then he looked over his shoulder at Kitty, grinning at her as though the two of them shared a secret. Kitty noted the envious glances of other children as they made their way through the crowded streets and felt her cup of happiness was full. Obedient to Miss Brogan's instructions, she slowed at every lamp post, though she had had to ask Bridget just what the woman had meant by 'going to the bathroom'.

'Oh! Then should I have said someone's gone to the bathroom and made a puddle on the floor instead of what I did say?' Kitty asked. The whole thing was such a puzzle; she felt as though she had been suddenly propelled into a foreign country where she would keep misunderstanding until she had learned the language. 'Is that what Sister Enda meant when she told me off for using a rude word?'

Bridget shrugged. 'I dunno, but I reckon you can't do right as far as the old bat's concerned,' she said, pulling Kitty to a halt. 'If we're all to get our fair turn wit' Fluffy, then I reckon you ought to hand over the lead to Jane now. It ain't far to the river from here.'

Kitty complied, trying not to show reluctance, but even though she was not holding the lead Fluffy kept glancing up at her as they walked. He likes me, Kitty thought. I've made three friends today, not just two, and Miss Brogan is most awfully nice, so she is. I'll tell Maeve how nice she is when I get home, though it won't make any difference; I still don't mean to come back to school again, where that horrible nun will hit me whenever she has a chance. I wonder if the teachers are the same in Our Lady's? I don't think they can be, or Clodagh and Grainne would have said.

The three children were walking along the riverbank whilst Fluffy pottered happily amongst all the entrancing smells, when a diversion occurred: a skinny, grubby lad approached them, greeting them cheerfully. 'Hello, 'ello, 'ello, girls! Where's you goin' on this fine mornin'?' His glance singled Kitty out and he addressed her directly. 'Ain't you supposed to be in school, Kitty? I's certain sure Miz O'Keefe said you were startin' today, though I see you ain't got no school uniform.'

Kitty stared at him, then recognition dawned. 'I *am* in school. This is me lunch hour, Nick Mooney,' she said indignantly. Nick was a neighbour who often played in Handkerchief Alley; Kitty knew him well. 'Come to that, why ain't you in school? You're only eight.'

The boy grinned. He had a thin, mobile face, very bright light brown eyes, and hair the colour of the taffy sticks which Maeve sometimes made for the children. Kitty had always liked him; they had played together when they were small, but of late they seemed to have grown apart. 'Eight's old enough to sell newspapers an' I were doin' that earlier in the day,' he said. 'Where's your uniform, then?'

'We don't have none at St Joseph's,' Bridget said, butting in when she saw Kitty looking baffled. 'Who's you, anyway, apart from a perishin' rude boy, I mean?'

Nick grinned, showing surprisingly white and rather pointed teeth. 'Didn't you hear me little pal? I'm Nick Mooney an' I sell newspapers to the early workers an' folk on trams up and down O'Connell Street.' He turned to Kitty. 'But why's you at St Joseph's when your sisters are at Our Lady's? That Grainne could have passed her uniform down to you and got a new one for herself.'

'Can't afford it,' Kitty said briefly. 'They ain't my sisters, not really; I'm adopted, like, an' Caitlin can't afford to send me to Our Lady's . . . well, Maeve can't, 'cos it's her that took me on when I were a little baby. Now why don't you buzz off an' leave us alone, Nick? Askin' stupid questions when you should have known the answers.'

'Oh, keep your hair on, Pigtails,' Nick said rudely. 'Who did you steal the dog from then? If it is a dog. It looks more like a perishin' wolf in sheep's clothing.' He laughed raucously, then bent down and rubbed Fluffy behind the ears.

'Leave him alone,' Kitty said sharply. 'He don't like horrible, dirty boys, 'specially ones what sell newspapers on O'Connell Street.' She turned to her friends. 'Thanks to him holdin' us up, we shall have to run if we ain't to be late,' she said. 'Come *on*, Fluffy, be a good little feller then.'

But it now appeared that Fluffy could be as

235

perverse as any other dog. He had leapt up to lick Nick's unsavoury chin, and now he was dancing round the boy, behaving as though he had known him for years.

'I'd best walk back wit' you seein' as how the dog don't want to be parted from this horrible dirty boy,' Nick said, grinning at them. 'Step out, young ladies . . . which you ain't, of course, but I'm a gent, I am. I don't call names.'

'You did, you did. You called me Pigtails,' Kitty said furiously, her voice rising. 'Bugger off, Nick Mooney, or I'll tell your dad you've been pesterin' me an' me pals.'

This was a blow beneath the belt and both children knew it, for Mr Mooney was a huge man, a docker, more often out of work than in, and known for the beatings he administered, on the smallest excuse, to his wife and family whenever the drink was strong in him. Nick tried another grin but it lacked conviction. 'Okay, okay, I'm goin',' he said. 'See you around, Goody-Two-Shoes.'

Much ruffled, Kitty apologised for Nick's interference, but neither Jane nor Bridget had taken much notice. Both had brothers of their own and knew how irritating boys could be, and thought nothing of the revelation that Kitty was adopted, and that Mrs O'Keefe could not afford to send a third girl to the expensive fee-paying school. They brushed Kitty's apologies aside and the three children were back in school well before the bell went for afternoon lessons, but when Bridget asked if they might walk Fluffy again next day, Miss Brogan shook her head. 'Not tomorrow, dear; two children from Sister Elizabeth's class will take him tomorrow. But you may take him again next Monday, if you wish.'

The afternoon wore on. Kitty tried to blend in, as Bridget had advised, but with very little success, for Sister Enda suddenly noticed that Kitty was holding her pencil in her left hand. This seemed to infuriate her even more. 'What on earth are you doing? You're using the devil's hand and not the angel's,' she said accusingly. 'Every Christian soul knows the right hand is the angel's hand and is the one we use to hold a pencil. The left is the devil's hand – why do you think I caned you on your left hand? It was to drive the devil out of you.'

When the bell rang to indicate that the children could go home, Kitty, Jane and Bridget tumbled out of the classroom and made for the door as fast as they could, bursting into the sunshine like prisoners released from gaol.

'Well, if it ain't little Goody-Two-Shoes! Can I walk you home?' Without turning her head, Kitty aimed a swipe at Nick and was rewarded by an indignant shout. 'Hey, who d'you t'ink you're hittin', eh? What's wrong wit' wantin' to walk you home? Or is you goin' to wait for your new pals and cast off the old 'uns?'

'In case you've forgot, you haven't took much notice of me for . . . oh, for a year or more,' Kitty said. 'I dunno why you're bein' so particular now, neither. I've not come into money, not as I know, anyhow.'

She had heard the twins say this, and was rewarded by seeing a faint flush steal into Nick's dirty cheeks. 'That's a horrible t'ing to say, so it is,' he said reproachfully. 'You were a nice little kid afore you started school, but already it's changed you. Aw, come on, Kit, lemme walk home wit' you. Mebbe there's something I could do for your Maeve – bring in water, or carry up a couple o' buckets o' turf. What d'you say?'

'I say Maeve will have a cup o' tea and a currant bun waitin', and it's that what you're after,' Kitty said, but she grinned at her companion. 'Only I've got to talk to her, so you can't stay. Just come in, grab a bun, and go. Pat's fightin' wit' the army in France and the money ain't so good, so Caitlin doesn't like us bringin' kids back wit'out we asks first.'

'Oh. Right you are,' Nick said, rather dolefully. Kitty felt mean, for her old friend, she remembered now, was always hungry. So she said she would ask whether he might come to tea the following day, and then changed the subject.

'Why don't you go to school, Nick?' she asked curiously. 'Oh, I know you sell newspapers, but you must have gone to school once. Can you read?'

'A bit,' Nick said. 'I don't hold wit' school, though. Me brother Sean went and he came home wit' his bum striped all red where one o' them bleedin' brothers what call themselves teachers had hit him wit' his belt. The buckle end,' he added morosely. 'So I thought, that ain't for you, Nick old feller, and I give school the go-by.' He looked at her, a smile glimmering in his eyes. 'Same as you've got it in mind to do,' he finished.

Kitty stared, mouth opening. 'How did you guess?' she said at last. 'Why, if that old nun had hit me bum . . . but she hit me hand. Look.'

She held out a tiny, and by now rather grubby, paw and saw Nick's eyes widen. 'Why, the wicked old bitch,' he said in a low voice. 'Fancy hittin' a little kid like you so hard you bled! I'd like to punch her on her big old snout so I would.'

'Well, I reckon Maeve will tell her off, even if she don't punch her on the nose,' Kitty said complacently. 'And I'm sure she'll tell me never to go to that wicked school again. Why, Caitlin taught Maeve to read and write, so I guess Maeve can teach me . . . if it is really important to learn, that is,' she added. 'And if it isn't important for you why should it be for me?'

But Nick just shrugged; it was clear he did not intend to agree with her that reading and writing might not be as important as their elders claimed, and presently Kitty found a promising stone in the gutter and the two children played kick-ball the rest of the way back to Handkerchief Alley.

Once there, Kitty and Nick hurried up the long flights of stairs and were greeted by a bright-eyed Maeve. She hugged Kitty and began to ask how her day had gone, but Kitty said that Nick would be glad of a buttered scone, or a bun, if Maeve had such a thing by her, but then he would leave so that the two of them could enjoy a good crack about the day's happenings.

'You could ask him to stay . . .' Maeve began, but was quickly shushed.

'I've explained we want to talk, and I've asked him back to tea tomorrow, when he's sold all his papers,' Kitty explained. 'I – I can't talk about school wit' Nick standin' there, all ears.'

So Maeve buttered a bun and a scone and handed them to Nick. 'I don't like to turn you out,' she said awkwardly, 'but Kitty says you understand that she needs to be private, and you're to come to tea tomorrow. Proper tea, not just a bun,' she finished.

The boy grinned and hurried back down the stairs, thanking Maeve at the top of his voice as he careered down the flights, and the two females settled themselves comfortably at the kitchen table with a mug of tea and a buttered scone apiece. Maeve had four of the neighbours' babies in a homemade playpen on the rag rug in front of the fire, though this was banked down as the day was warm, and she gave each of them a piece of hard rusk to chew on, then looked hopefully at Kitty. Her cheeks were very pink and her eyes very bright and Kitty thought she had never seen Maeve looking prettier.

'Well? Start at the beginning and go on to the

end,' Maeve said, her voice husky with excitement. 'You went to your classroom . . . and then what?'

Very slowly, very regretfully, Kitty lowered her left hand into her lap. She wanted to show her poor palm to Maeve, to get it kissed better, to hear Maeve's wrath over the way she had been treated, but she had suddenly realised that she simply could not do it, could not shatter all Maeve's dreams in such a cruel and final way. Maeve had never been to school, but she thought it was a marvellous place, where all the teachers were kind and good, and wanted their pupils to succeed. Kitty knew she had made big sacrifices so that she, Kitty, might learn to read and write, to do sums, to be taught such mysteries as history and geography. If she showed Maeve her hand, explained that she did not mean to go back, then Maeve's heart would break. She looked wistfully down at her bruised and scarlet palm, then straightened her shoulders. She would put up with school – and the hateful Sister Enda – until she could read and write better than anyone else in her class, and then she would tell Maeve that they were all wicked and hateful, that they beat their pupils for no good reason, and Maeve would say . . .

But there was Miss Brogan; she was really nice. And another nun, a young and pretty one, had been friendly to the three little girls when they had taken their carry-out into the yard. And above all, there was Fluffy. Every Monday, if they were good, she and her pals could take him for a walk down to the Liffey! Perhaps school would not be too bad . . . perhaps she could find a way to get round Sister Enda so that the nun no longer itched to beat her. Or I might get Nick to come into school and punch her on the snout, and tell her that he'd do it again if she kept on being mean to me, Kitty dreamed . . . then saw Maeve's anxious eyes on her and began to speak.

'Well, the first thing the teacher did was to chalk up letters on the blackboard, only of course I've already learned me letters so I were a bit ahead of the rest of them . . .'

When Caitlin returned from work it was to find Kitty playing with her pals out in Handkerchief Alley whilst Maeve, pink-cheeked and smiling, was cooking a huge pot of pigs' trotters, onions and potatoes over the fire. Maeve turned and beamed at her as Caitlin entered the kitchen and slung her coat on to its hook.

'Kitty had a grand day, just grand,' Maeve said contentedly. 'I don't mind admittin' I were dreadfully worried, 'cos she's a bright kid and sometimes teachers don't like it when their pupils are a bit ahead of the class, and I don't know anything about St Jo's, though what wit' Clodagh and Grainne both going to Our Lady's I reckon I could answer an examination on how things are done there. But it were all right! She's made two good friends, Jane and Bridget, who both live near here, and the school secretary, a Miss Brogan, let the children take her dog for a walk in their dinner hour. Imagine that, on their very first day! Oh, Cait, all me worries disappeared like mist in summer! You mark my words, she'll be readin' as well as I can meself by Christmas!'

Caitlin agreed that that was just grand, but inwardly she was less sure. One of the women with whom she worked had a child at St Joseph's and Caitlin had heard a number of horror stories about the nun who took the intake class – Sister Enda, wasn't it? But she knew Kitty to be a truthful child and could think of no reason why she should pretend to have had a good day if she had not. In any case, she did not mean to let Maeve see her doubts.

Presently, Maeve picked up the youngest of her charges, took the hand of another and bade the two oldest to hold on to each other firmly and follow her downstairs. Caitlin tutted, shaking her head reprovingly. 'I'll take two down and you bring the others,' she said, 'then you'll be able to use your crutch without clouting anyone. It won't take me but a minute, and then I'll shout my lot in so they can lay the table, mash the tea and carry up water. By the time we've done that, you'll be back and we can eat.' So the two women and four children descended the wobbly, creaking flights of stairs. At the foot, they piled the children into Maeve's trusty handcart – the twins had lost interest in it long ago – and Caitlin walked with her young friend as far as Francis Street. By the time she turned back, she was determined to have a word of her own with Kitty. As usual, boys and girls had separated into two groups, the boys playing kick the can with a tin which had once contained peaches whilst the girls lined up to play piggy beds on the squares which they had marked out in the dirt with a stick. Kitty was almost at the head of the queue, waiting to play, so Caitlin stood back and watched critically. She had been a dab hand at piggy beds as a youngster and thought she could probably do pretty well still, for the game had not changed one iota since her day. The girls were playing with a flattened-out piece of tin whereas Caitlin, a country child, had used the flat-test piece of stone available, but otherwise it was exactly the same. There was a howl from the children as the piece of tin skidded through the dust and landed touching one of the lines. 'You're out, Dilly Morgan, you're out, you're out!' they shouted. 'You're touchin' the line. So you're out.'

Dilly, a fat, untidy girl, wearing a man's cut-down overcoat, seemed resigned to her lot. She picked up the piece of tin and handed it to Kitty, then scuffed, barefoot, across to where another group of girls were skipping with an orange box rope and chanting a rhyme which was as familiar to Caitlin as the piggy bed game had been. Kitty took her time, got the piece of tin into the square she wanted, hopped round it and beamed as she completed the course successfully. 'I goes on to the next round,' she shouted gleefully, then saw

Caitlin and went across to her, her face anxious. 'What's the matter, Auntie Cait?' she asked. 'Where's Maeve?'

'She's taken the kids home. There's nothing the matter; everything's fine. It's just that I could do wit' a bit of a hand. Where's the others?' She had already gathered, from a quick glance round, that neither her daughters nor her sons were present.

'Clodagh's gone to Mrs Maloney's sewing circle, an' so's Grainne,' Kitty said, ticking the children's names off on her fingers. 'They're rolling bandages to send to the soldiers in France, but they'll be home afore it gets dark. The twins went off wit' Mr O'Sullivan to play a proper game of football against St Xavier's boys, and Colm had a penny left from the money you gave him Sat'day, so he and his pal have gone to Thomas Street after an orange.'

Caitlin laughed. 'What a mine of information you are,' she said teasingly. 'Well, if you're the only one around, I'm afraid you'll have to help me with all the chores.' She looked hard at Kitty but could see nothing unusual. 'Tell you what, your legs are younger than mine. If you come upstairs wit' me now and take a bucket down to the tap can you half fill it, just enough for a kettleful, and bring it up again?'

'Sure, I can manage half a bucket,' Kitty said at once. 'And I'll come straight back up and give you a hand wit' the tea. Did you see me win at piggy beds?'

'Yes, I was watching,' Caitlin admitted. 'I've had a better idea, alanna: you go up and fetch the bucket and I'll carry it back full. In fact, bring two buckets; that will balance me better and it'll mean I shan't have to come down again.'

'Oh!' Kitty said, rather blankly. 'Are – are you sure, Auntie Cait? Only two buckets is pretty heavy, you know.'

Caitlin smiled at her. 'And I won't have a hand free to pull on the banister rail, except that there is no banister rail,' she said. 'Don't worry about me, alanna – I've been running up an' down them perishin' stairs ever since Patrick and I moved to Handkerchief Alley, and that's a good few years. Just you run up and fetch me those two buckets – unless you feel two empty buckets is more than you can manage, of course.'

Kitty gave her a very odd look, but before Caitlin could question her she had disappeared into the building. When she re-emerged, Caitlin saw that she was carrying both buckets in one hand; saw also that the buckets were banging painfully against Kitty's thin little legs. However, she said nothing until she had taken the buckets from the child, carried them to the tap at the end of the alley, and begun to fill the first one. Only then did she turn to Kitty. 'Show me your hand,' she said quietly. Kitty hesitated, then held out her right hand. Caitlin shook her head. 'The other one,' she said.

Kitty, after a considerable hesitation, held out

her left hand, breaking into speech as she did so. 'Oh, Auntie Cait, you won't tell Maeve, will you? I didn't do anything wrong, honest to God I didn't, but perishin' old Sister Enda picked on me because I moved me feet out of a – a puddle. And I uses me left hand to hold me slate pencil and – and she says that's the devil's hand an' I mustn't use it or she'll whup me again.'

Caitlin examined the small palm held so trustingly out to her and felt honest fury welling up. 'The wicked old – old nun,' she breathed. 'Why, you're only five years old, and why shouldn't you move your feet out of a puddle, indeed? I'd like to go up to St Joseph's and give her a piece of my mind. And you've not told Maeve, you say? Why not, alanna? Maeve would have been round there first thing, telling the creature what she thought of her.'

'I know. She'd likely make Sister Enda promise never to hit me again,' Kitty said wistfully. 'But I *can't* tell her, Auntie Cait, because she'd be so upset. She's worked ever so hard, teaching me my letters, and 'splaining about numbers, and getting me decent clothes to wear for school. If she knew I were unhappy . . .'

Caitlin pulled the now three-quarter-full bucket out from under the tap and replaced it with the empty one. Then she bent and gave Kitty an impulsive hug. 'You're a good little soul, so you are,' she said. 'Look, alanna, if that woman makes a dead set at you again, you're to tell me, understand?'

She turned the tap off, lifted both buckets and began to walk back towards the house. 'Now, I've had an idea. You said Clodagh and Grainne are rolling bandages for the soldiers in France; well, that's what gave me the idea, actually. If you go along to Mr Farrington, the chemist on Francis Street, and ask him to sell you a piece of bandage – I'll give you a penny – enough to wrap round your hand, then I'll do it up for you. I'll put some butter on your palm first, which will ease the pain, and I reckon your teacher won't be too pleased. You see, it will be a sign that some grown-up person has seen the wounds on your hand and knows how they got there, and that's the last thing Sister Enda will want. I remember my brothers saying that their teachers pulled hair, pulled ears, twisted arms, but very rarely left marks – except when they had a genuine reason for beating a boy, of course.'

'Oh, but what about Maeve? I can't bear her to know,' Kitty said, much distressed. 'She'd want to know at once why I was wearing a bandage.'

'We'll say you fell over playing piggy beds and cut your hand quite deeply, and we'll say I've dressed it very carefully and don't want anyone to take the bandage off because it will heal quicker if left undisturbed. And if sister asks why you're wearing it, say your Auntie Caitlin is afraid infection may set in; can you remember that?'

'Ye-es, but I hope she won't ask me,' Kitty said. 'And I don't think she will, Auntie Cait; I think she'll just ignore it.' She grinned up at Caitlin, her expression suddenly extremely mischievous. 'She's a bully, ain't she? And Maeve says all bullies are cowards at heart. She won't dare to hit me, not while I'm wearing the bandage, so I reckon she'll just pretend I'm not even there.'

By this time, the two of them had reached the big kitchen, and Caitlin reached down her purse from the mantel and handed Kitty a large brown penny. 'Off wit' you,' she said cheerfully. 'And hurry back, 'cos I want that bandage in place before Maeve and the others get home.'

Chapter Nine

Spring 1919

Brendan looked around him as the long column of soldiers in which he marched reached the quayside. It was good to be going home at last, though he would be returning to a country smitten by the terrible influenza epidemic which had decimated both armies since the signing of the Armistice on 11 November.

Brendan had lost many friends over the past few years, but when he climbed aboard the ship which would take him on the first leg of his journey home he was delighted to recognise Patrick O'Keefe amongst a great many other soldiers. Brendan immediately forced his way through the crowd until he was able to clap Pat on the shoulder, and tug out a packet of Woodbines from his pocket. 'Well, by all that's wonderful! We haven't met for four years, despite the fact that I knew your battalion and mine had fought in the same battles,' he said breezily. 'An' now here we are, headin' home, and the first feller I see on the ship is you.' He flipped a cigarette out of the packet and handed it to Patrick. 'Here, hold still while I gets out a lucifer.'

Pat took the cigarette. 'Thanks, Brendan, old

feller,' he said. 'We've run out of baccy – haven't had a smoke for a week.' Then he gestured to the small man beside him. 'Can you spare one for me pal Barry? Only he's as desperate for a fag as I am meself.'

'Sure and he's welcome,' Brendan said easily, for though it was the last cigarette in the packet, he was sure he would be able to buy more as soon as they landed. The man named Barry stuck the cigarette in his mouth, and then grinned as Brendan searched his pocket for matches only to find he had none. He was beginning to apologise, to look round for help, when Barry leaned towards him, striking a match as he did so. He held it first to Brendan's cigarette, then to his own, then turned to Patrick. Even as the match flamed against the cigarette, Brendan said sharply: 'No!' and Pat jerked back his head. But it was too late – the cigarette was burning well.

Barry looked horrified and, for a moment, so did Pat. He had taken the cigarette out of his mouth and was staring at the lit end as though he could not believe his eyes, but then he gave a rueful laugh. 'That superstition was fair enough when bullets were whizzing round your ears and a lighted match gave your position away,' he observed. 'But we're not at war now; as far as I'm concerned you could light a dozen cigarettes from one match, and be none the worse.'

'That's true,' Brendan said, but he said it largely for Barry's sake because the other man was still looking uneasy over what he had done. He turned to Pat. 'Are you going straight back to Ireland? They tell me we'll get a suit of civilian clothing and a bit of money, so I'm staying for that, and then I reckon I'll go back to Liverpool to see Sylvie and my old landlady, but afterwards it's Connemara for me, and no messing.'

'I'm wit' you there,' Pat said. 'Only I'll not be going back to Connemara, not with Caitlin and the kids waiting for me in Handkerchief Alley.' He turned to his friend. 'Where's you going, Barry?'

'The big smoke . . . London town,' Barry said. 'I've a gal there – Betty, her name is. Me an' her mean to marry as soon as we've got ourselves a bit of a room somewhere – I can't wait.' He drew deeply on his cigarette then coughed noisily, thumped himself on the chest, and sucked again on his cigarette. 'Yes, to think I volunteered for this little lot! Well, it's the last time I volunteer for anything; from now on, it's home and family, and I hope to God the dairy have kept me job open, like they promised.' He looked interrogatively at Brendan. 'What do you do, mate? I know old Pat here is in a bank, an' they said they'd keep his job open, but you can never tell.'

'I'm a copper, a bobby – a scuffer, as they call us in Liverpool,' Brendan said. 'But it's too like the army and I've had enough of the army, so I have. I can't see meself walking the beat again, not unless I were desperate. So I'm going back to me daddy's farm and I'll be looking to buy a small place of me own in Connemara. I'd like to be near the sea wit' a little boat so I can fish when the land don't need me,' he added dreamily. 'I'd keep a few hens, a couple of pigs, a donkey to pull the plough . . . I know I'd never make a fortune but at least I wouldn't go hungry. Country folk don't, you know.'

'Except when the potato crop fails,' Pat reminded him. 'That was when my family left their farm and went to Dublin, and I guess it were the worst move they could have made because we ended up in the slums an' it took us forty year to fight our way back to any sort of decent life.'

'Why don't you and your family join me, once I've got settled?' Brendan suggested, though there was a twinkle in his eye. He was pretty sure that nothing would turn Pat from the relative comfort of an office life to the hard work and hardships of a small farm. Besides, there was Caitlin's job to consider. He knew her employers thought highly of her and paid her accordingly. Then there were the children, growing up fast and wanting jobs of their own, which would be easier to find in Dublin than in the wilds of Connemara.

Pat blew a smoke ring and watched it curl hazily upwards. 'If they haven't kept my job for me, mebbe I'll take you up on that offer,' he said idly. 'Aha, we're movin'! Next thing, we'll be seein' the dear old white cliffs of Dover. Eh, I can't wait!'

Sylvie was about to start peeling potatoes when Becky burst in through the back door, but she

253

immediately turned to give her daughter a peck on the cheek and to relieve her of her smart leather satchel, for Becky now attended an expensive private school. 'You're early, queen? But I've got the kettle on and you shall have a nice cuppa in one minute,' Sylvie said, helping her daughter out of her navy blue coat and hanging it on the hook behind the kitchen door. 'Grandma Dugdale is sitting with your father, reading the paper to him whilst he waits for his tea, so if you'd like a snack with your cuppa . . .'

Becky said she would and Sylvie watched affectionately as that young person went over to the pantry and helped herself to a couple of ginger biscuits from the tin. Becky was growing up; she had always been clothes-conscious, but now she was serious about her appearance, spending a great deal of time combing the big department stores in the city centre for exactly the right shade of ribbon to go with a new jersey, or a pair of shoes which had the modern heel but which were not so high as to attract disapproval from her mother. She frequently consulted Sylvie as to what suited her best, and her mother was always delighted to give her opinion and to see Becky becoming a proper little lady, young though she was.

'I'll take his tea in when it's ready,' Becky said, nibbling her biscuit. 'Dad likes ginger biscuits; I'll put a couple on a plate for him.'

'Right,' Sylvie said. 'I'll do a couple of slices of

thin bread and butter for your gran as well, since she says biscuits give her indigestion.'

'I'll fetch the loaf,' Becky said, suiting action to words, and presently she carried a laden tray through from the kitchen into the parlour. A year or so earlier, because Len had improved so much, they had decided that he would be more comfortable if he had a room of his own, though they always left the connecting door open so that they would hear if he called them. He had a small bell by his bed which he could ring at need, for his speech was still uncertain, though it was very much better than it had been. He was still partially paralysed but could now get out of his bed with assistance. Each morning, Bertie or Sylvie helped him to dress, and he sat in a wing chair close to the parlour fire, which was now kept burning winter and summer. He could read a little and enjoyed crossword puzzles, though these had to be the simple ones which some of the newspapers ran for children, and he liked doing jigsaws provided the pieces were large.

Consequently, he had become very much easier to nurse, although, as Brendan had predicted, he had changed, and was no longer the man Sylvie had married. He was gentle, grateful for every small service performed for him, and eager to do as much as he could to help. Not that there was a lot he could do. He had tried peeling potatoes but had cut himself so badly that Sylvie would not let him attempt it again. But he was working his way slowly through his mother's large collection of brasses, polishing them with such enthusiasm that they gleamed like silver. Once, Mrs Dugdale had provided him with a bowl of hot soapy water so that he might wash the Dresden figurines which she kept in the china cabinet, but this had not proved a success and now Mrs Dugdale had a shepherdess without a nose, and a goose girl with only three fingers and no thumb on her tiny hand. Still, you had to give it to Len, Sylvie mused now as she turned back to the sink, still full of potatoes waiting to be peeled: he really did his best, never complained and ate whatever was put in front of him without a murmur.

She had realised a long while back that she was much fonder of him now than she had been when they were first married, and knew that this was at least partly due to her friendship with Sam Trescoe. He had been a wonderful friend to her and Len since that first meeting, calling in every time his ship docked, bringing small presents, recounting stories of shipboard life and telling her and Len of the ports he had visited.

As time passed, Sylvie became aware that her feeling for him was growing warmer and knew that he felt the same, though he never showed his emotions by anything other than the warmth of his glance. Once or twice, when she had been very down, exhausted by the double demands of her work in the factory and the various tasks in the Ferryman, he had given her hand a consoling squeeze. It had become her habit to walk back to his ship with him to wave him off when she sailed, and these were the only occasions when they could discuss their lives, with any sort of freedom. Sam was full of suggestions for helping Len to improve and encouraged Sylvie to give Len all the help and support she could, and somehow this made nursing Len easier to bear because by so doing, she was pleasing Sam.

It was impossible, of course, not to think wistfully of how things might have been had she met Sam a dozen years earlier, for Sylvie now knew that she had never been in love before; knew also that her love for Sam was deep and abiding, the best thing in her life. They had never exchanged a kiss or a hug, had never spoken of their longing for one another, yet her feeling for Sam brightened every aspect of Sylvie's life and, paradoxically, turned nursing Len into a labour of love.

As she began to run water on to the bowl of potatoes, the letter crackled in her pocket and she smiled to herself – in two more days, Sam would be back in port! Presently, she would go into the parlour and tell Len the good news, but now she had best get on with her preparations for the meal.

Brendan's ship docked and the men disembarked. 'We might as well keep together,' Brendan suggested, as the three of them marched towards the temporary camp from which they would be demobbed. He grinned at Pat. 'You'll be wanting to come up to Liverpool so's you can catch a ferry back to Ireland. Isn't that right?'

Pat shook his head and gave an enormous yawn. 'No, man, I'll be catching the boat train from Euston and the ferry from Holyhead. It's quicker if you're headin' for Dublin. But we'll meet up tomorrow for a last crack before we part.' He gave his small companion a nudge. 'But Barry here will leave us as soon as the train draws in to Waterloo.'

'That's right,' his friend agreed, with a cheerful grin. 'Don't you envy me, fellers? I'll be back with me old mum tomorrer an' mekkin' wedding plans wiv' me girlfriend the following day.'

'You won't be so far ahead of me, you know,' Pat pointed out mildly. 'Say they give us our civvies and send us off on the first train, I could still be in Dublin by late tomorrow night.' He yawned again, jaw-crackingly, then turned to Brendan, a slight frown etched between his brows. 'That's odd! When I yawned just now, I sort of saw double . . . two of everything. It only lasted a moment but it was real weird.'

'You must have hid a bottle of French plonk in your kit bag,' Brendan said, grinning. 'Though how you managed to drink it with me and Barry so close, I can't imagine.' They had been marching as they talked and now entered the camp. There were a number of large temporary buildings and tents scattered everywhere across the site and the ground between them was soggy, for it had been raining throughout their voyage and was raining still. 'That looks like the cookhouse, that building over there. Let's get ourselves a meal before we join the queue for signing off.'

They joined the jostling crowd heading for the cookhouse, but had a half-hour's wait in the rain before getting inside and by then Pat said he was no longer hungry. Brendan saw that the other man's face was flushed and thought he had probably caught a cold, for all the men were soaked through. He thought no more of it as he himself finished a hearty meal, bade Pat and Barry a cheerful good night, and made his way to where his division was quartered.

Next morning, he looked for Pat but could not see him, though eventually he ran Barry to earth. 'Me pal's been took to the hospital in Southampton,' Barry said miserably. 'By the time I woke up, he were delirious. Didn't know me from Adam, thought he was back in the trenches, and kept waving his rifle around – before they took it off of him, that is. I meant to catch the first train out of here but now I reckon I'll nip along to the hospital first. You comin'?'

Brendan agreed at once to go and the two men made their way through the dark streets, dodging enormous puddles and turning up the collars of their greatcoats, for there was a raw wind blowing which chilled them to the bone. They arrived at the hospital and asked for Private Patrick O'Keefe and were sent to a waiting room where they sat, uncomfortably, on stiff little wooden chairs, wondering why they had not been allowed to go to the ward where their friend lay.

Presently, they knew. Private Patrick O'Keefe had died at midnight, one of the victims of the killer flu which was sweeping Europe.

Brendan was numbed with shock and pain. On hearing the news, Barry had turned to him, his eyes wide with horror and grief. 'It's my fault,' he had said. 'I lit three cigarettes with the same match and the third man died.' Brendan had tried to rally him, to reassure him that whilst that old soldiers' tale might have been true when the enemy was on the watch for anything that might pinpoint his target's position, it could have no relevance when the killer was a pandemic disease, but Barry had refused to be comforted. Even Brendan, without precisely blaming himself, felt all the guilt of the survivor. Pat had been a good bloke, he thought, admired by his fellow soldiers, liked by his officers. I could have been spared with a few tears, a few regrets, Brendan told himself humbly, but it's different for Pat. Caitlin needs him desperately and so do the children. Oh, his wages were important, of course they were, but Pat himself was even more crucial to their happiness. Good God, he joined up in 1914 because he knew how vital it was to win the war. He was in just about every battle in France and Belgium you could mention. I remember thinking that he and I had had the devil's own luck to get through without a scratch ... but that was before we were both wounded, of course. Pat had a shell splinter dug out of his back after Passchendaele, and I had me collarbone broke by a bullet a few weeks later. But small wounds like that scarcely count, compared with what some fellers went through. And now he's dead and I've got to go back to Ireland and tell Caitlin, because things are in such a state down here that they might not send news of his death for a week or more. And anyway, it'll be easier for her if I'm there.

He had intended going back to Liverpool before setting off for Ireland but the terrible news of Pat's death had changed everything. He would follow the course that Pat himself had meant to follow. He would catch the boat train to Holyhead and the Irish ferry to Dublin. He would make his way to Handkerchief Alley, bracing himself to give Caitlin the dreadful news. He would stay with his cousin as long as she needed him, and then he would make his way back to Connemara. He would visit his parents for a week or so, but then he would have to return to Liverpool, for not only were his savings deposited in one of the city's banks, but he needed to speak to the police authority, though he was pretty sure that he would not again become a beat constable, but would take his chance on the land.

Accordingly, Brendan said a sorrowful farewell to Barry on Waterloo Station and set off on the long, sad journey home. For the first time in his life, he realised as he climbed into the boat train, he was dreading a return to Ireland.

When Brendan boarded the Irish ferry in Holyhead, it was a cold and windy day, and the Irish Sea was covered, as far as the eye could see, with white horses. A good many of the passengers looked apprehensive, for even in the shelter of the harbour the ferry was rocking in an ominous manner, and when they surged out into the open sea she began to bucket and cavort, which sent a good few of the passengers to hang over the rail and lose their breakfasts. Brendan, however, had not gone out in his father's black-tarred sailing boat without getting his sea legs, and now he viewed the sick passengers with pity, but with no desire to join them. Instead, he went below to the almost empty saloon, bought a large cup of coffee and a couple of buns, and settled down to enjoy a good gossip with the elderly bartender. The man hailed from Dublin and knew the Liberties well, though he had moved out from there some years back and now lived on Conyngham Road, with the River Liffey at the end of his garden and Phoenix Park not a stone's throw away. Brendan told him his sad errand and mentioned Handkerchief Alley and the bartender was immediately helpful. 'Sure and don't I know the old place as well as any man alive,' he said genially. 'You'll want to make for Bridgefoot Street, and at the junction turn left into Thomas. Then you turn right into Francis Street. Handkerchief Alley's off

Francis Street; you can't miss it.' He looked curiously at Brendan. 'I wouldn't be after telling you it's a rough area because it's a mix, same as the rest of the Liberties, but it ain't a place to linger in after dark, not if you're a stranger. Have you heard of the gangs? They behave like animals, have pitched battles in the streets, thieve from anyone not known to them, and have killed their man many a time.'

'No, I haven't heard of them. But it ain't likely me cousin Caitlin would talk of such things,' Brendan said. 'I shan't be around there after dark – not if you've give me right directions, that is.'

The other man grinned. 'You won't get lost, not in daylight,' he assured the younger man. 'But I don't envy you having to break such turble news to your cousin. It's not as though she'll be expecting it, since the war's been over for months.'

Brendan nodded. 'That's the worst part,' he admitted. 'Everyone spent the war years braced to get bad news, but it's different now. Caitlin and the kids will be expecting him home any day; in her last letter she said the kids had got out the paper chains they made at Christmas, and one of the little lads had sneaked into Phoenix Park and dug up a bowlful of crocuses. She had made a grand big fruit cake at Christmas, but they didn't eat it because their daddy wasn't at home, so she'd skimmed off the top of it and written *Welcome home, Pat* in pink icing sugar.'

The bartender drew in his breath, then released

it in a long, sibilant whistle. 'I don't envy you,' he said again. 'I t'ink, if I were you, I'd let the aut'orities break the news.' He paused, then shook his grey head, and Brendan saw that his eyes were shiny with tears. 'Poor woman. No, I reckon you're doing the right thing. There's little comfort in a telegram.'

Brendan found Handkerchief Alley without difficulty, for the bartender's directions had been clear and concise, and far sooner than he wished he found himself mounting the stairs of No. 3 tenement and making for the top floor. He rapped on the door, heard a brief flurry from behind it, and then it was snatched open. His cousin Caitlin was almost in his arms before she recognised him, and Brendan realised, with sick dismay, that she had thought he was Pat. As he had suspected, the telegram from the authorities had not yet arrived, might not do so for several days. For a fleeting instant, he wondered once again whether he had done the right thing in deciding to break the news to Caitlin himself. If he had not done so, she could have gone on for a little while longer in happy anticipation of her husband's return. But it would only have been a fool's paradise, and perhaps the truth, when it came, would be easier to bear if he was present to comfort her distress. Now, though, Caitlin was giving him a hug, pulling him into the kitchen, telling him as they entered that she had been expecting Pat for ten days, that he might walk in at any moment, and how glad she was that it was her half day and she was at home when he called. She pushed him into a chair by the fire, and pulled the big blackened kettle over the flame. 'Sit there and warm yourself – you shall have a cup of tay in two minutes and a buttered oatcake, with some of me famous cherry jam on top. I was waiting for Maeve to get back with the messages – Maeve's the girl who helps me round the house and wit' the kids, including Kitty – but the kettle won't take a moment to boil, and everything else is ready.' She began to gather the tea things together, then turned back to Brendan. 'I suppose you've not come across Pat on your travels? I guess you realised I thought you were him when I first opened the door.'

She was gazing at Brendan as she spoke, her eyes alight with pleasant anticipation, her mouth curving into a smile. He cleared his throat and met her eyes squarely. 'I – I saw him in Southampton,' he said haltingly. 'He was – he was . . .'

The words would not come. A lump like a cricket ball blocked his throat. But even as he watched Caitlin's face, he saw the anticipation fade from her eyes as her smile faltered and died. She stared at him for what seemed like hours and he saw all the youth and pleasure drain from her face as the pink left her cheeks and lips, until she looked like a marble effigy, save for the big dark eyes, and the tears which ran from them.

Brendan had expected that Caitlin would want him to remain with her whilst she grew accustomed to the fact that she was now a widow and her children were fatherless, but she did not. 'Sure and I'll be terrible glad if you'll come back when you've visited your parents in Connemara,' she said in a small, formal voice. It was a bare hour since he had arrived in the flat and already Caitlin wanted him gone. He might have been hurt, might have thought the help he offered was being scorned, but Caitlin assured him that this was not the case. 'I need to be alone for a while before the kids come in from school and that,' she explained. 'I've got to tell them, obviously, but first I've got to tell myself. And when will they bring his body back so's he can be buried on Irish soil? They'll send him home, won't they?'

'I'm sure they will, but if they don't, I've got savings . . . I'll do anything I can. Oh, God, Caitlin, I'll do anything to make things easier.'

Caitlin gazed at Brendan and for a moment her lips tightened. He imagined, without rancour, that she must be wishing that it had been he, a single man, who had died, but then her gaze softened once more and he saw that she had been merely fighting back tears, though she had cried a river when he had first broken the news. 'I've got savings, too, but I probably won't need to touch them,' she said tightly. 'You've never lived in the Liberties, Bren, so I'm telling you, these people have no money but they've got the biggest hearts in the world, and they stick together. As soon as they know Pat's gone . . .' her voice wavered for a moment, 'they'll start a collection, and believe me, there'll be enough money in it, even if we have to give up the thought of a wake.'

'But I'd like to help,' Brendan said awkwardly. 'I've always been mortal fond of yourself, Caitlin. Don't deny me a chance to give you a bit of a hand.'

Caitlin, however, shook her head firmly. 'If I need help, it's to yourself I'll turn, I swear it,' she said quietly. 'One thing you can do for me, though: you can tell that Sylvie of yours that she'd best take young Kitty back, because I'll have enough to do wit' keeping me own kids fed and clothed, and I'll need Maeve to help me as much as she can. To own the truth, Brendan, Maeve spends all her time lookin' after Kitty, an' all her earnings go on the child as well, and it won't do, not now I'm widowed and alone.'

Brendan stared at her, feeling helpless. He could not possibly expect Sylvie to take the child. If she had been thirteen or fourteen, she could have been introduced into the Ferryman as a young relative of his own who needed a job and would work hard for very small wages. But with a child of almost eight this was simply not practicable. Still, it was clearly useless to say anything of the sort to Caitlin in her present mood, so he just nodded.

Caitlin, however, continued to muse aloud. 'Now that Pat has gone, everything will have to change,' she said slowly. 'I could put Kitty in an orphanage, I suppose – at least they'd clothe and feed the kid, which is more than I'm going to be able to afford to do. I know you think the sun shines out of Sylvie, Brendan, but you've never had to live with her. She was real selfish, honest to God she was. I don't see why she shouldn't shoulder responsibility for Kitty.' Caitlin turned sharply to the door, which was not quite closed. 'What was that? Did you hear something?'

'No, I can't say I did,' Brendan said, rather stiffly. 'But you know very well Sylvie can't acknowledge Kitty while her husband is alive. He's a very sick man and it would break his heart if he believed Sylvie had played fast and loose while he was in prison. Look, the last thing I want is to reproach you, because you've done marvels for Kitty, but Sylvie made it plain right from the start that she wanted the child adopted. I know she did because she told me so, and Sylvie is no liar.'

Caitlin sniffed and dabbed at her eyes with the corner of her apron. 'I guess you're right,' she said wearily. 'I suppose I'm hitting out, trying to hurt someone else the way I've been hurt. Anyway, if I tried to send Kitty away, then Maeve would leave, that's certain. She thinks of Kitty as her own child and I can't say I blame her since she's brought Kitty up from birth. You've not seen her yet, have you? You'll be pleasantly surprised when you do, for though she only goes to St Joseph's school she's at least as bright as any of my kids were at her age.'

Brendan got to his feet. 'Look, if I'm to catch a train to Connemara which will get me home before dark, then I'll have to leave now,' he told her. 'The t'ing is, I'm happy to stay if it will help, but if it won't, I'd sooner go now than in a couple of hours. No point in getting lodgings just for one night, if you don't need me. But as I said, I'll spend a week or so wit' my parents, so if you need me you can send a telegram and I'll be back before you can say knife.' He took a note from his pocket and placed it on the kitchen table. 'Now don't start making a fuss. That money's to pay for the telegram if you need to get in touch,' he said firmly. 'If you don't, I'll come in again on me way back to the ferry, all right?'

Caitlin nodded. 'All right, and thank you for everything, Brendan,' she said in a small husky voice. 'I think you were very brave to bring me the awful news, and you've been ever so kind and understanding, the same as you always were. As for all the nasty things I said about Sylvie, please forget them. I'm – I'm not meself, an' shan't be, mebbe for days. You see, I've kept me guard up all through, waitin' for bad news, preparing myself to hear the worst. And then, when the Armistice was signed, I relaxed. I thought Pat was safe, that it was simply a matter of time before he walked through that door. So it was all the harder to face up to your news, and I reckon I let meself down.'

'You did nothing of the sort; you were bloody wonderful,' Brendan said warmly. 'Don't forget, now, that I'll always be here for you, even if we're separated by the whole width of Ireland.' He had stood his kit bag down on the kitchen floor, and hung up his coat and hat, but now he began to struggle into his outer garments. 'I must hurry or I'll miss the train. Are you sure now that you want me to leave?'

Caitlin nodded her head and ushered him to the door. 'It's sorry I am that it looks as if I'm pushin' you out,' she said as they reached the top of the stairs. 'I'm not ungrateful, Bren, an' I'll probably be glad of you later, but right now I need to be alone.'

'I understand, and I'm not hurt,' Brendan said, with false cheerfulness. 'I'll be seeing you.' He clattered down the stairs and was about to cross the hallway when a small figure entered in rather a rush. They almost collided; he put out a hand to steady her, for it was a girl, and saw that she was heavily burdened with a large marketing bag and that she walked with the aid of a small crutch, though she wielded the latter so efficiently that she did not seem lame when she approached.

Vaguely, he remembered something Sylvie had told him concerning a child with a crutch, but this was no child. She was a young woman, probably seventeen or eighteen, though she was so slight she might have been older. He was still trying to puzzle out just who she was when she whisked past him without so much as a glance, and began to climb the stairs. 'Hey, missus!' he called, rather affronted to realise she had not even noticed him. 'Let me give you a hand with that bag; it looks heavy.'

She continued to mount the stairs but half turned to look at him over her shoulder, giving him a mischievous smile as she did so. 'Don't you be troubling yourself, I'm not a cripple! I'm fit as a flea so I am, and more used to climbing stairs than a grand big feller like yourself,' she said airily. 'But t'anks for offerin'.' And with that she disappeared round the first landing.

Brendan bristled; so she wasn't a cripple? Then why did she have a bleedin' crutch? Cheeky young varmint. You'd think a girl with a lame foot would be grateful for any help she could get, but not she! Oh no, she's too proud to accept an offer of assistance. Someone should teach her a lesson, but it won't be me since I've better things to do than to bandy words with a kid of her age. Brendan went out into the alley.

Halfway to the station, he realised he had still not seen Kitty, but that was no longer important. She would doubtless be there when he returned. And he had done what he had set out to do; the fact that Caitlin had more or less dismissed him, and his proffered help, was hard to accept, but it was her wish and he must abide by it.

By the time he climbed aboard the train his thoughts had taken a new turn, and as the carriage travelled through the lush Irish countryside he began to look, with more than a passing interest, at the little farms and smallholdings he could see through the grimy window. Now he must begin to look for somewhere which would suit him.

Chapter Ten

Kitty had never mitched off school in her life and she was not mitching off school now, since she had a legitimate excuse for being out on the street instead of in her classroom. Since starting school she had worked as hard as she possibly could and had actually gone up a class at the end of her second year, happily leaving the hateful Sister Enda behind. Now she was a pupil of Sister Jeremiah, whose dreadful name was belied by her nature, which was sunny, helpful and under-standing, and this was the reason why Kitty was making her way to the Iveagh Market when she should, by rights, have been in school for another hour. But Sister Jeremiah trusted her and had given her a sum of money in a small purse, and told her to go along to the market and to explain to Mrs Fish, a large red-faced woman with a squint, that Sister Jeremiah wanted material which she could make into painting smocks. Painting was an activity previously unknown to any of the children, but a benefactor, a rich woman who had been educated at St Joseph's many years before, had presented Sister Jeremiah with six large pots of powder paint, a great many brushes and a quantity of beautiful cream-coloured paper. In the accompanying letter, which Sister had read them, she had told how she had won a prize, whilst at St Joseph's, for an essay about the River Liffey. The prize had been a tiny paint box and a small pad of paper and she truly believed that this was what had started her off on her career as a water-colourist. Now she made a great deal of money by selling her paintings, and she wanted other children to know the pleasures of creating a beautiful picture, even if they never became artists like herself.

She had sent her gift to Sister Jeremiah because she must have guessed that Sister Enda would simply have locked the stuff away and forgotten all about it. And Kitty was thoroughly glad that she had done so, for only the previous day, Sister Jeremiah had found up some bits of broken pottery from somewhere. She had carefully spooned a little powder paint on to each fragment, had mixed it with water to the right consistency, and had then told the children to use one colour at a time, and to wash their brushes, between colours, in the jam jar of water she had provided.

Unfortunately, the children's enthusiasm and lack of previous experience had led them to scatter paint everywhere, including over their clothing, and though many of the garments they wore were old and shabby they were not improved by daub-ings of paint, so Sister Jeremiah had decided to have smocks made for them out of any cheap, second-hand material available. Accordingly, she had sent Kitty off on her errand, which included taking the material to an old friend of the sister's who lived on Dame Street, and was a noted needlewoman. 'She's got a sewing machine,' Sister Jeremiah had said proudly. 'A wonderful, modern one! She was one of my pupils and is always eager to help, so if you explain that we want as many painting smocks as she can make out of the material you will give her, then I dare say they'll be ready for collection in a week.' She had glanced, speculatively, at Kitty's eager face. 'Your home is quite near Francis Street, isn't it? Then once you've left the material in Dame Street, you might as well go straight home.' This had been an unexpected treat but typical of Sister Jeremiah's thoughtfulness and Kitty had thanked her from the bottom of her heart.

Now, she was heading for Handkerchief Alley, having concluded her mission successfully. She knew it was Auntie Cait's half day and hurried up the stairs, knowing that for once the kitchen would not contain any other schoolchildren. Because she was early and the day was chilly, she would sit by the fire whilst explaining to Auntie Cait and Maeve all about her errand, and toast slices of bread. It would be lovely; a little treat, for hot buttered toast was a rarity when all the children were home.

Kitty went as quickly as she could up the long flights of creaking stairs, but halfway up the last flight she heard voices and one of them was the voice of a stranger. Startled, Kitty stopped half a dozen steps from the top landing and glanced upwards. The kitchen door was ajar but now she could make out a man's voice. For one glorious moment, she thought it must be Uncle Pat, and actually retreated a step since she had no wish to barge in on a reunion such as she knew Pat and Caitlin would enjoy. Then she heard her Auntie Cait's voice, raised and angry, and realised that whoever the man was, he could not possibly be Uncle Pat. She crept up a couple more stairs, listening intently, and heard her own name. Auntie Cait was speaking more quietly now and her words brought a cold, shrinking feeling to Kitty's heart. '. . . you can tell that Sylvie of yours that she'd best take young Kitty back, because I'll have enough to do wit' keeping me own kids fed and clothed, and I'll need Maeve to help me as much as she can. To own the truth, Brendan, Maeve spends all her time lookin' after Kitty, an' all her earnings go on the child as well, and it won't do.'

For a moment, Kitty felt so cold and alone that her head whirled. She knew that her real mother's name was Sylvie, that Brendan was the name of the man who had sent her mother to Caitlin in the first place, but other than that Caitlin's words did not seem to make sense. Or rather, they made a horrible sort of sense, the sense that she was a nuisance, unwanted . . . but why? She had not been a nuisance yesterday . . .

But her aunt was still speaking. Kitty crept a

little further up the stairs and this time the words came far too clearly for Kitty to misunderstand them. 'Now that Pat has gone, everything will have to change,' her aunt said slowly.

Uncle Pat was dead! Kitty felt tears form in her eyes and begin to trickle down her cheeks, and she clung to the stair in front whilst she fought a terrible feeling of nausea. Then Caitlin was speaking again, and at the sound of her own name Kitty simply had to listen once more.

'I could put Kitty in an orphanage, I suppose – at least they'd clothe and feed the kid, which is more than I'm going to be able to afford to do . . .'

But Kitty could bear to hear no more. She turned and stumbled down the stairs, trying to go quietly, though without really caring whether she was heard or not. She shot out of the door and into the alley, then rushed round the back of the tenement building, knelt on the cold hard ground and vomited violently and painfully. Then, as if by instinct, she made for the bustle of Francis Street, wanting to lose herself in the crowds whilst she thought about what she had heard. As she stumbled along the pavement, she told herself that Caitlin had rejected her not from a lack of love but because, as the overheard conversation had made clear, she had lost her beloved husband and thought she could no longer manage. For the first time, Kitty became aware that she was a burden. She only had to look down at herself to realise that Caitlin had spoken no more than the truth: Maeve spent all the money she earned on seeing that Kitty was as well dressed as any child who attended Our Lady's school, and a good deal better dressed than anyone else at St Joseph's. Many a time Maeve had looked proudly at Kitty, saying as she did so: 'You're a credit to me, so you are. Now don't forget to change as soon as you come back from school, 'cos you wouldn't want to spoil your nice t'ings, would you?'

Kitty had thought she would be able to think more clearly among the scurrying crowds, but now she found the people a distraction. She needed peace and quiet to think out what she should best do, so she turned her footsteps towards Phoenix Park. The one thing that she most dreaded had been threatened. An orphanage! There was an orphanage in the Liberties, probably more than one, and Kitty had seen the children occasionally as they were marched through the streets, and had been horrified by the dullness of their eyes and the air of weary hopelessness which seemed to emanate from them. Yet she could understand how Auntie Cait felt, for without her beloved husband things would be hard indeed. As for returning Kitty to her mother, how could she possibly do so? If her mother had wanted her, she could have sent for her any time, but she had never so much as written a line to her small daughter; Kitty had heard Clodagh and Grainne discussing Sylvie, and Clodagh had made that very remark. Kitty had thought it unimportant at the time, but now she realised its significance. Her mammy did not want her. Maeve occasionally talked about the woman called Sylvie; she had told Kitty that her mother was very beautiful, very elegant, a real lady. But once Auntie Cait had overheard her and had snorted, saying that though Sylvie was indeed pretty as a picture, she was also selfish and idle. Maeve had waited until Auntie Cait had left the room and had then told Kitty, so softly that only she could hear, that this was not true. 'While your mammy was in Dublin, she took work in a laundry, which was real hard,' she said earnestly. 'Auntie Cait didn't mean what she said. She – she's a bit upset because money's a bit short this week.'

Nevertheless, Kitty thought that being returned to her mother would be as bad as being sent to an orphanage, and she knew that poor Maeve would do anything to save her from either fate. Maeve was so good! But how could she expect Maeve to do even more for her than she had already done? Maeve was lame and could not hold down a proper job, nor earn proper money.

Hurrying along the pavement, she turned her thoughts to a possible solution of the problem: she could run away! Maeve had passed her love of books on to her adopted child and Kitty read anything she could lay her hands on. Many of the stories told of children, oppressed by adults, who had run away and made everything right by so doing. But where would I run to, Kitty thought, rather pathetically. I certainly don't mean to go to

279

England, but perhaps I could make my way into the country and find someone who wanted a little girl of their own, someone who could afford to look after me. This seemed so unlikely, however, that she was on the verge of giving up the idea when she saw a familiar figure mooching along the pavement in front of her. Immediately, she began to feel almost cheerful, for it was her old friend, Nick Mooney, and Kitty did not doubt that he would advise her. Joyfully, she called his name.

Nick turned and came back towards her, a grin spreading across his dirty face. 'Hello, kid. Why you ain't you in school?' he asked, as soon as he was near enough. 'Don't say little Goody-Two-Shoes is mitching off? Sure, and I never would have thought it!'

Kitty opened her mouth to explain, and felt tears rush to her eyes. She turned her head sharply, ashamed, for it was a well-known fact that Nick despised weakness and she did not wish to annoy him. However, it seemed that he was in a generous mood for he put his arm round her shoulders and gave her a gentle squeeze. 'What's up, alanna?' he said. 'Why's you cryin'? Don't say that old devil of a nun has started beating you again?'

'N-no, it's much worse than that,' Kitty said, her voice breaking. 'A man came – his name's Brendan – to tell Auntie Cait that Uncle Pat's dead.'

'That's awful sad,' Nick said. 'I liked your Uncle Pat; he were a grand feller. Is there anything I can do? To help your family, I mean?'

'I don't know,' Kitty said. She felt deeply ashamed. She had loved Uncle Pat dearly, as indeed she loved Auntie Cait, but the truth was, her own predicament had chased her sorrow out of her mind. She looked hard at Nick. He was her best friend, and despite being older had always stood by her, sharing her sorrows and joys. Since the day he had met her out of school, after the nun had whipped her hand until it bled, they had been good friends. Kitty often saved some of her carry-out for Nick and he liked nothing better on winter evenings than to go home with her after school and share the high tea Auntie Cait provided. Then they would all sit round the fire in the kitchen doing homework, playing games or telling stories, until it was time for him to make his way home. Kitty knew that quite often, when he got home, Nick would be greeted by a flood of abuse from his short-tempered mother or by physical violence from his drunken father, and then Nick would join the other young vagrants sleeping in the entrance lobby or on the landings of one of the tenement houses. Not much of a life, but still infinitely preferable, Kitty thought, to living in an orphanage, or to being sent far away to a foreign country to live with a woman who did not want you. 'Nick, can I tell you a big secret? It's a really, really big secret, so you'll have to promise not to tell.'

'Cross me heart an' hope to die,' Nick said immediately, drawing one finger across his throat in the time-honoured fashion. 'Not that you need to ask me, 'cos I've never split on a friend, and I don't mean to begin with you,' he added, a trifle reproachfully. 'What's this big secret then?'

'I'm going to Phoenix Park . . .' Kitty began, and was interrupted by a shout of amusement from her companion.

'Sure and if that's your big secret, I don't know why you're worried I might tell,' he said, grinning. 'I'm going to Phoenix Park meself!'

Despite her misery, Kitty giggled. She was very glad she had run into Nick, for even though her troubles still loomed large she felt more cheerful, certain that he would help her. 'Idiot! What I meant to say was that I'd tell you when we reached Phoenix Park,' she explained. 'There's rather a lot to tell, you see, but there's nice places to sit in the park and not nearly as many folk around.'

Nick acknowledged the truth of this, and neither child spoke again until they were settled on a bench in a little arbour with a stretch of grass before them, and a stout beech hedge at their backs. Kitty plunged into her story halfway through, but Nick stopped her short by clapping a grimy hand over her mouth. 'Start at the beginning with why you aren't in school and go on until you reach the bit where you caught me up,' he said firmly. 'You say you want me to tell you what you should do; well I can't do that unless I know the whole story.'

As soon as she began to marshal her thoughts,

Kitty realised how clever and sensible her companion was. Simply by going carefully through the events of the day, she grew calmer and was able to explain what she had overheard without starting to cry once more. Indeed, her situation actually seemed less desperate when put into words. She still felt rather ashamed of the fact that Pat's death had seemed less important than her own plight, but Nick told her that this was perfectly understandable. 'There's nothing you can do about your uncle's death, 'cos it's happened,' he assured her. 'But what you're afraid of hasn't happened yet. Are you certain Caitlin meant it? She's ever so nice, your auntie; surely she wouldn't just turn you out?'

'No, of course she wouldn't,' Kitty said, rather impatiently. 'I *told* you, Nick, that she'd either put me in an orphanage, or send me back to my real mammy, who lives far across the sea, in England. The t'ing is, she don't want me.'

'What makes you say that?' Nick asked. 'You're a nice little thing, so you are, and you're useful. Oh, I know you're still in school, but you could mitch off like I does, so's you could run her messages, help in the house and that. I agree wit' you that an orphanage would be real terrible, but if your mammy's a nice lady . . .'

'If she were a nice lady, would she have left me here as a burden on me Auntie Cait?' Kitty asked wildly. 'She could have took me to live wit' her any time.'

Nick nodded reluctantly. 'Right, then you can't go back to your mammy,' he agreed. 'And there's no way you can go into one of them bleedin' orphanages. I wish I could say you could come home wit' me . . .'

'It's all right, Nick; just talking to you has cleared me mind something wonderful,' Kitty said. She stood up, dusting down her skirt automatically as she did so. 'I'm going to run away. It's the only thing left to do, isn't it? Only will you do one thing for me: will you go round to Handkerchief Alley and let Maeve know that I've gone and tell her not to worry?'

'No I will not!' Nick said, looking horrified. 'D'you think I'd let you run away all by yourself? A kid of your age? I'm coming wit' you. It's not as though I shall be missed,' he added bitterly. 'My mam and daddy would give three cheers and help me on my way wit' a kick on me backside.' He, too, rose to his feet, and took Kitty's hand in his. 'Summer's coming; we'll live off the land, help the farmers in the fields, earn ourselves a bed for the night, or snuggle up in a haystack,' he said enthusiastically, and Kitty saw that his eyes were shining at the prospect. 'As for your Maeve, you can write her a note, an' I'll deliver it.'

Kitty squeezed Nick's hand. The prospect of running away, alone, had been terrifying, for she knew herself to be ignorant of real life, having lived such a sheltered existence. But Nick had been fending for himself for years; she doubted whether he ate more than one or two meals at home in a week. She knew that he not only cadged, but also stole, and knew, too, that for Nick there was no alternative. If he did not steal, he did not eat, and if one did not eat, one starved. The O'Keefe family knew that it was wrong to steal, but to the Mooney family it was a way of life. Mr Mooney stole from the docks, though no docker ever really considered they were stealing; it was thought to be a perk of the job. Mrs Mooney worked as a cleaner and stole from her employers, and the kids . . . well, they too had to eat. Kitty remembered Uncle Pat, home on furlough, saying that the poorest kids in the Liberties would steal anything that wasn't nailed down. And though he had said it jokingly, Auntie Cait had told him off, reminded him how the war had forced up the cost of living without also raising wages, and Uncle Pat had looked sad and said she had made him eat his own words; a phrase which had had Kitty in fits of laughter, because if there was one thing she did know, it was that words would make a pretty poor meal.

'You are good, Nick,' she said gratefully now. 'I was ever so frightened at the thought of going off by myself, but with you along as well it will be grand, a proper adventure. Only . . . how can I write a note? I've got no pencil nor no paper. And we've got no money, either.'

Nick laughed. 'We've got to go back into the Liberties to deliver the note, so we'll nip down Francis Street. The stalls will still be there, so I'll borrow a pencil and a scrap of paper off one of the stallholders; that's no problem. And if we hang around till they begin to pack up, we'll likely get give some bruised fruit, mebbe even a tatty or two.'

Kitty frowned. 'But Nick, I can't eat raw potatoes, even if you can. And I don't want to be cotched by Clodagh or Maeve or someone. I thought *you* was goin' to deliver the note, not me.'

'So I am,' Nick assured her. 'But I can't write the note, can I? Your mam . . . I mean your auntie would know it weren't your writin' at once, let alone your spelling, 'cos mine's chronical bad, I'm tellin' you.'

Kitty giggled. She could well imagine what Nick's writing must be like, since he could only read with difficulty. 'All right, I'll come along to the market and write the note,' she agreed. 'Only then I really must hide somewhere, Nick. You know how it is – whenever you want not to be seen, you run slap bang into your best friend, your worst enemy, and the feller next door. I've heard Maeve say so, many a time, when she's in a hurry to get the messages done.'

Nick looked at her measuringly. 'You're difficult to miss with them clean clothes an' all, and your hair tidily plaited,' he agreed. 'We'll have to change all that afore we take to the road, else we'll be picked up within five minutes.'

Kitty looked rueful. 'I know what you mean about me clothes. Don't get me wrong, I've always been grateful to Maeve for the trouble she takes and the money she spends seein' I look respectable, but it makes me stand out and that's the last thing anyone wants really, not just when you're running away, but in school even, or when you're playing out.'

'Yes,' Nick said, giving her his broadest grin. 'Only wit' me it's the opposite way round, so it is. I get picked out 'cos I'm the filthiest kid for miles. Still, there you are, it's something we can both of us change. I've not bothered much about me appearance 'cos it hasn't mattered up to now, but if we really are goin' to run off we want to blend in wit' each other, so I'll clean up a bit and you can get muckier.'

'All right,' Kitty said. Like most children, she had no objection to a bit of dirt, but she did not fully understand how her pal could clean himself up. He was wearing a ragged jumper full of holes and an equally ragged pair of trousers. Kitty did not see how such garments could possibly be improved and said so, causing her companion to give a snort of amusement.

'You're a dafty, so you are,' Nick said derisively. 'Haven't you ever heard of washing lines?'

Now it was Kitty's turn to snort. 'Oh, I'm sure you'd look ever so smart dressed in a washing line,' she retorted. 'What'll you do wit' it? If you take off all your clothes and put the washing line on, do you think you'll be like that king in the story books, the one who bought invisible clothes off of the swindler, and walked down the street in his birthday suit?'

Nick gave a growl of pretended annoyance and leapt on her, and for a moment the two of them rolled around on the grass, giggling and exchanging half-hearted punches. Then Nick fended her off, got to his feet and pulled her to hers. He was still grinning. 'Trust a girl to miss the whole point,' he commented. 'Washing lines have clothes pegged to 'em? Right?'

'Right, I suppose,' Kitty said. She was brushing twigs and dust off her skirt, thinking as she did so that she already looked a good deal less tidy than she had done five minutes earlier. 'Wet clothes, I suppose you mean?'

'Not necessarily,' Nick said. 'But it don't matter if they're wet or dry, really. The thing is, there's always the odd careless housewife about what forgets to take her washin' in. When I feel the need for a change of clobber I goes out in the dusk, quiet like, walkin' round the tenement blocks, till I find a line wit' washin' on it. I don't want good stuff, nor nothin' that stands out, I just find a decent enough shirt and trousers, and an old jumper, with only the odd hole.'

Kitty looked thoughtfully at her companion. This was definitely stealing and would, she knew, have been frowned upon by both Maeve and Caitlin, especially since they had suffered losses from their own clothes line once or twice. By now, they were walking along the crowded pavements once more, so she slid a cautious look around her before saying softly, in Nick's ear: 'But the tenements is full of poor folk what can't afford to lose such t'ings. An' you say you take clothes wit' holes, so that's robbin' the poor, isn't it?'

Nick pulled a face. 'I never take all me clobber off the same line if I can help it,' he said right-eously. 'So put that in your pipe an' smoke it, Miss Goody-Two-Shoes, and if we're goin' on the road together, you'll soon have to learn that folk don't give much away to a couple o' hungry kids. Of course, we'll earn whenever we can, but often it'll be take what isn't yours or go hungry.' He pulled Kitty to a halt and swung her round to face him, looking extremely serious. 'Do you understand that, Kitty? Once we're on the road, it's every man for hisself, and if you don't like it, say so now an' go home to your Maeve wit' no harm done.'

He sounded so grave that Kitty was frightened. She had quite made up her mind to leave the city before Caitlin could incarcerate her in an orphanage, or send her back to her mother, but Nick's words had impressed her. Alone, she would never have the courage to rob so much as a fruit barrow, let alone a washing line. With Nick beside her, she would dare anything. She assured Nick, eloquently, that she understood what he meant and agreed with everything he said. And indeed, by the time they reached Francis Street, they had decided that she, too, should take appropriate clothing from a washing line. She did not add that she meant to leave her own nice clothes in the place of those she had taken. After all, she reasoned, no one could turn from a good little girl into a robber overnight; doubtless wickedness would grow on her.

Despite Kitty's fears, they saw no one they knew amongst the jostling crowds round the stalls in Francis Street. In an effort to disguise herself a bit, Kitty had unplaited her hair and combed it through with her fingers until it hung forward over her face in draggly witch locks. She had then had the brainwave of buttoning her grey cardigan on the wrong buttons, so that it looked bunched up and peculiar, and she had rolled up her sleeves and hitched up her skirt on one side, though she had refused to take off her shoes and stockings, despite Nick's urgings. 'Me legs is as white as peeled celery sticks, and me feet's the same, so everyone will guess I isn't used to goin' barefoot. And besides, me feet are so tender I'll be hobbling like an old woman,' she said pathetically. 'Honest to God, Nick, it wouldn't do.'

Nick had shrugged but said he understood and presently they arrived at a large, well-laden stall selling all sorts of delicious-looking fruit. There was a fat red-faced man, without one hair on his head, serving the customers, many of whom were buying a quantity of goods, for his prices were all a penny or two cheaper than those on surrounding stalls. Nick waited patiently until there was a lull, and then stepped forward. 'Mr Marriott, give us a lend of your pencil and a bit of paper for five minutes, will you?' he bawled.

'Me cousin here is after gettin' a load of messages for her gran and we wants to write 'em down afore we forgets 'em.'

Mr Marriott turned to the back of the stall and picked up a large sheet of paper which had been covering a box full of rosy apples. He handed the paper and a pencil to Nick, and the two children moved into an adjacent doorway. Kitty saw Mr Marriott's gaze following them and muttered apprehensively to Nick that she thought they had been rumbled, but after flicking a quick glance behind them, Nick shook his head. 'No, he's watchin' his bleedin' pencil,' he explained. 'There's kids what'll nick anything and though he knows me better'n most . . . well, pencils cost money. Now stop imagining things and get on, do, or I'll be delivering your message at midnight, when the hue and cry is already up and your family's frantic.'

So Kitty settled down to write her note, which speedily became quite a long letter as she strove to assure the O'Keefes and Maeve that she had gone for their sakes, would be perfectly safe and quite all right, and would never forget their kindness to her.

Nick watched with awe as Kitty, crouching in the dusty shop doorway, wrote line after line, almost covering the paper by the time she had signed off and handed it to him. He folded it into a four-inch square and shoved it into his pocket. By now, darkness had fallen, and as he gave the pencil back to Mr Marriott he suggested that she might as well accompany him to Handkerchief Alley, since he had no desire to lose her yet did not think it advisable for her to hang around in one spot. Mr Marriott, who had not appeared to be listening, turned to the apple box behind him and picked out two very nice fruits, handing one to each of the children. 'Little missy here looks as though she could go gentle with me apples and pears. I'm going to start putting the fruit back into its boxes any minute now, so if you want to go off on your errand, she can give me a hand and I'll keep an eye on her,' he said jovially. 'If she's careful an' gentle, like, wit' me fruit, she shall have an orange or two as well.'

Kitty looked a little doubtfully at Nick but he was nodding enthusiastically and Kitty saw his eyes examining the oranges, and guessed he was choosing the two largest, in case he should be invited to pick his own. 'Thanks, Mr Marriott. She's a real good kid. She won't bruise your fruit, an' I'll be back afore you can say knife,' he said, and before Kitty could put in a word he had vanished into the crowd.

By the time he got back, Kitty and Mr Marriott were chatting like old friends. Kitty, emboldened by Nick's story, had invented a large family living several streets away from Handkerchief Alley. It was her grandma, she had explained glibly, who lived in the alley, and she had reeled off a list of messages half a mile long. Nick had taken the list she had written round to her gran's to make sure she had left nothing out. Mr Marriott, for his part, had talked about his customers, his fruit, which he said was the best anywhere in Dublin, and his friendship with Nick. This had come about because the boy had taken to appearing late on a Saturday night to help him dismantle his stall, and they had become so friendly that Mr Marriott had asked his wife, 'a generous critter, so she was', to pack up a bit of new bread, a good slice of cold bacon, and a couple of pickled onions for his young helper.

Kitty was about to expand on her own usefulness, for as they talked she had been gently transferring the piled-up fruit on the stall to the boxes which Mr Marriott had indicated, when Nick reappeared. 'It's all right, alanna, you hadn't misremembered,' he said breathlessly. 'Now we'd best get on or the shops will be closed before we're through.'

When they left the bustle of Francis Street behind them, Kitty demanded to know just what had transpired in Handkerchief Alley. 'Nothin',' Nick said, sounding surprised. 'I went up them stairs like a bleedin' ghost – good thing I know the creaking ones off by heart by now – and shoved the paper under the door. I could hear voices, but they weren't angry or frightened, they were just chattin'. Then I made off down the stairs, still quiet like, and come straight back here.'

'I expect they think I've gone round to a friend's

place,' Kitty said, trying not to show the disappointment she felt. She was *never* this late; if they truly loved her, surely they would have grown anxious by now. Maeve had always stressed that she must let them know if she intended to visit a friend. But then she remembered the terrible news of Uncle Pat's death and thought that that probably explained it. They would be so busy deciding on details for the funeral and the wake which would follow it that they might not even notice she had not come in at her usual time. She turned to Nick, eager to ask what he thought, but he was already speaking.

'. . . so we'll go straight round to Handkerchief Alley, because there's a line of washing, looking awful droopy, behind the first tenement block,' he said. 'Is that all right by you?'

'No, it is not,' Kitty said indignantly. What on earth was Nick thinking of, planning to rob a washing line so close to her home? 'For one thing, the moment they open that note I reckon they'll come flying out to see if they can find me. And for another, when the neighbours start asking questions about who robbed their washing line, they'll think it's me.'

Nick started to speak, then stopped short, gazing thoughtfully at Kitty. 'That's an idea,' he said, though Kitty was very certain that she had said nothing to give him any sort of idea. 'And you're right, of course, there's no sense in hanging round here any longer. We'll leg it for the Coombe, or even to Marrowbone Lane; is that sufficiently far for Miss Goody-Two-Shoes?'

Kitty punched him. 'Don't call me that,' she said, trying to sound severe but failing dismally. 'And what's this bright idea that I give you, eh?'

Half an hour later, she knew. Nick had taken the clothing he wanted from various lines and had shoved three garments at her. There was a blue shirt with no collar or cuffs, and precious few buttons; a man's much washed V-necked pullover, which had shrunk until it more or less fitted Kitty; and a pair of quite decent trousers, though they were much darned and patched. Kitty had donned the first two in the dirty little yard of the tenement from which Nick had taken the clothing, but now she brandished the trousers, giving a scornful sniff. 'You are an idiot, Nick,' she whispered. 'There were a long skirt on the next line; did you think you'd got that?'

'No I didn't; put 'em on,' Nick said briefly, and as soon as Kitty, much mystified, had obeyed, he got out his old pocket knife, which had a minute pair of scissors folded in the back, and proceeded to chop at her hair, strand by strand, saying as she protested: 'Sure and isn't this the best disguise you could hope for? If anyone twigs that we've both run off, they'll be lookin' for a girl and a feller, not two lads. What's more, when we've made ourselves a few pennies doing odd jobs, we'll buy you an old cap. It'll keep the rain off and you'll look completely different. Isn't that what you want?'

Kitty sniffed and knuckled the tears from her eyes, for the cutting of her hair had been a painful business, but she was quick to realise that Nick was absolutely right. No one, not even her darling Maeve, would look twice at a scrawny lad in the dreadful clothing which Nick had stolen for her. She said as much to Nick, who beamed approvingly at her, though it was now so dark that she could really only see the flash of his teeth in the gloom. 'But now I know the very place where we can lie up until we set out for the country.' He put a comforting arm round Kitty's waist and began to propel her out of the little yard. 'I reckon you're tired, old Kitty; you'll sleep like a log tonight.'

Maeve came home with the messages, having first delivered the babies in her care to their respective homes. She hurried up the stairs, gaily refusing an offer from a strange young man to give her a hand with her marketing bag, and burst into the kitchen to find Caitlin sitting at the table like a wax image, staring at nothing. Immediately, Maeve realised that something was wrong. Was one of the children hurt? The twins had acquired roller skates the previous Christmas and terrified the life out of their elders by swooping in and out of the traffic along O'Connell Street. They had been forbidden to do so, of course, but Maeve and Caitlin both realised that forbidding was one thing and getting the twins to obey such instructions quite another.

So Maeve's anxiety was chiefly for the boys as she said: 'What's happened, Caitlin? I can see it's something bad.'

For a full minute, Caitlin stared at her as though she did not understand the question. Maeve was about to repeat it when her friend spoke. 'It's me darlin' Pat,' she said in a flat voice. 'He's dead of the flu, died a day or so ago in hospital. Me cousin Brendan came in on his way back to Connemara to tell me what happened.'

'Oh, Cait. Oh, you poor darling! And wasn't Pat the best husband in the world, to be sure? Oh, it's a terrible thing to happen, especially when he fought all through the war wit' scarce a scratch on him.' Maeve put both her thin little arms round Caitlin and tried to hug her, but the older girl pushed her gently away.

'I've not told the children yet, and I'm dreading it,' she said bleakly. 'He must be buried out at Glasnevin wit' all his family and friends. It'll cost, but folks is generous. I dare say everyone who ever knew him will put a few pence towards the cost of buryin' him.'

'Of course they will; everyone were real fond of Pat,' Maeve said, feeling the hot tears begin to slide down her cold cheeks. They had all been longing for Pat's return; it had never occurred to anyone that he might not come back. Why should it? The war was over. Men were being repatriated all the time and then demobbed, though it was a slow business. Oh, God, how would they explain to the kids? Her own beloved Kitty, though not even related to Pat, adored him, for wasn't he the nearest thing to a father she had ever known? Maeve knew Kitty wouldn't understand why Pat's life had been spared through all the terrible dangers of the war only to be struck down by an illness from which, surely, he could have recovered. He wasn't old not yet forty-five, and he must have been strong to survive the rigours of the war. Maeve thought that God had a lot to answer for.

Caitlin seemed to have pulled herself together, for she stood up and went over to the mirror which hung beside the kitchen door. She unpinned her hair, then reached for the comb on the ledge beneath the mirror, running it through her thick dark locks and pinning them back into a bun once more. Then she rubbed vigorously at her pale cheeks. 'We'd best get a meal going,' she said, and her voice was remarkably steady. 'I'll not tell the children until we're all sitting down together. Oh, Maeve, it's so hard. I've got to be brave, to pretend for their sakes, but inside I feel as if my life ended when I realised Pat was dead.'

'I'm hungry,' Kitty said plaintively, as Nick dragged her along the dusky streets. The lamp-lighter was ahead of them, but only just, and as the lamps bloomed gold it seemed to make the shadows between them more menacing, turning the sky from the palest of blue to indigo. Nick, with his arm round her shoulders, gave her a comforting squeeze. 'There's a soup kitchen a few streets away, don't you remember?' he said. 'You must have been there, 'cos it's not far from where you live. They give you a decent hunk of bread an' all.'

'I've never been to a soup kitchen; Caitlin makes our soup,' Kitty explained. 'What is a soup kitchen anyway? And how d'you get the soup home? You can't carry it in your hands.'

'You takes a pot or a bowl, but they lends cup things to kids, only you ain't allowed to take 'em away from the steps, and you have to hand 'em back as soon as the soup's done,' Nick told her. 'Often it's cabbage soup – well, mainly cabbage – wit' some spud to thicken it, like. It's good, I'm tellin' you.'

'But what if they ask us why we isn't at home wit' our mammies?' Kitty said, as they rounded a corner and saw a queue of children and adults waiting outside a lamplit doorway. 'What if the soup lady knows us?'

Nick chuckled. 'They know better'n to ax questions,' he said. 'They knows me awright an' I reckon they knows I don't go home that much.'

Kitty nodded. She had never visited Nick's home because both Maeve and Caitlin had absolutely forbidden it, and Kitty knew that such strictures were placed upon her for a very good reason. Nick's dad hit his mam and his mam hit the kids, and neither Caitlin nor Maeve wanted Kitty to be hurt. So now she trotted along beside

Nick and joined the queue whilst wondering at the strangeness of life. A week ago she would simply have accepted that Maeve and Caitlin did not want her to be hurt because they loved her, but what she had overheard today had called that love in question. If Caitlin had truly loved her, she would not have dreamed of sending her across the water to the woman who had given birth to her, or imprisoning her in an orphanage. Orphanages were awful places; everyone in the Liberties knew that. Huge families, all living in one room, and mostly half starved, would still take in a couple of kids, perhaps only distantly connected to them, when the children's own relatives died. The people of the tenements, particularly the women, would make room, somehow, for an extra mouth to feed. Yet Caitlin had talked of putting Kitty in an orphanage as though it were the only sensible solution.

'Here.' Nick pushed a cracked and rather dirty bowl into Kitty's hands. 'Did you notice? The woman handin' out the bowls never so much as glanced at either of us. When we shuffle past the ladle you hold your bowl out as near the pot as you can. Likely, they'll lay a chunk of bread across the bowl. Then we sits on them steps until the grub's all gone.'

Kitty was about to ask who would give her a spoon when she noticed that the line of children already sitting on the steps were drinking the soup straight from the bowls. Presently, she followed

Nick over to the steps, sat down in the place vacated by a child who had just finished his portion, and looked dubiously at the contents of her bowl. It was thin and watery, with bubbles of grease floating on the surface, and bits of what she hoped was cabbage clearly visible. The bread was hard and stale and was probably a day or two old, but when she cautiously tasted the soup it wasn't too bad, and she was so hungry that the bread disappeared in a trice. Even so, Nick's bowl was empty long before her own.

'Finished?' Nick stood up, then took her bowl. 'I'll take 'em back, Kit. You wait here.'

When he rejoined her the two of them set off into the dark streets once more. They walked slowly, for by now Kitty was very tired and Nick, obviously sensing this, regulated his pace to hers. However, halfway down a dark and particularly noisome alley, he pulled her to a halt and swung her to face him. 'Look, Kit,' he said seriously. 'Up to now, this has been a sort of game to you, wouldn't you be after admitting? You were upset and even angry about what you heard your Auntie Caitlin say, but surely in your heart you know she couldn't mean it? You isn't her daughter and Maeve isn't your mammy either, but they've been mortal good to you ever since you were born. Caitlin's got a good job, and though she'll miss Mr O'Keefe's money the family are still a heap better off than most. You've never gone hungry in your life, never had to visit a soup kitchen, never slept rough. Why, even friends you tek home get give a good meal – many a fine meal I've had meself in your kitchen – so why should they turn you out? Clodagh's earnin', even if it ain't much, and Fergal and Seamus get a bob or two selling the papers.'

Kitty shook her head hopelessly. 'I don't know why, I just know Auntie Cait said it weren't fair to expect her to look after me as well as all the others. And if I go back, I know she'll send me away, either across the water or into an orphanage. If you don't want to help me, Nick, just you say so and I'll go off by meself. But go off I shall, wit' or wit'out you.'

She expected Nick to make a sharp rejoinder, even to walk away from her, but instead he linked his arm with hers, and even in the darkness she could see his grin. 'That's all right then; we'll be off as soon as we're prepared,' he said cheerfully. 'I were testin' you because it's no use settin' off to live rough wit' someone whose heart isn't in it. I didn't hear what your Auntie Cait said but I dare say there's some other reason for her wantin' rid of you. Well, not wantin' rid exactly,' he added, clearly sensing his companion's distress, 'more likely needing your space in some way. I wonder if she's thinking of taking a lodger, perhaps?'

'I don't know,' Kitty said tiredly. She was beginning to feel that this day, the worst in her whole life, was going on for ever. 'Please, Nick, where's we goin'? I'm so wore out I could sleep on a clothes line, if you'd just peg me to it. I don't think I can walk no further.'

'That's good, 'cos we've arrived,' Nick said. He pulled her into a narrow passageway, too small to be lit by street lamps, but in the faint starlight Kitty saw a great heap of rubble and realised that this had once been a tenement block. She pulled back, for the place smelt most unpleasant and she was pretty sure that it must be haunted by the rats which immediately took over and thoroughly scavenged in any deserted building, but Nick firmly propelled her on. 'It's awright, it isn't as bad as it looks,' he said encouragingly. 'If we slide past that big block, there's like a little cave among the bricks. I keep some sacks there and a big pile of newspapers. We can be snug as bugs in rugs, I'm tellin' you.'

'What about rats?' Kitty quavered. Never had she wished so passionately for Tommy, and she said so. But Nick told her that Tommy was not like a dog, who would follow at heel and come to their command.

'Besides, Tommy belongs to Maeve really, you know he does,' he reminded her.

'Yes, I know,' Kitty muttered unwillingly. 'Only – only Tommy's me best pal, next to you, of course, Nick, and – and he's cleared all the rats out of Handkerchief Alley. Oh, I wish he could have come wit' us.'

But Nick only gave a deep, pretend snore, so

Kitty hunched the sacks up over her shoulders and closed her eyes, fondly imagining Maeve, in the little bed they shared, with Tommy curled up at her feet, and Clodagh and Grainne snoring in the next bed. I wonder if Maeve's t'inking of me? was Kitty's last thought as she sank gratefully into sleep.

Chapter Eleven

Maeve awoke to find daylight stealing into the room so that she saw the humped figures of Grainne and Clodagh as dark shapes against the dawn light. For a moment, she just lay there, conscious that the warm little body which usually cuddled close to her own was missing and thinking, hazily, that Kitty must have got up to use the chamber pot. Then suddenly everything came flooding back: the dreadful news that Pat O'Keefe was dead, the sudden realisation that Kitty had not come home from school, the breathless hurry through the streets to St Joseph's where Sister Jeremiah had placidly assured her that her worries were unfounded. 'Sure and you're believin' the child has been mitching off school, but you'd be wrong, alanna, for it was meself sent her off on a message,' she had said comfortably. ''Twould take her to Francis Street, which is so near Handkerchief Alley that there was little point in her returning to school.' She had given Maeve her kind and gentle smile. 'And if she's not home b' now, sure an' she'll be skipping rope or playing relievio in some back yard wit' a crowd of other youngsters.'

Comforted, Maeve had walked home in a leisurely fashion, scrutinising every group of children she met in the hope of seeing Kitty. She had not done so, but when she got back to the flat there was so much to do that she had almost forgotten the child's absence until the meal was on the table. Caitlin had put off telling the children of their father's death until they were all present, but Maeve had noticed that when they settled down at the table and she asked Grainne whether she had seen Kitty, a look crossed Caitlin's face which Maeve had been unable to interpret. Was it fear? Maeve knew awful things could happen to children; why, she herself as a child of five had been scutting a horse and cart with her elder sister, clinging on for dear life and thinking it great fun, when the carter had noticed them; his long whip had curled round and she had fallen into the road. A passing delivery boy had snatched her up but not before the wheel of the cart behind had caught her leg; she could still remember the agony of it. If something like that had happened to Kitty . . . but she was sure Kitty had more sense than to play at scutting, with the example of Maeve's lameness for ever before her.

There were other dangers, of course. It was not unknown for children to be injured when there was a falling out amongst dockers or the players in a toss school. Attracted by the shouts and yells, children would rush towards the ruggyup, as they called it, and sometimes as the fights swayed back and forth a child would get knocked to the ground unnoticed.

But this happened to smaller children, usually boys, and Maeve reminded herself once more that Kitty was sensible. She might watch the police breaking up a toss school because gambling was illegal, but she would never get involved.

By now, everyone was seated round the table. Caitlin crossed to the pot of stew simmering on the stove and dipped the ladle into it, then hesitated, glancing across at Maeve. 'I'm sorry, alanna, I wasn't really attending when you were telling me that Sister Jeremiah had sent Kitty on a message. Did you say she told Kitty to come straight home?'

'That's right,' Maeve said, rather mystified. 'I can't imagine why she didn't – come straight home, I mean. Sister suggested she'd have stopped to play relievo or something wit' her pals, but when I t'ink about it, I can't agree. Kitty's a good girl; she'd have come straight home to change out of her good skirt and blouse, and anyway most of her friends would still have been in school.'

'Oh.' Caitlin said. She looked stricken. 'Maeve, me love, I'm after t'inkin' . . . oh, janey mack, whatever have I done?'

Maeve stared at her. 'I don't understand,' she said slowly. 'You said you hadn't seen Kitty.'

'No, but . . .' Caitlin turned to Clodagh. 'Dish up the food, there's a good girl; I need to have a word wit' Maeve, in private like.'

Clodagh got up, came across to the stove, and began to ladle stew and potatoes on to a pile of tin plates her mother had placed in readiness. Maeve saw that the children were all beginning to look uneasy and guessed that they sensed something unpleasant had happened. She hoped that they would eat their food before Caitlin told them of Pat's death, because she was pretty sure that appetites would disappear when they heard the dreadful news. She followed Caitlin out of the kitchen and into Caitlin's own room, where the two of them perched on the bed whilst Caitlin, falteringly at first, repeated word for word, or as nearly as she could remember, the exact conversation between herself and Brendan concerning Kitty.

As her friend spoke, Maeve felt the hot blood rush to her cheeks. How dared Caitlin talk about Kitty as though the child were unwanted, a burden. But then she remembered that Caitlin had received crushing news herself, and after all it had been Brendan who had persuaded his cousin to take the child in. Yet she was not sure what this had to do with Kitty's disappearance and said as much, whereupon Caitlin's beautiful dark eyes filled with tears. 'I – I thought I heard someone on the stairs when I was saying those wicked things,' she stammered. 'I – I went to the door and looked down the flight and I thought I saw someone disappearing round the corner, but I was too upset to wonder who it could be. Honest to God, Maeve, if I'd known it were Kitty . . .'

Maeve got up and took the older girl's hands in her own. 'It isn't your fault and I know you didn't mean a word of it, and so will Kitty once I've had a chance to talk to her,' she said comfortingly. 'Of course she'll be hurt and upset, but when you tell her you spoke out of your pain . . .'

'I'll tell her the moment she gets back,' Caitlin said earnestly, getting to her feet and giving Maeve a hug. 'We'll sort it out as soon as she gets home. But right now, I've got to tell the children that their daddy's gone.'

It was a dreadful evening; quite the worst Maeve thought she had ever spent. The children had been stunned and horrified, even the twins who thought themselves so tough had wept bitterly, for they all knew how lucky they had been to have a father like Pat. He had worked hard for his family, seldom drank, and was truly interested in every aspect of his children's lives. They had all looked forward eagerly to his return from the war, anticipating the stories he would tell, longing to hear of the countries he had visited, the pals he had made. Now all that was over, and though their mammy had promised their daddy would come back to Ireland they knew the coffin would be fastened down; indeed, they had no wish for it to be otherwise, for, as Clodagh said, the picture of their daddy would be in their hearts for ever and they would need no reminders.

As soon as the meal was finished, Maeve took herself off to ask around the neighbourhood for any sign of Kitty. She walked up and down Francis Street questioning the stallholders, but though several said they thought they had seen a neatly dressed child with a couple of thick plaits it was little help, since they had no idea in which direction she had gone, or even whether she was alone or with a friend.

Maeve had returned to the flat very late, by that time desperately worried, certain that Kitty must have fallen into some scrape or other. She had visited the home of every school friend that Kitty played with, but no one had seen the child since she had gone off to do Sister Jeremiah's message. Maeve had dragged herself wearily up the stairs and pushed open the kitchen door. Late though it had been, everyone was still up, and as she entered Caitlin had swung round, flourishing a dirty sheet of crumpled paper. 'It's a letter from Kitty,' she had said excitedly. 'It had your name on the outside but I opened it – unfolded it, rather – because I knew you'd want me to do so. I were just beginning to read it to the children when I heard your foot on the stair.' She had gazed hopefully at Maeve. 'Have you any news, alanna?'

Maeve had shaken her head but taken the proffered sheet, scanned it quickly, and then begun to read it aloud.

Dear Maeve,
  I heared Auntie Cait saying poor Uncle Pat were dead. I am so, so sorry. I did love my Uncle

*Pat. I know things will be hard and I'm not real
family, but I don't want to cross the water nor go
to an orphanage. I'm not alone, I'm with a pal
what'll keep me safe, he's promised he will. And
I'll be real careful, Maeve. I can't get work yet,
I'm too young, but I'll be all right. Please don't
worry, and remember I love you very, very much.
I shall miss you and everyone but I'm sure it is
for the best. It's an adventure, after all, and I know
money will be scarce now Uncle Pat has gone but
Auntie Cait won't have to feed me, and when I'm
fourteen I'll be back, you bet.*

Love from Kitty.

Maeve had looked round at the faces; everyone
had been shocked, but it was Clodagh who had
spoken first. 'Who's she with, Maeve?' she had
asked. 'Do you think she's gone to your mam?'

Maeve had begun to answer but was rudely
interrupted by Fergal who had given a derisive
snort. 'Gone to old Ma Connolly? Are you *mad*,
Clodagh? She'll be wit' that perishin' young tear-
away, Nick Mooney. Who else would be hangin'
round when everyone else is in school? Mitching's
a way o' life for the Mooneys.'

Maeve had stared at him, then rushed across
the kitchen and given him a hug, despite his
vigorous attempts to hold her off. 'Nick! Nick
Mooney! Sure and aren't you the cleverest boy in
Dublin, Fergal O'Keefe! I should have thought of
him at once, 'cos the two of 'em's thick as thieves.

311

Well, all I hope is she's not spending the night in their room, because if she is, she'll be coming out wit' a good deal more than she went in wit'. Lice, hoppers, scab . . . the Mooneys have got the lot!'

Fergal had snorted again. 'What, go back to the Mooney room? I reckon young Nick sleeps under his own roof no more'n two nights a year. They'll kip down on a pile of newspapers in a tenement hallway, tucked out of sight. They'll be back for breakfast tomorrow, 'cos Nick never has a penny to bless himself with an' I reckon our Kitty's no better.' He had pointed an accusing finger at Maeve. 'And don't you go hugging me again or I shan't go out and fetch Tommy in for you.'

Maeve had beamed at him. 'You're a grand feller, Fergal, so you are.'

Now, Maeve slid out of bed and got to her feet. She was always first up in the mornings in order to light the fire, fetch water if necessary, empty slop buckets and get the porridge started. She would pull the kettle over the fire as soon as it was well lit because she liked to take Caitlin a cup of tea, even though the other woman was seldom actually in bed when she took it in but was already preparing for the day ahead. Usually she was careful to go quietly in order not to wake Kitty, but today there was no need to steal about the bedroom, for Clodagh and Grainne, no doubt exhausted by the horrors of the previous day, did not stir even when Maeve clattered the jug against the basin when pouring her washing water.

In the kitchen, she went about her morning tasks automatically. The flames began to take hold and the turfs burn steadily. She pulled the kettle over the flame, and presently heard the milk cart rumble past the end of the alley. Grabbing a jug off the dresser, and her crutch from the corner, she slid some coins into her apron pocket and hurried downstairs and out into Francis Street. Already, there was a short queue waiting to be served, and she took her place in it, watching as the ladle was dipped into the churn and the milk tipped carefully into various receptacles. When it was her turn, the milkman measured out the pint she wanted and then added a little extra. 'Summat for de cat,' he said jovially as he did every morning, taking the money.

'Thank you,' Maeve said, adjusting her crutch beneath her arm so that she would not spill the precious milk. 'You've not seen Kitty, I suppose? I'm – I'm a bit worried. I think she's stayed over in a pal's room an' it's not like her. She didn't ask, you see.'

The milkman thought, then shook his head. 'No, I ain't seen her,' he admitted. 'If I do, I'll send her home wit' a flea in her ear.'

Maeve thanked him and returned to the flat, moving much more slowly now and feeling suddenly uneasy. Surely Kitty should have been home by now? She would have to go round to the Mooney room if Kitty was not back by breakfast, because she did not mean to let Kitty's record of good behaviour slip, which it certainly would if the child mitched off school. She reached the kitchen and opened the door, praying that she would find Kitty within, but the only person present was Caitlin. Across the room, the two women stared at one another. 'No, she's not come back,' Maeve said quietly, answering the unspoken question. 'I really am worried, Cait. I'm goin' to the polis as soon as we've finished breakfast. There's that many kids in Dublin, you could search for a week – a month – and never find her.'

Caitlin took the kettle off the fire and poured bubbling water into the teapot. 'I think you're right to go to the polis,' she observed. 'Mind you, there aren't many kids in Dublin dressed as nice as she is.'

'That's true,' Maeve said, cheering up a little. 'But I'll be that grateful to see her face appear round that door. I dare say I shan't even scold her for giving me such a fright.'

Brendan walked along the well remembered lane with his heart full to bursting. It had been five long years since he had last visited his family home, but every stick and stone, every cushion of moss and patch of wild flowers, was as familiar to him as the backs of his own hands. He saw the rosettes of primroses and the tiny sweet-smelling violets which grew on the grassy bank to his right, and saw the bright buds on the quickthorn hedge which would presently hide the rough pasture on which his father's beasts grazed from the view of anyone walking along the lane. He had dreaded having to tell Caitlin that Pat was dead and it had been every bit as bad as he had feared, but once it was over and done he could turn to his own affairs once more and begin to consider what his next move should be.

Yet now, with less than a mile to go to reach the long, whitewashed cottage where he had been born and brought up, he found himself thinking back to the moment when he had left Caitlin's flat. He had not given another thought to the girl he had met until now, when, for some reason, the sight of the primroses and the sweet scent from the tiny violets reminded him of the girl with the elfin face, who had scorned his help, despite the heavy marketing bag, and the little crutch which she had wielded so expertly. And of course, now that he thought about it, it had been a good few years since Sylvie had given birth to Catherine Mary in the O'Keefes' small back bedroom, which meant that the child with the crutch had almost certainly grown into the young woman he had recently met.

He wished he had seen Catherine Mary, though – he must remember to call her Kitty, as Caitlin had – because it would be nice when he returned to Liverpool to be able to give Sylvie a description of her little daughter. This thought so surprised him that he stopped short in his tracks. He had told himself, over and over, that he might not return to Liverpool at all; why should he? Sylvie had managed very well without him for the past four years, and though she had written regularly enough he had sometimes thought that her missives read like 'duty' letters, and occasionally even suspected that she wrote the same one to a number of people, merely changing the name of the recipient. Yet she had somehow managed to get into his blood, he told himself crossly, and knew that he would go back to Liverpool, even if only to sever his final connection with the Liverpool Constabulary. And whilst he was there, he would of course visit Sylvie and Len; he really must not forget to visit Len. Before the war he had become quite fond of the poor feller and thought his feelings were reciprocated; Len was glad to see him, and always sad when he left.

Just before he reached the cottage he had to ford a small stream, and he saw, without surprise, that the water was running fast and deep. There were stepping stones, but these were awash, so he had to take care because should he slip he would be wet to the knees. It was always the same in winter and spring, he reminded himself as he reached the further bank almost dry-shod; the rain from the moor drained off into the stream and made crossing it a difficult business. The stream put all thoughts of Liverpool and Sylvie out of his mind, for from here he could actually see the cottage and his heart lifted in delighted anticipation of the welcome he knew he would receive. His father and brother might well be working on the land but his mother would certainly be home. The cottage was a single-storey building, heavily thatched, and now that he was so close he could see the peat pile which leaned against the end wall, and was still only half used, and his mother's vegetable garden, empty now of everything save a few draggly cabbages. There was a potato clamp in the back yard but he could not see that from here, though he guessed that a good deal of it would have been used by now for it was March, when the seed potatoes would be planted, and then his mother used the potatoes as sparingly as she could until the new crop could be harvested.

But we're luckier than most, he thought contentedly as he swung open the tiny wicket gate and walked up the path and round past the peat stack to the back yard. We've got a grand sturdy fishing boat, half a dozen goats and two cows – mebbe more by now – so even when times are hard the mammy can drive the donkey cart into town on market days and sell her goat's milk cheeses, her fine butter and even a little cream around Christmas, when the rich folk will buy it for the festivities. Even as the thought came to him, he pushed open the back door, and there was his mother in the large and homely kitchen, scooping flour out of a sack and sprinkling it on to the big wooden table; clearly she was about to start her weekly bake. He had telegraphed her to say he was coming home but had been unable to name the day, and now she gave a shriek, dropped the flour scoop and rushed across the room, her face flushing, her eyes bright. 'Oh, Brendan, me darlin' boy, you've growed,' she gasped, throwing her arms round his neck.

She was a small, plump woman, but he lifted her off her feet with ease and swung her round, kissing her resoundingly on one rosy cheek. 'Oh, Mammy, it's grand to be home,' he said contentedly. 'But where's Daddy and Declan?'

'They're ploughing. It's been a wet winter so they've took the donkey to the driest field and they'll plant the spuds tomorrow,' his mother said. 'I've tried to tell you about all the changes we've made in me letters, but I've not said nothing about Declan's young lady because I wanted you to meet her for yourself. She's a grand girl, so she is, and will make him a good wife. They plan to marry in twelve months, and when they do they will go to a place of their own.' She gave him a twinkling look. 'She's a woman of property, so she is, and her father means to give them some land and a bit of a cottage as a wedding gift. You must meet her before you go off again, if we can arrange it. But what am I t'inkin' of? Sit yourself down and I'll put the kettle on ... eh, but it's a grand t'ing to see me boy again, so it is.'

Brendan sat down in the old rocking chair which was his father's favourite seat. 'Sure and I'll meet the young lady just as soon as you like,' he said.

'But what makes you think I'm in a hurry to be off? I'm sure I told you in me letters that I wasn't going to re-join the police force and that I meant to look for a bit of land of me own in these parts.'

His mother clapped a hand to her mouth, then turned to the mantel and took down a telegram which had been propped against the clock. Brendan had noticed it and had assumed that it was the one he had sent telling of his impending arrival, but now he realised his mistake as his mother handed it to him. 'Sure an' I'll be forgettin' me own head next! This came for you a couple o' days back. We opened it, your daddy and meself, because we thought it was from you, and when we realised it weren't . . . but you'd best read it for yourself.'

Brendan stared down at the piece of paper in his hand. The message was short but succinct: *Mother-in-law Len and Becky very ill stop I am desperate stop Please come stop Sylvie*

'I don't know how she knew you'd be here,' his mother said.

'I wrote from Southampton saying I'd be returning to Connemara so wouldn't be in Liverpool for a week or two,' Brendan said heavily.

He looked up and met his mother's anxious gaze. As he did so, he realised that she did not know who Sylvie was, for in his letters home he had referred to her as Mrs Dugdale and had tried to avoid mentioning her very often since he had no intention of letting his mother know that he had fallen in love with a married woman. But now he must make some explanation, for the naked fear and emotion in the telegram would have made any woman suspicious. If only Sylvie had thought, she should have signed the telegram *Dugdale*, but it was pretty clear that she had sent the epistle in a state of desperate anxiety and had never expected eyes other than his own to see it.

'Well, son? You'll go, of course?'

Brendan took a deep breath. 'I'll have to go,' he said quietly. 'Sylvie is Mrs Dugdale. I'm sure I mentioned her in my letters – I got involved with the family when I found her husband and father-in-law left for dead in an alley during the riots back in 1911. The father-in-law died but the husband lay for months in a hospital bed. He did improve a little, enough to be taken home, but the two Dugdale women have had quite a struggle, and whilst I was in Liverpool I visited them regularly. I imagine she's turned to me because there's no one else.'

'I see,' his mother said quietly, but Brendan thought her face spoke volumes. She knew him too well, that was the trouble. She had known him bring in a half-drowned fox cub which he had come across out on the moor and hand-raise it himself, going to infinite pains to release the little creature back into its natural habitat as soon as it was strong enough. At one time, he had taken a two-mile detour on his walk to and from school so that a younger boy might have a companion on the long trek. And there had been another boy in school with whom he had shared his bread and cheese and apple, because the lad was a town-dweller and seldom got enough to eat. She would know that he would have helped anyone in Sylvie's position, whatever the circumstances; it was his reticence on the subject that would have told her he cared. Now, she abandoned the pastry she had been making, dusted flour off her hands and came over to him. She put an arm round his shoulders and gave him an affectionate hug. 'You like her, but she's a married woman doin' right by a sick man,' she said gently. 'You'll have to go . . . but this telegram arrived two days past; by the time you reach Liverpool the crisis may be over. If so, you'll maybe come home almost at once. Oh, Brendan, don't you think that's best?'

'I do, Mammy, but you need never fear I'd get between a man and his wife,' Brendan assured her. 'Remember, I've only seen Sylvie once in the past four years and I'm certain she thinks of me as a friend and nothing more. But you'll not mind if I go at once? She – she says she's desperate and she's never appealed to me for help before. I can't let her down – and it would be letting Len down as well, wouldn't it?'

His mother nodded and rumpled his hair. 'You'll do the right t'ing, whatever that may be,' she said. 'I suppose you'll catch the train from Clifden first thing tomorrow, but at least you'll see your daddy and Declan this evening and explain how it is.'

Kitty awoke and, for a moment, could not imagine where she was. The bed seemed unusually hard and uncomfortable, the covers were scratchy, and the delicious warmth which was engendered by Maeve's body was missing, though there was something nice and warm pressing against the back of her knees.

Cautiously, Kitty opened her eyes and stared around her. Of course; she was in the little cave which Nick had made in the ruins of the tenement building, and she was lying on newspapers and covered in sacks, and not in her own beautiful comfortable bed at all. For a moment, tears of self-pity filled her eyes, but then she sat up on one elbow, her body creaking with stiffness for she had been so tired she had scarcely stirred all night, and looked around her. She supposed that it was quite a good little place to sleep if the alternative was some draughty landing where you might be disturbed in the early hours by a tenant stumbling home after spending the night in a shebeen, one of the unlicensed drinking dens that abounded in the Liberties, or by a policeman with a grudge against kids who slept rough on their patch. Last night it had been too dark to see anything much, but now she glanced about her thinking that Nick had done pretty well. The ground was covered in newspapers, a thick wad of them, and the tumble of brick walls had been roughly insulated by pushing crumpled up sheets of newspapers into the cracks. Nick, lying not a foot away from her, was rolled up in a quantity of sacks, some of which had contained potatoes, and she herself was covered in similar sacks. She put out a hand to pull the sacks over her shoulders once more for she guessed that it must be very early since the light filtering through the entrance hole was grey, and as she did so she realised she was very dirty indeed. But I'll have a good wash later, she told herself, then thought that a nice wash with soap, hot water and a towel was a luxury that she would have to learn to do without. She tried to lie down again and the warmth behind her knees shifted. Kitty half turned, her heart jumping into her mouth. Rats! She had heard of children who slept rough finding themselves cheek by jowl with rats who had sought to share their warmth during the coldest part of the night and the thought filled her with such horror that she tried to jump to her feet, cracking her head painfully against the ceiling of old boards and lurching forward to collide heavily with Nick. Behind her she saw, out of the corner of her eye, a grey shape, and clutched desperately at her companion. 'Rats!' she shrieked. 'Oh, Nick, there's rats, a huge rat; it was lying . . . lying . . .'

It was Tommy. He was standing up, arching his back, yawning with a great curling and uncurling of his pink tongue. Then his great golden eyes swung round to meet hers and he began to reverberate with his astonishingly loud purr.

Nick sat up. 'Whazzat? Whazzermarrer? Oozat?'

Kitty giggled and picked Tommy up, cradling him against the ragged jersey which, she now remembered, Nick had made her swap for her nice white blouse and clean grey cardigan. But Tommy did not seem to mind her change of attire and reached up to rub his broad head beneath her chin, then gave her neck a little lick with his rough tongue, as though to reassure her that he was still her friend, even when she chose to sleep in horrid places instead of their cosy bed at home. 'Sorry, sorry, sorry,' she said quickly. 'I thought it were a rat cuddling up against me, but it were only my dear old Tommy. Oh, I'm so glad he's come to join us after all. I say, Nick, it isn't even properly light yet, but I'm awful hungry. Think we might find something to eat somewhere?'

Nick glanced towards the doorway. 'That's dawn light, that is,' he said knowledgeably. 'Tell you what, we's quite near Ringsend Bridge. D'you know it?' Kitty shook her head doubtfully; the name was familiar but she could not imagine that they might find a free breakfast sitting out on a bridge. She said as much, making Nick give a snort of laughter. 'You're daft, you are, girl! It's where they keep the coal what fuels the engines, great glistening heaps of it. It's no use during the day,

324

of course, but I reckon if we set off at once we can prig some before anyone's about.' He rose to his feet as he spoke and began looking at their bedding, critically surveying each sack, until a particular one seemed to take his fancy, for he folded it and shoved it down the back of his trousers. 'C'mon, we want to get to work before anyone's about,' he urged, pushing her ahead of him into the tenement yard.

He began to make his way across the cobbles but Kitty jerked at his sleeve. 'What d'you mean, heaps of coal?' she asked plaintively. 'I said I were hungry, and I can't eat coal. Not even Tommy can eat coal,' she added, for the cat had followed them and was close at her heels.

Nick looked affectionately down at her. 'You're so green I can't hardly believe it,' he said. 'We're goin' to rob the coal so's we can sell it for someone to burn on their fire; or we can swap it for a nice big plate of porridge, or half a loaf of bread an' a chunk of cheese. Now d'you understand?'

'Ye-e-es,' Kitty said slowly. 'But suppose we's seen, Nick, suppose someone recognises us?'

Nick shook his head grimly. 'Sure and do you think I was born yesterday?' he asked incredulously. 'I don't mean to sell coal round the Liberties, 'cos most folks there is like us Mooneys and doesn't have two pennies to rub together. Nor we won't go to the really posh houses 'cos they'll guess the coal is stole – ha, ha, I just made a poem – and might tell on us to the polis. No, we'll go to the little houses . . . but what am I doin' tellin' you? You'll see for yourself presently.'

Kitty had never stolen anything in her life, though she had often enough been in Nick's company when he had walked close to a fruit stall, purloining a couple of apples, an orange, or even a few potatoes as he went past, but this time, it seemed, she must be directly involved, for now she too was a street child living on her wits and must steal what she could no longer pay for.

By the time they reached the coal yard, the light was definitely strengthening, but when they sneaked under the bridge there was no one about. Nick climbed the wall and dropped lightly down on to a mound of coal, telling Kitty tersely that she must keep nix for him. 'If you see anyone, anyone at all, just give a little low whistle,' he instructed her. 'I'm an old hand at this, and believe me I'll be out of that coal yard an' runnin' like a rabbit before you can blink your eye.'

In the event and much to Kitty's relief, there was no need for anyone to run anywhere, for not a soul appeared and Nick climbed back over the wall and dropped down beside her with enough coal in his sack to make him lean heavily to port as they walked along. Kitty continued to feel nervous until they were well clear of the area, but just as she had begun to relax Nick headed for a respectable-looking house and once more poor Kitty's heart jumped into her mouth. Suppose the householder was someone she knew? Not that this seemed likely . . . and then Kitty glanced down at herself and was comforted, for a dirtier, more ragged urchin she had never seen. And when their knock on the door was answered by a thin, anxious-looking woman with a child clinging to her skirt, she was even more reassured.

'Yes, little fellers?' the woman said. 'Ah, I see you're sellin' coal. How about half that sackful for a bright sixpence and a morsel o' bread an' cheese?'

Little fellers! The woman had taken a good look at them and then unhesitatingly accepted Kitty as a boy! What was more, the promised cap was still just a promise, so the woman had seen Kitty's hacked-about hair yet had not given her a second glance. This gave Kitty more confidence than anything else could have done and she shot a triumphant look at Nick, but he was too busy bargaining to so much as glance at his smaller companion.

'How about a great deal of bread an' cheese, a big bowl o' porridge each, an' a nice cup o' tea?' Nick said promptly, giving the woman what he no doubt considered a beguiling smile, though Kitty thought it was more like a leer. 'That and a quarter of me coal is fair dealin', I'm after thinking.'

Not unnaturally, the woman disagreed, but in so half-hearted a fashion that Kitty was not surprised when Nick continued to haggle and finally settled to hand over a quarter – so far as he could judge – of the coal in his sack in return for a sixpence, half a loaf and a good chunk of cheese. She wished he had insisted on the tea, and the porridge too, for despite walking briskly she was feeling very cold indeed, and the warmth wafting out of the doorway was tempting, but Nick tipped a pile of coal out on the doorstep, the woman handed over the money and the bread and cheese, and the two children left, one at least well satisfied, for Nick turned to her, beaming.

'Ain't that just grand?' he said contentedly. 'Where d'you want to eat your breakfast, eh? There's a back alley back the way we come . . .'

'Why didn't you let her have half the perishin' coal so's we could have tea and porridge?' Kitty said ungratefully. 'Poor Tommy's nigh on starvin', but he don't like bread and cheese.'

'Because I didn't want her sittin' us down in her kitchen an' plyin' us wit' questions and mebbe takin' a good look at us,' Nick said promptly. 'You don't use that head of yours, 'cept in school, seemingly. Why, it were you who kept on about bein' recognised . . .'

Kitty had to acknowledge the truth of this, and apologised unreservedly, particularly when they found themselves a ramshackle wall in a narrow little alley and, perching upon it, settled down to eat. She offered Tommy a small piece of cheese which he ate, though Nick called him a greedy pig since, he said, the cat had no doubt had his fill of the mice and other vermin which dwelt in ruined buildings. 'And if we see a milk cart we'll find a bit of broken delft what some kid's left out after playin' shop, and swap a couple of bits of coal for a drain of milk. Then Tommy will be set up for the rest o' the day,' he said as they humped the sack of coal along the road, for Kitty had offered assistance and had been gratified when her help had been accepted. 'Now look, Kit – I'm a-goin' to call you Kit in future, 'cos that's a boy's name and Kitty ain't – we can't go off into the country wit'out a penny to our names, and since neither of us have got anything to sell we're going to have to earn some money somehow. That means hangin' around the markets and shops, which you don't want to do and I can't say I blame you, for that Maeve of yourn will be settin' the polis on us today and combin' the Liberties for a sight of you. Are you certain sure you don't want to go back home?'

'Certain sure,' Kitty said stoutly, though her heart quailed a little at the thought of poor Maeve's distress. But it was for the best, after all, she told herself, and hugged Tommy so tightly that his great golden eyes bulged and he squawked to be put down, which she was happy enough to do since he was heavy and so was the sack of coal. 'But how can we earn money, Nick? I's nearly eight, but not really strong, like you.'

Nick looked gratified. 'Well, that's what I were goin' on to say,' he admitted. 'We can't earn money, or not enough to be useful to us on the road, at any rate. But we can rob . . . apples off stalls, a few spuds here an' there, stuff off a washin' line when darkness falls. If you're game, then I reckon we can set out for the country in a week, mebbe less.'

'I don't see why you should think I'd hold back from pinching a few apples considering we just robbed this great sack of coal,' Kitty pointed out. 'I'm game for anything, so long as we don't get caught.'

Nick laughed and gave her an affectionate punch on the shoulder which made her suck in her breath sharply, and this made Nick laugh again. 'It's no good you lookin' at me all reproachful like, 'cos I'm goin' to have to treat you just like I'd treat another feller,' he told her. 'Of course, you're a fair bit younger'n me so I reckon we'll tell anyone what asks that you're me little brother. We'll tell 'em you're Christopher Mooney an' I'll call you Kit. But what we're goin' to do about that blamed Tommy of yourn I can't imagine. Does he always follow you?'

'Not always; not when I'm headin' for school, anyway,' Kitty said after some thought. 'I dare say he'll go back to Handkerchief Alley as we move out towards the country, but he may not. Cats aren't like dogs – they make up their own minds and do what they want, not what anyone tells them. If Tommy were a dog I could probably get him to go home, but a cat . . . well, they're just different. But why is he a problem, Nick? We shan't have to feed him, you know, not while there's mice and rats about, though he does like a sup of milk from time to time.'

'He's a problem because it ain't usual to see a

couple o' kids wit' such a huge cat marchin' along o' them,' Nick said frankly. 'We can't disguise him, either . . .'

Kitty gave a shout of laughter. 'Oh, Nick, did you ever read Puss in Boots? When you said that about disguising Tommy, I got a picture of 'im in me head with a pair of wellingtons on his back paws and a red spotted handkerchief tied to a little stick across his shoulder. But I dare say he'll go home if we don't pay him much attention.'

'I don't know nothin' about a puss in boots, but I do know a nuisance when I see one,' Nick grumbled. 'Still an' all, there's nothin' we can do about it, and if you do decide to change your mind . . .'

'I shan't!' Kitty shouted, thoroughly annoyed that Nick had not accepted her determination to leave Dublin. 'After all, Nick, this were my plan not yours. For all I know, you might turn round after a week or two 'cos you's missing your mammy and daddy, so if I believe you, why can't you believe me?'

''Cos you've got something to lose,' Nick said bluntly. 'You've a good home and folk what love you; in the Mooney household, I'm tellin' you, there's more kicks than kisses. The only food what comes through our door is the liquid kind 'cos it's cheaper'n bread or spuds or porridge. Me daddy visits the kips in the Monto if he's any money to spare after he's had a bellyful of booze, and me mammy hits out at any kid silly enough to be within reach when she's feelin' naggy. Believe me,

I'm better away. Dunno why I didn't go years back, when I were your age.'

'You're hardly ever home anyhow,' Kitty pointed out. 'An' running right away all by yourself would be horrible – frightening, I mean. But when it's the two of us . . .'

'The t'ree of us, you mean,' Nick said, grinning and jerking a thumb towards Tommy, who was trotting along behind them, tail up in the air as straight as a poker, and not appearing to give them so much as a glance.

Kitty grinned too. 'Where'll we get rid of the rest of the coal?' she asked, for the weight of it, slung between them, was a nuisance and every time the sack banged her leg coal dust drifted from it, blackening her feet – for she had abandoned her shoes and stockings, taking Nick's advice that street children went unshod.

'We're going to take it back to our little cave; I've plans for it,' Nick informed her. 'And after that, I think we'll see.'

Chapter Twelve

Brendan arrived in Liverpool two days after he received the telegram. As he hurried to the tram stop at the Pier Head, the sun was shining warmly on his back and the sky was blue overhead, whilst a gentle breeze ruffled his hair. It was impossible not to feel hopeful, but when he drew near the Ferryman worries and doubts began to return. The pub was shut, which was normal for this time of day, but somehow it bore a menacing look, though at first he thought this merely fanciful. When he got close, however, he noticed that the shutters on the bar windows were closed across, and then he saw, with a lurch of sickening apprehension, that an untidy white curtain of some description hung across the large windows on the upper floor. He quickened his pace, and even as he raised a hand to bang on the door it opened. Sylvie stood there. He had never seen her look so dreadful, for her face was white as a sheet, her eyes were red-rimmed, and her mouth drooped so forlornly that it was all he could do to stop himself from snatching her into a comforting embrace. She looked up at him for a moment as though she had never seen him before, then she stepped back, gesturing to him to follow. He obeyed, smelling the familiar odour of the bar – alcohol, cigarette smoke and dust – and, impulsively, tried to take Sylvie's hands, but she shrank back, shaking her head. 'Better not touch me,' she whispered. 'I've just been helping Mrs Bywater with . . . with . . .'

Brendan saw great tears form in her eyes and slide down her pale cheeks. He watched with a sort of fascinated horror as the tears soaked into the grimy blouse she wore. Grimy! In all the years he had known her, Sylvie had made sure that her clothing was always spotlessly clean and beautifully ironed. Now – he took in the black cardigan, half unbuttoned, the draggly grey skirt, the dirty, down-at-heel slippers – she looked as though she had slept in her present outfit for weeks.

'What's happened?' His own voice sounded creaky with disuse. 'Someone – someone's passed away; I saw the white sheet in the bedroom window. Oh, dearest Sylvie, was it – was it poor old Len?'

Sylvie shook her head, then nodded it. 'Yes. He died yesterday. But today . . . but today we lost Becky. We . . . we fought very hard, Mam and me; we thought she'd turned the corner. When I saw her this morning, her little face, which had been red with the fever, was pale and cool, and I thought – I thought . . .'

'Oh, my dear,' Brendan breathed, stricken. He knew how she adored her small daughter, how proud she had been of the little girl's quick intelligence. And he knew how fond Mrs Dugdale was of her granddaughter; it must have been a terrible blow for her, too.

He said as much, but Sylvie shook her head. 'Granny Dugdale was the first to go,' she muttered. 'There's only Mam and me here now. We sent Bertie and the other fellers home because of the infection, and anyway, there's no point in opening the pub.'

'You said you were helping Mrs Bywater?' Brendan said.

'She's – she's laying Becky out,' Sylvie whispered. 'She's been rushed off her feet. There's ever so many ill, Brendan, and the hospitals are full, you know. But she did do her best to give me a hand and my mam's been wonderful. She's not been home since Len took ill – he were the first to get it – but it seems to me that she and meself must have some sort of immunity, if that's the right word, and the doctor says we've got to wash our hands twenty times day and disinfect all the rooms and maybe it'll pass us by.' For the first time, she smiled tremulously up at him. 'Oh, Brendan, it's so good to see you! But I knew you'd come – I knew you'd not let me down.' And then, as though the effort of talking had been too much for her, she swayed, gave a little choking cry, and collapsed into Brendan's arms.

Sylvie was ill for a week, though it was not the influenza as Brendan and Mrs Davies had feared, but the result, the doctor said, of the strain of continuous nursing and the agony of losing the fight three times over. 'However, the best thing you can do, young man,' he added, 'is to get in touch with the brewery and explain what's happened. They'll likely send someone in to manage the place until they decide what to do, because with the landlady gone they'll want someone else in charge.'

'I'll speak to the brewery,' Brendan said. 'You're quite right: it's something that needs to be sorted out.'

When Sylvie had collapsed, Brendan had carried her up the stairs to her own room, accompanied by her mother. 'You're a grand feller, Brendan, so you are,' Mrs Davies had said. 'I dare say Sylvie told you when she wrote that a seaman, Sam Trescoe, popped in to visit Len whenever he were in port. Well, Sylvie and meself reckon he brought the infection since Len sickened a couple of days after his last visit. We've not heard a word from him since, and when he left he was complaining of dizziness, so I fear he's gone the way of all flesh, too.'

This seemed very odd to Brendan for Sylvie had never so much as mentioned a seaman called Sam in her letters, yet he must have known the family well. He decided to ask Sylvie about Sam when she was well enough to answer questions, but then Mrs Davies suggested that he should stay in the spare room, so that the two of them might share the nursing of Sylvie, and he quite forgot his puzzlement.

With Sylvie on the mend, the brewery advised them that a temporary manager would be coming in at the end of the week, and Brendan told Sylvie that when the man arrived he himself would leave. 'Your mam will look after you, alanna, and when I was in Ireland I hardly set eyes on me father or me brother because I came straight back to see what I could do to help you,' he said quietly one evening. 'You and your mam will be simply grand, but if you need me . . . well, you know I'll come running, don't you?'

Sylvie thanked him but said, rather stiffly, that she and her mother intended to apply to the brewery to become joint licensees and their request would, she felt sure, be acceded to. Then, unexpectedly, she flung her arms round his neck and pulled his face down to hers. 'I don't know how I'd have managed without you,' she said in a small, choked voice. 'It wouldn't be fair to ask you to stay because in all your letters you talked about buying some land of your own and I know your heart is in Ireland, really. But oh, Brendan, how on earth will I go on without you? I – I'm so alone, and though it wouldn't be true to pretend that Len and I had an ideal marriage I do miss him, and I scarcely dare think about Becky because it hurts and hurts like a sword in my heart. D'you know, every morning when I wake I have to convince myself all over again that she's gone. She – she was so alive, so quick and clever, so very, very sweet.'

Brendan held her gently in his arms, feeling his heart begin to race. He knew it was not the moment to ask her to marry him, not even the moment to declare his love for her, though he was sorely tempted. Instead, he put her gently away from him, then smoothed the silky white-blonde hair back from her forehead and gazed steadily into her large blue eyes. 'I t'ink you know I'd do anything for you, Sylvie,' he said quietly. 'And I'll be back when I've had a chance to settle me affairs in Connemara. Now, I know you'll t'ink I'm being hard, but Becky wasn't your only child. How would you feel if I came back and brought your daughter Catherine Mary – they call her Kitty now – with me? Or would it hurt too much, reminding you of your loss?'

'I – I don't know,' Sylvie muttered. 'I think it's too soon . . . but later, I might be glad to have her here. Only – only would Caitlin be prepared to part with her?'

Brendan remembered Caitlin's despair over Pat's death and how she had threatened to put Kitty into an orphanage or to send her back to her real mother. He took Sylvie's hands in his and squeezed them gently. 'Caitlin's got a heart as big as a bus, so she has, and quite enough children of her own to satisfy any woman,' he said, bracingly. 'And she's lost her man, remember? Things will be as difficult for her as they are bound to be for you, but if you truly want Kitty Caitlin would be the first to acknowledge your right.'

'I don't know about right . . .' Sylvie was beginning, when her mother entered the kitchen.

'Letter for you, Sylvie,' she said cheerfully. She turned to Brendan. 'It's from Dublin, so it'll be from your cousin Caitlin I expect.'

'I suppose she'll want to tell you that Pat's dead, since she doesn't know that I've returned to Liverpool,' Brendan said. He hoped that Caitlin did not mean to reproach Sylvie for leaving the child, for he'd had no opportunity to write to his cousin to tell her of Sylvie's tragic losses. Sylvie, however, having quickly scanned the letter, pushed it into his hands, her eyes darkening with some emotion which Brendan could not interpret.

'She's run away!' she said urgently. 'Me little girl's run away! She's not yet eight years old and a prey to any bad person who might get hold of her. Oh, Brendan, I were a terrible mother to the little creature and I don't deserve to have her back after the way I treated her. But – but you said you'd do anything you could to help me; will you go back to Ireland, my dearest friend, and find my little girl for me? Will you tell Caitlin I'll pay for my child's keep until she's a woman grown, if Caitlin's willing to have her? If not, she'd be welcome to make her home with me.' She turned towards her mother. 'Isn't that true, Mam? Wouldn't you welcome your other granddaughter if Brendan brings her home to us?'

*

339

By the end of the week, Kitty was getting to know Dublin almost as well as Nick. Maeve had protected her from so many things! She had never had to queue at the soup kitchen before, never had to line up in Buckingham Street for a mug of stew, nor follow a milk cart round the streets until the milkman left it for long enough for a child to nip in and dip a small quantity of milk out of the churn. She grew to know which stallholders could be relied upon to turn away for a moment just as one passed the stall, so that a fruit or vegetable could be slid into one's pocket without starting an outcry.

In that first week of freedom, she learned that the children of the streets stuck together. One would collect wood for a fire, another would steal potatoes to cook on it, others would share anything they could obtain. Nick told her that often, in winter, children who were afraid to go home because of drunken and abusive parents would gather in some quiet spot to pool their resources, try to get some sort of hot meal inside them, and sleep together, curled up like puppies amongst piles of newspaper, straw or rags. She, who had been told by Maeve and Caitlin that the police were her friends, learned that this did not apply if you were a child sleeping rough. Authority did not approve, wanted you back in your parents' room, even when a return might mean a beating or worse.

Then there were the street fights, generally

regarded by the young as a grand form of entertainment. Maeve and Caitlin had not approved of such ruggyups, but now Kitty followed Nick's example and wriggled through the crowd of watching adults to get a good view, though this was a pastime which they had to abandon after Kitty found herself elbow to elbow with a boy called Jimmy who lived in Handkerchief Alley and would undoubtedly have recognised her, despite her altered appearance, had she not seen him first and beaten a hasty retreat.

Nick had said they would stay in the city for a week, collecting money so that their flight into the country might not be a penniless one, and sure enough, after eight days, they had managed to accumulate almost five shillings in coins. They had slept every night in the little cave formed by the ruined tenement building, but after the eighth night Nick decreed that they should move on at last. 'The fact is, alanna, that I wanted to be absolutely certain sure we were doing the right thing by getting out of Dublin,' he explained. 'You're not used to the sort of life I live, but I must say you've took to it like a duck to water. I reckon we've been dead lucky not to have bumped into the twins, or Maeve, or one of your neighbours, but our luck's bound to run out if we hang around much longer. The polis will have been told to look out for you, and though they aren't going to reckernise you it's daft to take chances, so tomorrer we'll start movin' out, headin' for the real countryside.'

Kitty touched her raggedy head cautiously, yet with a certain pride, for Nick had done as he had promised, and she now had a splendid cap which obscured half her face as well as her hair. They had been sitting in the mouth of what Kitty thought of as their sleeping quarters, and now she turned to Nick, eyes rounding, for the remark about the police had just sunk in. 'The polis? But why should they be looking out for me? I've done nothing wrong.' She saw a gleam in Nick's eyes and added hastily: 'Well, nothing that anyone knows about, I mean. We robbed the trousers and shirt and that, but we left my clothes instead. And there was the coal . . . but I don't see why the polis should be looking for me if they aren't looking for you.'

Nick grinned and gave her a shove. 'Whatever Caitlin may have said, she wouldn't want you goin' off on your own, or with me, come to that. She might send you over the water or put you in an orphanage, but she wouldn't just let you wander off, like. So you see, she'd tell the polis to bring you home.'

'Well I *won't* go home,' Kitty said mutinously. 'So let's leave at once, Nick. Five shillings is a lot of money and you think we can earn more in the countryside? Let's go right away!'

They went, with Nick carrying the sack into which they had put their few personal possessions, Kitty close to his side and Tommy strolling along at their heels, trying to look as though he were not in the least interested in the two scruffy kids ahead of him.

As they neared Dolphin Barn, where open country started, Nick looked hopefully behind him. 'He won't follow us much further; he'll turn back soon,' he said, with a confidence which Kitty was sure he was far from feeling. 'You said yourself that cats ain't like dogs; they like places, not people. Oh aye, I reckon he'll turn for home quite soon.'

An hour later, walking down a country lane and enjoying the sweet fresh air, Kitty glanced back, then turned to Nick, suppressing a giggle. 'I thought you said he'd go home? Of course, it might be some other cat, but it looks remarkable like Tommy to me.'

Nick's head whipped round and he stopped short then swore, colourfully, beneath his breath. 'The old bugger,' he said, and Kitty recognised admiration in his tone. 'I was sure he'd turned back ages ago, but I reckon he'd just nipped off on some ploy of his own. Don't he look smug, though? Wicked old devil – I'd swear he were grinnin' if he weren't a cat.'

'Cats can grin,' Kitty remarked sagely. 'Think of the Cheshire Cat in Alice . . . oh, I forgot, you can't think of him 'cos you can't read. But the Cheshire Cat was famous for his grin.'

'I can read – well, a bit – if it's in print,' Nick said indignantly. 'And I can write me name; not Nick, of course 'cos when I were in school I had to use my real name, but I can write that, I'm tellin' you.'

'Your real name? I didn't know you had one,' Kitty said and then, realising that this was rude, added hastily: 'I thought Nick was your real name, I mean. But I suppose it's just a nickname, like Kitty is. I'm Catherine Mary; what's you?'

'Mumble mumble,' Nick said. 'It don't matter, but I can write it.'

'Of course you can,' Kitty said soothingly. A while back, Nick had cut himself a hazel wand from the hedge and, at Kitty's request, had cut another for her. Now she pulled him to a halt and pointed to the smooth mud at the side of the road. 'Write it in that, with your stick,' she said cunningly. 'Go on, write your real name.'

Nick gave her a suspicious stare, then took his stick and began to trace letters in the mud. At first, Kitty could not make out what they were meant to be and said so, whereupon Nick said crossly: 'It's Cyril. C Y R I L,' and then fell on Kitty, making a spirited endeavour to box her ears as she crowed with amusement. 'What's so funny? Oh, I know it's a stupid name, that's why they call me Nick, but I told you I could write it and so I can.'

Kitty saw that her friend was beginning to be truly embarrassed and hastily straightened her face. 'I'm sorry. It's a very nice name, really,' she said, and then, changing the subject, 'As for Tommy, I'm afraid he's here to stay. The further we get from Dublin, the more he'll depend on us.

Oh, stop it, Nick. You nearly knocked my cap off and this lane's awful muddy.'

Nick stopped trying to box her ears and glanced back at Tommy. 'Well, when we find a barn to sleep in there's bound to be mice so at least one of us will have a good supper,' he observed. 'I've got a box of matches so's we can light a fire but we'd best start searching for a potato clamp so we can rob a few for us supper.'

Kitty was about to ask how they were to cook potatoes when they had no saucepan but then remembered the night Nick had taken her along to a communal fire in a tumbledown tenement block, where a number of ragged boys and girls had been cooking potatoes by thrusting them into the hot ashes, hooking them out with sticks when they were done, dusting the ash off them and eating them eagerly, despite the danger of burned fingers. So instead of questioning him, or asking what a potato clamp was, for she had never heard the word before, she nodded enthusiastically and continued to trudge beside him.

Brendan arrived in Dublin on a fine spring day, though it must have rained overnight for the sunshine glinted off the wet cobbles and there were puddles on the quays.

He reached Handkerchief Alley and hurried up to the flat, hoping that when he saw Caitlin she would assure him that the child was safe. For, despite himself, he was beginning to believe that if he returned with Kitty to the Ferryman he would be rewarded by Sylvie's unequivocal gratitude. If that was so, he meant to ask her to marry him at once, planning to tell her that the bringing up of little Kitty should be shared by them from the start. The fact that the child knew neither of them occurred to him but was speedily banished. Who could fail to see Sylvie and not love her, he reminded himself. And though Caitlin was a wonderful woman, she had children of her own who must have come first in her affections. Once, when Becky had been alive, he would have doubted whether Sylvie could give Kitty the love she had known in Dublin, but it was different now. Now Sylvie had only memories, and would, he was sure, welcome Kitty and love her as she had loved poor Becky. However, when he reached the flat and was ushered into the kitchen by a pale and red-eyed Caitlin, it was to be told that there had been no sign of Kitty, not so much as one sighting, since the fateful day when he himself had visited her.

'And glad I am that you've come back, Brendan,' Caitlin said tearfully, sitting him down at the kitchen table with a mug of tea and a piece of soda bread. 'For 'twas my fault, mainly, that she ran away. I couldn't put it in a letter, but actually Kitty overhead the conversation between you and myself. Oh, Brendan, I wasn't after meaning the half of it, you know that, I was just so upset over losin' me darlin' Pat that I talked wildly. Only –

346

only a child takes everything literally, and she thought I meant it, so she did. She lit out that very day and no one's seen hide nor hair of her since. I felt I ought to search for her meself but I dare not risk losin' me job 'cos work is awful scarce now that the troops are comin' home. And I'm tellin' you, me kids have scoured the city; Maeve's searched from Clontarf to Sandymount.' As she talked, Brendan's understanding of the situation grew and he felt dismayed. If the child had fallen into the wrong hands, she could be anywhere. But Caitlin was continuing to talk. 'We do know one t'ing though; she's not alone, she's with Nick Mooney, an old pal of hers. He's ten years old, very self-reliant, and he'll look after her, keep her safe. But I was forgetting; she pushed a note under the kitchen door – it was addressed to Maeve – on the evening of the day she ran away. I'll fetch it so you can read it for yourself.'

She hurried out of the room, leaving Brendan to consider Maeve and to wonder just what her part was in all this. He remembered Caitlin's saying she looked after the children, spoiled Kitty and spent a good deal of time with her, but he saw no reason why Kitty should have addressed the note to Maeve rather than to Caitlin herself. He would have to ask his cousin when she returned – and when he had read the note, of course.

Presently Caitlin came back, somewhat flushed, holding out a worn and crumpled sheet of paper covered in untidy pencilled handwriting. Brendan took it and scanned it quickly, then crossed the kitchen to put a comforting arm round his cousin. 'When you remember how young Kitty is, this is a grand letter, so it is. She's explained she's run away because she doesn't want to be a burden on you, and she reassures you that she knows she must be very careful. She's also said she'll come back when she's old enough to earn, but I t'ink she'll come back sooner than that. This boy she's with, Nick Mooney – tell me about him.'

'Well, he comes from a bad home – and I mean really bad, Brendan, so he's not often there,' she said. 'But despite living on the streets he's managed to survive, get himself some schooling. Knowing Nick, he probably tried to persuade Kitty to come home and, when she wouldn't, decided to go with her. He's a good lad, honest to God he is.'

Brendan nodded thoughtfully. 'He sounds a good lad, which is a great comfort,' he acknowledged. 'But what about this Maeve? I remember Sylvie saying that a young woman called Maeve looked after the children for you, but I thought she had probably left you as the children grew up. I t'ink I saw her on the stairs when I was here last: just a slip of a girl wit' a crutch under one arm and a great heavy marketing bag. Kitty seems mortal fond of her; well, it stands to reason she must be, since this letter' – he waved the sheet – 'is addressed to her.'

Caitlin nodded. 'Yes, Kitty looks on Maeve as a

sort of foster mother,' she said. 'Maeve's brought her up, you know; she's clothed her, even paid me something towards the child's keep, though I told her it wasn't necessary. Oh, Brendan, I'd never have put Kitty in an orphanage, or sent her away, I'm sure you know that, but if I had tried to do so Maeve would never have allowed it. Kitty's the only child she's ever likely to have and she adores her.'

'Why do you say Kitty's the only child Maeve is ever likely to have?' Brendan asked curiously. 'Sure and she can't be more than seventeen or eighteen; she's got all her life in front of her.'

'She's twenty, and she's a cripple,' Caitlin said bluntly. 'No man's likely to take her on because they'd see her as a liability, not an asset. Not that Maeve would care; I don't believe she's ever so much as glanced at a feller . . .' Despite his worries, Brendan grinned. She had certainly not so much as glanced at him, even though she had called him 'a grand big feller'; he had realised even at the time that this was comment rather than compliment. You had to admire the kid, he reflected; she might have a limp and a twisted foot but it hadn't impaired her self-confidence. Caitlin, however, was still talking. '. . . so you see, we've all done our best to find Kitty. We've told the polis and put the word about in schools, at soup kitchens and of course amongst the tenement kids. There were one or two young fellers who said they'd seen Nick, or thought they had, but that was only very soon after Kitty had run off. And even though she's really shy, and hates putting herself forward, Maeve's been up to the polis station every day, pestering them for news.'

'Shy?' Brendan said incredulously. 'I wouldn't have called her shy meself. I offered to help her wit' her marketing bag and she cut me down to size right away. Told me she weren't a cripple and had climbed more stairs than I'd had hot dinners, or words to that effect.'

Caitlin stared at him. 'Maeve said that?' she said disbelievingly. 'She must have taken a liking to you, Brendan, because she's awful shy with strangers and hates to mention her poor old foot. Are you sure it was her?'

'Well, I can't be certain, but she was in your block and she did have a crutch, and there can't be many like that,' Brendan said, rather stiffly. 'Anyway, it doesn't matter. Where is she now? I t'ink we ought to have a council of war before we do anything else because I've promised Sylvie I'll find her daughter and I mean to do so if I have to search all Ireland.'

'And you'll need Maeve's help, because you've never set eyes on Kitty,' Caitlin said, nodding. 'She's got a photograph, though. We had it done as a Christmas present for Maeve two years ago; it cost a lot but it were worth every penny 'cos she were tickled pink with it. Here, I'll show you.' She rushed out of the room once more but returned seconds later, empty-handed. 'I forgot; Maeve took it to the polis station and left it with them. One of the constables is takin' it round the city, showing it to shopkeepers and so on. Still an' all, she'll get it back when she knows you're going to help.'

Brendan was about to reply when he heard footsteps ascending the stairs. He glanced interrogatively at Caitlin just as the kitchen door flew open and a dark-haired young woman limped into the room, talking as she came. 'I've bought up half the market stalls on Francis Street, and I've actually heard news of—' She stopped short, suddenly realising that she and Caitlin were not alone. Her face flushed deeply and she bent her head. 'I'm sorry, I didn't realise you had company,' she muttered. 'I'll just put these t'ings away . . .'

'Oh, Maeve, this is me cousin Brendan – Brendan, Maeve – so you needn't stand on ceremony. In fact, he's come to help us find Kitty, so you might as well tell us your news.'

Maeve put the heavy bag down on the kitchen table, then turned to stare thoughtfully at Brendan. 'So it was you I met on the stairs the day Kitty ran away,' she said. 'Why for do you want to find Kitty? I'm tellin' you now, she's stayin' with me, here in Ireland. She's not being put into an orphanage or taken to England. I know Sylvie's her real mother, but she's been glad enough to leave her with Caitlin and meself these past years . . .'

'I understand how you feel, but t'ings change, and so do people,' Brendan said quietly. 'You were kind to Sylvie when she was in Dublin years ago, I know. It wasn't possible then for her to take Kitty home, but it's different now. Sylvie's quite alone. She lost her husband, her mother-in-law and her daughter in the flu epidemic, and when she heard—'

'That's very sad, but our Kitty is a person, not a parcel, and I won't see her handed over to anyone else without a fight,' Maeve interrupted firmly, though Brendan noticed that her voice trembled a little. 'You're welcome to search for her, but I'm telling you straight, Kitty won't want to cross the water, she'll want to stay here in Dublin with the people she loves around her.' She glared defiantly at Brendan as she spoke, but before he could put her in her place, remind her that Kitty was Sylvie's child, no matter how bad a mother Maeve might think her, Caitlin cut in.

'Maeve,' she said roundly, 'you said you had some news. Tell us, please. No point in arguing about Kitty's future until we've found her!'

Maeve hesitated and Brendan could see that she was considering either refusing to tell or making up a story which would be acceptable to her audience, but then she shrugged, gave Caitlin a small smile, and began to speak. 'I met Timmy Two-Shoes – the tramp, you know. I asked him if he'd seen Nick and Kitty – he knows Kitty quite well because many a time she's give him her Saturday penny, kind little thing that she is – and he couldn't bring them to mind. Then I said it were an odd thing but Tommy the cat seemed to have took himself off as well, and old Timmy slapped his leg and began to laugh. When he'd got over chokin' and wipin' his eyes, he said he'd seen two lads walkin' along a country lane wit' this big old cat at their heels. He called out to them, askin' which of 'em was Dick Whittington, and the little lad pushed back his cap and laughed and said that he was the Marquis of Carabas and old Tommy here was Puss in Boots. Then the older lad nudged him and pushed the little lad's cap down over his eyes, and they went their ways.

'I asked him if the older lad could have been Nick Mooney but he just looked shifty and said he couldn't tell one lad from another, but he did know a girl when he saw one and he'd not seen our Kitty, not for weeks.'

'Could the smaller boy have been Kitty, wit' her plaits tucked under the cap?' Caitlin asked eagerly, even as Brendan opened his mouth to put the same question. 'She's a bright kid is our Kitty, and so's Nick. We guessed ages ago that they would have disposed of her decent clothing and got some raggedy stuff from somewhere, but wouldn't it make sense now if she dressed herself as a boy? No one would look twice at two young boys – though the cat would raise eyebrows.'

'That's what I t'ought,' Maeve said, a trifle grudgingly. 'And dressed as a boy she's safer than if folk knew she were a girl. So tomorrow I'm going to head for the part of the country where old

Timmy saw the lads and the cat. I'm sure we're on the right track at last, so I am.'

'I t'ink you're right,' Brendan said eagerly. 'Whereabouts was this boreen?'

Maeve hesitated, then said flatly: 'I'll not be after telling you, 'cos I don't want you gettin' there first an' scaring the living daylights out of me darlin' girl wit' talk of takin' her over the water. But don't worry yourself; I'll bring her back to Handkerchief Alley, 'cos it's the only home Kitty and meself know.'

Brendan felt the heat rise up his neck and into his face and longed to give the girl a good telling off; if necessary, to shake the truth out of her. This was his chance to prove to Sylvie that he loved her and cared deeply what happened to her little daughter, and this slip of a girl was trying to undermine him. But Caitlin was looking warningly at him and he realised that if he became aggressive he would only antagonise this small, determined creature. So he smiled placatingly, and assured her that nothing was further from his thoughts than to rush out to find a child he had never seen in his life before. 'But if you'd let me go wit' you, sure and I'd be grateful to my life's end,' he said humbly. 'And I promise not to so much as mention crossing the water until we're back here in Handkerchief Alley.'

'Very well,' Maeve said, after a pause so lengthy that Brendan feared she was not even going to reply. 'Where's you stayin' in Dublin?'

'He's stayin' here; he can sleep on the sofa,' Caitlin said at once. 'Then the two of you can set off as early as you've a mind tomorrow morning.' She glanced apologetically at Brendan. 'There's been so much talk that I've not had chance to prepare food for supper; how's about if you nip down to Thomas Street for me, Bren? There's a fried fish shop only a few doors along.' She hesitated and Brendan saw the pink begin to stain her cheeks. 'I'm a bit short of money right now, but if you could . . .'

'I'd be glad to buy for us all as a small thank you for lettin' me stay in your house,' Brendan said heartily. 'Shall I go now?'

'Yes please,' Caitlin said. Maeve was beginning to unpack the huge marketing bag, carrying potatoes, swedes, carrots and other vegetables to their places on the pantry shelves. He noticed that, in the house, she dispensed completely with her crutch, and though she limped a little and occasionally clutched at the furniture, he thought that a stranger would not have realised that she was disabled. He wondered about offering to help her, then remembered his errand. 'I'll buy for eight; that's right, isn't it?' he said, as he opened the kitchen door. 'I shan't be long.'

Next morning, Brendan woke when sunshine slanted in through a gap in the curtains and fell across his face. For a moment he was confused for, of late, he had woken in so many different places:

in tents, in trenches, in forward dressing stations, and of course in the attic bedroom at the Ferryman, as well as his own little room in the cottage where he had been born. But as soon as he looked round, he remembered. This was his cousin Caitlin's kitchen and he was spending the night here so that he and Maeve might set out early in their quest to find Kitty.

He lay back on the rather lumpy pillow with which Caitlin had provided him, thinking lazily how very much he had enjoyed the previous evening. When he had returned from his shopping expedition the children had been home and he had been really impressed by them. Clodagh was a tall, willowy girl with a mass of dark hair and her mother's big brown eyes. She was quick and competent about the house and had told him about her job – she made sacks in a large factory down by the quays – with a good deal of tolerant humour and a quantity of easy charm. Her sister Grainne was round-faced and chubby, with black curls and an infectious giggle. Neither girl was shy, and nor were the twins or Colm. They were polite, never interrupting their elders, and later in the evening he had told Caitlin he thought she had done an excellent job in the upbringing of her children. She had blushed with pleasure, though she had quickly disclaimed. ''Tis Maeve you should be congratulating, for she's had the rearing of them whilst I worked,' she pointed out. 'And the boys' manners were dinned into them when they were little lads by me darlin' Pat. But they're grand kids and I'm glad you've took to 'em.'

But now, hearing a noise from the room next door, Brendan swung his feet off the sofa and stood up. He'd better get himself dressed and ready before the family invaded the kitchen. It wouldn't take long, since he had not stripped off but had merely removed his trousers and shirt.

He went to the sink and had a quick wash, then dressed and padded across to the fire, which was smouldering dully, and poked it into life. Then he picked up the heavy black kettle and pulled it over the flame. He imagined that Maeve would be the first up and it would do their future relationship no harm if he greeted her with a friendly word and a nice cup of tea. But when the kitchen door opened, it was Caitlin and not Maeve who stepped into the room.

'Mornin', Caitlin,' Brendan said breezily. 'I've pulled the kettle over the fire so's we can all have a cup of tea . . . I thought it would be best if Maeve and meself took a bite of breakfast before setting off.'

Caitlin stared at him for a moment and Brendan saw the colour rise in her cheeks. 'Isn't – isn't Maeve here?' she quavered. 'I heard her get up a couple of hours ago. I didn't expect to see you still here, Bren; I thought the pair of you would be well on the road by now.'

Brendan stared back, feeling his own face flush and knowing that this was with rage. How dared she leave without him! She had promised they should go together . . . well, no, thinking back he realised she had made no promises, had just appeared to comply with his suggestion that they should search together. In fact, the only promise she'd made – if it was a promise – was to bring Kitty back to Handkerchief Alley since this was the only home that she and Kitty had ever known. But Caitlin was speaking, and he guessed she had read the anger in his face and was worried by it. 'It'll be all right, Brendan. Don't t'ink Maeve was trying to steal a march on you or prevent you from finding Kitty,' she said urgently.

'Oh, really?' Brendan said. 'I'd have thought different meself, but I'll take your word for it.'

'I told you earlier, she's never so much as glanced at a feller and it's my opinion that she's scared of men. Oh, she loved our Pat and she's fond of the boys, but she's shy as a little bird wit' fellers she don't know, honest to God she is.'

Brendan slumped down at the kitchen table and put his head in his hands. 'But she never said she'd bring the child straight back here and it's my belief she'll do no such t'ing. Oh, I don't doubt she'll bring her back eventually, but not while I'm here, for as you know, Cait, I need to work, same as we all do, so I can't stay here indefinitely. An' who's to say she'll find the kid anyway? If only I'd been straight with her . . . but I weren't, an' that's the truth. She – she made me mad so I sort of pretended I meant to take Kitty back to her real mammy for good, though all I truly meant to do was to take her to Liverpool for a few days so that Sylvie could see her daughter were alive and well. Then I'd have brought her back to Ireland, if that was what she wanted.'

'It's a great shame you didn't say so,' Caitlin said sadly. 'For I'm afraid you may be right. Maeve's a resourceful young woman; she could get a job, hire a room somewhere, and stay away from Dublin for months, maybe years. Brendan, my love, you must go after her.'

Brendan sat up and stared at his cousin. 'But I don't know where she's gone, and neither do you,' he said heavily. 'Sure and I'd search the whole of Ireland if I could, but . . .'

'But I do know Timmy Two-Shoes,' Caitlin said triumphantly. 'And I know where he'll be sleepin' of a night when he's in Dublin. Can you make porridge? But it doesn't matter. Clodagh was getting dressed when I passed her bedroom door. She'll do it, only I'll have to go at once before Timmy's up and has had a chance to get going. And don't worry that he'll not tell me, 'cos he's a grand old feller and wouldn't want me worrying.' As she spoke, she was rushing across to the pantry, taking out a chunk of cheese, removing a loaf of bread from the crock, and hurrying back to the table. Quickly, she made a hefty sandwich which she wrapped in a sheet of newspaper. Then she crossed the room, took a coat off the back of the door and pushed the sandwich into a pocket.

'Besides, I'm after thinking it's not every day that Timmy Two-Shoes gets his breakfast served by a pretty woman,' she finished, and whisked out of the door before Brendan could thank her.

Chapter Thirteen

When Kitty awoke in the early hours of the morning, it was raining; the fine, soft Irish rain which penetrates every garment on your back, yet falls so gently that it seems more like a mist than proper rain. She and Nick were curled up in the middle of a nice haystack into which they had burrowed the previous evening, but despite the fact that she was warm and cosy – though a trifle itchy, for hayseeds down the neck are not the best of bedfellows – she was depressed by the sight of the rain. She had thought that sleeping under the stars would be romantic but she had not bargained either for rain or for the extreme cold that sometimes descended as darkness fell. When they found property owned by someone with sufficient money to have outbuildings it was usually well fenced against intruders, and the smaller places did not run to such luxuries.

Cautiously, Kitty shifted Tommy's warm body from the curve of her stomach and crawled down the short passageway through which they had entered the haystack. It was difficult to tell what time it was for the grey clouds hid the sky completely, but she guessed that it was early; no cock crowed, no dog barked, and there was no sound of human beings stirring.

Satisfied, Kitty crawled back into their warm nest; you never knew, in a couple of hours the rain might have cleared. Tommy, who had uttered a mew of protest as he felt her warmth withdraw, began to purr deeply and resoundingly as she cuddled against him once more. She was actually drifting back to sleep when a thought occurred to her and gave her a certain amount of satisfaction. This was the very first time since she had left Handkerchief Alley that she had woken in the morning and not thought immediately and wistfully of Maeve and the O'Keefes, of the comfortable life she had lived and of the good food that had arrived on the table morning and evening. But now I'm not only growing accustomed, I'm beginning to enjoy the freedom, she told herself. Sister Jeremiah was kind and gentle but the other nuns had been real horrors, so though she regretted that she would not be properly educated she thought life 'on the hoof', as Nick called it, might well prove a good deal more amusing. Nick had warned her pretty often that when winter came they would have to find some sort of work or refuge, but it was not yet the end of April and winter seemed a long way ahead. Kitty drifted off to sleep.

The second time she awoke, it was to hear definite indications that the outside world was awakening. A cow lowed, then a rooster began to crow and Kitty heard the distant sound of a bucket clanking as someone went to the well. Hastily, she sat up. They had chosen a haystack as far away from the farmhouse as possible but, even so, Nick made it a rule that the three of them should be well away from their sleeping place by the time people were astir.

'Nick!' Kitty shook her companion's shoulder and he woke at once, sitting up and knuckling his eyes and glancing around him as though he, too, wondered for a moment where he was. But Nick was an old hand, and did not waste time asking questions. 'Out!' he said. 'Grab your stuff; c'mon, Tommy.'

As the three of them emerged from the haystack, Kitty realised that the rain had stopped and the sun was shining, though there was a chilly breeze and the long wet grass felt ice-cold to her bare feet. They were halfway across the meadow, heading for the little lane which bordered it, when they heard a shout behind them. Nick kept determinedly on, but Kitty glanced back and saw a large, heavily built man carrying what she assumed to be a milk pail in either hand, staring at them. There was a black and white dog at his heels and when they did not answer his shout he uttered a sharp command and the dog streaked towards them, ears flat, mouth opening to show a remarkably fine set of teeth. Kitty had always liked dogs but there was something in the way the animal covered the ground that made her give

Nick a sharp dig in the back. 'He's set the perishin'
dog on us,' she said. 'Let's run!'

They ran. Had it not been for Tommy, Kitty
dared not think what might have occurred, but
Tommy undoubtedly saved them. He had been
loping along behind them, seemingly unaware
of the dog, but when it got within ten feet of
them he stopped dead, fluffed out his body and
arched his back, uttering a fearful squawk as he
did so. Kitty hesitated, would have turned back
to snatch her pet to safety, but Nick grabbed her
hand and urged her on. 'Forget it; Tommy's been
dealing wit' dogs since he were a kitten. He's
goin' to save our bacon for us,' he said breathlessly, as the two of them thundered towards the
gate which led on to the lane. 'Keep runnin';
don't look back.'

But Kitty, unable to resist, glanced behind her
and saw Tommy, when the dog was only feet away,
suddenly turn and streak to the left. The dog
changed direction so fast that his paws must have
smoked, and as she and Nick threw themselves
over the gate Tommy arrived on the lane beside
them. Kitty would have continued to run but Nick
pulled her to a halt. 'The dog won't follow us into
the lane 'cos it ain't the farmer's property,' he
gasped, a hand to his side. He bent to caress the
cat, who did not appear one whit the worst for the
chase. 'Good old Tommy. I said you'd save our
bacon and so you did. Now we'd best be goin',
'cos something tells me the feller with the milk

pails ain't a-goin' to let us earn ourselves a bite o' breakfast by workin' for him.'

Kitty chuckled. She bent and picked Tommy up, then strolled along beside Nick, though she could not help glancing nervously at the hedge which bordered their late adversary's field. It was diamonded with drops from the recent rain, sparkling now in the sunshine, but there were several gaps through which a dog could squeeze should it so wish and she could see the animal keeping pace with them on the other side. 'He won't come through to worrit us,' Nick said reassuringly, following Kitty's glance. 'It's wishful t'inking, so it is; he's hoping either us or the cat will wriggle through that hawthorn hedge so that he can take a nice mouthful out of us.'

Kitty smiled. 'Tommy would make a pretty prickly mouthful,' she observed. 'Isn't he brave, Nick? He stood his ground until the dog were almost on him, then he whipped round like a – an adder, and ran like a hare. I know you thought he might give us away, but like you said, he did save our bacon, didn't he?'

Nick nodded, though he was looking rather serious. 'Sure and he's a grand feller,' he agreed, rather absently. 'But I dare not nip into a field to rob a cow of some of her milk, and I must have left that half loaf we were saving in the haystack. We came away in a bit of a hurry. Oh well, it'll be a treat for the rats.'

Kitty shuddered. 'Then we'll just have to walk

until we get to another farm, or a village,' she said. And as soon as she saw through the hedge that the dog had deserted them, she put Tommy down, for he was heavy. 'Remember the last potato clamp – oh, and the woman in that terrible little cottage who gave us soda bread and goat's cheese? Isn't it odd, Nick, that poor people will often give us a crust whereas rich people chase us off their land?'

'It's the way of the world,' Nick said airily. 'Wish it were blackberry time. Still, we've not starved yet so likely we shan't starve today. Best foot forward, Kit!'

A couple of miles further on, the little lane they were following veered to the east and Nick stopped in the middle of it, staring about him. They were approaching wooded country now, with little sign of human habitation, and Kitty thought sorrowfully of the large chunk of soda bread nestling in the haystack, and of the cows which might have given up some of their milk to three hungry travellers, but Nick told her they would have to tighten their belts until they were through the woods. She smiled as bravely as she could. 'The food'll taste all the better if we're really hungry,' she said, and Nick flung an arm round her shoulders and gave her a quick squeeze.

'You're a brave kid, so you are,' he said approvingly. 'And don't worrit yourself; we'll find somethin' to eat afore nightfall.'

Shortly after this conversation they left the lane and took to the woods, and Kitty began to sing.

At first Nick joined in, but suddenly he tugged at her arm and put a finger to his lips. 'Hush! Can you hear that noise? I reckon there's a woodcutter quite close at hand; if so, he might give us a share of whatever food he's got, or maybe let us gather a big bundle of firewood to sell in the nearest village. Then we could buy our own breakfast.'

'It won't be breakfast now, it'll be dinner,' Kitty pointed out, but she followed Nick's lead with alacrity. Suppose the man has bread and cheese and apples? Her mouth watered at the thought, for they had found country people to be a good deal more accommodating than city folk when it came to sharing food.

Presently, they came upon a rutted track between the trees and followed it since it was pretty plain that it led in the direction of the thuds they had heard. But now the thuds were accompanied by other sounds: whimpering, wailing, shouts and yells. Left to herself, Kitty would have turned tail, but Nick grabbed her arm. 'Best see what's going on,' he muttered, 'though I don't like the sound of it. Kit, if I pinch your arm, you're to simply follow me as fast as you can. No turning back for Tommy, 'cos he'll be in no danger. Understand?'

Kitty whispered that she understood. Ahead of them she could see a pool of sunlight, and within a very few minutes they came to a clearing in the trees and took shelter behind the trunk of an enormous beech tree. Peering round it, they were shocked by what they saw. The first thing Kitty noticed was the gypsy caravan, the second thing the large hindquarters of a piebald horse, and the next thing the man and woman. The woman had fallen to the ground where she lay trying to cover her head with her arms. The screaming they had heard was fainter now. The man was belabouring her with an enormous stick, bringing it down mercilessly on any part of her body he could reach. There was blood on the woman's ragged clothing and instinctively Kitty stepped forward, shouting 'Stop that!' as she did so.

The man could not have heard her or, if he had, cared not at all, for his stick continued to rise and fall. The woman's body shuddered with every stroke, but now her cries had dwindled to the occasional sobbing moan. Kitty broke from cover and ran across the clearing. She grabbed for the stick and clung on to it with all her might. 'You're killing her,' she shouted. 'Stop it at once, do you hear me? I tell you you'll kill her.'

For answer, the man growled a stream of invective, his brogue so thick that Kitty only half understood what he was saying, but she could not mistake his intention as he tried to raise the stick and hit his victim again, even though by now Nick was clinging to his other arm and kicking out with all his force at his shins.

The woman on the ground had ceased to move. The man turned his attention to Kitty and Nick, and clearly thought he could handle a couple of youngsters. He wore long leather boots to the knee, old and battered but still a protection against Nick's bare feet, and Kitty thought, desperately, that presently he would break free, kill the woman, and then start on themselves. She tried to explain this to Nick, but Nick had dropped the man's arm and joined her on the end of the stick. 'Get it away from him,' he muttered, his mouth close to Kitty's ear. 'Pull wit' all your strength, alanna. Pull, pull.' And then, to Kitty's astonishment, he hissed: 'Let go!' It was just luck that Kitty obeyed instantly, even though she did not understand why Nick should have said such a thing. However, his strategy became clear the next moment, for as they suddenly released their hold on the man's cudgel he was taken completely by surprise and fell heavily backwards, striking his head on the trunk of the tree behind him with a rather sickening thud.

'That'll teach him to hit his poor wife,' Nick said breathlessly. His chest was heaving from the struggle and his eyes darted uneasily from one still figure on the ground to the other. 'Tek a look at her, Kitty, while I see if I can find something to tie the old bugger's arms and legs together with, else he'll give us a fearful hidin' as soon as he comes round.'

Kitty knelt obediently by the woman's side and put a tentative hand on the scarf which covered her head. It fell back, revealing the fact that this was no young woman as Kitty had supposed, for her attacker appeared to be in the prime of life, but a woman of perhaps seventy years of age, for her hair was sparse and grey as a badger, and her thin, bony face was seamed with wrinkles. However, despite the beating she had taken, Kitty saw with immense relief that she was still alive, for the transparent lids flickered up, revealing a pair of eyes so dark that they appeared black, and Kitty realised that the face into which she peered had once been beautiful, though time and bad treatment had left their mark. She turned to Nick, who was leaning over the man on the ground. Kitty wished Nick would hurry up and find some rope to tie him with, for even though he was worsted for the moment she could see now that he was both young and strong, with a pelt of black hair, curly as a ram's fleece, swarthy skin, and the shoulders of a man used to physical labour, for they were broad and strong. She began to speak, and Nick straightened and came towards her, his expression troubled. 'I'm after thinking we'll not be needing so much as a length of string,' he said quietly. 'I've took a good look at him, alanna, and he's stone dead. His neck's broke. He won't be hittin' anyone again, not his wife, nor a pair of kids. How's the woman?'

'She's alive; she's breathin', and her eyes opened for a second just now,' Kitty said tremulously. 'But she's *old*, Nick, really old. 'I t'ought she was his wife too 'cos I know bad men do beat their wives. Sometimes you hear the yells from some poor woman what's done nothin' wrong 'cept to be there when her man comes home drunk, but even the worst of fellers don't beat their mammies.'

Nick knelt down beside her and peered at the woman. 'I dunno; they ain't much alike,' he said uncertainly. 'They're both tinkers, though. Maybe a tinker might marry an old woman to get her money, 'cos they say tinks keep gold under the floorboards of their caravans, or – or mebbe he were drunk and mistook her for his wife.'

Kitty thought that this sounded reasonable but it still left them with an insuperable problem. The man was dead and the woman in a bad way. They knew better than to take her to a hospital, even if they could find one in these parts, because that would have meant telling the whole story, and admitting that a man lay dead. Kitty told herself that she and Nick were innocent, had done nothing save to let go of the cudgel with which the man had been beating the woman, but she knew that if the authorities heard of their involvement it would be the end of their freedom; Nick would be sent back to his parents and the hovel in which he lived, and she would be put in an orphanage, or sent across the water to England. She glanced at Nick and saw immediately that he shared her own feelings. 'It weren't our fault that the feller tripped over his own cudgel and broke his neck agin that tree,' he said. 'But if we goes an' tells, likely they won't believe us and we'll find ourselves in Mountjoy Prison or swingin' on the end of the hangman's rope. No, we've got to get out of here and forget we ever met 'em.'

'But we can't just leave the old woman here,' Kitty objected. 'What if she's been hurt mortal bad and goes an' dies? Let's carry her to the caravan, and if there's a spade or some such I suppose . . . I suppose we'd best bury the feller. If we leave him here someone's bound to find him, and then they'll start looking for us.'

Nick, however, shook his head. 'If we bury him, there'll be nothing to prove we didn't stick a knife in him, or kill him in some other way,' he pointed out. 'I reckon if we leave him where he is – don't move him so much as an inch – then when he is found, it'll be pretty plain he fell and broke his neck. Besides, this is a pretty remote part o' the woods. It could be days, weeks even, before someone comes this way again.'

Kitty looked doubtful. 'But they'll know he wouldn't have come here by hisself and on foot,' she said fearfully. 'Oh, Nick, I'm scared, really I am.'

'Don't worry, we'll think of something,' Nick said bracingly, though Kitty noticed that there was a deep worry line between his brows. 'Let's get the old girl into the caravan for a start, then we'll decide what to do. You take her feet, 'cos that's the lightest end, and I'll carry her shoulders.'

The two of them carried the old woman into the caravan. They laid her upon a narrow bench seat which, Kitty guessed, became a bed at night, then Kitty fussed about finding a brightly coloured, hand-knitted blanket to put over her and used one of the cushions with which both seats were decorated as a pillow. Then she looked about her. She thought the caravan was delightful, for there was a little blackened stove, and a board pulled out from one end of the van so that the occupants could sit along the bench seats with their plates of food upon the table in front of them. It was all very neat and compact. The walls were hung with kitchen equipment – pans, ladles and the like – and from the ceiling depended a number of hooks upon which hung a string bag of onions, another of potatoes, a third of turnips and carrots, and – oh joy! – what looked like a side of smoked bacon. Kitty grabbed Nick's arm, seeing his eyes as wide as her own. 'Isn't it lovely?' she whispered. 'I wish we could stay in this caravan – I wish it were ours! Do you – do you think the old woman would mind if we spent a bit of time and made ourselves a bite of dinner? That there smoked bacon looks so good I could eat it just as it is, and the vegetables could be in the pot in a moment, if you give the word.'

Much to Kitty's disappointment, Nick shook his head. 'I don't think we ought to hang around here, not with that feller dead out there. You settle the old lady comfortable, tuck the blanket in tight so she won't fall out when we move, an' I'll get the horse backed into the shafts and harnessed up. We'll take the track we came into the woods on because it's already thick with wheel marks, so another set won't bother anyone. But just to be on the safe side, I'll drive the caravan a bit along the track and then I'll walk back and brush out any traces it's left in the clearing. Then there'll be nothing to say he weren't just a tramp making his way alone across country.'

'Right,' Kitty said, her brow clearing. 'But will we be able to stop later, Nick, and make a meal? I'm tellin' you, me belly's flappin' against me backbone an' me stomach thinks me throat's been cut.'

This made Nick laugh, since they were expressions he commonly used himself but had never heard before from Kitty's lips. 'We'll stop as soon as we've put enough distance between us and this clearing,' he promised. 'For one thing, the old 'un's took one hell of a beating and when she comes round she'll be wantin' her dinner. All right? If so, I'll start harnessing the horse.'

Kitty glanced round the caravan. So neatly was it arranged that it was easy to see movement would not bring anything tumbling down, so she nodded. 'Yes, right you are, Nick; only can you drive a horse? I know you say you've been on the hoof on and off for years, but surely no one's ever let you drive a caravan before?'

Nick, already descending the steps, looked back. 'As it happens, I shan't be driving for a bit 'cos mostly the horses is led, but I joined up with a band of tinkers a year back – grand fellers they were, up to every rig – and though I never drove a cart meself, I often sat up by the driver and it's dead easy.' Kitty looked at him sceptically and his grin broadened. 'Well, it might not be so easy wit' a young horse or a mettlesome one,' he admitted, 'but wit' a placid old feller like the piebald, I reckon I can't go far wrong.'

With that, he disappeared, and Kitty turned back into the caravan. She looked speculatively at her patient. She supposed that the best way of ensuring that the old woman stayed on the bench would be to stand against it, or even to sit on the edge, but when she did so her nose wrinkled with disgust, for the old woman stank. She looked around for something to tie round the bench seat, then glanced back and stared. Was it her imagination or had the old woman's eyes actually closed as she turned? She was pretty sure they had, and if so, she realised with a stab of dismay, the woman had probably overheard the conversation between herself and Nick. Desperately, she tried to remember just what they had said. She was pretty sure they must have mentioned that the woman's companion – if you could call him that – was dead. Would the woman think they had killed him? But Kitty could not imagine that she would object; after all, the man had beaten her mercilessly with a cudgel, ignoring the fact that his victim was old and frail. Bones grew brittle with age, Kitty knew; the old woman would be lucky if she had escaped with only bruises and abrasions. She comforted herself with the thought that the attacker had intended murder, so his victim ought to be grateful she was still alive and not quibble over the unfortunate accident that had ended his days, which had been no fault of theirs.

There was a slight jolt as Nick backed the horse between the shafts and Kitty, keeping her eyes on the woman, saw her wince. Presently, as the cart began to rock a little, she groaned and opened her eyes again. Kitty went to her at once, taking hold of the woman's filthy, almost skeletal hand, and smoothing the hair back from her swarthy brow. 'It's all right,' she said gently. 'We're not stealing your cart or anything – me pal's movin' it because . . . because it seemed best to move on. We don't know how bad you're hurt but mebbe we ought to find you a hospital?'

The old woman began to shake her head, then muttered something in a strange tongue which Kitty assumed must be Romany. 'Do you know how bad you're hurt?' she asked timidly. 'And I'm afraid you'll have to speak English, 'cos that's the only language me and Nick understand.'

The old woman's dark eyes fixed themselves on Kitty's face. 'I've broke me arm,' she said in a tiny whisper. 'And I t'ink me collarbone's gone. I heared it snap. There's a couple o' ribs what took a cruel blow too, but no hospital, nor no doctor; me nephew will see to me once he's over his temper.'

Kitty stared at her incredulously. Assuming that it was her nephew who had inflicted her hurts, surely she could not expect him to doctor those same injuries? But then she looked more closely at the old woman, and though the eyelids immediately descended, Kitty thought she could read the answer in her eyes. The old woman was no fool; she knew her nephew was dead, must have known it was he who beat her up, yet for some reason that Kitty could not fathom she was pretending ignorance. What would be the best thing to do? Join the old lady in her strange game of pretence, or tell her the truth and see how she reacted? But then the cart began to lurch and bump as the horse circled the clearing, heading for the cart track, and the old woman gave a cry of pain and reached out to grab the table. Immediately, Kitty sat down in the curve of the woman's body and put her own arm round the skinny shoulders. 'Keep still!' she commanded. 'I must tell you right now that your nephew isn't here and won't be able to help us to nurse you back to health. What was his name?'

'Was? *Was?*' the old woman said, confirming Kitty's suspicion that she knew more than she was prepared to let on. 'Why for does you say "was", darter?'

Kitty stared; clearly the old woman had not been fooled by her cropped hair, or her trousers, since she had known her at once for a girl. But it did not really matter so long as Kitty impressed upon her, later, that her sex must not become common knowledge. She looked again at the old woman's face. 'I believe you know very well that your nephew is dead,' she said bluntly. 'Indeed, if it hadn't been for Nick and meself you'd be the dead one, because his next blow would have crushed your skull like a walnut. Why was he beating you? What had you done?' And then, as the old woman closed her lips tightly: 'I think you'd better tell me, because if you don't, then I shan't feel able to stay with you in the cart and look after you until you're well again.'

There was a long, long pause. Kitty, who was beginning to realise that the old woman was as wily as a fox, thought that she was considering how much to tell, if anything. But suddenly she seemed to make up her mind. She had shut her eyes, as well as her mouth, probably realising that both could give her away, but now she opened them, though she did not look directly at Kitty, but kept her gaze fixed on her own bony fingers. 'Me nephew's name were Jacky Smith and he were beatin' me because I found out something about him,' she said slowly. 'I didn't mean to let on I knew; in fact if he hadn't raised the cudgel to me and broke me arm with the first blow, I might ha' kept my mouth shut.'

'I don't understand,' Kitty said, thoroughly bewildered. 'If he didn't know you knew what you knew . . .'

The cart jolted again and the old woman cried out and held out her arm. Kitty could see that it looked strange, though the bone, she thanked God, had not broken through the skin. 'You'll find a little plank what I use to prop the door open in hot weather,' the old woman said faintly. 'Lay me arm on it, straighten it as best you can, and tie it in place; tie it tight so it can't move. Then I'll tell you the rest.'

Kitty found the plank easily but did not feel able to touch the painful-looking arm herself. Luckily, after no more than a couple of minutes, the jolting and rocking stopped and Nick opened the caravan door. 'I'm going to walk back and get rid of any wheel marks . . .' he was beginning, but Kitty interrupted him.

'Nick, can you tie this arm to that plank? I'm so afraid of hurting her that I dare not touch it, but you know much more than I do and you're older. I'll go and wipe out the wheel marks if you'll do the arm.'

Nick came right into the caravan and looked at the pitifully scrawny limb held out for his inspection. 'Fetch me some strips of material,' he said brusquely, and Kitty saw that he was looking rather pale. 'Tear up a bit of old sheet, or a petticoat, or something. Then we'll both go and wipe out the wheel marks; it'll be safer.'

Kitty looked wildly round her, then at the old woman. 'Are you wearing a petticoat?' she asked. 'If so, I'll help you out of it. It's all right, Nick – she knows I'm a girl.'

The old woman made a scornful sound, and pointed to the bench opposite the one upon which she lay. 'Lift the top off that seat,' she said faintly, and sure enough, when Kitty did so, she found a squirrel's horde of material scraps. Soon enough, the old woman's arm was bandaged tightly to the board, but she would not let Nick leave the cart until they had had the explanation which the old woman had promised.

It seemed that Jacky had invited the old woman to share the caravan with him, cooking, cleaning and doing other housewifely tasks, because, he told her, his common-law wife, Miranda, had left him. The old woman had been happy to agree, since her own husband was long dead and her children were scattered. She had been living in a tent, too cold in winter and too hot in summer, so the prospect of sharing the cart, which she knew Jacky's wife had kept beautifully, was irresistible, and she had agreed.

At first, all had gone well, but then Jacky had begun to complain that her cooking was not to his taste. He had hit her several times, and then one night, returning to the cart very drunk indeed, he had actually boasted that he had killed Miranda when he had seen her whispering to a young farm worker, because he had been sure she was telling the man that Jacky was a brute and that she meant to run away from him.

The old woman had been horrified, for it had explained many things that had worried her, but the next day it was soon clear that Jacky had completely forgotten his confidences of the night before. She had thought herself safe, had actually believed that she now knew something which she could hold over his head, but this had not been the case at all. Jacky had used his fists on her several times and had abruptly decreed, the next time he came home drunk, that he did not mean to let her continue to sleep in the caravan, but had decided that she must bed down beneath it 'like the dogs'. She had pleaded with him to remember her old bones but he had simply laughed, and in the course of a night crouched beneath the caravan whilst the rain beat relentlessly down, and the wind constantly blew the wetness in upon her, she had decided to rebel. By the time she had emerged, every bone ached and she was as cold as if it had been midwinter.

Jacky had been in a reasonable mood until she said, flatly, that she did not mean to cook his meals, do his washing, or fetch and carry for him, until she was allowed to sleep in the cart once more. He had punched her in the face, knocking her to the ground, and as he raised his cudgel she had played what she thought of as her trump card. 'Don't think you can kill me as you killed Miranda,' she had shrieked, staggering to her feet. 'Ho, yes, you told me all about it your own self, you wicked bugger, and so I'll tell Miranda's fambly an' anyone else what's interested.'

She had seen his look of astonishment and chagrin turn to red rage, had realised her mistake and tried to run, but it had been useless. He had knocked her down and begun to beat her with his cudgel, exclaiming as he did so that he would see she never told anybody anything.

After that, she remembered nothing until she came to herself inside the cart, with her poor head throbbing and her whole body afire.

Kitty and Nick listened to the story in respectful silence, but when it was over Nick spoke out firmly. 'We saved your life, missus,' he said. 'Jacky's cudgel was about to descend on your head when Kitty and me grabbed it and stopped the blow short. Jacky were a strong man and we couldn't wrest the cudgel away from him, so when he jerked it back sudden like we had to let go. He weren't expectin' it so he fell straight backwards and broke his neck agin the nearest tree. And I hope you aren't going to pretend to be sorry,' he added, 'because if so, you're mad as bedlam and ought to be shut up.'

The old woman whimpered. 'I ain't sorry, 'cos another night spent under the cart would probably have kilt me wit'out a doubt,' she said. 'What's youse names? I's Granny Trotter; Trotty they call me, or Granny, dependin'.'

'Nice to meet you, Granny,' Nick said, and Kitty echoed the sentiment. 'We're willin' to take care of you until you're well but you'll have to give us your word you won't never mention what happened to Jacky. If anyone asks, you're to say he went off to get drink and didn't return. So after hangin' around for three days, you set off to find the rest of your band.'

The old woman nodded wearily, but Kitty doubted whether she had taken it all in, for the bruises were beginning to come out and there was a very large lump on Granny Trotter's forehead. 'Will you be all right if we leave you for half an hour, Granny?' she asked. 'I want to help Nick hide all traces of the caravan back in the clearing. I'd like to make a meal but Nick says we must move on for a few miles before stopping again.'

The old lady gave what might have been a tiny nod. Kitty decided to take it as that, anyway, and the two children left the cart. The horse was still between the shafts but Nick had tied the reins to a low bush, enabling the animal to graze, provided he kept within ten feet of his tethering place. Returning to the clearing seemed strange and Kitty, glancing at Jacky, realised that she was afraid he might suddenly jump to his feet and pursue them. Like all children reared in the Liberties, she had had her fill of ghost stories, and knew that if the banshee threw her comb at you you'd die within twenty-four hours, whereas if the wailing lady who walked the walls in Gardiner Street pointed a long scarlet finger at you, then you'd die within six months. She had always been told that such tales were invented to keep children in their place, and had not given much credence to the stories. But Jacky was real all right, and he looked so natural lying there, so strong and malevolent! If he were to jump to his feet . . .

Fortunately, he did no such thing, and very soon

Kitty was so busy helping Nick to eradicate all signs of their presence, that she almost forgot the still figure on the ground. Because of the rain, and the fact that the cart had stood in the clearing for at least twelve hours, if not more, they might have had difficulty filling in the ruts it had left save that Nick suddenly remembered something. He smote his forehead with his hand, exclaiming: 'Sure and what a fool I am, for didn't I know that tinkers store such things as spades, turf-cutting tools, scythes and even buckets underneath their caravans; I'll bet Jacky and old Ma Trotter did the same. Because of last night's rain the mud's really thick, but if I can find a spade we'll be able to get rid of all the signs that the cart was ever here.'

He disappeared and presently returned with a spade and an implement that he told Kitty was used for cutting turf. 'You take this because it's lighter,' he said, handing her the strangely shaped tool, 'and I'll take the spade, and soon it'll be as though we were never here.'

Kitty began to work, then stopped short, glancing round wildly. 'Nick, where's Tommy? I've not seen him since we first arrived in the clearing. Oh, poor feller, he must have made off when he saw Jacky beating the old girl.'

She began to call the cat's name, but Nick shushed her impatiently. 'He'll turn up. He's probably gone off to hunt himself some food,' he assured her. 'Cats don't like folks fightin' an' swingin' cudgels, but don't worry, he'll be back.'

'I do hope you're right,' Kitty said dolefully. 'I can't bear to think of Tommy lost and alone.'

The two children set to work, and soon they were satisfied that they had left no trace of their recent occupation. Then they returned to the caravan and drove until they came to open heath, and here Nick decreed that they should stop and eat. They were now both so hungry that they could have devoured the vegetables raw, but this was not necessary. Nick lit a fire, using some dry wood he had found under the caravan as kindling, and very soon they were tucking into a vegetable stew, though Granny Trotter was only able to drink the broth. Throughout the meal, Kitty kept glancing behind, hoping to see Tommy's small figure coming purposefully towards them, but there was no sign of him. Nick joked that he was unlikely to reappear for vegetable stew but would undoubtedly turn up when they fried the bacon; he had decided that they'd save this for another day since, as he pointed out, there were vegetables enough to last a week, but meat was not something you could nick from a farmer's field when no one was about.

Since they had no particular destination in mind – though Nick had said vaguely that they must get as far away from Dublin as they could – they simply let the horse take whichever path across the moor appealed to him. Nick tried to ask Granny to point out a good spot to spend the night but she merely gave him a malevolent glance out of the only eye she could open; the other was black and blue, the lids so swollen that it remained closed, giving her the appearance, Kitty thought, of a pirate in a storybook.

'I can't t'ink straight wit' me poor body broken in a dozen places, like as not, and me half blinded an' achin' in every limb,' she grumbled. 'I wouldn't be surprised if I upped and died in the night, so you'll have to make up your own mind where you stop. Only mek it soon 'cos the joltin' o' the cart is likely to kill me, else.'

Nick shrugged. 'Right. I can see trees on the horizon so we'll make for them. If there's a stream and a bit of cover, we'll stop there.' He left the caravan, gesturing to Kitty to follow him, and they both went to the horse's head and began to lead him towards the distant clump of trees. 'If her arm's really broke, then I reckon we ought to take her to see a doctor whether she likes it or not,' Nick said in a low tone. 'She took a terrible beating, Kitty, and I don't fancy having another corpse on our hands. How bad is she, do you think?'

'I don't really know, but I think she's pretty tough. After all, she told us about Jacky without once getting muddled, so her brain's all right,' Kitty said. 'But she is awfully old and I reckon she knows she'll need help until her hurts heal, so she'll do her best to keep us on her side. But she must be hurtin' quite bad, so I 'spect that's what's making her niggly and cross. But oh, Nick, it's such a relief to have the 'van to sleep in and the horse to pull it along, I think we'll just have to put up with Granny Trotter's crossness for a bit.'

Nick agreed that this would be sensible, adding that the old woman's temper would doubtless sweeten as her hurts healed. 'You want to see whether she's got any cures for bruises and wounds in them cupboards in the 'van, 'cos they do say tinkers have remedies for most t'ings, and do all their own doctoring,' he said. 'You can do it when we settle down for the night, 'cos you can't go spreading a salve on a wound when you're being jolted and jounced.'

Kitty agreed, and presently they reached the spinney and found that it was an ideal camping site. The trees were pines, bent against the wind, and when they backed the caravan into their shelter they discovered that a stream ran nearby. Nick unharnessed the horse – Granny Trotter told them its name was Tugger – and hobbled him since they had no wish to discover, next morning, that their sole means of conveyance had gone off on some private spree. Then he fetched a couple of buckets of water and returned through the trees with Kitty trotting beside him. As they approached the caravan, Kitty looked hopefully round once more; surely Tommy had not turned back? Nick would say the cat's home was in the Liberties, that cats were attached to places and not to people, but she knew he was wrong. Tommy had accompanied them for miles and miles and probably had no more idea than she had of how to return to the city. She wondered whether to suggest that they should go back to look for him, but this would mean revisiting the clearing where Jacky's body lay. So she said nothing but followed Nick up the steps and found Granny sitting up and looking a good deal more cheerful. She held a bottle in one hand and a cup in the other and she actually smiled at them as they entered. 'It's me elderberry wine; it's grand for pains, so it is,' she informed them. 'How about makin' a fire in the stove so's we'll be warm overnight?'

Kitty looked hopefully at Nick; it would be fun to light a fire in the little black stove and she imagined that Granny would feel the cold more because of the battering she had received, but Nick shook his head. 'Not tonight; we'll need the dry wood to cook our breakfast porridge tomorrow morning,' he pointed out. 'I see you managed to get out of bed to fetch your elderberry wine.'

Granny looked somewhat self-conscious. 'It weren't easy, but the two of youse weren't around to give an old woman a hand and the pain drove me,' she mumbled. 'Well, if you won't light me a fire in me stove then I'll take another swig o' this to warm me.'

She waved the bottle at them as she spoke but Nick stepped forward and removed it from her grasp, despite her indignant wail. 'No you don't, Gran,' he said grimly. 'We'll have you drunk as an owl if you keep on guzzling strong liquor. Kitty's goin' to see if she can find something to spread on your bruises so I'll mek meself scarce while she does that.'

Granny sniffed but raised no more objections, and presently Kitty began to spread an evil-looking concoction over the old woman's hurts. When this was done to Granny Trotter's satisfaction, she tucked the old woman up warmly and went and called Nick. For a moment there was no answering hail and Kitty's heart began to beat fast, but then she saw Nick's small figure approaching from the direction in which they had come. He must have seen her watching, though dusk had fallen, for he quickened his pace. 'I were just takin' a look round to see what I could see,' he said guardedly. 'You sleep on the bench, Kitty; I'll curl up on the floor wit' me blanket an' one o' them pillows.' He shot Kitty a quick glance, then gave her hand a comforting squeeze. 'Don't worry,' he said, 'cats is independent. He'll find us again when he's good and ready.'

Kitty sniffed, hating the thought of curling up to sleep without Tommy's warm body vibrating gently against her. She imagined him returning to the clearing, finding the caravan gone, casting about wildly, and perhaps being attacked by badgers or foxes, or even by farm dogs . . . were there wolf packs in Ireland still? She did not think so, but there were many other perils for a small cat who suddenly found himself alone in the world.

She buried her head in her cushion and felt tears

begin to fall from her eyes, but then she gave a watery chuckle. Little cat, indeed! Tommy was a very large cat and he had very sharp claws and excellent teeth. He would be all right; he had to be all right. Sighing, Kitty disposed herself for sleep.

Chapter Fourteen

Brendan had meant to pursue Maeve on foot and, indeed, he would have done so had it not been for the twins. They had pointed out that Maeve had a good three or four hours' start on him. 'And she'll have hurried because she's desperate keen to get her precious Kitty back,' Fergal had opined. 'You'd best catch the bus.'

It had seemed like good advice and Brendan had taken it, but it had meant another half-hour wasted while he waited for the vehicle to start and then the journey almost drove him mad, for the bus was crowded with country folk and their belongings and it stopped at every lane, cottage and tiny hamlet, picking up and putting down with such frequency that Brendan thought he would have been a good deal quicker on foot.

Arriving at the village nearest the spot where Timmy Two-Shoes had told Caitlin he had seen the kids and the cat, he climbed thankfully down. There was no sign of Maeve, and he asked an old man sitting on a bench whether he had seen a young woman with a crutch. The ancient replied, balefully, that the only people he had seen had just got off the bus.

So Brendan swung along the road, enjoying the gentle warmth of the sun, and thinking about Sylvie. She was very alone right now, and very vulnerable, but she must have known that he had loved her from the very first night they had met. She had been too honourable to even think of returning his regard, for she had been a married woman, but now she was a widow and could follow her heart. If he went back to Liverpool to report that he had found Kitty, safe and well, surely she would show her relief and delight. Then he would declare himself and she would agree to marry him and they would live happily ever after. His imagination working overtime, he could actually feel her slim body in his arms, touch the silken floss of her pale hair and see the love for him shining out of her big, blue eyes. He walked on without so much as glancing to left or right. After some miles he remembered, with a pang of dismay, having passed a neat little bakery close by an inn of some description. Damn, I could have bought meself a meat pie or gone into the pub for a pint of ale and a sandwich, he thought, dismayed. But that was what happened if you let your imagination run away. He could go back, of course, but he did not want to lose any more time and there was doubtless another village not too far ahead. Resolutely, Brendan strode on.

Maeve was in the bakery buying tea brack when a movement outside in the street caught her eye.

She turned her head, the way one does, then froze, for she recognised the passer-by instantly. It was Caitlin's cousin, Brendan O'Hara!

Maeve shrank against the counter, holding her breath, then glanced quickly away, afraid that her gaze might be felt by Brendan and cause him to look her way. Her fears were needless. Brendan had a half-smile on his face and he was striding out as though he was in a hurry. Maeve had guessed he would try to find her but had not worried overmuch since she had been careful not to give anyone even the vaguest idea of where she was bound. In fact, it had not occurred to her, until she had actually reached this village, that there was one person who knew all too well where Kitty, Nick and Tommy had been seen. Timmy Two-Shoes! Brendan would not know him from Adam, but Caitlin and Timmy were old friends. If Brendan were to ask for information, Timmy would clam up or even lie, but if it were his old friend Caitlin, who had made him cups of tea and fed him with hunks of gur cake, that would be different. Timmy would tell her anything, and why should he not? So if Brendan were here – and he plainly was – it would be because Caitlin had got information from old Timmy.

Maeve sighed and turned towards the door just as the baker came back into the shop. He carried some soda bread and a loaf of brack, all of which he placed upon the counter. 'Here y'are, alanna; they come out of the oven no more'n ten minutes ago,' he said jovially. 'I'll pop 'em into the bag, but you'd best leave it open till they cools.'

Maeve thanked him and produced her money, and was quite glad of the delay when he had to go next door to the pub to get change, for it gave her the chance to consider what she should best do. Brendan was ahead of her and would doubtless draw further ahead as the day advanced. But he was hunting for her, she realised, and not for the runaways. He had never seen Nick or Kitty so would not recognise them even if they walked slap bang into each other; though if they still had Tommy with them she supposed they might be identified by the cat. However, the children had a good start on them; she reckoned it would take her at least a week, and maybe more, to catch up with them, especially as she would have to ask everyone she met if they had seen a couple of lads and a cat. The only description of the 'boys' which Timmy had been able to give her had been that the younger of the two wore a faded blue jersey. But, as yet, it was only the cat which folk remembered.

So what to do? Finally, she decided that, for the moment at least, she would simply continue on her way, questioning everyone she came across. If she caught up with Brendan, which seemed unlikely when she compared his pace with hers, then they must have a truce. She would explain slowly and carefully that Kitty must not be taken back to her birth mother against her will. She would remind him that there was no written proof that Kitty was Sylvie's daughter, because she was pretty sure that Sylvie had given a false name when she had registered the birth. Yes, she remembered now that the authorities had been told the child's name was Catherine Mary O'Keefe, which was how she had been known throughout her short life.

'Thanks, m' dear. Here's your change.'

Maeve jumped. She had been so intent on her own thoughts that the baker's return had taken her by surprise, but she took the money, crammed her purchases into the bag which contained her nightdress, a clean blouse and skirt and some underwear, thanked the baker and left the shop. She had already asked in the village and knew that Timmy had been right; the children had passed this way, complete with cat, though no one was able to say how long ago this had been. But at least she knew she was on the right track.

She set off in the direction Brendan had taken, then paused by a grassy bank. She might as well stop here and eat some of the food she had just purchased; it would give her time to think. Maeve settled herself on the bank and fished out a portion of soda bread and the bottle of cold tea she had made that morning. She was munching away when she saw two young men approaching. They were clearly farm boys and when they saw her they greeted her cheerfully, though there was something in their manner that worried her a little, especially when they sat down on the grassy bank, one on either side of her, and exchanged sly glances before untying large and rather dirty handkerchiefs to reveal hunks of soda bread and cheese and beginning to eat. But she returned their greeting, finished her soda bread, then re-capped the cold tea and stood up. To her dismay, both young men followed suit, cramming the uneaten food into their pockets. 'We'll come wit' you a bit of your way,' the one on the left said, thickly, through a mouthful of bread and cheese. 'Where's you bound? A pretty colleen like yourself shouldn't be all alone-io.'

Maeve settled her crutch firmly under her arm and turned to glare at him. 'I'm not alone,' she said crisply. 'Please don't stand so close or you'll get in the way of me crutch.' The young man gave a hoarse laugh, but stepped back when she dug the crutch into the ground, grazing his large booted foot. The other man simply moved closer, remarking as he did so that there could be no harm in his lending her an arm since it looked as though they were all three going in the same direction.

Maeve had been moving forward but now she stopped short. 'Leave me alone or I'll yell,' she said, trying to make her voice sound firm and steady. 'I've – I've had a row with me young man but he's not far ahead. Did you see him? He's a well set up young feller – he's a policeman, in fact – and he went through the village, oh, twenty minutes before I did, so if you'll kindly get out of my way . . .'

The two young men exchanged glances once more. One was fat and red-faced with a squint. The other was shorter and thinner, with a strange ferrety face, and a loose mouth which hung open revealing bad and broken teeth. 'We aren't doin' no harm,' the fat one said, sounding injured. 'We only wants to be friends, doesn't us, Kev?'

'Aye, that's right, us only wants to be friends, to be sure,' ferret-faced Kev agreed.

'That's all very well, but my young man has a very jealous nature; that's why we quarrelled,' Maeve said, inventing as she went along. 'He's a big feller wit' a short temper and a nasty way wit' anyone what looks at me twice, so if I were you . . .'

She left the sentence unfinished because there was clearly no need to say more. Both young men moved smartly away from her, though Kev said reproachfully: 'We don't mean no harm, missus, it's just that us farm lads don't see many girls, 'specially strangers. And my mammy would say that good girls don't go wanderin' country lanes wit'out so much as a dog to keep 'em company.'

Maeve felt a flush rise to her cheeks. The young man was probably right, for country and city ways were very different. In the Liberties, a girl would not walk around alone after dark, for that would be dangerous; asking for trouble, as her elders would say. But during the day, with people constantly surrounding them, unaccompanied girls and women were safe enough. In the country, however, it was clearly very different; she would be well advised to catch Brendan up before she had trouble with someone not as easily vanquished as the farm boys, who had taken her story to heart and were shambling off the way they had come, not so much as glancing back.

Maeve heaved a great sigh and felt her heart begin to slow to a more normal rhythm. She knew she could not possibly catch Brendan up if he continued to walk as fast as he had been doing when she saw him in the village, but he would have to stop at some point, even if it were only to beg a bed for the night at some inn or similar hostelry. And he would have to eat. Determinedly swinging her crutch, Maeve hurried along the quiet road, looking hopefully as she rounded every bend for Brendan's tall – and suddenly reliable – figure.

Ever since he had left the bus, Brendan had been aware of a steadily growing contentment, for the day was fine and he was in the countryside he loved. At first he had walked quickly, but then he slowed to a more comfortable pace, for there was little point in hurrying. The children, he knew, were well ahead of him, but it was Maeve he sought, and because of her limp – and the fact that she had a mere three or four hours' start on him – he would probably catch her up without having to hurry. He knew the children would sleep rough, of course, but he did not imagine for a moment that Maeve would do so. She would ask for a bed in a cottage, or perhaps even an inn, so when he came to any sort of habitation he would enquire, but until then he would simply enjoy the day and be glad that he was no longer walking a beat or dependent upon the Liverpool Constabulary for his weekly wage. It was not long before his thoughts darted ahead to the little farm he meant to buy and the life he would lead there, and the miles went by unnoticed.

He reached a tumble of small cottages as the sun began to sink and bought soda bread and cheese at a neat little dwelling whose owner proved garrulous. No, she had not seen a girl with a crutch, but a week or two before strangers had passed that way: two young lads with a big grey cat. They had offered to weed her garden in return for bread and cheese and they had done a good job, though she had had to speak sharply to the younger one – a little lad in a blue jersey – who had started to root out some seedlings which had only just begun to poke their green noses above the soil.

Considerably heartened by this information, Brendan continued on his way, deciding that the next time he reached a dwelling he had best arrange a bed for the night. But first he would eat the food he had purchased. He glanced around him for a suitable spot and presently found a great oak tree spreading its branches half across the road. The roots formed a comfortable seat and he sank into it and began to eat. Presently, his mind strayed back to Liverpool and Sylvie, and he realised, with a sense of shock, that he had managed somehow to divide the desires of his heart into two quite separate sections. In one, he imagined himself married to Sylvie, and in another he was the owner of a neat little Irish farm, yet he had never even attempted to reconcile the two, to imagine Sylvie feeding the hens on his small farm, digging potatoes, cutting cabbage. In fact he had no idea how Sylvie felt about country living, but now that he had leisure to think, he realised he could only see her against the background of the Ferryman. If he managed to find Kitty and take her back to Liverpool so that Sylvie could meet her, and if as a result Sylvie agreed to marry him, then he supposed that he would have to help her run the pub and would, perforce, become a citizen of Liverpool once more.

Of course, the pub was a thriving business in which he would make very much more money than was possible on an Irish farm. His time in the army, and in the police force, had taught him organisation and efficiency and he knew, without really having to think about it, that he could build the pub up to be as successful as it had been in old Mr Dugdale's day. But did he want to? With Sylvie as the prize, he supposed that it would be bearable, yet it was not his dream.

Uneasily, he tried to banish the thought, but

once he had let it enter his mind it would not go away. He had longed and longed for Sylvie, longed for her still, but it would be hard to have to give up his dream of living once more in his own country, farming his own land, being truly independent for the first time in his life. However, there was no need to despair; he had never even suggested to Sylvie that she might enjoy life as a farmer's wife, but he would do so as soon as he had found Kitty, and who knew what she would say?

Brendan ate the last of his food, leaned back against the trunk of the tree, and closed his eyes. It would be another couple of hours before it grew dark. Presently he would set off again, and this time he would walk faster, for he was determined to catch up with Maeve before nightfall. But he had travelled a long way today and was beginning to feel weary. He would just close his eyes for a moment, just have five minutes' rest . . . Brendan slept.

Maeve came round a bend in the road and was almost dazzled by the dying rays of the sun. For a moment, she stopped short, astonished by the beauty of the scene before her, for the sun was sinking into a bed of tiny pink cloudlets, and painting the countryside in rose and gold. There was a great oak tree, its branches just bursting into coral bud, which seemed to have snared some of the sunset's glory to itself, for its rough bark reflected the sun's rays so that it almost looked as though it were on fire. Maeve sighed deeply and began to move forward, but when she came within a few feet of the oak tree she stopped once more. There was a man sitting against the trunk, his legs stretched out before him, his chin on his chest. Maeve saw at once that he was fast asleep, and that it was Brendan O'Hara.

She leaned over him, a hand out ready to shake his shoulder, but then she had second thoughts. If she disturbed him, he might wake angry; better to sit quietly down beside him and let him wake naturally, and then she would explain why she had fled from the house in Handkerchief Alley. She supposed he might be annoyed with her, but hoped that an explanation of her early departure – and an abject apology – would be enough to calm his wrath. Carefully and gently, she sat down beside him. She leaned against the trunk, then turned her head sideways so that she would watch his face. She knew that her gaze might well wake him, for one of Kitty's favourite ploys when she wanted Maeve to be up and about was to stare fixedly at her sleeping face until she awoke. So she allowed her gaze to travel slowly around Brendan's face.

It was a nice face, the eyes deep set, the brow broad, the nose straight. She let her eyes linger on his lips, and liked the fact that even in sleep the corners of his mouth tilted up so that he looked almost as if he were smiling. His chin, however, was square and forceful, with a deep cleft: a determined chin, the chin of one who would not be turned aside from his purpose once he had made up his mind.

He had rather thick, black eyebrows; last time she had seen him they had formed a bar across his forehead and had frightened her almost as much as the sparkle of annoyance in his dark blue eyes. But now that the eyes were veiled by lids, she could tell from his smooth brow that he was not a man who frowned often. Indeed, had he not threatened her beloved Kitty, she thought she could have liked him, could have been his friend. As it was, however, she meant to make use of him, albeit without his knowledge. She would need his help and protection to find Kitty and Nick, but once they had met up she meant to get Kitty back to Handkerchief Alley where she and Caitlin must persuade him to leave Kitty with them, secure in the knowledge that she would be best among her own folk, would be miserable across the water. 'If you take her, she'll bide her time and run away again, and she's only a kid after all,' Maeve imagined herself telling him. 'She might get into terrible trouble because she won't have Nick to keep an eye on her. She could get into bad company . . . tell Sylvie we love Kitty and won't ever ask her for a penny piece, if only she'll leave our girl with us.'

But all that was for the future; first they must find Kitty. And God knew what trouble the child might already have fallen into. It was all very well having faith in Nick, but he was only a kid. In the last village through which she had passed, they had told her of a band of tinkers making their way to a horse fair many miles off – if Kitty and Nick had fallen in with any of them ... Maeve shuddered. Some tinkers were undoubtedly grand folk, but there were others who would rob their own mammies and probably slit a throat for sixpence.

'Well, would you know me again?'

The remark, coming from a man whom she had thought to be fast asleep, made Maeve jump six inches, and give a muffled shriek. She tried to scramble away from him and fell, whereupon he jumped to his feet and reached out and picked her up, giving her a little shake before setting her with her back against the tree once more. 'It's all right, alanna; I didn't recognise you for a moment. In fact, I thought you were one of the fairy folk, come to enchant me,' he soothingly. 'But how did you find me? I was searching for you! You'd had several hours' start of me, but though I walked fast and questioned everyone I met, no one could remember seeing you. I don't understand it at all, at all.'

Maeve's heart was still beating uncomfortably fast, but she could not help laughing a little at the puzzlement in Brendan's voice. 'That's easily answered,' she said. 'Sure and you were in such a hurry, some miles back, that you passed me by; I were in the baker's buying soda bread and brack.

I – I meant to try to catch you up, but the baker had to go next door for change and by the time I got out of the shop you had disappeared.'

'Right, but why did you sneak out of the flat this morning when I t'ought we'd agreed to travel together?' Brendan said, in an injured voice. 'And what changed your mind? You could have walked quietly past me just now wit'out wakening me. Why, if you'd not stared at me I dare say I'd have slept till dark.'

'I know, and I'm very sorry I didn't wait for you,' Maeve mumbled, hanging her head. 'But you said you were going to find Kitty and take her across the water and – and I couldn't bear that and nor could Kitty. You say Sylvie wants her now because she's lost her own little girl, but she never gave Kitty a thought for years. So – so . . .'

'I reckon we neither of us gave the other much of a chance to explain,' Brendan said. 'I should have said I only wanted to take Kitty across the water for a couple o' days so that her mammy could see she was safe and well. Then I'd have brought her back to Handkerchief Alley, I swear to God I would.'

'You'd bring her back if Sylvie would let you,' Maeve said shrewdly. 'And why couldn't she come over to Dublin, if she only wants to make sure that Kitty's safe and well? She's a girl who's used to getting her own way is Sylvie, and if she made up her mind when she clapped eyes on Kitty that she wanted her, you'd mebbe not find it so easy to get the child out of her clutches. I don't mean to say that Sylvie isn't a nice kind of person, for to be sure she's grand, so she is. But as you know her well – and you must do or you wouldn't have come chasing after Kitty for her – then you'll know she's always got her own way, right from the time she was a child. Why, look what you did for her. And she told me you met her quite by chance and had hardly known her for more than a few days when you packed her off to Ireland,' she ended triumphantly.

Brendan looked startled, as though none of this had occurred to him. 'I admit Sylvie may have been spoiled as a child, but she's had it hard recently,' he said. 'As for coming to Ireland to see Kitty for herself, she can't possibly do that at the moment because of the pub, you see. It's her liveli-hood and she's trying to persuade the brewery to grant her the licence, now that her mother-in-law's gone. Of course, I can't promise you that Sylvie wouldn't want to keep Kitty, but I can promise you that she would never do so against the child's will. And none of that explains why you came meekly over and sat down beside me if you think I mean to take Kitty away from you.'

Maeve twisted round so that they were facing one another. 'I'm not very big and I'm not very strong, and I'm a bit of a coward, so I am,' she said haltingly. 'When I set off in the early hours of this morning, I was after thinking it all a great adventure. I'd got me savings so I could pay a bob or two for a hot meal and a night's lodgings, and I'd a bottle of cold tea and a few apples to keep me going until I needed something more solid. I stopped outside the village to eat the soda bread I'd bought, because I wanted you to get really well ahead, for at that stage I didn't mean to catch you up. But then, as I sat there . . .' She told the story of the two farm boys flatly, without exaggeration, and saw Brendan's eyes widen as he took in the implications. '. . . so I saw, then, that if I went on alone I might end up in real trouble or even wit' a knife between me shoulder blades,' she concluded, giving him a rueful smile. 'And there were you, hurrying ahead of me, a big strong chap what would put the fear of God into half a dozen ploughboys, or a whole band of tinkers. So when I saw you asleep under this tree . . .'

She said no more, since Brendan was nodding his comprehension. 'You're right; a thousand bad things could happen to you and we must pray to God they've not happened to Kitty,' he said. 'So we'll strike a bargain, shall us? I'll keep you safe while we're on the road, and when we find Kitty and Nick we'll persuade them to come home with us, back to Handkerchief Alley. As for crossing the water, what say we put it to Kitty, ask her if she'd like to visit her real mammy, just for a few days. Will that do?'

He was looking down at her so kindly that for a ridiculous moment Maeve feared she would burst into tears, but she pulled herself together as

Brendan got to his feet and helped her to hers. 'There's one thing you've not explained,' she said huskily. 'Why are you doing all this for Sylvie? Caitlin said you were talking about buying a farm in Ireland . . . why did you go back to Liverpool at all?'

There was a long pause whilst Brendan gazed down at the ground, almost as though he did not know how to answer her question, but at last he looked up. 'I've been in love with Sylvie for years, but it weren't no use 'cos she were married,' he said quietly. 'Only now she's a widow and, as I'm sure I've said, very alone. She begged me to find Kitty, to bring her back to Liverpool if that was what the child wanted, and I do believe that when I show her her daughter is safe she'll agree to marry me.'

'I see,' Maeve said, after a longish pause. So engrossed in her thoughts was she that she did not speak again as they walked along the lane. She was tired from the unaccustomed exercise and glanced at Brendan a couple of times to see whether he, too, was again growing weary, but he seemed unaffected.

Presently, he looked down at her, giving her a wry smile. 'You'll be tired, alanna, for you've been on the road longer than I have and your legs are a good deal shorter than mine. The next cottage we find we'll see if they can put us up for the night.'

'If I'd not caught up with you, Brendan, when would you have stopped for the night?' Maeve asked. 'I'm not tired, you know; I can go on for a while longer.'

'Oh, if I were by meself, I'd walk till dark, or until I came to a hamlet or a decent-sized farmhouse,' Brendan said. 'But I've not been walking since dawn.'

Maeve tightened her lips; she would not hold him back, would not admit that she was tired until she reached the end of her tether, which was not yet. 'We'll go on,' she said decisively. 'If I can't keep up, though, I'll tell you and mebbe you could slow your pace a little.'

Brendan laughed but nodded. 'Right, you set the pace,' he said cheerfully. 'But remember, you'll do Kitty no favours if you try too hard and collapse on me.'

'I know that,' Maeve said scornfully. 'But we'd best not talk; I'll need all me breath for walking.'

Kitty and Nick were beginning to enjoy life in the caravan, though Granny Trotter was a demanding invalid who seldom allowed them to rest. She told them she wanted to rejoin her band, who would be on their way to the horse fair, but Nick told Kitty, privately, when they were out collecting turfs for the fire, that he did not think this a good idea at all. 'Once she's wit' her own folk, she'll either turn us off or treat us like her servants,' he said. 'I know we saved her life an' that, but tinkers aren't like ordinary people. They'll close ranks agin us, and mebbe drive us out.'

'We aren't much better'n servants now,' Kitty pointed out, seesawing the turf-cutting tool which she had been given into the soft tobacco-coloured peat. 'It weren't our idea to come out cutting turf on a day when the sun's shining so hot, and we may not need it if we're going to pass through wooded country; wood burns a lot easier than turfs.'

'It's not for burning now; it's for puttin' in the nets under the cart, so's it can dry out for later,' Nick said, rather breathlessly. 'She knows an awful lot, old Granny Trotter. I thought I knew a thing or two, but she's taught me no end.'

'We've got more work than we can manage to keep the queen of the tinkers as idle as the day is long,' Kitty said rather bitterly; it was, after all, she who did all the cleaning and cooking, she who carted Granny out of the caravan so that she could point out the best potato clamps to rob, the driest turf to steal, or the best cabbages to cut, for now that spring was well advanced, living was easier for travellers who had no gardens or animals of their own.

At first, Granny had nagged them to go in a certain direction, but Nick soon realised that if they listened to her they would end up with her band, and this he had no intention of doing, so quite often they let old Tugger have his head for miles and miles, despite Granny's screeching and wailing, and when they came across a tempting woodland path which was wide enough to take the caravan they would turn down it, gathering wood as they went.

'But we can't stay with the old girl for ever,' Kitty pointed out as the two of them lugged a sack of turfs across the patchy, boggy moorland, back to where the caravan waited. 'I often get the feeling that one day the old devil will send the pair of us miles away on some wild goose chase or other, and when we get back we'll find that Tugger and the caravan have gone.'

Nick stopped short and stared at his companion, round-eyed. 'I reckon you're right,' he said slowly. 'It's just the sort of thing she would do, though at the moment she really does need us. The beating she took means she can't even bend down to light the cooking fire without gasping and groaning, and she'd never manage to dip water out of the stream and carry it back to the cart. Why, it takes the pair of us, and I reckon I'm a good deal stronger than her. That's another good reason for not catching up wit' the band. We'll bear it in mind, old Kitty, because I don't fancy finding us alone on the moors without so much as a cottage for a dozen miles.'

Kitty was about to reply when she heard a plaintive miaow and saw Tommy trotting towards them, tail erect, eyes blazing. Even in this desolate moorland country, the cat never hung around asking to be fed, but caught frogs and field mice, though he was happy to accept a saucer of milk when they managed to get to a cow before the farmer did. Kitty had been overjoyed, the day after the fight in the clearing, to find him sitting expectantly outside the caravan when she opened the door in the morning. He looked none the worse for his temporary absence, and, not for the first time, she wished that he could talk. Even Nick had been pleased to see him, although he said philosophically that cats would always avoid trouble if they could, and he had known all along that Tommy would turn up. Cats, he said darkly, knew when they were well off.

Now, Kitty dropped her end of the sack in order to give Tommy a welcoming hug. 'If the old girl ever does abandon us somewhere, we'll get Tommy to hunt rabbits for us,' she said, only half jokingly, for the cat had brought in young rabbits a couple of times when they had been in pastureland. He had eaten part of the animals and had seemed quite happy for Granny to commandeer the rest for her cooking pot. She had shown Kitty how to skin, joint and prepare the carcasses, and though Kitty had made no secret of her dislike of the task Granny had insisted that she should do it in future since 'me finger bones aches whenever I moves 'em . . . ah, Jacky, may he burn in hell, has a lot to answer for.'

Because they were on moorland they could see the cart, with its bright yellow and green paintwork, a good way off, so they knew they had not been abandoned by Granny today. Indeed, when they reached the caravan, Kitty popped inside for a moment and found the old woman still in her bed, though she stirred herself when she saw Kitty. 'I didn't get up 'cos I knew you'd be wantin' to spread ointment on me hurts,' she said querulously. 'You should ha' done it afore you went gadding off, but you young 'uns never give a t'ought to another's pain.'

Kitty gave a gasp of indignation. 'If you think cutting turf is gadding off then you're even stupider than you pretend to be,' she said roundly. 'And a fat chance I had of anointing your bruises 'cos you just gobbled up your breakfast porridge, pointed out the best peat hag, and then snuggled down again under your blanket. Why, you were snorin' before we were through the doorway.' As she spoke, she had been getting down the various ointments and salves from the cupboard at the end of the caravan and now she took off the clean rags she had bound round the worst of Granny's hurts, noticing as she did so that the bruises had largely disappeared and the wounds had pretty well healed over. Even the damaged arm was less painful than it had been, and Granny did not mention it more than three or four times a day. Nevertheless, Kitty smeared the ointment as she was bidden, ignoring Granny's frequent moans, small shrieks and urges to 'treat me careful 'cos I's been hurt bad'.

She might have spoken sharply to the old woman had not Nick entered the caravan, saying as he did so: 'Fancy a nice rabbit stew, Granny?

There was a fine fat doe in the trap this morning. I'll do the skinning and jointing while Kitty prepares the veg.'

The old woman's eyes lit up, but it seemed she did not intend to show any appreciation of the meal to come. 'I could do wit' some nourishment after the rubbish you've been feeding me,' she grumbled. 'Is rabbit all you know? Eh, but I wish I were back wit' me band. Alecky-jem is a grand robber, so he is, and I just fancies a chicken stew.'

'In that case we'll get off this moor and into the hills,' Nick said, ignoring the old woman's howl of protest. 'If you ain't satisfied with rabbit, Granny, then we'd best get on to farmland once again, though I don't mean to go robbin' farm-yards when there's a fine big rabbit in the pot.' He turned to his companion. 'Kitty, you make all fast in here; it seems we're movin' on.'

Maeve and Brendan fell into a comfortable routine. They walked and questioned, lost the trail and found it again, were cheerful in good weather and made the best of bad, and Brendan noticed that Maeve would not give in and admit she was tired even when her face was white with fatigue, and her crutch faltered with every step. Tales of two young people in a colourful gypsy caravan had given them pause for thought. They had reached wild and lovely country, and had stopped a young man in a donkey cart. He had been surprised to be hailed by a couple of walkers, but obligingly drew his equipage to a halt. 'If it's a lift you're after looking for, then you've chose the wrong feller, for me cart's crowded enough with the old sow and her bonaveens,' he had said jovially and Maeve, standing on tiptoe, had seen that the cart was indeed well filled with an enormous sow and at least a dozen piglets, all cuddled up together in the straw, with a net slung over them to prevent escapes. Brendan, peering as well, had laughed, but shook his head. 'It's information we're after, not a lift,' he had said. 'We're searchin' for a couple of kids – lads they are – what have gone adventuring when they should be in school. They've a big old grey cat with them, and the little chap is wearin' a blue pullover. This young lady' – he had indicated Maeve with a jerk of his thumb – 'is their auntie, doin' her sister, their mammy, a favour, for she's in mortal dread they'll fall into bad company and end up dead.'

The young man had laughed and shaken his head, but then stopped short, an arrested look on his face. 'Wait on; I have seen a strange t'ing, only a couple o' days ago. I seen two young fellers wit' a green and yellow caravan pulled by a big old piebald. It struck me as strange, 'cos tinkers' carts is like gold dust to 'em; they wouldn't go trustin' a decent cart like that to a couple o' kids. Come to that, it's very rare you see a tink by hisself; there's safety in numbers, so they say, especially when they're stealin' from every man whose land they pass through. Why, even when autumn comes

415

and there's acorns aplenty in the woods, I doesn't let the pigs to graze on the nuts if there's tinkers abroad.'

'That sounds as if it might be – be me nephews,' Maeve had said excitedly. 'Was there a cat wit' them?'

The young man had considered this, but only for a moment, before nodding vigorously. 'Now you mention it, I did see an animal of some sort. I thought it were a dog, but it could've been a cat.'

Maeve had beamed at him and thanked him profusely, and the young man had driven on with a cheerful wave. As soon as he had gone, Brendan had turned to Maeve and given her a hug. 'Now we know we're not far behind them, 'cos he said he saw the cart a couple o' days ago,' he had said exultantly. 'They'll be a bit faster than us in a cart, I dare say . . .'

Maeve had smiled and returned the hug, but then she had shaken her head at him. 'They're in a tinker's caravan wit' a horse pullin' it, I'll grant you that,' she had said, 'but they'll go at walking pace because I reckon neither of them would dare to drive the horse, and, of course, they don't know we're after them. If they had an adult with them it might be a different story, but as it is – well, a cart's a deal easier to find than a cat. Oh, Brendan, we're getting near 'em, I feel it in me bones.'

So here they were, two days later, penetrating deep into the wildest county Maeve had ever seen. Steep hills reared about them, rivers had carved deep valleys between. There were lush water meadows and pastures where fat beasts grazed. And there were woods, already brightened by bluebells which, seen from a distance, made the trees look as though they were standing in lakes of brilliant blue.

So far, they had found it easy enough to find a lodging each night, though the beds had often been just a couple of straw pallets laid down in the family kitchen. At first, folks took them for either husband and wife or father and daughter, and Brendan would have been happy not to challenge this, but Maeve was firm. 'If you let folk believe that we're related, then we'll be given a pallet to share and that would never do,' she had said crisply. 'I know it's a bit more awkward because they have to provide each of us with a separate bed of some description, but it's better that way.'

'Why?' Brendan had said baldly, but there was a twinkle in his eye. 'I don't mind sharing a bed wit' you, alanna; we share just about everything else.'

'I snore,' Maeve had said, with equal bluntness. 'And I kick like a mule; sure and wouldn't you be black and blue by mornin'? Anyway, folk is happy enough to provide each of us wit' a pallet when they realise they can charge a bit more.'

'Oh well, if it makes you happy, then we'll continue to say I'm a family friend, helping you to search for your nephews,' Brendan had said easily. 'Good thing it's getting towards summer, you know, 'cos if it were cold I reckon we'd be glad enough to cuddle up under the same blanket.'

Maeve had snorted but vouchsafed no reply, and they continued on their way. Though he always vowed he never slackened his pace to suit hers, Maeve knew that Brendan did just that. But with the children only a couple of days ahead, both were determined to walk as fast as they could and to continue walking well into the long evenings. 'For as you say, they don't know we're after them,' Brendan reminded Maeve, as dusk deepened that night. 'And one good thing about this country is that the cart has got to keep to the tracks. We can cut corners by goin' cross-country, but they won't be able to do that because hills and valleys would be dangerous for the caravan. How do you fancy walking all night?'

They were making their way along a leafy lane and the sun was already sinking in the west. It was deserted country so far as human habitation was concerned, so it might be quite a while before they came across a farmhouse, or even a cottage where they might ask shelter for the night. Yet already she was tired. Her crutch arm ached abominably, as did her left leg, but she was determined not to slow Brendan up, not even if it kills me, she vowed to herself, plodding on.

'Well, alanna? Shall us walk all the night?'

Maeve glanced up at the face above her own; was he joking, or did he honestly intend to keep going right through the hours of darkness? 'Sure and if you're set on walking all night I'll keep up wit' you, so I will,' she said. 'Only when morning comes, I dare say we'll want nothing more than a good sleep, and no one won't give us a bed during daylight.'

Brendan looked down at her and she saw his grin spreading with some relief; so he had been codding her after all and had no more intention of walking all night than of pretending they were man and wife so they could share a bed. He was a real joker and she supposed that this fact had made it easier for them to remain on good terms, for when she grew desperately tired towards the end of a day she also grew cross, quick to snap out an answer, quicker to argue and contradict, even when she knew perfectly well that Brendan was right. But he was chuckling, his glance mocking. 'Eh, you're a grand, brave little girl, so you are, but I could tell you anything and you'd swallow it hook, line and sinker, like a trout jumping for a mayfly.' He began to laugh again, then sobered suddenly. 'But I know this part of the country from a visit I made here years ago, and I'm tellin' you we could tramp ten miles and not find a place to rest our heads. Only 'tis a fine night, so it is; what say we make ourselves a nest when we reach that woodland ahead? I know how to make a shelter from thin branches, moss, dead leaves and the like. We'll be snug enough in there while it's dark, and can set out at dawn, long before most folks is up. But how's the food lasting out? I don't want to see you starve.'

'If we could find a stream, I could fill the water bottles and mebbe you could kindle a fire so's I could make a hot drink,' Maeve said longingly. She missed a hot cup of tea more than anything else. 'And there's soda bread and some farm butter, so we shan't starve.'

'Right, then I'll start making a shelter at once,' Brendan said briskly, as they reached the trees. 'It'll be our first night in the open, but I dare say not our last, for we'll get on quicker if we leave as soon as we wake.'

'I'll fetch wood for a fire,' Maeve said eagerly; it would be bliss to lie down, even on the hardest ground, to ease the ache in her left leg. And the thought of camping out in the open air made their trip seem more of an adventure than ever. She was looking forward to getting inside the shelter which Brendan was building, though she knew that the only blanket in her possession was a thin and skimpy affair. But then the fire crackled up and she perched Brendan's old tin billy-can, filled with water from the stream they had crossed a short while before, on top of the flames, and presently the two of them sat by the fire, sipping tea and eating buttered soda bread, whilst around them the small sounds of the night were carried to them by a gentle breeze. The fire crackled and sank, a sleepy bird twittered, a hunting owl hooted a soft warning, and, far off, a vixen screeched.

When the last morsel of food was eaten, Brendan showed her inside his shelter, his pride obvious. He had floored the place with dry bracken, over which he had spread his own blanket, and now he indicated that Maeve should climb inside before him, keeping a good foot of distance between them. He had arranged their knapsacks in place of pillows and the two of them lay down, a little self-consciously, and prepared for sleep. Maeve was snug enough wrapped in her blanket, but presently began to feel guilty; she really ought to share her covering with her companion. After all, if they could share the shelter, and the bracken couch, why should they not share their covering as well? She said as much in a shy whisper, but it seemed that Brendan was already fast asleep and, as he had said, it was a warm night. Maeve cuddled down once more and very soon fell asleep.

Chapter Fifteen

Nick was examining the traps which he had set the night before whilst Kitty rifled through the beech mast in search of acorns, for their latest acquisition – stolen, of course – was a little fat porker. Kitty had come across him a few days before when he had strayed away from his mother. He had followed Kitty back to the caravan where Granny had immediately seized him, ordered Nick to construct a pen for him, and told them that they would remain in this particular clearing for a few days until the bonaveen grew used to them; only then would they move on.

Kitty had realised, with a sinking heart, that this meant sharing the caravan at night-time with the pig, whom she had christened Percy. She had been brought up to believe pigs were smelly creatures, but Percy was clearly an exception to this particular rule for he smelt of milk and grass, and even of the acorns he so loved. The only real disadvantage to having him in the caravan was his extreme friendliness and excessive love of the human race. He insisted upon sleeping as close as possible to either Kitty or Nick, although he apparently did not consider Granny a human being at all and seemed to avoid her by instinct, as if he knew that when she looked at him she saw bacon, sausages, hams and chitterlings.

Kitty would not have minded Percy's proximity had he not also woken as soon as light touched the sky and begun to wander about, treading indiscriminately with his extraordinarily sharp little hooves on any hand, foot or indeed face which protruded from the blanket. Tommy he regarded as a brother pig, and constantly nuzzled up to him or followed him around. Tommy had tried spitting, swearing and lashing out at the piglet, though always with sheathed claws, but this had availed him nothing. The only way to be sure that he was beyond Percy's reach was to scale a tree, and this he had frequently done, squatting in the branches like some furry but furious owl, and ignoring Percy, who would stand on his hind legs with his front legs resting on the trunk whilst he squealed at the cat to come down.

So now, Kitty was filling her bag with last autumn's acorns, and picking large handfuls of dried grasses whenever she came across them. Percy would eat most things but he drew the line at hay, so the dried grasses were for Tugger. He often wore a nosebag, but the grain which usually filled it was running short, so until autumn came and it was possible to steal wheat, corn and barley he would have to make do with hay.

They had been pressing deeper into the wood, for Nick had laid his traps with care, each one near some obvious landmark so he could find it again. Now, however, he turned to Kitty with a puzzled frown, holding up an empty trap. 'That's real odd, Kit. It's the first time since Granny taught me how to set a snare that there's been nothing in any one of them.' He glanced cautiously around him, as though expecting to see a trap thief lurking behind every tree. 'Well, there are only two more traps left unvisited, and they're both deeper in the trees. I wonder . . .'

'What do you wonder?' Kitty asked curiously, as they went further into the wood. 'Perhaps this isn't the sort of place where you find rabbits and such. Perhaps you'd have been better to set your traps nearer the fringe of the wood, instead of so deep in.'

'I thought that, but you must admit Granny knows all about traps. Because this was our first time in this particular camping spot she came out wit' me herself last night. Don't you remember? She showed me the best runs, even told me I'd find a blaze on every tree close by where the tinkers had found an animal run . . .' Nick stopped speaking. 'Oh, be Jaysus! What a fool I am! What fools we both are! If I'm right, I'm after thinkin' we've been tricked. We're two babes in the wood, and if we're covered up wit' nothing but leaves by mornin' . . . come on, run!'

'I don't know what you're talking about,' Kitty panted, as the pair of them began to dodge back and forth between the trees. 'Nick, you're going in the wrong direction, I'm certain of it; the clearing's more to our left. If we'd been heading towards it, we would have been able to see the caravan by now.'

Kitty was right, and the children might have taken even longer to find the clearing they had left had it not been for Tommy, who came wandering through the trees at that moment. 'Hello, Tommy,' Nick said breathlessly, bending down to rub the cat behind the ears. 'Which way is home, old feller?'

As though he understood, Tommy turned straight round, and in a very short time had led them out of the wood and into the clearing, where Kitty stopped short, a hand flying to her mouth. She had guessed that Nick thought Granny had deliberately encouraged him to set the traps deep in the wood because she was trying to get rid of them, and now she saw he had been right. The clearing had been vacated in a hurry, for the ashes of the fire still glowed red, though of the cooking pot which had stood amongst the embers there was no sign. Kitty looked round wildly; surely Granny would have left their personal possessions? But there was no sign of Nick's knapsack, or her own bag. The stout piece of canvas which they had rigged up on wet nights had been rolled up beneath the caravan, so Kitty supposed, sadly, that it would not have occurred to Granny to leave that for them. But it was clear that the old woman had simply abandoned them, just as Nick had feared she would.

'But we can follow the cart tracks,' she said eagerly, pointing to the marks in the dust, for it had not rained for several days. 'But – how did she manage, Nick? We didn't leave Tugger harnessed up; she would have had to catch him, back him between the shafts, take the cooking pot into the van, and round up Percy. How on earth could she possibly have done all that in such a short time?'

Nick shrugged. 'I don't know, but it's the first thing I'll ask her when we catch her up,' he said grimly. 'C'mon, Kitty, because if we're going to eat tonight we'll have to find the cart within the next hour or so. She won't walk by Tugger's head – she'll drive him hell for leather until she reaches some spot where she can hide up.'

He set off at a smart pace, but though Kitty followed him obediently she soon began to giggle and presently had to stop, a hand to her aching side, to have her laugh out.

'Janey mack, whatever's got into you?' Nick howled. 'There's nothing to laugh at, you daft girl. Why *is* you laughing, anyway?'

'At the thought of Granny driving hell for leather, like someone in a cowboy fillum,' Kitty said breathlessly, mopping streaming eyes. 'Think of poor old Tugger even trying to trot or to canter, when a walk is all we've ever seen him do.'

Nick grinned reluctantly, but very soon neither of them was laughing, for Granny had indeed got a long way ahead, and the sun was low in the sky.

In no time at all, dusk would be upon, and then they might easily miss the caravan if Granny had hidden it well.

In fact, had it not been for Tommy, they might have walked into a veritable wasps' nest, for as they rounded a bluff the cat stopped short, gazing ahead of him with ears pricked up, and then looking up at the two children as though he were actually saying: 'Can you hear that noise? What does it mean? I don't like the sound of it at all, at all!'

Kitty bent to pick the cat up, beginning to say that he was tired, but Nick shushed her. 'There's something going on up ahead,' he whispered. 'You stay here wit' Tommy while I go and tek a look.'

Kitty obeyed, settling herself as comfortably as she could on a fallen tree trunk, whilst the light ebbed away and she became uneasily conscious of how dark and strange were the woods about them, and how ill-equipped she and Nick were for whatever lay ahead. When Nick rejoined her, she jumped to her feet, eager to question him, but he shushed her, took her arm and led her some way back along the track to where another fallen tree formed a sort of seat. They settled down upon it, Kitty glad of the warmth of the cat, for the evening breeze was chilly. She looked enquiringly at her companion. 'Well? It can't have been Granny or you'd have made me go on instead of drawing back.'

'It were Granny, but not just her, a whole band

of perishin' tinkers,' Nick said with a groan. 'If you count the kids, there must've been fifty of 'em, and Granny acting like a queen, the miserable old thing. I don't know how she got in touch with 'em, but I reckon she knew they were close. Perhaps one of them dropped behind, and she made some sort of sign to him to come back once we were out of the way.'

'That's why there was nothing caught in the traps,' Kitty breathed. 'If the band were just ahead of us, they would have set their own traps in that wood the previous night, and not only taken all the rabbits which passed that way, but left signs as well. D'you remember Granny grumbling that young tinkers don't have the sense of the old ones? The old 'uns are careful not to handle the undergrowth so as to leave a scent, but the young 'uns don't think of such things and spoil hunting for others.'

'Yes, I remember something of the sort,' Nick admitted. 'But oh, Kitty, I've let you down, so I have. We're miles from anywhere and the only folk around would cut our throats as soon as look at us, so we can't get any help from them. We'll have to sleep rough tonight, and then tomorrow make our way back to the nearest village in the opposite direction and see if we can find work of some sort. It were all my fault, 'cos I'm older'n you, and I never trusted that wicked old woman! I just knew she'd plan to dump us if she found herself amongst tinkers again. But I thought she were too weak to do it on her own, like.'

Kitty patted his arm comfortingly. 'It weren't your fault, because I didn't trust the horrible old woman either, and I knew her bruises and cuts were better because I dressed them each night,' she said. 'I should have told you she was getting stronger all the time. But anyway, Maeve always says *What's done is done*, so we'll just have to put up with what's happened. And you know what, it were poor old Tugger's fault really. We gave him his head, let him go whichever way he chose; we should have guessed that he'd follow the paths and lanes he'd always followed. And we should have realised that whenever we stopped for the night it was in a place that Granny knew quite well, 'cos she could point out streams, fields where crops grew and woods where fuel could be found. And maybe it's for the best, because we always meant to find ourselves work on farms. I thought it were good luck when we moved into Granny's caravan, but maybe it were too easy, like. Maybe we'll be best on our own.'

Nick flung his arm round her and gave her a brotherly hug, then got to his feet and pulled Kitty to hers. 'You're a grand kid, so you are,' he said. 'But I'm afraid we're going to be pretty hungry by the time we reach easier country. So what'll we do? We could bed down here, there's dry leaves aplenty, but we can't eat dry leaves and what's more, we're a bit near the tinkers. If you can manage it, I'd like to put a couple of miles between us and them before we settle down for the night.'

'Right you are. Off we go, then,' Kitty said stoutly, falling into step beside him, but secretly feeling frightened and uneasy, as well as extremely hungry, for they had not eaten since breakfast, which seemed a very long time ago. 'If we were pigs, we could root for acorns, or eat beech mast, but never mind; you once told me how horrid it was to be hungry and I pretended to understand, but I didn't, not really. Now, I shall!'

Nick gave her another hug and then rubbed his cheek against hers. 'You're the best, Kitty,' he said quietly, 'and don't worry, I'll see you through this if it's the last thing I do. Why, when we reach . . .'

He stopped speaking and gave a muffled gasp as a tall figure suddenly emerged from the trees and came towards them, menacingly. Nick gave Kitty a violent push. 'Run, Kit,' he screamed. 'I'll hold him off then follow you. Run for your life!'

Brendan awoke to find sunshine streaming through the tiny window of the kitchen where he and Maeve had spent the night; the previous day they had left the woods behind and had begged shelter for the night in a turf-cutter's cottage. Their hosts were an elderly couple, scraping a living as best they could from the moorland on which their home was situated. The old man was often paid for his turfs in kind, and though their natural desire to offer hospitality to strangers was strong they were persuaded to accept some money both for the meal they provided and for the beds of dried heather they prepared for their guests.

Brendan thought that the sunshine had wakened him, but then the smell of cooking alerted him to the fact that the old woman was already up and stirring porridge over the fire on the hearth.

Brendan sat up, greeted his hostess and looked about him for Maeve, but she was nowhere in sight. The old woman followed his glance and grinned, revealing a mouth almost devoid of teeth. 'Sure and doesn't yourself sleep like the dead?' she said. 'The young woman has gone to the stream to wash but you never stirred, not even when me husband kicked you by accident when he went out to feed the hens.'

Brendan laughed. 'Me niece is an extraordinary person,' he said, struggling out from his makeshift bed. 'She's years younger'n me and not nearly as strong, but she never complains or lags behind. As I told you last night, we're searching for a couple of young lads who've gone off on the spree. Maeve has looked after the younger of the two from birth, and looks on her – him – as her own. But I reckon we'll find them in the next day or two, because at the last village they reckoned they had passed through not long before.'

The old woman nodded. 'And the tinkers came by day afore yesterday. Some folks is scared of them but we're not, 'cos we're too poor; we've got nothin' to steal, see? Besides, there's good tinkers and bad, like there's good folk and bad. But tell me, why do your young woman walk wit' a crutch? Seems to me she nipped round the kitchen last night spry as a blackbird and her feet look both straight and strong, yet when she first come in it were hop and go one.'

Brendan stared at her. The same thought had been occurring to him for at least a week, and yesterday he had realised that she did indeed manage better without the crutch when under a roof. Watching her, it was easy to see that the crutch was far too short and must have been made for her when she was only a child; in order to lean on it, she had to throw her whole body into an awkward, lopsided position, and this, of course, made her lameness appear very much worse than it really was. He had tentatively suggested that she might try to use a stick instead of the crutch, but she had given him a cold glance, very different from her normal friendly look. 'A stick wouldn't support me like the crutch does,' she had said stiffly, and had changed the subject so quickly that he had not referred to the matter again.

Now, however, he watched Maeve coming across the yard, using her crutch as a matter of course, and, probably because the old woman had remarked upon it, he noticed that Maeve's left foot was as straight as the right one, and not turned in as Sylvie had assured him it had once been. I believe her foot has cured itself and she's never noticed because of that damned crutch, he thought wonderingly. I'll have to say something, because otherwise she'll go through life believing she's crippled, might even become crippled, whereas without the crutch I do believe she could walk as straight and upright as any other girl.

At this point in his musing Maeve re-entered the cottage, her face glowing from its recent wash, and her eyes bright. 'That porridge smells good, so it does, missus,' she said, beaming at their hostess, 'and I've a good feeling, so I have, that today we'll catch up wit' Nick and Kitty.' Brendan gave her a warning glance, but though she clearly understood his meaning, she continued to smile. 'As soon as we catch up with them, she'll be my little girl again. Don't worry, Brendan. You were asleep when I first woke, but Mrs O'Regan was on her way out for turfs and kindling to make a fire. I went with her and we had a good chat. I told her all about Kitty and why she'd run away, and she wished me luck, so she did, and said she was sorry she couldn't see me darlin' child for herself.' She turned to the old woman, still beaming. 'Isn't that so, missus?'

The old woman nodded and smiled, and presently, when Mr O'Regan came in from the hens, the four of them sat down to bowls of porridge, though it was poor, thin stuff compared to some they had been given as they journeyed, for the O'Regans only had two goats and a dozen or so hens besides the potatoes from their patch of garden. Still, it was all they needed, and all they could manage, furthermore.

As soon as they could do so without appearing

rude, Maeve and Brendan packed up their belongings and left the cottage. It was a glorious morning, and the sun was warm on their heads. They soon left the moorland and found themselves in woods once more. Only the lightest of breezes stirred the branches of the trees. As they walked, Brendan kept glancing at Maeve, wondering when would be the best time to tackle her about her use of the crutch. Now that Mrs O'Regan had pointed it out, he saw how very bad for his companion the support was. She had to lean heavily to her left to make any use of it at all, and this resulted in her right shoulder's heaving up and her left shoulder's drooping down so that she appeared, when walking, to be badly deformed. The trouble was, Brendan could not help remembering how very annoyed she had become on the only occasion that he had mentioned the inadequacies of the crutch. His offer of a stick had been contemptuously rejected, and since she had abruptly changed the topic of conversation he had not liked to revert to it.

Now, however, it was different. Before, he had simply noticed that the crutch was too short for her and not helping; now he could see that it was actually doing her harm. He told himself that she was a nice little kid, brave, sensible and loyal, and he did not see why should she go through life branded as a cripple when she was no such thing. He realised he would have to be extremely tactful, but he had been a policeman for many years, and when he thought of all the domestic quarrels he had had to sort out without offending either party he felt sure he could make Maeve see reason, persuade her to try to manage without an aid which was doing her more harm than good.

Several times Brendan tried to raise the subject, but on each occasion something occurred to prevent him. When they stopped by a stream to drink and to eat bread and cheese, he began to suggest that Maeve might like to try walking a short way without her crutch, but before he had got to the nub of the matter Maeve had noticed that the cart track they were following showed distinct signs that a large number of caravans had passed that way, and after that all she was concerned about was whether her beloved Kitty – and Nick, of course – had joined up with a tinker band. 'Sure and wouldn't it be just our bad luck to catch up with 'em as darkness fell,' she moaned, hastily cramming the remainder of her bread and cheese back into her bag. 'Oh, Brendan, I'm sorry to rush your dinner, but do you mind if we get on?'

It was now or never. Brendan took a deep breath. 'Maeve, me love, I've been thinking,' he said, as they began to hurry along. 'That crutch . . . it's a deal too small for you. When was it made?' He gave an indulgent laugh, looking down at the curly head bobbing along level with his shoulder. 'You're not very big now, alanna, but I reckon that crutch is at least six inches too short. You'd do better—'

'Wit' a stick; I know, you've said it before,' Maeve said. 'Are you trying to tell me I'm holding you up? Don't think I'll be offended, because cripples are used to being blamed when they drag behind. Only I'm doing my best, and you've never said . . .'

'Don't be so touchy, alanna. You've never held me up; indeed, sometimes you've insisted we go on walking when I'd have been glad to seek a bed for the night,' Brendan said hastily. 'But that crutch is making you walk crooked because it's too short. In order to use it at all, you have to lean to your left and that jerks your right shoulder up. Do you understand? Honest to God, alanna, it's doing you more harm than good.'

'Well I'm the one using it and I couldn't go more than a few yards without it; I'd either fall flat on me face or keel sideways, because I'm used to its support,' Maeve said obstinately. 'And now just stop talking about it, will you? I can't help me foot being twisted, can I? It's all very well for you, you're a big strong feller; you can't understand that a cripple needs a crutch.'

'But you needn't *be* a cripple, not if you'll just chuck the bloody crutch over the nearest hedge,' Brendan said, thoroughly exasperated. 'Why won't you listen to reason, you silly girl? I've a good mind to use that crutch to light our fire if we have to sleep rough tonight. Can't you see how pig-headed you're being? All I'm asking is that you walk a few hundred yards without it! Sylvie told me years ago that you'd been injured in a road accident which had twisted your foot. Well, I dare say it were twisted, but it isn't now. Haven't you noticed, you stupid girl, that your left foot's as straight as the right one?'

They had stopped walking and were facing each other across the little boreen they had been following. Both were furious; Brendan knew he was scarlet with rage and he could see Maeve was pale with it. Now, before he had time to consider the action, he snatched the crutch away from her, snatched it so roughly – and so unexpectedly – that she fell. Instantly, remorse seized him. He threw the crutch to the ground and went to help her to her feet, but she eluded him, slithering out of his grasp and going to pick up the crutch once more, literally spitting with fury, like an enraged wild cat.

Having gone so far, Brendan was determined not to give in. He snatched up the crutch before she could reach it and began to apologise, saying he had done wrong to take it from her so abruptly and offering his arm for the hundred yards or so it would take to convince her that she had no need of it. His apology went unheeded, however. Maeve wrenched the crutch out of his hold, and before he had time to duck or dodge she had swung it in a vicious half-circle, catching him so sharp a blow across the head that for a moment he saw stars, and swayed on his feet, fighting to regain his balance. Maeve was trembling, actually raising the crutch, possibly to deliver another blow. He sprang at her and snatched the crutch back and before she could prevent him he broke it in two across his knee. Then he hurled both pieces, as far as he could throw them, into the nearest thicket. 'And now you can take me arm, you little wild cat,' he said breathlessly, 'and I'll prove to you that you've no more need of that bloody awful little crutch than I have meself.'

He held out an arm but Maeve made no attempt to take it, and to his horror he saw that tears were pouring down her cheeks. 'You're a wicked devil, Brendan O'Hara,' she hissed. 'Pat made me that crutch when I were twelve. He made it with love and care, to help me when I were doing the messages, and now you've gone and bust it. I shall hate you to me dyin' day, so I shall.'

Brendan, beginning to come out of the red rage which had consumed him, went towards her, half afraid she would shrink from him, for he knew he had behaved badly. But she stood firm, glaring up into his face, and he could read the fury in her eyes, even though tears were still pouring down her pale cheeks. 'Get away from me,' she said. Her voice still wobbled, but he could see she was rapidly regaining her self-control. 'And just you find my little crutch because I shan't stir a step until you've done so. Oh, don't say you can't mend it because I know that, but just as soon as we're back in Dublin someone who knows about such things will put it right for me.'

'I'm sorry. I don't know what came over me . . .' Brendan began. Poor kid, she looked so helpless standing there, with her small heart-shaped face as white as a ghost, and her big dark blue eyes brimming with tears. And she was such a darling; so brave, so loving, that she had been prepared to limp across half Ireland in order to find Kitty, no child of hers, and fetch her back to Handkerchief Alley. He began to speak, to hold out his hands towards her, and the next moment he had snatched her into his arms and was kissing the tears away, loving the feel of her slim, strong body close to his own, filled with a feeling of protective love such as he had never known.

But the embrace only lasted a moment. Maeve tore herself free and gave him a hard push which sent him staggering back a couple of paces. 'How dare you!' she shouted. 'How dare you kiss me when everyone knows you're in love with horrible Sylvie Dugdale! Oh, I pretended I liked her because I didn't want to hurt your feelings. I didn't want you to know what I really thought. But I don't mind you knowing now, because you're as horrible as she is. She came over to the O'Keefes and took, took, took, and never gave nothing. She said pretty things, bought the kids a few presents when she was in the money, and then swanned off back to Liverpool wit'out giving a thought to the poor little baby she'd left behind. That's why I won't let Kitty cross the water, not if you paid me a hundred pounds.'

Brendan stared at her, almost unable to believe his ears. It was incredible that meek little Maeve Connolly could turn into this harridan, but it had happened, and he knew it was largely his own fault. What in God's name had made him pull her into his arms and kiss her? He knew, of course, that he'd grown fond of her during their journey, but it was not until he had seen her standing there, defenceless and in tears, that he had wanted to kiss her, to hold her, to show her that he cared. Oh, not in the way he cared for Sylvie, but . . .

As they stared at each other across the small space that separated them, he saw the roses begin to bloom in her cheeks. He took a step towards her, beginning to apologise again, trying to take her hands in his, wanting desperately to wipe away the tears, to see her elfin smile tremble once more on her lips, but she was backing away, shaking her head. 'You shan't make me love you,' she whispered, her voice so low that Brendan barely caught the words. 'I don't want to love you. You're going to marry Sylvie Dugdale, so loving you would only break my heart.' And with that, she turned away from him and disappeared into the trees.

Brendan shouted at her to come back, that he was sorry, that he had behaved like a brute, that they must talk, but she was fleet as a deer and Brendan, crashing through the undergrowth, soon lost her altogether. He returned to the cart track, his mind in a whirl of mixed emotions. The words she had spoken had not seemed to make sense. As though his desire to marry Sylvie was any concern of hers, or had anything to do with the relationship that he and Maeve had begun to build up! He told himself crossly that women – all women – were the very devil. Maeve might be young and inexperienced, but she was still woman enough to thoroughly confuse him.

Regaining the lane, he considered, uneasily, what he should do and decided that the most important thing was to find the two pieces of the crutch. She'll never forgive me unless I find them, he told himself distractedly, trying to remember where he had been standing when he had hurled them from him. After all, she's bound to come back to the boreen because she knows the tinkers came this way, and she's desperate to find Kitty, so she is. So if I find the pieces of crutch and promise to get it mended for her, I'm sure she'll forgive me. How on earth did we ever get into such a situation, though? We've been grand companions through thick and thin, sharing everything, and I go and ruin it all by telling her she doesn't need the one support she believes she relies on. He headed towards the thicket, then stopped, remembering the last glimpse he had had of her. Why, she had run through the woods ahead of him swift as an arrow, and as straight. He knew his size and bulk had held him back, for she had been able to slip between the saplings and young trees in a way which he could not, but even so, surely this would convince her that she had no need of any help in order to walk or run. Oh, if only it had! He realised he wanted Maeve's friendship more than he had wanted anything for a long time, could not contemplate her regarding him as an enemy. He must find her, but how best to do it? Should he stay here and hope she would return? But now that he considered this, he realised it might not be a good idea. The boreen wandered along, sometimes through woodland, sometimes down into valleys and up amongst the high hills. She could rejoin it at any point and he be unaware, standing here until moss grew on him, very like, whilst she – and the children – made their way back to Dublin.

So what to do? Crashing through the trees in search of her was useless, for he had penetrated sufficiently into the woodland to realise that in less than a quarter of a mile the trees thinned into open ground. Once there, she could go even more swiftly, and in any direction. No, what he must do was to follow the tinkers' tracks, because he knew Maeve's sole aim was to find Kitty and Nick. If he found them first, then she would run straight into his arms, so to speak, but if she found them, especially if they were with the tinkers, she might be extremely glad of his support before the day was over, for tinkers, he knew, did not readily surrender their prey. He took a couple of strides along the track, then hesitated and turned back, shoulders drooping. He must find the pieces of crutch; the wretched thing had meant a lot to her because Pat O'Keefe had made it, and perhaps it was a sort of symbol, he did not know; he only knew that she valued it and that his best hope of retaining her friendship was by returning it to her. Resolutely, he advanced on the thicket.

Maeve had not known she could run so fast; in fact, by the time she was clear of the trees, she was feeling so proud of herself that she began to soften towards Brendan. He had been *right*! She had had neither crutch, nor stick, nor a helping hand, yet she had easily outdistanced her pursuer and was now so far ahead of him that it would take ages for him to catch up. Maeve hugged herself, then realised that the tears were still wet on her cheeks, and wiped them away with the heels of both hands. If only he had not kissed her! Until she had felt his mouth on hers, she had supposed her feelings for him to be largely gratitude and admiration; almost the sort of hero worship which young girls often feel for an older man. But when she had found herself in his arms, felt his lips on hers, love had surged over her like a great wave. She tried to rekindle her anger against him by remembering how he had grabbed her and kissed her without even considering that she might not like it, might resent such an act. He had made no secret of his love for Sylvie, nor of his wish to marry her, so how dared he kiss her and fill her with longings which he had no intention of satisfying?

Then there was the crutch which Pat had made for her with such loving care. He had told her that it would help her to walk straight, and she was sure it had done so at first. If Pat had not gone to the war, he would have realised she had outgrown it, so it was scarcely his fault if it had done her more harm than good, as Brendan had put it.

Loping along steadily in the direction she thought the tinkers had taken, she told herself firmly to forget the whole incident and concentrate on finding Kitty. She glanced down at her feet as she hurried on, and could not prevent either a gasp of astonishment or a small, half-guilty smile. Brendan had been right and she had never noticed before! Long ago, her left foot had turned inwards, but now it was, as he had said, as straight as the right foot. And being no longer burdened with the crutch, she could see that her left foot was as capable of bearing her weight as the other. Maeve stopped for a moment to consider what she should do. Should she retrace her steps, make her way through the trees, and try to find Brendan again so that she could apologise to him? But surely by now he would have moved on. And the track she was following seemed to run level with the boreen, so if she just continued on her way they would probably meet up before nightfall. She acknowledged now that he was a good man and would not leave her alone out here, a prey to all sorts of dangers. Yes, he would search for her, as indeed he would continue to search for Kitty and

Nick, knowing that she, too, would be on their trail; yet he would not want her to reach the tinker encampment before he did, for they had heard bad reports of this band as they had travelled.

It would be hard to show Brendan an indifferent face when she knew, now, that she really loved him. It would be easier, she decided, to continue to pretend that he had truly upset and insulted her by throwing away her crutch. She would forgive him for the business of the crutch, of course, but remain cool towards him and then they would be able to continue to travel together without embarrassment. Yes, that was what she must do. And she would go with him across the water – if Kitty consented – and once she saw Brendan and Sylvie together, saw the love they shared, it would be easier to turn away, take Kitty and herself back to Handkerchief Alley, and return to her old life. She had never expected to marry or have children of her own, so she should embrace the life of a single woman, an aunt to Caitlin's brood and a foster mother to Kitty, and not repine.

Brendan found the pieces of crutch at last and emerged from the thicket with great relief. It had been hard, hot work; he was scratched and bruised and had leaves in his hair, but he told himself sturdily that it should have taught him a lesson. Losing one's temper never helped anyone. It happened to him rarely, but he had certainly lost control of himself that afternoon and had, consequently, wasted at least an hour. However, he shoved the pieces of broken crutch into his knapsack, picked up the bag which Maeve had left behind in her wild flight, and set off at last along the boreen.

He walked as softly as he could, watching the woodland, for he hoped that presently he would see Maeve's slender figure making her way back to him through the trees. Soon, however, the woods on his right thinned out and he began to be seriously worried about Maeve, for evening was drawing on and he wanted to find her well before dusk. All her possessions were in the bag he carried, and though there were streams in plenty from which she could drink, he had the round of soda bread and the remains of the cheese, and the blanket which covered her when they stopped for the night. However, it was still light, and now that the woodland had thinned out she would not be able to hide from him, even if she wished to do so.

At this point, the boreen began to run steeply downhill, and at the foot there was a stream and a wooden bridge. On the opposite side of the stream the woods began again, and Brendan sighed with frustration. He could see quite a way from the eminence upon which he stood, but there was no sign of either Maeve, the green and yellow cart, or the tinker band. Yet he knew that tinkers always camped near water and had confidently expected them to take up their position near a decent-sized stream such as this one. Then he thought again and nodded, a trifle grimly, to himself. Someone had built that bridge, presumably so that stock could cross in safety during the winter months when the stream would be swollen to twice or even three times its normal width, and that almost certainly meant that there was a farm nearby. Tinkers might prey upon farmers – well, they did – but they would not linger near such a place; too dangerous. No, they would move deep into the woods before setting up camp. Brendan hitched up his burdens, then took the longer piece of crutch in one hand and began to move forward once more. You never knew what lay ahead, and if he needed a weapon the business end of the crutch might come in handy. Resolutely, he crossed the bridge and plunged into the trees.

A short while later, he saw definite signs that the tinkers had passed this way: wheel tracks, broken twigs, some fragments of dried peat which must have fallen from a net of the stuff when the vehicle carrying it bounced over a rut. Hastily, Brendan left the track itself and began to creep forward with the utmost caution, moving silently from tree to tree, watching the ground ahead so that he did not tread on dry twigs or give himself away by a similar blunder, and presently his care was rewarded. Ahead of him but well to his left, he saw that the last of the light was falling into a clearing, and in that light he saw movement and the brightness of painted carts. Even more cautiously now, Brendan stole forward. Then he saw the oak: a massive tree with a trunk split in two by its great age to form a cavity which could almost be called a cave. He shrugged himself out of his knapsack and pushed both bags into the oak; he would move both more quickly and more quietly without luggage. He had shoved them well back, but now he carefully picked up leaves and twigs off the ground and piled them in front of the knapsacks. He moved a few feet away then glanced back, and having assured himself that his possessions were well hidden he continued to advance through the trees. Presently, he was close enough to smell wood smoke, and after another few yards he could see the camp clearly. There were a great many tents and seven caravans; he had caught up with the runaways at last!

Maeve crossed the bridge and moved quietly forward through the trees. Her legs were beginning to ache dreadfully but she gritted her teeth and kept on, for she had read the signs – snapped twigs, cart tracks in the dust – and knew that she was nearing the end of her search at last; that was, if Kitty and Nick had really joined up with the tinker band. It seemed unlikely because, from earliest childhood, Kitty had been warned that tinkers were dangerous people, people best avoided, particularly by the young:

> My mother said, I never should
> Play with the tinkers in the wood.

If I did, she would say,
Naughty little girl to disobey.

It was an old rhyming game, probably a good deal older than the wood through which Maeve was passing, and she was still repeating it beneath her breath when she saw, through the trees, the flames of a camp fire. Immediately, she looked round for good cover and saw a tangle of bushes to her right. Quickly and silently, she slid amongst them until she reached a spot where she was well hidden but could see the encampment clearly. The very quietness and stealth with which even young children went about their various tasks meant that they were up to no good, though she could see no sign of Kitty or Nick.

She had noticed that the camp seemed to consist mainly of women and children and presently understood why, as the men began to return. One or two heaved sacks of peat, others were laden with buckets of milk, hares, rabbits and even hens for the pot. One man carried a fat black and white puppy under each arm; another led a wide-eyed calf. Maeve sucked in her breath at the boldness of it, but then realised that the camp was being dismantled. The tinkers must have been here reconnoitring the land around for several days, finding the weak spots in the local farmers' defences. One housewife might be careless with her hens, another had not collected the eggs on this particular day. A turf pile could be robbed of the best dry turfs whilst the family slept, and barns could be explored, puppies taken, even a calf detached from its mother, provided it was weaned.

But the tinkers' thieving, though it distressed her, was not her principal concern, for unless the children were actually imprisoned in one of the caravans she soon saw that Kitty and Nick were not travelling with the band. She had been watching a green and yellow cart since, according to report, they had travelled a good way with such a vehicle. But after a while the door had swung open and a very skinny old lady, helped by a buxom wench in a scarlet shawl, had descended the steps and tottered over to another cart. There had been some conversation which Maeve could not hear and then someone had handed the old woman a clay pipe; someone else had filled it with tobacco and lit it, and the two women had settled down on the caravan steps, both puffing away.

Soon enough, Maeve had seen that each caravan door had been left swinging open long enough to enable anyone inside to escape, had they so wished, and she was certain that even if Kitty and Nick had once been with the tinkers, they were with them no longer.

Her thoughts turned to Brendan. She longed to get up from her crouching position amidst the saplings and go back to tell him that the children were no longer with the band, that they must search elsewhere, but she dared not do so. Now that the tinkers had raided the farms and were clearly about to depart, they had ranged their children all round the camp, looking outward and not inward, so that they might warn their elders of anyone approaching through the thick woodland. Maeve guessed that the children would spot the slightest movement, hear the smallest sound, and resigned herself to remaining just where she was until the band abandoned the camp. Sighing to herself, she realised for the first time that she was both hungry and thirsty, and thought wistfully of the food and drink in the knapsack she had left behind. Then she remembered that without her knapsack she had no money and her eyes filled with tears. Damn, damn, damn! But even hunger was not as bad as the fear that either Kitty and Nick, or Brendan himself, might walk straight in on the tinkers. Maeve dreaded to think what they might do to anyone who caught them red-handed with stolen property.

But there was absolutely nothing she could do about it, so she settled deeper into the undergrowth. She would have loved to go to sleep but was frightened to do so in case she snored, or made some involuntary movement which would give her away. Evening was drawing on and it was noticeably colder. Pins and needles attacked her extremities. Maeve gritted her teeth and clenched and unclenched her fists; soon, the tinker children would leave the clearing in the wake of their elders, and she would be able to stand up and shake the stiffness out of her limbs, and try to make her way back to the boreen and Brendan. Soon it would be over. And suddenly a little glow of warmth within her made itself felt and a small voice spoke in her head: *You'll find the children today and you'll find Brendan as well, so stop worrying*, it said. *You know the kids were with the green and yellow cart which you seen wit' your own eyes; they can't be that far away.*

One by one, the tinker children were slipping away. Soon, it would be safe to move. Maeve waited.

Chapter Sixteen

'Run for your life!'

Kitty was so terrified by Nick's shriek that she actually started to run, but then a quick glance back showed her that Nick, far from following her closely, appeared to be fighting with a huge man who held what looked like a cudgel in one enormous fist. Kitty was no coward and Nick was her best and dearest friend. Without a second's hesitation she turned and flew back to the fracas. She grabbed the cudgel, then sank her teeth into the hand holding it whilst Nick did yeoman work, kicking the man's shins and punching anything he could reach, even though the man's fingers were gripping the neck of his shirt.

'Leggo me pal!' Kitty shrieked, as the man dropped the cudgel and tried to grab her as he had already grabbed Nick. 'Leggo me pal, and me, or – or I'll fetch the polis!'

The man gave a short laugh. 'Will you get your perishin' teeth out of me hand,' he said, as Kitty snapped at his fingers once more, having been forced to loosen her bite in order to threaten him. 'I am the polis, or I was rather, and I don't mean you no harm; it were a case of mistaken identity. I thought you were me pal Maeve Connolly; I didn't realise there were two of you.'

At the mention of Maeve's name Kitty stopped biting and Nick stopped kicking and punching. It was dark and they could make out very little of the man's face, but they could see he was not a tinker. For what tinker would wear a knapsack on his back and carry another slung over his shoulder? There was a moment's silence as all three stared at one another, then Kitty spoke. 'Did – did you say your pal were called Maeve Connolly? But if so, where is she? If she's Maeve Connolly from Handkerchief Alley then – then she's our pal, too.'

The man began to answer but Nick hushed him impatiently. 'Who's you?' he demanded aggressively. 'Maeve don't have no feller and you ain't an O'Keefe, 'cos I knows 'em all, and so does Kit here.'

The man let out his breath in a long, low whistle. 'Well if that ain't the weirdest thing,' he said in a wondering tone. 'Here's me and Maeve trekked halfway across Ireland searching for Kitty and her pal Nick, and I reckon I've walked straight into you. Am I right?'

Kitty opened her mouth to assure him that he was right indeed, but Nick pinched her hand warningly. 'A minute ago you said you were the polis; now you say you're a friend of our Maeve's,' he said gruffly. 'And I asked you who you were;

454

that means, what's your name and what are you doin' here?'

The man sighed. 'Me name's Brendan O'Hara, though I don't suppose it'll mean much to you,' he said. 'And I was in the polis, though I'm not now. And I'm wit' Maeve, helping her to search for you two, because it's not right for a pretty young woman to go crossin' the country without a feller to see she's not troubled.'

'Oh,' Kitty said, digesting this. 'But where's Maeve? You said you and she were searchin' together, so where is she?'

'We had a bit of a disagreement,' Brendan said. 'Sure and it was all my fault, though I meant well, I can promise you that. But she – she took offence and ran off and I've been searchin' for her ever since.' He grinned at Nick; Kitty could see the flash of his teeth, even in the dark. 'That's why I grabbed you, young fellow-me-lad, 'cos I thought you were Maeve.' He sighed and looked about him. 'If Maeve hears the row we've been making, perhaps she'll . . . oh, thank God!'

Kitty and Nick turned to follow Brendan's gaze and saw a slim figure emerging, hesitantly, from the trees. She was too far away to be identified at once but neither Kitty nor Brendan had any doubts. They both ran towards her, but Kitty reached her first, flinging her arms round the older girl's waist and giving her a hard hug. 'Oh, Maeve, Maeve, I'm so sorry if you worried when I ran away but I meant to come back when I was old

455

enough to earn me livin' and I couldn't bear to be put in an orphanage or to go across the water to that Sylvie woman.'

Maeve cuddled Kitty close for a moment, then kissed the top of her roughly shorn head and held her back. 'You should have known your Auntie Caitlin better,' she said reproachfully. 'She didn't mean a word of it; she'd never have let you go to an orphanage any more than I would, and as for crossing the water, that's entirely up to you. But we can't talk about it now.' She turned to Brendan. 'It's a long way back to the nearest village, and anyway I don't feel inclined to go knocking on doors when everyone is likely to be abed. What do you think?'

Brendan agreed. 'There must be a farm not too far distant, because when I was hiding in the wood I saw the tinkers coming back with hens and such that they had stolen. I thought at first that they had just arrived and were making camp, but I soon realised they were moving on because you don't steal and then sit waiting to be caught. We could try to get a bed there, I suppose – it's nearer than the village – but I reckon you're right and everyone in the house will be asleep by now. It's a fine night. Mebbe sleeping rough, just for the one night, would be best.'

Maeve nodded. 'I'm agreeable. But Brendan, where *were* you when you were watching the tinkers? I was laid down in a sort of thicket when they were preparing to go, keepin' an eye on them like, in case Kitty and Nick were being held prisoner. I was too scared to move so much as a muscle because the kids had eyes everywhere. And then I reckon I fell asleep because next time I raised my head and looked, the clearing was deserted.'

Brendan laughed. 'Isn't that just the strangest t'ing? I were crouched down behind some blackberry bushes; I got scratched by the thorns and stung by some nettles. Pity I didn't yell out, then we might have met earlier.'

'We took a quick peep at them as well,' Nick said, grinning. 'I don't know whether you realise, but we'd been travelling with an old woman in a green and yellow caravan, only she did the dirty on us – sent us off on a wild goose chase, and then lit out with all our belongings, wicked old thief. We didn't realise the rest of the band were so close, or we'd have taken more care. As it was, we followed in the hope of catching up with Granny Trotter before she reached her pals, but we were too late. So when we came back along the cart track and you' – he pointed to Brendan – 'jumped out at us, we thought you were one of the tinkers come to get us.'

'I'd come to get you all right, even if I didn't know it,' Brendan said.

They made their way back along the cart track, and though Kitty did her best to keep up she was beginning to think she would have to admit she could go no further when Brendan, who had been bringing up the rear with Maeve, suddenly said in a low voice: 'Hang on a minute, you two. There's a hollow tree not far from here which might do us very well; I'll show you.'

They followed him into the wood and presently came to a mighty oak. 'That's where I stashed our belongings,' Brendan said, pointing. 'It's like a cave, so it is, being hollow, and there's a heap of dry leaves which you kids can burrow into.' He looked enquiringly at Maeve. 'It's a warm night, alanna. If you and meself wrap up in our blankets and lie within the curve of the hollow, do you reckon you'd be able to sleep?'

'I could sleep on a clothes line,' Maeve said. 'I could do with a drink, though, and a mouthful of bread.'

'So could I,' Kitty said, in heartfelt tones, and was delighted when Brendan produced a water bottle, half a loaf of bread, and a chunk of cheese, which he divided into four portions. They took it in turns to gulp down some water, gobbled the food, and settled down. Kitty's last thought before she fell asleep, Tommy purring blissfully against her back, was that there had been something different about Maeve, but she could not put her finger on it, and slumber claimed her whilst she was still wondering. Soon, all four of them slept.

Now that they had found each other, it took the small company a couple of days to reach a point where they could catch a train back to Dublin. And it was during those two days that the four of them sorted out what had happened and how they meant to behave in the future.

Maeve explained, frankly, that Brendan had pointed out the uselessness of her crutch, had made her see that she had no need of it, could in fact walk better without it. In their turn, Nick and Kitty told of their encounter with Granny Trotter and her horrible nephew, including his unfortunate death, for which they had felt responsible though it had been the man's own ferocity that had caused his end. Kitty asked, anxiously, whether they should tell anyone, but Brendan thought it was unwise. In fact, he doubted whether the man had suffered anything more than a deep concussion and this cheered both Kitty and Nick considerably.

Brendan asked Maeve which of them should explain to Kitty that they would very much like her to visit her mother in Liverpool, just for a couple of days so that Sylvie could see for herself that her daughter was alive and well, and after a great deal of thought Maeve said, a little brusquely, that she would do it herself since she wanted to make sure that Kitty thoroughly understood the situation and would not be jockeyed into doing something against her inclination.

Brendan was hurt by this seeming lack of trust, but when Maeve put the point to Kitty he had to admit that she was completely fair. 'She's your mammy, alanna, even if she did leave you to Caitlin and meself,' she said gently. 'Brendan wants her to see what a lovely little girl you are, but I'm going to come with you so that we can travel back home to Ireland together, because it's possible that Brendan himself may be needed in Liverpool for rather longer than you would wish to stay.'

Kitty looked doubtfully from Brendan's face to Maeve's, as if trying to read from their expressions whether they were agreed on the course of action Maeve had outlined. Then she gave a quick little nod, and said: 'All right, I'll go and visit me real mammy, because she's lost her own dear little girl, but I wouldn't stay wit' her if you paid me a hundred pounds. Ireland's me home and Maeve's me mammy, or as good as, so I'll be coming back just as soon as it's polite.'

Brendan and Maeve both chuckled and Brendan was turning away, well satisfied with what had been arranged, when Kitty spoke again. 'But what about me pal Nick, what's stood by me through thick and thin?' she asked. 'Can he come wit' us? Only his mammy and daddy don't care what happens to him, you know. I asked him if his family would be worried 'cos he weren't around and he just said that they probably wouldn't even notice. When I'm in Dublin, Auntie Cait gives me food for him an' he comes to tea an' that, but while I'm across the water . . .'

'It's all right, it's all arranged,' Maeve said quickly, shooting a glance at Brendan. 'Brendan here means to keep an eye on Nick. If – if he comes back to Ireland to buy a farm, he'll get Nick to go along wit' him, to give him a hand and help him build a house, and so on. If he stays in Liverpool, of course . . .' She cast a desperate glance at Brendan for they had not, in fact, discussed this possibility. 'If he stays in Liverpool . . .'

Brendan cut in quickly. 'If I stay in Liverpool I'll send you money, Maeve, because I know that you and Caitlin, between the pair of you, will see Nick right.'

Nick had gone off to buy food at the nearest village so it had been safe to discuss his future, but now Brendan saw him hurrying back along the road with a bag of groceries clutched in his arms, and a big grin on his face. 'Only another two miles and we'll reach a railway station,' Nick shouted. 'In the whole of me life, I've never been on a train; janey mack, wait till I tell the fellers at home where I've been. Tommy, we're going on a train!'

'Mam, Mam, they're coming! The post's just arrived and there's a letter from Brendan,' Sylvie cried. 'He says Catherine Mary – Kitty, I mean – has agreed to come to Liverpool with him, and they're bringing Maeve as well. He says he doesn't think for one moment that Kitty will stay, but I'm not so sure. The pub's doing well so we could afford to pay Maeve to work in the bar; not as a barmaid perhaps, because she wouldn't suit at all, but as a cleaner or someone to wash up. Then we could keep Kitty even though we'd have to have Maeve as well.'

Mrs Davies had just come into the kitchen and was taking off her coat and hat as her daughter spoke. She smiled indulgently at Sylvie's bright-eyed excitement, but shook a warning finger. 'Now don't you go getting all excited, love,' she said prosaically. ''Cos in his last letter, when he found the little lost girl, Brendan made no secret of the fact that she'd run away because she didn't want to cross the water and come to us. I don't doubt that Brendan's talked her into it for your sake, because of what you've gone through. But that don't mean to say the kid will want to stay here. All her pals are in Dublin, and from what Brendan's told us, she's mortal fond of that cousin of his, that Caitlin, and of the other kids. Why, she's been brought up to think of them as her brothers and sisters. You can't expect her to simply cast them aside for a woman she scarcely knows.'

Sylvie sighed and went over to pull the kettle over the flame. 'I know you're right, but we can give her a really good life here,' she pointed out. 'All right, so she would have to make new friends, but she'd have us for family, she'd have Maeve, and . . . and I suppose she'd have Brendan, too.'

The kettle began to boil and Mrs Davies got the tea caddy off the shelf and began to make a brew. 'So you mean to marry Brendan, do you?' she asked mildly. 'I'm not saying I'm blaming you, queen, because it's plain as the nose on your face

462

that he worships the ground you walk on, and he'll make an excellent landlord. You and meself and Bertie do our best, but there's nothing like a well set up young man, who gets on with folk, to bring in the business. Oh, aye, if you decide to make Brendan the happiest man on earth, we'll all be well pleased. Only before you agree to marry him, wharrabout Sam? I know you keep saying he brought the flu here and must have died of it himself, else he'd have been back long since, but you can't be certain sure. You don't want to do the same thing twice . . . marry in haste and repent at leisure.'

Sylvie shot her mother an indignant glance. 'How can I find out if Sam's dead or alive when all I know about him is that he comes from Plymouth?' she asked. 'It's not as if I could take time off to go and search for him because we're far too busy building up trade in the Ferryman. Don't think I haven't thought about it, though.'

'Aha, but there's another way of tracin' people,' Mrs Davies said complacently. 'Last night I were havin' a chat wi' a young fellow what's a journalist on the *Echo*. I told him as how we'd lost touch wi' a seaman what sailed from Southampton and he said we should advertise in the local paper down there. So how about it, eh? Even if Sam don't read the papers, you can bet your life there's others what do. If he's dead – sorry, love, but I know it's what you fear – then by the same token someone will write and tell us.'

Sylvie stared at her mother and felt her cheeks grow warm. If only Sam were alive! She loved him, had loved him almost from their first meeting, and she knew he had loved her too. So why, if he were alive, had he not returned to the Ferryman? But now she supposed there could be a thousand reasons. She jumped to her feet, for she had been sitting at the kitchen table opening the post, and flung her arms round her mother's neck. 'You're a wonderful woman, Mam,' she said breathlessly. 'I'll draft the advertisement right away.'

'What's them, Brendan? Ooh, what's that? Janey, it's huge so it is, much bigger than Dublin. An' look at all the ships, and the people, and the towers and spires and great tall buildings!' Kitty turned towards Brendan. 'Don't you know? Is that why you aren't answering me?'

Kitty, Maeve and Brendan were standing on the deck of the Irish ferry as it nosed past the Liverpool waterfront. Brendan laughed and put an arm about Kitty's slender shoulders. 'Of course I know what they are; I didn't live here for God knows how many years without learning the name of practically every building in the place. And remember, this was my beat when I was a scuffer – scuffer is the name Liverpudlians give to the polis.' He took her small hand in his and pointed with it. 'Them's the Liver Birds – they say they flap their wings whenever . . .' he suddenly realised that the remark he had been about to make was not a suitable one for a youngster to hear, and continued somewhat hastily, 'and the next building is the offices of the Mersey Docks and Harbour Board and all the towers and turrets are on the Cunard building. I expect you've heard of the Cunard liners – big ships that travel all over the world. Well, that's where the company that runs them plans out their voyages and books passages.'

'I see,' Kitty said, round-eyed with the wonder of it all. She had thought Dublin a wonderful city, the biggest city in the world, but this place dwarfed it with its tall impressive buildings, to say nothing of the masses of shipping moving to and fro, or lying at anchor, and the docks themselves, black with people and vehicles. She glanced quickly at Maeve, who was staring with equal amazement towards the shore. She tugged at the older girl's sleeve. 'I know it's huge but it's not as pretty as Dublin, is it? I love the Dublin quays, so I do, and – and the Custom House. Then there's the Four Courts on the northern quays and the National Library, and the Chapel Royal at Dublin Castle . . .'

Brendan cleared his throat. 'Dublin's grand, so it is, but remember, Kitty me love, that comparisons is odious. I'm off for a stroll along the deck. I shan't be long, so don't move from here; we don't want to lose one another when it's time to go ashore.' And with a cheerful wave, he detached himself from the throng hanging over the rail and disappeared.

'Oh, alanna, the size of a place isn't important, nor the splendour of the buildings,' Maeve said warmly. 'It's the people that really matter and we're Dubliners, so we are. Well,' she amended, glancing somewhat diffidently at Brendan's back, 'perhaps I should say we're Irish. But we're not here to criticise, we're here to meet your real mammy and to see the sights. And then we'll be off home again to our own place in Handkerchief Alley. Only – only it might be nice to visit your mammy again from time to time, 'cos I know she's after hoping the pair of yez will never lose touch again.'

'That's right, Maeve; it's just like a sort of holiday, isn't it?' said Kitty, clinging tightly to Maeve's hand. She had already made it clear as clear to everyone who would listen that she had no intention of remaining in Liverpool, but she knew, too, how powerless a child can be if it comes to a battle of wills. It was all very well to say she would run away if Sylvie tried to keep her in England, but where would she run to? A great expanse of sea separated Liverpool from Dublin and a ticket to cross on the ferry would, she imagined, be unbelievably expensive. What was more, there would be no Nick to help her, not this time, for he had been left behind in Handkerchief Alley with the O'Keefes; another good reason for returning home, she thought rebelliously, clutching Maeve's hand so tightly that the older girl winced. A friend like Nick was a friend indeed, and not to be cast off lightly. But it seemed that Maeve had divined the thoughts which were running through her head for, quite suddenly, she lifted Kitty off her feet, big girl though she was, kissed her cheek, and whispered into her ear, 'Will you stop your worritin', alanna, for I would swear on a stack of Holy Bibles that you an' meself shan't be parted, for aren't you my own little girl, who's been lost and found again, like it says in the Bible. Think of this as a holiday, and when it's over we'll be getting aboard the ferry and going back to Ireland, no matter what.'

She stood Kitty down, smiling reassuringly at her, and Kitty returned the smile almost gaily, for she knew that Maeve would never lie to her. 'But what about the wedding?' she enquired anxiously. 'Weddings take some arranging, so they do – I've heard Auntie Cait say so many a time – and we can't be after hanging around in Liverpool while Sylvie and Brendan make plans.'

Maeve's eyebrows shot up. 'Whatever makes you think there's going to be a wedding, alanna?' she said gently. 'I'm sure I never said any such thing.'

'No, but remember, I sleep in the same room as Clodagh and Grainne, and we goes to bed before you come in,' Kitty said. 'Auntie Cait told Clodagh that she was certain Uncle Brendan meant to ask my real mammy to marry him and of course she was sure Sylvie would, because Brendan's a dote. They wondered if they'd be bridesmaids wit' bunches of flowers an' pretty dresses. And then Clodagh started on how she meant to get married herself, and Grainne said she'd best find herself a rich feller first, and he'd best be blind an' all, else he'd never take on such a scarecrow. And Clodagh thumped her, an' Grainne hit back, an' someone's foot got me right in the back an' knocked me and Tommy out of bed. So you see, Auntie Cait thinks there's goin' to be a wedding.'

Maeve sighed deeply and squeezed Kitty's hand. 'I suppose it must look that way; in fact, you're probably right and Sylvie and Brendan will get wed,' she said, and Kitty thought she sounded sad. 'But that's for the future, alanna, for as Caitlin says, weddings take a deal of arranging. And we shan't be lingerin' in Liverpool for weeks and weeks, I can promise you that.'

'Good,' Kitty said contentedly. 'Though I'd like to be a bridesmaid all right, with a pretty dress and a posy of flowers. Might we cross the water again, d'you suppose, just for the wedding?' She looked up at Maeve, then had to peer round her, for her friend had turned her head away and was gazing steadfastly towards the stern of the ferry. To her horror, Kitty saw that there were tears trembling on Maeve's long lashes, but then her companion produced a handkerchief, blew her nose vigorously and brushed a hand across her watering eyes.

'I got a smut from the perishin' funnel in me eye when I was facing forwards,' she said. 'As for returning for the wedding, I don't think that'll be possible, alanna. You see, when we go back, I'm going to try to get a proper job. You're old enough to fend for yourself after school, and in the holidays, so I shan't feel guilty at leaving you. Look how you coped when you ran away. Your Auntie Cait is going to try to get me some work in Switzers. Oh, I dare say I'll only be a cleaner, but Cait reckons if I work at me brogue and spend me wages on decent, respectable clothing, then I might end up on the shop floor, like she did.'

'Well, that would be grand, so it would,' Kitty said. 'I suppose it's because you walk just fine wit'out needing the crutch that's made the difference. Aren't you grateful to Brendan, darling Maeve, for making you see that you didn't need it no more?'

But it appeared at this point that another smut had got into Maeve's eyes for she became very busy with her handkerchief and it was several moments before she remarked, in a voice which trembled a little: 'Oh yes, I'm *very* grateful; and – and I wish him joy of Sylvie, so I do.'

Kitty had begun to agree with this generous sentiment when the ship drew close to the quay and Brendan re-joined them. He had told her he thought that her mammy would meet them and now Kitty found herself glad that Maeve had insisted on their remaining in Dublin until her hair had grown and been properly cut. 'Appearances have always mattered a lot to Sylvie, and if she sees you looking like a ragged little boy she might think I've not taken proper care of you,' Maeve had said.

Kitty had thought this pretty silly but now, eyeing the elegant blonde lady in the fur wrap and expensive leather boots, she realised that Maeve had been right, and was glad of the smart new coat and boots which Brendan had bought, and of her shining, neatly cut curls.

Mother and daughter simply stared. Kitty could not move though she clutched Maeve's hand convulsively and Sylvie, too, was motionless for a moment. Then she came forward, took both Kitty's hands in her own, and kissed her cheek. Then she stepped back, her beautiful blue eyes filling with tears even as her mouth curved into a generous smile. 'Welcome to Liverpool, Catherine Mary, only I believe I'm to call you Kitty,' she said, her voice trembling a little. 'The last time I saw you, queen, you were a red-faced, squawking baby, only a few weeks old. But now I see you're a beautiful little girl and one day you'll be a very lovely woman. I'm glad and proud that you've come to visit me and I promise we'll see you have a grand time whilst you're with us. But now we'd best get back to the Ferryman because me mam – that's your granny, Kitty – has a capon roasting in the oven, and strawberry tart and cream ready on the side. We'll walk, since you've not got a great deal of luggage and waiting for a tram at this time of day can be a lengthy business.'

Then she turned to Kitty's companions. 'Maeve, how very pretty you've grown! I wouldn't have recognised you, but of course the last time I saw you you were twelve years old.' She gave Maeve a hug and a kiss and Kitty, observant as always, saw that Maeve held herself rather stiffly, scarcely responding at all to the embrace. Then Sylvie turned to Brendan and it seemed to Kitty that Sylvie's whole being relaxed into warmth. 'Brendan, my dear,' she said, and her voice had a sort of throaty purr. 'I've been so anxious that Maeve or Kitty might have changed their minds, decided not to come, but I should have known better; you wouldn't have broken my heart in such a way.'

Kitty saw the tide of colour rise in Brendan's face, saw how he shuffled his feet, and wondered why he should be so obviously embarrassed. But then Sylvie tucked her arm into his elbow, Maeve took Kitty's small paw, and they headed away from the quayside and towards what Kitty assumed to be the Dock Road.

Sylvie had been pleasantly surprised by her daughter's appearance, though she had been unable to stop herself from thinking, sadly, how different the meeting might have been had Becky been alive. Her older daughter had had golden hair and blue eyes; Kitty's eyes were green and her hair chestnut brown, but their faces and movements were very similar indeed. This was not surprising since they were half-sisters, yet it had shocked Sylvie for a moment so that she had simply stared at her small daughter instead of rushing forward and kissing her, as she had planned. She had been aware that the child had not responded when she had hugged her, but told herself that this was natural. She and Kitty were strangers; she thought they should spend the next few days getting to know one another, and even if love was too much to hope for, perhaps liking and friendship could follow.

But if Kitty had been a bit of a shock, Maeve had been even more of one. Sylvie remembered Maeve very well indeed, as a skinny, hunched-up, crippled child, dependent upon a crutch, and plain as a boot with draggly limp dark hair, a pale little face and a brogue so thick that at first she had had difficulty in understanding a word the child had said. Yet now, what a contrast! Maeve stood almost as tall as Sylvie herself and straight as an arrow, with no sign of the awkward limp which had contorted her body years ago. Her dark hair was cut short and curled crisply round a small elfin face, and her eyes, which Sylvie had never particularly noticed before, were large, deep blue, and framed with dark and curly lashes.

And she was young! For the first time in her life, Sylvie was suddenly conscious that she herself was no longer a girl. Oh, she felt like a girl, considered herself a girl, but seeing the freshness of Maeve's skin, the shyness of her smile, Sylvie knew that she herself was a woman of the world. She had not undergone the privations which Maeve had known, but her life had never been easy, not since Len's accident, at any rate. But she comforted herself with the recollection that Brendan loved her and that Sam had loved her too, once.

As they walked back towards the Ferryman, she chatted easily with Brendan, now and again turning her head to include Maeve and Kitty in the conversation, but all the time her thoughts were elsewhere. She had advertised in the Southampton paper, but so far had received neither a reply from Sam himself, nor word from some friend or shipmate telling of Sam's death. She knew of course that being a seaman he could easily have taken a berth and sailed to foreign parts, but if he had done so, surely he would have written?

'Here's the Ferryman.' Brendan's cheerful voice as he turned his head to address Kitty and Maeve broke into her thoughts. Sylvie followed his glance and thought that, compared to Handkerchief Alley, her home should really impress the young people from Ireland. With its fresh coat of paint, and the bar door open and her mother framed in it, one could tell at a glance that this was a popular and prosperous place. Sylvie remembered how shocked she had been on first entering Handkerchief Alley, and looking over her shoulder saw that Maeve's large eyes had rounded in appreciation and that Kitty, too, seemed impressed. We've done all right, me, Mam and Bertie, she thought as she ushered her companions in through the open door. It's been hard work but we've done all right.

Maeve and Kitty were given a large, airy bedroom which had once belonged to old Mrs Dugdale, but it had been freshly whitewashed, newly carpeted – a great luxury – and there were flowers on the dressing table. The only thing missing, Maeve thought, was a washstand, but this was explained when Sylvie took them a little further along the corridor to where there was a proper bathroom. Maeve gazed at it with awe and knew that Kitty was doing the same. The floor was covered in dark blue linoleum. There was a large hand basin, an enormous lavatory with a mahogany seat set on a small dais, and a wonderful bathtub. There was a strange contraption on the wall above the bath and Sylvie explained that this object was called a geyser. It was powered by gas which one had to light with a long taper – she demonstrated – and after a few moments you turned one of the big silver taps and hot water gushed forth. Maeve, admiring it, thought she would never dare use it, though Sylvie said it was safer than it looked and hardly ever blew up. 'I'll come and run it for you until you've grown used to it,' she said kindly, and Maeve saw Kitty's face become troubled and realised it was because of the implication that they were meant to stay until the geyser no longer frightened them. And that would be a mortal long time, she thought, and gave Kitty's hand a quick squeeze. As soon as Sylvie had finished giving them the tour of inspection, they would go to their room and then they could discuss freely what they had seen.

When Maeve had first set eyes on Sylvie as they crossed the quay to her side, she had been surprised by the change in her. Sylvie was still as beautiful as Maeve remembered her, but there were lines on her forehead which had never been there before. And you could tell that she knew her way around and was a capable and businesslike person. She's grown very much harder, Maeve thought, which is odd because I used to think her selfish. But it isn't selfishness I read in her face now so much as a determination not to let anything stand in her way. It's easy to see she means to marry Brendan, but I'm not at all sure that she loves him. Well, I shall watch carefully and make up my mind what to do – not that I mean to stay here, nor to persuade Kitty to. But – but I'm real fond of Brendan, so I am, and I'm not at all sure he would enjoy being a pub landlord. Brendan isn't hard, for all his size and strength; he's as soft as cream cheese. Still, if he's really deeply in love with Sylvie, then not all the persuasion in the world will make him leave Liverpool and return to Ireland.

Presently, she found herself alone with Kitty in

their bedroom and they began to unpack the few clothes they had brought with them and hang them in the large wardrobe. As they worked, Maeve glanced interrogatively across at the child. 'Well? What do you think? I told you your mother was beautiful and it was true, wasn't it? And the Ferryman is a thriving business, so your mother isn't short of money. Did you see the photograph of Becky on the mantelpiece in the parlour, when your mam showed you where they sit when they've got company? I never met her but it did strike me how very alike the two of you are. It's awful sad because you're half-sisters and I'm sure you would have been great friends. I know you don't want to stay in Liverpool and I don't blame you, but it might be a kindness to your mam to say you'd come over, say twice a year, and spend a couple of weeks with her. Would you like to do that?'

'No I would not,' Kitty said baldly. She was changing out of the old dress which she had worn under her green serge coat into a grey pleated skirt and white blouse, but now she stopped buttoning the blouse to stare defiantly at Maeve. 'You think she's beautiful . . . Sylvie I mean . . . but I think she's cold, and nowhere near as pretty as you, Maeve. As for Becky being me half-sister, I've got two half-sisters already, Clodagh and Grainne. I know you say they're not me half-sisters but that's how I think of them, so I do.'

'Yes, I know what you mean, but in fact you

and Clodagh and Grainne aren't blood relations, whereas if Becky hadn't died . . .'

'Oh, Maeve, do stop it,' Kitty said irritably. 'I know I'm only a kid but you've always said I'm sensible, and I am! If Becky hadn't died, I'd never have come here – never have met Sylvie, let alone her precious daughter. She only wants me because she's lost Becky, and she only wants Brendan because that Len of hers is dead.'

'Oh, alanna, that isn't true,' Maeve said, horrified by the child's cynical remark. 'I know it looks like that but it really isn't fair to judge on such a short acquaintance. I suggest we keep our eyes open and our mouths closed for at least three days and then we'll talk the matter over again. Only, one thing I must say. I truly believe that Sylvie and Brendan loved each other even when her husband was alive, but of course they could do nothing about it, not then. It would have been dishonourable, and Brendan is an honourable man.'

Regrettably, Kitty gave a loud snort. 'Well, darling Maeve, don't try to pretend that my mammy is an honourable woman because you know very well that Len Dugdale wasn't my father, but some other feller,' she said roundly. 'And that's dishonourable if you like.'

Maeve stared at Kitty as though she had never seen her before. 'I know what you say is true, but it all happened a long time ago and – and Sylvie's a different person from the one who ran away to Ireland all those years back,' she said gently. 'Try not to hold it against her, alanna, otherwise this whole trip will have been a waste of time.'

'So it is,' Kitty muttered, but then she must have noticed that she was upsetting her companion for she flung both arms round Maeve's neck and kissed her cheek resoundingly. 'I'm sorry, I'm sorry, but I'm all mixed up,' she gabbled. 'You're right, I've come over here which means I'm willin' to give it a try, so I'll do just as you say: I'll keep me eyes open and me mouth shut for three days and forget me mammy abandoned me all those years ago and then we'll talk again.'

'That's my good little girl! But remember, your mammy had no choice but to abandon you. She couldn't take you back to Liverpool because you were the living proof that she'd been unfaithful to her man, and she paid towards your keep for a long time, you know, even though she was nursing a sick husband and bringing up her other little girl.'

Kitty had been hanging her coat in the wardrobe, but turned at these words. 'No one ever told me before that my mam paid Auntie Cait towards my keep,' she admitted. 'Then she must have loved me a little, because she could easily have just walked away. I'm glad you told me, Maeve, because it shows she's not all bad and I did think that a good person like Brendan wouldn't go falling in love with a really bad one.'

Maeve felt the warm colour flood into her cheeks and bent her head to stare intently down at the jumper she was folding. 'Yes, you're right, of course Brendan is a very good person. But sometimes men do fall for a pretty face and scarcely notice the character behind it. But I'm sure that isn't the case with Sylvie. She may have been heedless in the past, when she was young, but she's changed a lot.'

Kitty shot her a quick glance and began to speak, then bit the words off short and headed across the room towards the door. 'I've hung up all my stuff so I'm going down to see if I can help get some dinner, 'cos I'm starving, so I am,' she said cheerfully. 'I like that Mrs Davies, so I do; she wants me to call her Granny, but like you said, I'll have to get to know her better first.'

For the rest of the day Kitty was unusually silent because she had so much to think about. When they had crossed the water, she had been full of both excitement and apprehension at the thought of meeting her real mother, of visiting a great city and of seeing all the sights, for both Brendan and Maeve had impressed upon her that this was to be a sort of lovely holiday and that her mother meant to give her a grand time. Sylvie had written to her and had said she meant to take Kitty to the big stores in the city centre and kit her out with some really nice clothes. She said they would visit theatres and cinemas, parks and museums, and any other places of entertainment that Kitty would like to see. Consequently, Kitty's mind had ranged ahead during the voyage on the ferry, and she had not thought very much about Maeve and Brendan, save to be glad that they were clearly good friends.

Then they had met Sylvie on the quayside, and when she had tucked her arm into Brendan's so possessively Kitty had happened to glance at Maeve and had seen the stricken look on her friend's face. At the time, she had merely thought that Maeve had resented being virtually ignored by Sylvie, who had once known her well, but later she had wondered if it were not something more. And just now, in the bedroom, she had read something in Maeve's face which she had not wanted to see. For the naked pain had spoken volumes; Maeve did not like the thought of Brendan falling into Sylvie's hands any more than Kitty did.

Or could it be more than that? Kitty did not know very much about grown-up people's emotions, but she was beginning to have a shrewd idea that Brendan meant more to Maeve than Kitty had imagined.

After a week in the city, Kitty's attitude towards Sylvie began to change. Granny Davies had told her, sadly, that apart from colouring she was really very like Becky, so it was understandable that the sight of her brought back bittersweet memories, but she was beginning to believe that Sylvie actually liked her for herself. Her mother had accompanied her, Brendan and Maeve to cinemas and

480

theatres but she had insisted that, when they visited the big stores, it should be she and Kitty alone. 'We'll probably have different ideas, but two sets of ideas are easier to deal with than four,' she had said decisively, so on the day that she took Kitty shopping Brendan and Maeve were left to their own devices. Kitty thought this a good thing; if Brendan and Maeve really liked one another then they stood a better chance of sorting things out by themselves. So she set off, on that bright summer day, skipping along beside Sylvie and chattering nineteen to the dozen, determined to enjoy herself, to have high tea in a café or restaurant and to keep Sylvie away from the Ferryman for as long as possible.

Because she and Sylvie had been getting on so well she had expected to enjoy the day, and it was living up to her highest expectations. Kitty had never chosen her own clothes, or if she had done so it had been from the second-hand stalls on the Iveagh or Daisy Markets, but now they went into Lewis's, Bunney's, and a great many other shops, taking their time. Kitty tried on half a dozen dresses before she took Sylvie's advice and chose a blue gingham dress which had a white Peter Pan collar and fastened at the waist with a big bow. That was for summer, of course, so the second dress was a lovely woollen one, honey-coloured, with a chocolate-brown sash round its middle and a neat little collar, a bit like an Elizabethan ruff, which Kitty thought the height of fashion. Never

having owned a pair of leather gloves in her life
– Maeve always knitted cosy mittens for the winter
– she was equally impressed by the pair which
Sylvie insisted on buying for her and which
matched the neat leather boots with the fur tops.
The purchase of the boots was followed by the
buying of a lovely earth-brown coat which Sylvie
suggested might be bought a little large to allow
room for growth. The hat which went with it was
shaped like a pudding basin with a small,
upturned brim, and though Kitty thanked Sylvie
prettily she knew she would never wear it, not in
Dublin; Nick and her other friends would die
laughing, and she did not mean to let that happen.
In fact, as they sat over their high tea in a café
Sylvie had chosen, she confided in her mother that
she thought she ought to leave the winter clothes
behind, in Liverpool. 'Because you did say you'd
ask me and Maeve over again, around Christmas
time,' she pointed out. 'And – and if I wore lovely
new clothes in Handkerchief Alley, they'd probably get nicked, or maybe I'd drop food down
them. I'd rather they was here, honest I would,
and you'd know that I meant to come back,' she
finished in rather a rush, feeling the hot blood rise
to her cheeks.

Sylvie leaned across the table and clasped
Kitty's hands. 'Oh, Kitty, you are a darling,' she
said softly, 'and I'm delighted that you'd like to
come back. But remember, Brendan – if he decides
to stay in Liverpool, that is – and meself will be

glad to see you any time – any time at all. I don't suppose Maeve will want to come over again; she came this time to make sure I didn't kidnap you, or try to persuade you to stay, and I know she's going to get a full-time job when you go home. It's not that I don't value Maeve, because I do,' she added hastily, 'but good jobs are hard to find and she won't want to risk losing hers by being away around Christmas.'

Kitty stared at her. 'But Brendan wants a farm. He doesn't want to be in the police any longer.'

Sylvie smiled. 'Oh well, I'll be delighted to see you anyway. But if Brendan were to ask me to marry him, he'd be the landlord of the Ferryman,' she pointed out. 'That's a much nicer job than being a policeman and a good deal better than scratching a living on a poor patch of ground somewhere in Ireland.'

Kitty looked down at her plate, upon which reposed a large doughnut, oozing with jam – she and Sylvie had already eaten their way through an assortment of sandwiches, a plateful of sausage rolls and some tiny pork pies – then raised her eyes and looked challengingly at her mother. She would have to speak out, even though it seemed ungrateful when Sylvie had bought her lovely things and was treating her to this delicious high tea. 'Has Brendan asked you to marry him?' she said bluntly. 'Because, if so, he's said nothing to us.'

'No, he's not asked me yet, but I believe he will,'

Sylvie said, with a quiet confidence which Kitty found frightening. 'He's wanted to marry me for years, but as you know, until recently I had a husband, a husband who needed me. It's different now. I'm a widow, you see, and that means—'

'I know what it means,' Kitty said brusquely. 'But Sylvie, do – do you love him? Oh, I know you're very sweet to him and take his hand in the cinema when the lights go down, but – but if you really love him, surely you'll go back to Ireland with him and help him to buy his farm? He could do wit' a bit more money to start with, I've heard him say so, many a time.'

Sylvie laughed, but shook her head. 'I wouldn't make a good farmer's wife at all,' she said firmly. 'As for loving, what does a child like you know about that, may I ask? Why, Brendan is a dear man and I'm truly fond of him. Sometimes, two people marry from fondness and end up deep in love.'

'And sometimes people marry and end up hating one another,' Kitty pointed out. 'Auntie Cait says you've got to love a feller to marry him 'cos all men has horrible habits; I don't think Brendan has any horrible habits, but I don't think he wants to be a landlord either, and you wouldn't want to make him unhappy, would you?' Privately, she thought that Sylvie had never even considered Brendan's feelings when she had decided to marry him. She wanted a husband to help her with the pub and Brendan was so kind that he might even give up the thought of his farm rather than disappoint her. It seemed very unfair to Kitty and she repeated her question in a rather more belligerent tone. 'You wouldn't want to make him unhappy, would you?'

'I'm going to make him the happiest man on earth,' Sylvie said, but there was something in her tone which made Kitty look at her closely, and to her astonishment she saw that there were tears on her mother's cheeks.

Remorsefully, Kitty leaned across the small table which separated them and gave her mother's hand a squeeze. 'I didn't mean to upset you, but I'm really fond of Brendan and I like you as well, Sylvie. But why are you crying? All I did was ask whether marrying was a good idea.'

Sylvie sniffed, then got out a dainty lace handkerchief, dried her eyes and blew her nose. 'Until a few weeks ago, I truly thought I was going to marry someone else, someone I loved very much,' she admitted. 'He came back from the war and visited us at the Ferryman; it was he who brought the flu, I believe, because he felt ill and left early – earlier than he had intended, I mean – and soon after that Len and Granny Dugdale sickened . . . well, you know the rest.'

Kitty stared at her. Maybe there was a way out of this tangle after all. 'Don't you know his address?' she asked. 'What's his name, anyhow?'

'Sam Trescoe, and he came from Plymouth. He was a seaman, sailing from Liverpool during the war, only when it ended he went back to his old ship, whose home port was Southampton; it was always to his ship that I wrote. And I have tried to contact him; I put an advertisement in the *Southern Evening Echo* – that's Southampton's local paper – but I haven't had any replies at all.'

Kitty nodded thoughtfully. 'Did you try the Plymouth papers?' she asked.

Dully, Sylvie shook her head. 'No, because I don't know how often he gets enough leave to go home, so Southampton seemed the obvious choice.' Suddenly, she jumped to her feet and began sorting out the money in her purse so that she could pay for their tea. 'Now, Kitty darling, I've trusted you and I want you to trust me. I'll make Brendan happy, I promise you. I told you about Sam because I wanted you to know that I have loved someone very deeply, but you must forget I ever said anything, because that really might hurt Brendan, and neither of us wants to do that.'

Kitty smiled reassuringly and patted her mother's hand, but already a plan was forming in her mind. 'Don't worry. I wouldn't hurt Brendan for the world,' she said reassuringly.

Sylvie was beginning to wonder how she could get rid of Maeve and Kitty for a whole day so that she could have Brendan to herself. He was sweet to her, understanding and sympathetic, but he still had not asked her to marry him. I've given him every encouragement, too, Sylvie thought resentfully now, as she rolled out the ball of pastry she had just made, and began to line a pie dish. However, if she got him to herself she was certain that he would seize the opportunity and ask her to be his wife. *And suppose he doesn't?* a nasty, niggling voice in her head asked spitefully. *Suppose he's had to wait so long that he thinks his case is hopeless? Why, he might even have met someone else and it may not occur to him to ask you. What'll you do then, eh?*

I'll ask him myself, Sylvie told the niggling little voice. And believe me, he'll jump at the chance. Why, he's been in love with me ever since he rescued me from the Mersey; he isn't going to change now. She waited, but the niggling little voice was silent, and presently, when Kitty, Maeve and Brendan came back from doing the messages, she suggested brightly that Brendan might take her to see his Uncle Sean. 'I've always longed to meet him because he's been a good friend to you, Brendan, and a day in the country would do us both good,' she said. 'Mum and Bertie can manage the pub during the day and we'll be back before opening time.' She turned to Maeve. 'I thought you and Kitty might like to catch the ferry over to New Brighton and have a day at the seaside,' she said. 'It was one of Becky's favourite places, and . . .' her voice wobbled, 'she really loved the beach,' she continued bravely. 'And the truth is . . . I can't bear to go back there without her, but I wouldn't want to deprive you.'

Brendan looked uneasy. 'When'll we go?' he asked. 'Sure and we can't just turn up on Uncle Sean's doorstep wit'out a word of warning.'

'We'll go tomorrow,' Sylvie said firmly. 'After all, in three days' time you'll be back on the ferry, heading for the Emerald Isle. And I've often wanted to visit your uncle; I believe the surrounding countryside is very beautiful, so we can spend most of the day exploring and just pop in to see the O'Haras for a cup of tea and a chat.'

Brendan agreed to this, and to Sylvie's great relief Maeve and Kitty took to the idea of a trip to New Brighton, especially when Sylvie promised to pack them a splendid picnic and Brendan insisted on giving them money for tram and ferry fares and ice creams and rides on the funfair. Mrs Davies agreed that she and Bertie could manage the pub between them, though the look that she cast at her daughter was a quizzical one. Sylvie ignored it. 'I'm making this pie for tonight, but as soon as it's out of the oven, I'll make some small ones which you can take to New Brighton,' she said. 'I'm really looking forward to a long day out!'

Chapter Seventeen

The morning dawned brilliantly fine and warm, just the day for a trip into the country, or to the seaside. Brendan was no fool and had realised from the moment Sylvie had outlined her plan that she was giving him the opportunity to ask the question he had so longed to put to her, so why wasn't he feeling overjoyed? He told himself he was a lucky dog that Sylvie had grown more beautiful with every year that passed and that he would soon grow accustomed to living in the city once more, for he was pretty sure she would not wish to become a farmer's wife.

The two couples parted at the Pier Head, Maeve and Kitty sparkling with anticipation of the delights to come, and, waving them off, Brendan found himself wishing desperately that he could accompany them. He glanced at Sylvie, opening his mouth to suggest that they, too, should visit New Brighton, then remembered her saying that she could not face the place because Becky had loved it so.

Crossly, he turned back towards the bus stop thinking as he did so that he did not believe a word of it, though he had no intention of admitting as much. Poor little Becky must haunt these streets; there must be a dozen places which she and Sylvie had visited far more often than New Brighton beach, yet Sylvie had insisted on accompanying them wherever they went.

The bus drew up alongside and Brendan helped Sylvie aboard. As they settled themselves in their seats, he glanced at that perfect profile, that smooth pale golden hair, and tried to plan how he would put the all-important question. But his mind kept wandering. At first, he thought it was regret for the farm which, if he married Sylvie, he would never possess. And as the bus trundled on, he grew quieter and quieter. He told himself that he had always loved Sylvie, longed to make her his wife, but odd little pictures kept cropping up in his mind. He remembered the journey across Ireland when he and Maeve had been chasing after Kitty and Nick; how happy they had been! They had shared the bad times as well as the good, and Maeve had never complained, never suggested that he should carry her knapsack as well as his own, though he had often done so, made the best of inadequate food and nothing but water to drink. He admired her tremendously and was astounded to remember that he had once thought her plain; now, he thought her the prettiest thing, though it wasn't simply her looks, of course. She was so lively – so gallant, somehow. But he was supposed to be concentrating on Sylvie, sitting beside him, chattering away, so he had no right to keep thinking of Maeve. He tried to fix his mind on

Sylvie, but her prattle, which had always amused and delighted him, suddenly bored him.

Presently, the bus drew up in a town which Brendan told Sylvie was Ormskirk and they got to their feet. 'You said you'd like to take a look at the town. It's quite close to where my uncle and aunt live,' he said, helping her down the step. 'We can have a wander round – they hold a market here today – then have a bite of lunch, and after that make our way across to Uncle Sean's place.' He looked anxiously at Sylvie, noting that she wore her best coat, which was cream-coloured, and dainty black patent leather high-heeled shoes. Brendan indicated the shoes with a jerk of his thumb. 'I thought you said you wanted to explore the country; in *those* shoes?'

Sylvie glanced down at her feet, then smiled brightly. 'It's a lovely fine day, so I thought . . . but if these won't do, there's bound to be a shop somewhere which can sell me something sturdier.'

Brendan sighed; this did not augur well for the day ahead. Then he brightened. Perhaps, after he had proposed marriage and she had accepted, she would no longer wish to visit Uncle Sean and his family. So he smiled down at her. 'We won't do no buying until we're sure of what we want to do,' he said. 'We'll go down to the market first and then see how your feet feel after we've been round the stalls.'

Late that night, when Maeve was putting Kitty to bed, Kitty voiced the thought that she suspected both of them had been harbouring. 'We talked an awful lot about our day, didn't we, Maeve? But Brendan and Sylvie said barely a word. Oh, I know Brendan said that they'd had to come home early because Sylvie's shoes weren't suitable for country walking, but even so, it seems really peculiar that neither of them wanted to talk about what they did.'

'Yes, I thought it were odd meself,' Maeve said. She chuckled. 'Mind, when I saw that pale-coloured coat and them shoes, I thought mebbe they'd changed their minds and were off to see a play, or a picture show, which weren't suitable for the two of us. But never you mind, alanna, only three more days and we'll be back on the ferry to Ireland.'

'Two of us, or three of us?' Kitty said. She had washed and was clad in her long white nightgown, and now she sat on the edge of the bed so that Maeve could give her hair the customary one hundred strokes of the brush.

Maeve smiled. 'Before today, I'd have thought maybe only two, but after today . . . well, I reckon it'll be three.'

Kitty nodded contentedly, then squawked as the brush caught her ear. 'Go steady, Maeve,' she said. 'Do you really think Brendan will be coming home with us? 'Cos if so, I've had an idea, only . . . could you help me? I don't believe I can do it by myself. You see, I feel awful sorry for Sylvie . . .'

*

When Maeve had finished brushing Kitty's hair, heard her prayers and tucked her up, she made her way down the stairs, intending to go straight into the kitchen, for she had taken on the washing-up of the glasses and the later it got, the more work would be awaiting her attention. She nearly jumped out of her skin when someone stepped out of the shadows and put a restraining hand on her shoulder. She drew in a breath to scream and then suddenly knew that it was Brendan, and gave a small husky giggle. 'How you frightened me! I didn't see you standing there and for a moment I thought it was some drunk who had managed to get in. I'm sorry I'm late, but . . .'

'Come with me,' Brendan muttered, towing her towards the side door. It was always kept locked and bolted at night, but opened easily beneath Brendan's hand and Maeve guessed that he had dealt with it earlier. He pulled her out into the gathering dusk, but when she began to ask him where they were bound he placed a finger across her lips. 'Tell you in a minute,' he whispered. They walked on in silence, hand in hand now, and crossed to the nearest dock. 'Ah, this will do nicely,' he said, sitting on a wooden seat and pulling Maeve down beside him. 'Maeve, you little witch, do you know you've enchanted me since the first moment we met? This afternoon, Sylvie asked me to marry her. I felt real ashamed, because I knew she was waiting for me to do the asking, but I couldn't do it . . . well, all of a sudden I realised that I – I loved someone else, so I told Sylvie no.'

'Was she very surprised?' Maeve said timidly. 'She's been so sure of you . . . she must have been terribly upset.'

'That's the odd thing,' Brendan said slowly. 'I don't think she was. I think she was almost relieved. Of course I promised never to tell a living soul that she had been the one who did the proposing, so you'd best forget it.' He turned to face Maeve and took her by the shoulders, looking straight into her eyes. 'Did you hear what I said, alanna? That I loved someone else, I mean?'

'I heard,' Maeve said steadily. 'Then hadn't you better ask her if she'll marry you?'

Brendan gave a snort of laughter and took Maeve in his arms. He began to kiss across her face and down her neck, then homed in on her mouth and Maeve, who had never expected to have a boyfriend, let alone a husband, returned his kisses and thought she was probably behaving shamelessly and found she did not care in the least. But presently they drew apart and Brendan put out a gentle hand and stroked the hair back from her hot face. 'Will you marry me, Maeve Connolly?' he said quietly. 'I'm hopeful that you like me at least a little bit, though I did wonder, when you were so furious the first time I kissed you.'

'I was furious because I did love you. I knew – or thought I knew – that you couldn't possibly

494

love me,' Maeve told him. 'The only thing is, Brendan, that I'm a city girl and know almost nothing about farming. Shouldn't you wait a while and maybe choose someone who could really help you?'

She had hated making the suggestion, but Brendan gave her a little shake, then stood up, took both her hands, and pulled her to her feet. 'You're a daft wee thing, so you are,' he said robustly. 'You can't turn love on and off like turning a tap, you know. Besides, it's years since I farmed meself, so I reckon we'll learn together.'

He put an arm round Maeve's waist, pulling her close, and they set off back towards the Ferryman. They had crossed the dock road and were heading for the jigger when Maeve gave a squeak and pulled him to a halt. 'Brendan, we can't tell them, you know; everyone expects you to marry Sylvie, even her mam. And Sylvie's got her pride. I think we ought to pretend tonight never happened. When we're back in Dublin, it will be different.' She glanced up at him, smiling wickedly. 'The O'Keefes may all think you're as mad as a hatter, but that's not important. What is important is that we mustn't hurt Sylvie any more than she's already been hurt.'

'Sure and aren't you the kindest, sweetest creature?' Brendan said. 'And you're right, of course. But how I shall manage to hide me feelings I don't know.'

'Nor me,' Maeve said contentedly. 'But we've

only got to do it for two more days, darling Brendan. Oh, it'll be wonderful to go back to Ireland and to know we'll be together for always.'

Sylvie stood on the quayside and waved them off; she was glad to see them go, for though Brendan and Maeve had done their best to hide the way they felt about one another, Sylvie had been doing the messages up and down the Scotland Road when she saw a familiar couple coming towards her. It was Brendan and Maeve, and Brendan had had an arm possessively about Maeve's shoulders, and had been looking down at her with great tenderness, whilst Maeve had been looking up at him, and there had been something in her look which told Sylvie that this was no casual friendship, but the real thing. She had shot into the nearest shop, aghast and amazed, for to have crippled young Maeve preferred to herself had been a bitter blow indeed. But thinking it over, she had realised that Maeve was no longer either a child or crippled, and had also realised that the younger girl was both pretty and engaging. Besides, it was foolish to wonder what one person saw in another. She had better start learning to live alone, for she had no intention of making another mistake and marrying the wrong man again. She had always been fond of Brendan, was convinced they could have had a good life together, but he had chosen someone else, and now, making her way back to the Ferryman, she told herself that, in a way, marrying Brendan would have been to cheat him, since she could never feel for him the true love which she had felt for Sam.

But Sam was dead and must be forgotten, and I'm lucky I've got Mam and Bertie to help with the business, and though Kitty insisted on going back to Ireland she's going to come again for Christmas, bless her, so one way and another I won't be entirely alone.

She returned to the Ferryman and spent a hectically busy evening trying to serve in the bar, wash up the glasses, and do everything else which, until today, either Brendan or Maeve had taken on. By bedtime she was exhausted, and went to her room confidently expecting to go straight to sleep, but instead she kept thinking about the future, the bleakness and loneliness of it, and the contrast between what she had, and what Brendan and Maeve would enjoy. Towards daybreak, she fell into a restless doze and was rudely awoken by her alarm clock, which seemed to be screaming right into her ear. She lay for a few minutes longer, trying to pull herself together, then got out of bed and went to the bathroom to wash, seeing her bedraggled hair and pale face in the mirror and not caring, for once, what she looked like.

Alone, alone, alone, her mind kept repeating, alone, alone, alone.

The compartment in which Sam Trescoe sat was full of seamen, but he had managed to squeeze himself into a corner seat. He was looking forward to going home for he had not been back for three months and knew how his parents looked forward to his rare visits. The man next to him was reading a newspaper, and Sam remembered the last time he had come into port and read, in black and white, the news that had caused him more pain than anything else in his whole life. He had gone to London to catch the train for Liverpool and had bought a copy of the *Daily Post*, had skimmed through the news, and as he had turned the page had spotted the name Dugdale, and there it had been, in black and white: *A well-known publican, Leonard Dugdale, and Mrs Dugdale, along with their daughter Rebecca, are the latest victims to succumb to the influenza. Their funeral will be held at St Anthony's Church, next Tuesday, at 11.00 a.m. When the public house re-opens it will be run, for the time being, by a manager from the brewery, but the loss of the Dugdales will be sadly felt by their friends and customers.* Sick at heart, he had abandoned his journey and gone straight back to Southampton.

Now, Sam tried to fix his mind on his homecoming, tried to forget that his beloved Sylvie was gone, that he would never hold her in his arms. But it was a futile exercise, so to take his mind off his loss he leaned a little sideways so that he could read his neighbour's paper. It was today's issue of a west country paper, and even as he looked the man flipped over the page and, to his astonishment, Sam saw his own name. Intrigued, he leaned a little closer until he could read the entire advertisement, and then his heart gave an enormous bound and he felt tears of happiness rush to his eyes. He checked the date of the paper again, then re-read the announcement, incredulity giving way to belief:

> *If Samuel Trescoe will get in touch with Sylvie Dugdale at the Ferryman Public House, Liverpool, he will hear something to his advantage: she loves him.*

For a moment, Sam simply sat where he was, reading and re-reading the magical words, but then his neighbour spoke. 'Like the personal column, do you?' he said. 'I always turn to it first go off, even before the hatch, match and despatch section. Hang on a minute, and you can have the whole paper.'

Sam smiled at him, but shook his head and began to scramble to his feet, though this was not easy for the men were jammed in like sardines. 'Thanks, but I won't trouble you,' he said, a trifle breathlessly, heaving his ditty bag down from the rack and slinging it across his shoulder.

He made his way into the corridor and a seaman from his ship, seated upon his own ditty bag, greeted him cheerfully and scrambled to his feet so that Sam might get past. 'Headin' for the lavvy, are you?' he enquired. 'I'm tellin' you, there's a queue a mile long and if you leave your seat for a second some other bugger will grab it. Can't you hang on till we reach the next station? It's no more'n ten minutes off.'

Sam grinned at him but shook his head. 'I've just discovered I'm travelling in the wrong direction,' he said. 'So I'm getting off at the next station and headin' back the way we've come. I've got a rendezvous to keep!'

To find out more about Katie Flynn why not join the Katie Flynn Readers' Club and receive a twice-yearly newsletter.

To join our mailing list to receive the newsletter and other information* write with your name and address to:

Katie Flynn Readers' Club
The Marketing Department
Arrow Books
20 Vauxhall Bridge Road
London
SW1V 2SA

Please state whether or not you would like to receive information about other Arrow saga authors.

*Your details will be held on a database so we can send you the newsletter(s) and information on other Arrow authors that you have indicated you wish to receive. Your details will not be passed to any third party. If you would like to receive information on other Random House authors please do let us know. If at any stage you wish to be deleted from our Katie Flynn Readers' Club mailing list please let us know.

arrow books

Orphans of the Storm

Katie Flynn

Jess and Nancy, girls from very different backgrounds, are nursing in France during the Great War. They have much in common for both have lost their lovers in the trenches, so when the war is over and they return to nurse in Liverpool, their future seems bleak.

Very soon, however, their paths diverge. Nancy marries an Australian stockman and goes to live on a cattle station in the Outback, while Jess marries a Liverpudlian. Both have children; Nancy's eldest is Pete, and Jess has a daughter, Debbie, yet their lives couldn't be more different.

When the Second World War is declared, Pete joins the Royal Air Force and comes to England, promising his mother that he will visit her old friend. In the thick of the May blitz, with half of Liverpool demolished and thousands dead, Pete arrives in the city to find Jess's home destroyed and her daughter missing. Pete decides that whatever the cost, he must find her . . .

From the rigours of the Australian Outback to war-ravaged Liverpool, Debbie and Pete are drawn together . . . and torn apart . . .

arrow books

Darkest Before Dawn

Katie Flynn

The Todd family are strangers to city life when they move into a flat on the Scotland Road; their previous home was a canal barge. Harry gets a job as a warehouse manager and his wife, Martha, works in a grocer's shop, whilst Seraphina trains as a teacher, Angela works in Bunney's Department Store and young Evie starts at regular school.

Then circumstances change and Seraphina takes a job as a nippy in Lyon's Corner House. Customers vie for her favours, including an old friend, Toby.

When war is declared the older girls join up, leaving Evie and Martha to cope with rationing, shortages, and the terrible raids on Liverpool which devastate the city. Meanwhile, Toby is a Japanese POW, working on the infamous Burma railway and dreaming of Seraphina . . .

arrow books

ALSO AVAILABLE IN ARROW

The Cuckoo Child

Katie Flynn

When Dot McCann, playing relievio with her pals, decides to hide in Butcher Rathbone's almost empty dustbin, she overhears a conversation that could send one man to prison and the other to the gallows – and suddenly finds herself in possession of stolen goods.

Dot lives with her aunt and uncle, the cuckoo in the nest, abandoned to these relatives after her parents died. She feels very alone . . . until she meets up with Corky who has run away from a London orphanage. They join forces with Emma, whose jeweller's shop has been burgled, and with Nick, a handsome young newspaper reporter who is investigating the crime. The four of them begin to plot to catch the thieves . . .

But Dot and Emma have been recognised, and soon both are in very real danger . . . .

arrow books

A Long and Lonely Road

Katie Flynn

Rose McAllister is waiting for her husband, Steve, to come home. He is a seaman, often drunk and violent, but Rose does her best to cope and sees that her daughters, Daisy, 8, and Petal, 4, suffer as little as possible. Steve however, realises that war is coming and tries to reform, but on his last night home he pawns the girls' new dolls to go on a drinking binge.

When war is declared Rose has a good job but agrees the children must be evacuated. Daisy and Petal are happy at first, but circumstances change and they are put in the care of a woman who hates all scousers and taunts them with the destruction of their city. They run away, arriving home on the worst night of the May Blitz. Rose is attending the birth of her friend's baby and goes back to Bernard Terrace to find her home has received a direct hit, and is told that the children were seen entering the house the previous evening. Devastated, she decides to join the WAAF, encouraged by an RAF pilot, Luke, whom she has befriended . . .

arrow books

Two Penn'orth of Sky

Katie Flynn

Two penn'orth of sky is all you can see from dirty, cramped Nightingale Court where Emmy lives with her widowed mother. Her main aim in life is to escape and she sees marriage as her best way out. When Peter Wesley, First Officer aboard a cruise ship, proposes, she accepts easily.

The Wesleys have a baby, Diana, and all seems set fair for the small family, but Peter is killed and Emmy left penniless. She and Diana are forced to move back to Nightingale Court. Emmy has to take work as a waitress but she becomes ill and when suitors appear, Diana detests them all . . .

arrow books

Strawberry Fields

Katie Flynn

Liverpool, Christmas Day 1924. When twelve-year-old Sara Cordwainer, the unloved child of rich parents, sees a ragged girl with a baby in her arms outside her church, she stops to talk to her, pressing her collection money into the girl's icy hand. But from this generous act comes a tragedy which will haunt her for years.

When, years later, Sara meets Brogan, a young Irishman working in England, she feels she has found a friend at last. But Brogan has a secret which he dare tell no one, not even Sara.

And in a Dublin slum, Brogan's little sister Polly is growing up. The only girl in a family of boys, she knows herself to be much loved, but it is not until Sara begins to work at the Salvation Army children's home, Strawberry Fields, that the two girls meet – and Brogan's secret is told at last . . .

arrow books

Order further Arrow titles
from your local bookshop, or have them delivered
direct to your door by Bookpost

Free post and packing
Overseas customers allow £2 per paperback

Phone: 01624 677237

Post: Random House Books
c/o Bookpost, PO Box 29, Douglas, Isle of Man IM99 1BQ

Fax: 01624 670923

email: bookshop@enterprise.net

Cheques (payable to Bookpost) and credit cards accepted

Prices and availability subject to change without notice.
Allow 28 days for delivery.
When placing your order, please state if you do not wish to receive any
additional information.

www.randomhouse.co.uk/arrowbooks